I Got Lucky

A Gunns Blazing Novel

Jennifer Ryan

To you, my friends...

May your luck never run out,
you have love that never ends,
hopes and dreams and true friends,
and the one who will love you to the end.

Chapter One

T he bar was packed, the music loud, but not so much that you couldn't hear the person next to you. It wasn't a club, though there was a small dancefloor. Couples moved together, their bodies close, while a group of ladies danced their hearts out, a lot of men watching, a couple even sliding in close to test the waters with the tipsy women. Lucky tried to make herself as small as possible, so no one touched her as she followed her best friend Desiree to a high top table for two.

This was the last place she should be.

Gunn Brothers was a place where everyone went to be seen, to hang out with friends, have a cocktail to unwind after a hard day at work, bring a date for some conversation and fun, or maybe find someone.

She was the opposite of a social butterfly.

Crowds made her anxious.

Getting lost in a book was more her speed.

But this was *his* bar. Any chance to see *him* made her heart long. Even though she'd more than likely hide so he didn't catch her staring.

I'm so awkward. And a coward.

Not that he'd know her in a crowd. She'd only met him once in person about two years ago, but since then, she'd had a mad crush on him. He didn't know that of course. To him she was just his house-keeper. She showed up once a week to clean his place, do his laundry, and sometimes leave him something to brighten his day. It wasn't personal, really, because Hawk Gunn wasn't just out of her league, he was the definition of tall, dark, and broody. Handsome as sin. Quiet. Deliberate. Strong. Protective of those he loved and strangers alike. A hero. He'd saved twelve people from near death the past two years working with the search and rescue team.

And he was broken. Like her.

How did she know?

Town gossip, mostly. Though that was a mix of truth and speculation.

She mostly relied on the signs all over his home. Things she recognized about herself that she saw in him. The sweat soaked sheets that told her he suffered nightmares from his time in the military. The bottle of booze and dirty glass next to the bed. The stack of books that told her more often than not he couldn't sleep at all. The lack of food in the fridge that said he wasn't eating well enough for a man his size, who was always on the go, working at the Gunn Brothers distillery attached to the bar and for the local search and rescue team, doing anything and everything not to have time to think.

Thinking was overrated. Sometimes all you did was awaken your demons and let them feast on your self-worth while you second-guessed every decision you've ever made.

She might not really know Hawk, but she knew enough to worry about him. To care.

His dark moods, past trauma...she could relate. She'd been through some stuff herself. Things that left her afraid to trust anyone, let alone allow them close enough to hurt her. Except for the one person who'd stood beside her through everything. Even if their relationship was sometimes...all about Desiree.

Her best friend clasped her arm and tugged. "Do you see who's behind the bar?"

The Gunn Brothers bar had only been open a couple of months and already it was the place to be and be seen. Desiree had begged her to come tonight.

Lucky pulled her arm free, took a tiny step away before they could have the same conversation again about her aversion to being touched, and glanced over, hoping to see Hawk, but found his older brother Lincoln instead.

"He is so hot." Desiree practically drooled.

All three of the Gunn brothers were gorgeous. Lincoln and Hawk were probably the most driven and serious, while Damon seemed the life of the party. He wasn't around as much. He traveled for Gunn Brothers Distillery, making connections and drumming up business.

And Hawk...well, he'd obviously seen and done some dark shit and carried it on his back like the black cape of a broken hero.

"Don't start." She held her breath, knowing Desiree wouldn't let it go.

"What?" Desiree tried to come off innocent, but Lucky knew any minute the questions and digging about Hawk would start.

Lucky kept her mouth shut about her clients and respected their privacy. And her strange...friendship with Hawk. "If you think you've got a shot with Lincoln, go for it." She encouraged her friend with a shooing wave of her hands to get her moving.

Desiree's eyes narrowed. "It sounds like you don't think I'm good enough for him." Of course she took offense where none was meant. She did it all the time.

And, yes, sometimes Lucky said the wrong thing. "I didn't mean it that way. I certainly don't think it. You're my best friend. You could have any guy in the room."

It was true. Desiree had an hourglass figure that men couldn't help drool over. If that wasn't enough, she was wearing a tiny black dress that showed off those curves to perfection. She'd left her chestnut hair to its wild waves, used a light touch of makeup on her gorgeous brown eyes, and painted her pouty lips red to match her heels. She looked smoking hot compared to Lucky in her basic navy blue maxi dress. Pink shadow, mascara, and tinted lip balm were about all the makeup she could handle. Her thick golden hair hung stick-straight down her back. Nude wedge sandals completed her *I-tried* look.

There was no doubt who the guys in the room were staring at.

"Lincoln seems so...intense." Not in the way Hawk came off with his don't talk or fuck with me face. "He just doesn't seem like the kind of guy you'd date."

Desiree liked guys who were all about having fun and getting it on. For Desiree that worked.

If Lucky ever put herself out there, she'd want something more intimate. A real connection. Someone she could let her guard down with and have a real conversation. Like she did with Hawk, even if she was too skittish to dare to ask for more than the letters they left for each other at his house when she cleaned for him.

Never going to happen, but a girl could dream.

Desiree's lips dropped into a pout. "All the guys I've dated suck. So why not go for someone different? He's older, more mature, rich, handsome, owns multiple businesses, and drives a new Range Rover. He built that amazing house on his family's land."

Town gossip said it was stunning. All stone and wood with towering windows to take in the breathtaking Montana views.

But nowhere in Desiree's list of things that Lincoln brought to the table did she say anything about his personality. Because she didn't know him. She knew his reputation as a ladies' man and business owner, most of which was just gossip from the rumor mill and heavily embellished stories from his exes.

Those Gunn guys couldn't be as good in bed as the stories proclaimed.

Or maybe they were, because those stories were really flattering.

What did she know about really great sex? Her last boyfriend took her virginity at seventeen with kindness and care, then drugged her family, killed them, and went to jail where he killed another man. The only orgasm she'd ever had came from her own hand or her buzzy little friend.

She didn't want to think about how sad and pathetic that was right now. Or the fact that Neil was out of prison already because of police mishandling evidence, leading to Neil only serving time for lesser drug charges. He'd plead self-defense in the death of a fellow inmate who Neil claimed attacked him first. He'd gotten off on that, too. The asshole was living with his family one town over. Way too close for comfort.

The justice system let her down again and again.

"You've got that look on your face again. We are not going down Memory Lane. Stop thinking about the past and get drunk. Be a normal twenty-something. It's Friday night. We're supposed to be having fun." Desiree waved a waitress over. "Two double shots of vodka."

The waitress nodded and headed to the bar to retrieve some of the best of what Gunn Brothers Distillery had to offer.

She tried to distract Desiree. "Aren't you going to take your shot with Lincoln?"

Desiree glanced up at the bar where Lincoln was entertaining three ladies as he poured their drinks. "He looks a little busy."

"You could distract him." She winked at her friend, trying to be encouraging and not the Scrooge at the party. She'd seen Desiree stop men in their tracks just by walking past them. She had the kind of sex appeal that turned heads, for both men and women. "You're so...sultry. He won't be able to take his eyes off you." She hoped pumping her friend up would keep her in a good mood.

At first, Desiree eyed her. "And all the guys in here with protective streaks take one look at your sweet, angelic, little broken bird face and all they want to do is wrap you in their arms and take care of you." Strange how it sounded like pity coming out of Desiree's mouth, with a hint of anger and...jealousy? No. Couldn't be. Next to Desiree, Lucky was just...plain.

Everyone saw it.

Lucky, despite her name, did not lead a charmed life. Anything but. After her family was murdered, she'd taken over her mother's house cleaning business so she had an income and the women her mother employed didn't lose their jobs. Traumatized by what happened, she'd decided to stay in town instead of going off to college alone.

But you feel alone here, too.

She was so busy just getting through each day that she'd forgotten to ask herself what more she wanted.

She patted the purse at her hip where she'd tucked the note Hawk had left her in the book he thought she'd enjoy. It was something she'd started with him a couple years ago, when she realized he loved books as much as she did and used them to escape into another world. He used to read nothing but thrillers and suspense. She'd left him a romance where the military hero comes home, overcomes his physical and emotional traumas, and finds love and a whole new life. She wanted him to see that it could happen for him.

Everyone deserved a happy ever after.

Today he'd left her an urban fantasy about witches with a note she'd reread so many times she'd memorized it.

When I come home on the days you've been at my house, it feels like you've walked in, waved a wand, and made the whole place, not just clean, but feel better. It's like you leave a piece of yourself here and it's comforting.

This witch heals the hero in more ways than one.

I think you've done a little of that for me.

Thank you. H

She didn't know why she felt so connected to him. Maybe because they carried things that still ached inside them and always would.

His note and the book meant a lot to her.

She never saw him at the house. In fact, she'd only met him in person the one time. But she loved their interactions. It was like having a pen pal without needing to buy stamps. Lucky felt a deeper connection because she spent so much time in his space, and saw him around town, even though they never spoke face to face.

Desiree snapped her fingers right in front of her nose. "Earth to Lucky!"

She startled at the sharp noise and her friend's scorching gaze. What were they talking about? Oh yeah. "You're the one who could walk out of here with any guy you wanted and you know it."

Desiree sat up straighter, smiling with confidence, beaming with pride. "Of course I can. But first...shots. Then seduction. I am going after Lincoln tonight." Her devilish grin said she had plans.

Lucky didn't want the details and remained quiet, preferring to watch others.

The waitress arrived and handed out their shots.

Desiree pulled out a wad of cash from her purse and deposited two twenties on the waitress's tray. "Keep the change."

Lucky wanted to ask where she'd gotten so much cash, but it was none of her business. Still, it seemed odd she'd have all that money on her. She didn't make that much working in the courthouse. Maybe Krystal's father finally paid his child support.

Lucky wasn't a big drinker, but she knocked back the shot with her friend, trying to put everything out of her mind and just have a good time. One of Lucky's favorite songs played and Desiree took her hand and pulled her out to the dancefloor. Even more than her aversion to being touched, she disliked crowds. She was too self-conscious. Too shy. Too aware of people staring at the scars she couldn't hide. But with a little liquid courage and the song she loved filling up her soul, she let loose for a few minutes, lost in the moment, the music, and the rare evening not spent alone.

When the song ended, some guy asked her to dance. He was cute. Tall. Dark hair with hazel eyes and a nice smile. She actually thought about saying yes, pushing herself out of her comfort zone, when Desiree took her hand and rudely tugged her away from him.

"We're headed to the bar. You're my wing-woman."

Lucky glanced back and mouthed *sorry* to the guy, then went with Desiree before she pulled Lucky's arm off. "What was that for? I thought you wanted me to have fun."

Desiree shrugged it off and rolled her eyes. "Like you were going to say yes."

She had intended to try. It had been on the tip of her tongue to agree. "He seemed nice." And she had to change something, or she'd end up twenty years from now still alone and closed off and even more miserable.

Desiree looked back at the guy, then her. "Not sure he's your type."

She wanted to say, "Murderous, you mean," but held her tongue. The truth was, she didn't have a type exactly. Except for maybe out of reach, like Hawk. They had a two year relationship going with no bumps or squabbles. Just notes and books exchanged like they lived worlds apart, though in reality she lived about three miles away from him. Granted, he had a gorgeous house and family and friends, and she lived alone in a dinky cabin that had more drafts than space. But it was hers.

Desiree pushed her way between two customers at the bar and leaned over, giving Lincoln a nice view of her cleavage. No one would accuse her of being subtle. "Hey, handsome."

Lincoln didn't take the bait and dip his gaze for even a second. "What can I get you and your friend?"

"Two double shots of vodka."

Lucky tried to avoid touching the guy next to her on the stool. "Actually, make that one. I'd like the new peach sangria you make with the Gunn Brothers peach vodka."

Lincoln beamed. "Good choice. It's our mom's new favorite. How'd you hear about it? We won't have it on the menu until next week." He pulled the bottle of GB vodka and poured out Desiree's double.

"My friend cleans Hawk's house."

Lucky blushed and wrapped her arms around her middle, shrinking in on herself. "He left a pitcher of it in his fridge and a note asking me to try it and let him know what I thought."

Lincoln's eyes went wide as he mixed her drink. "I've been meaning to get your number. Hawk says you're magic. Like you take stuff from his pantry and fridge and turn it into some decadent concoction. I had some of that beef and macaroni and cheese you left him last week. Oh my god." Lincoln's eyes rolled back. "So good. I'd kill for more of that."

Desiree turned to her, one brow raised. "What's this now? When did you add meal service to housecleaning?"

"It's...I...He...Um." *Is it hot in here?* "I...um...just sometimes do something nice for him...because..." She didn't know how to end that sentence.

"He needs it." Lincoln understood perfectly without her having to say anything. He knew his brother and what he'd been through better than Lucky ever would.

She tried to acknowledge that somehow. "I just...Yes. It's not a big deal." This was what happened around strangers. She forgot how to speak.

Lincoln slid her drink to her. "Yes. It is a big deal. And if he hasn't said it to you because he forgets to use his words, he does appreciate it. And I don't expect you to do the same for me, but if you want to, add an extra hour to the service. If you think that's fair. I'm happy to pay whatever you want. If you can fit me in. Please." He gave her puppy dog eyes. "I really need you." His earnest face told her how much he wanted her help.

Desiree downed her shot and slammed the glass on the bar.

Lincoln poured her another but never took his eyes off Lucky.

She blushed, pulled a card out of her wallet, and slid it across the bar. "You're in luck. I have one spot available on Tuesday at ten. Can we meet at your house and go over what you'd like done? I'll give you my quote and we can take it from there?"

"First, try the sangria."

Desiree snatched up the glass and took a sip first. "Delicious." She smiled at Lincoln, who narrowed his gaze and lost his smile as annoyance wrinkled his brow.

Lucky took the glass, sipped, and let her eyes roll back as the sweet, peachy taste exploded on her tongue. She hummed her approval, hoping Lincoln would appreciate how much she liked it. "That's fantastic. Reminds me of summer. You should make a strawberry, raspberry version, too." She didn't know why she said that, except she really loved sangria. She didn't normally talk to strangers so freely. But he felt like someone she knew because she knew Hawk and that made Lincoln feel familiar.

Lincoln's eyes lit up. "I'll get on that. We can put it on the summer menu."

"If you need a taste tester," Desiree purred. "I'd love to help."

Lincoln barely spared her a glance. "Thanks for taking care of my brother. Drinks are on me."

Lucky held up her glass. "Thank you. This really is my new favorite. I hope you keep it on the menu."

"Anytime you want one, come in and we'll make it for you."

"Thanks. I'll let you get back to work." The number of people waiting for a drink had tripled while she monopolized his time. "I'll see you Tuesday at ten."

"Actually, during the week is really hard for me. Could you come on Sunday, say four?"

Not like she'd be doing anything but binge watching *Virgin River* on Netflix. "Sure. No problem. Text me the address to the number on my card."

He held out his hand for her to shake. "Thank you. See you Sunday."

She wanted to take his hand, but hesitated.

Desiree piped up. "Yeah. She's not going to touch you. Hates it."

Lincoln's gaze met her shocked and embarrassed one as he dropped his hand and gave her a nod and a soft smile to let her know it was okay. "I get it. Hawk went through that for a while. Have fun tonight." He winked at her. "Let me know if you need anything else."

Before Lincoln went on to the next customer, she stopped him. "Actually..." She didn't know how being a wing-woman worked, but she owed Desiree for bringing her here tonight and getting her another job to fill the empty slot in her schedule. And with Hawk's brother. "My friend here...Desiree...she was hoping you two might hit it off."

Lincoln's smile dimmed. "Yeah."

Desiree's eyes lit up. And then...

"I'm actually taking a break from dating for a while. No hard feelings. I just—" He shrugged his massive shoulders.

"You don't have to explain. Thank you for the drinks." Lucky hated when people put her on the spot and wanted Lincoln to know he didn't owe them any kind of explanation.

He hadn't asked for one about why she didn't want to shake his hand.

Lincoln leaned in close. "Sunday. And be safe. If you need a ride home later, let me know. I'll call you a cab." He waited for her nod of agreement, then walked to the other end of the bar and started filling orders.

Desiree gripped her arm like a vice and pulled her away from the bar. "How could you humiliate me like that?"

She was going to have bruises. "What? I didn't. I was just trying to set you up. Isn't that what you wanted?"

"Not like that. Not in front of everyone. Not with you bungling your way through it. And then I had to watch him eying you and you flirting with him."

"I wasn't flirting. I was trying to get a job." She didn't know why Desiree was acting so mean when Lucky had tried to do her a favor.

Desiree rolled her eyes. "Come on. Maybe we can salvage this night."

Their table had been taken by another group. Desiree led her closer to the dance floor where a two top had just been vacated. They took their seats and Desiree people-watched, seemingly ignoring Lucky and sulking. She was really good at that.

The guy who'd come up to Lucky earlier appeared with a buddy and asked for a dance. Lucky took a chance and danced with the handsome ranch hand out for a good time while Desiree hung back with the friend. Lucky's partner tried to get a little handsy, but she backed away enough times for him to get the hint. After a couple of songs, they went back to the table.

Desiree and her guy were sitting close together, chatting and laughing, their chemistry palpable.

Lucky was parched after dancing and downed most of her drink in a few gulps. "God, that's good."

Desiree eyed her. "Looks like you were having fun."

"I'm trying." She really wished she didn't have so many hang-ups.

"Let's hit the ladies." Desiree slid off her stool. "You boys want to get us another round?"

They enthusiastically agreed and waved for the waitress.

Desiree turned to her. "Finish your drink."

Lucky took the last sip, knowing she should never leave her drink unattended.

Desiree looped her arm around Lucky's and they headed across the dance floor to the restroom.

Lucky did her business, then met her friend at the sink where Lucky washed her hands, really feeling the alcohol now.

Desiree didn't look at her.

"Please don't be mad about Lincoln. I was only trying to h-help y-you." She suddenly felt lightheaded and dizzy and leaned into the counter.

Desiree didn't even look up from her phone as she texted someone. "God, you're such a lightweight. It's time to go."

"I thought we were having a-another r-r-round-d." Lucky planted her hands on the sink and looked into the mirror, seeing nothing but a blur of lights and her outline. Lucky felt even woozier. "I think I've h-had t-too m-much to d-drink. The wine thing was s-stronger than I th-thought. I-I need the restroom." She turned back to the toilet.

Desiree snagged Lucky around the waist and turned her toward the door. Lucky blanked out, then had a vague sense of the hardwood under her feet moving. Or maybe her feet were. It was hard to tell up from down and in between anymore.

Time disappeared again and she was lying on...a table, looking up at wood beams, her calves and feet dangling off the end, swinging back and forth.

"Finally," Desiree shouted, rousing her. At least it sounded that way in the quiet room.

"Are you finally going to let me see her?"

Wait. I know that voice.

Panic made her heart stampede in her chest as the ceiling turned into a kaleidoscope of swirling wood beams.

What's happening?

Why can't I focus?

What's wrong with me?

He can't be here.

I don't want to see him.

It can't be him.

Lucky let her head loll to the side. She spotted him by another door, standing in front of Desiree. "W-what's h-he d-doing here?" She tried to get up, but just fell back down, her heart racing, her limbs numb. She wanted to run. Needed to run. Far and fast and never look back.

Oh god, he's going to kill me.

She didn't want to remember what happened to her family, how she woke up groggy and confused—like now—and found them all dead around her.

No.

Not again.

"What the fuck! What is this?" The anger in his voice didn't match the memories she had of the kind, nice, loving boy who swore he loved her.

Their faces swam in front of her and the room started to spin.

Lucky closed her eyes to try to stave off the nauseous feeling in her belly, while whispers hit her ears but made no sense in her muddled brain.

Someone put their hands on her knees and spread her legs wide.

Her eyes flew open and she tried to move, tried to lean up, to get away.

He loomed over her, his gaze roving over her body, then landing on her face as he reached a hand out toward her.

Fear spiked. "D-don't t-touch m-me. No one touches m-me." Not anymore.

He reached for her.

She screamed. At least she tried. Did it come out or get swallowed in the terror engulfing her.

Everything went black.

Lucky opened her eyes just as someone shoved her legs into a car. She was lying on the back seat, staring at the sky out the back window.

"This isn't right."

I know that voice.

What's hap—

Cold. Everything felt cold.

It felt like someone was jostling her. Everything smelled like pine. Maybe the poky things biting into her feet were pine needles. Rocks?

Am I outside?

She tried to open her eyes but they wouldn't obey. They opened and closed like the shutter on a camera.

The sky and land swirled into a swirl of colors.

Where am I?

She came to again. Seconds, minutes, hours later. She didn't know.

"You deserve this after everything I've done for you. You selfish bitch."

Suddenly the person holding her under the arms as her legs and feet scraped against gravel and dirt pitched her forward and she slid down a slope, unable to maneuver her arms or legs. She felt like a rag doll or Jill tumbling down a hill. One that never seemed to end. It was nothing but pitch black as her leg smacked a large rock, her hip skidded against the dirt and debris as she rolled this way and that, her head bounced off a tree, and her chest slammed into the ground, something sharp speared into her shoulder, and her forehead smacked into stone. Everything stilled with a jolt and an explosion of pain and the lights went out again.

She couldn't move. Everything felt battered, broken, and bashed. Cold. She'd never felt so...frozen. Like ice ran through her veins. She couldn't even open her eyes, but she knew she was outside. In a forest maybe. Crickets chirped and bugs buzzed. Occasionally she heard the rustle of a bush, an animal pulling off leaves or berries or something.

Where am I?

What's happened?

Everything hurts.

An eagle or hawk screeched overhead. Blinding light seared her eyes and made the pounding in her head worse. She tried to move her arms, but a searing pain shot through her shoulder, so sharp and piercing it sent her down into the black abyss again.

Night again. The cold. The throbbing pain. The ache in her belly. The desperate need for water. Her lips cracked as she tried to call out, her voice nothing but a rasp.

She opened her eyes and stared at the black ooze on the rock she lay on. It hurt like hell, but she lifted her head and stared at the tree root that had stabbed through her shoulder. She was lying in a pool of her own dried blood. Ignoring the pain, she shifted her shoulder, hoping to break the root so she could move, maybe sit up and eventually try to find help. But the thick root kept her trapped. The best she could do was curl her left arm into a makeshift pillow and wait.

For what, she wasn't sure.

No one is coming.

I'm alone.

Like Always.

Night turned into day, turned into night, then day again. Maybe.

It was hard to keep track of time when she spent so much of it unconscious. Her tongue felt thick and dry. Everything hurt, including her hair, even her fingertips and toes. Everything in between. She tried to catalogue her injuries. Her head. Her shoulder. Something was wrong with her knee and thigh. Her back and side.

An animal skittered nearby.

Smelled like a skunk. Or maybe that was just her.

Something thrashed through the brush. Maybe it was only the wind. She tried to move her head, but it was too heavy. Her neck and back were sore from lying in the precarious position on the downslope of the hill. She'd landed in front of two trees growing out of the hill before it dropped about five feet down to another level spot that looked like a creek bed or an abandoned trail of some kind.

She had no idea where she was or how long she'd been here.

Too long.

Too isolated.

She hadn't heard a car or person, a plane or ATV. Not even a hunter or hiker.

Whatever happened, whoever left her here, knew exactly what they were doing.

I'm alone.

No one is coming.

Another wave of nausea and thirst hit her.

She repositioned her head on her arm and was just about to close her eyes, probably for the last time when she spotted something red bobbing far ahead of her. Her vision was blurry at best, but in a sea of greens and browns, that red ball cap stood out.

In her desperation, she used the last of her energy and called out before she passed out, knowing she probably wouldn't make it out of here alive, but at least she wouldn't die alone.

"I'm here. Help me! I'm here. Help me!"

Chapter Two

Hawk wanted to kill his brother. Not the first time he'd felt that way. Wouldn't be the last. But as he stared at his brother, knowing he'd probably done something to piss off the woman who cleaned his house, he wanted to wrap his hands around Lincoln's throat and strangle him to death.

He didn't have a lot of good things in his life. The bad seemed to squeeze out all the good. But he had his family, the businesses they ran, his work with the local search and rescue team, and he had Lucky.

She made his life, his week, his black heart brighter.

And Lincoln had somehow fucked that up.

"Listen, man, it's like I said. I saw her at the bar on Saturday night. I asked her to clean my place. We were supposed to meet on Sunday. She didn't show or respond to my texts. I was nice to her. I don't know why she blew me off."

"Not just you. Me. She didn't clean my place yesterday like she always does. Every Monday like clockwork. No exceptions."

"Maybe she's sick."

"She'd have texted me and rescheduled." His gut felt like a knot he'd never unravel.

Lincoln grinned. "You really like her and you're pissed that I tried to hire her, too. Admit it. You're jealous."

"I'm pissed that you did something to make her not want to work for me anymore."

She'd never missed cleaning his place, except once when she broke a tooth on a piece of almond brittle and texted that she'd reschedule to do his place on Thursday instead of Monday, like usual. She was responsible and kind. She wouldn't just leave him hanging.

Lincoln put his hand on Hawk's shoulder. "First, I didn't do anything. Second...do you two have something going that I don't know about?"

Hawk tried to hold on to his patience, even as he shook off his brother's hand. "It's none of your damn business. I knew I shouldn't have told you about her leaving me food and stuff."

Lincoln's grin grew. "Hold up. 'And stuff?' All you shared was that she sometimes makes you something to eat. What else does she do?"

Make my whole fucking world a little better with her notes and books and reminders to eat and try the meditations for sleep in the book she left me.

"Nothing. Forget about it."

"No. Not happening. You've been a brooding asshole who's pushed everyone away for way too long. We get it. You needed space when you left the military to find your way out of the trauma of what happened, but we're way past that and you're still so closed off and..."

"What? Let me guess. Moody."

"You're being a straight up asshole right now. I talked to your girl for like five minutes. That's all. I know you have a thing for her, even if you don't want to admit it. You know how I know that? Because she's the only person you talk about outside of your coworkers and us."

"It's not like that." *You want it to be like that.*

"You want it to be," his brother echoed the voice in his head. "You just don't want to admit it. Or give in to it, because you think you're broken or whatever else you tell yourself that keeps you from asking out that smokin' hot, nice, kind, real woman. And when I mean real, I mean someone who is exactly what she seems."

Hawk took a chance and admitted. "While we have this kind of running conversation going, I haven't actually seen her in person in two years." He'd been working on getting better, getting his head straight after two tours of duty overseas left him with flashbacks and nightmares to go along with several surgeries after he'd crashed his chopper. Not to mention the other times he'd been shot or wounded in the line of duty.

"Maybe you should change that. She seems really nice. You could use some of that."

I have some of that. She leaves it behind every time she's at my place.

Lincoln prodded some more. "Does Lyric know about her?"

Hawk shook his head. His cousin's wife had taken it upon herself to be his best friend. At first, it was mostly one sided. But the woman wore him down a little at a time until they were exchanging phone calls a couple times a week and she and Mason visited him in Montana once a month. He went down to Wyoming a few times a month, usually when Mason or Nick needed his help on one of their FBI cases.

"If you need more encouragement, or a woman's perspective, you know Lyric would tell you to go for it. She's been trying to set you up every chance she gets, but you keep turning her down. Now I know why."

"It's not about Lucky. It's about the baggage that comes with me."

Lincoln hooked his arm around Hawk's shoulders. "We all have baggage. If you expect her to carry some of yours, you might remember that she'll expect the same. It's called a relationship. And if you haven't noticed, you're already in one with her."

Am I?

Yes.

Sort of.

And the thought of it made him…happy?

He hadn't felt that way in longer than he could remember.

"I need to get out of here for a while. I'm going for a hike. I've been meaning to up my training anyway—now that the weather's improving, search and rescue is going to be inundated with calls from hikers. Some of the places they get lost in are rough terrain. And my stamina isn't what it used to be."

Lincoln eyed him critically. "Not from what I'm seeing. You're probably in better shape than when you left the military."

He kept in good shape for a reason—so he could help those in need. He loved working at the distillery with his brothers, but he loved his search and rescue work even more. It gave him a sense of purpose. One he needed after his military life.

"Let me clear my head. I'll call Lucky's service and see if they know why she didn't show on my way out."

Lincoln's eyes filled with concern. "Let me know what you find out. She didn't seem like the kind of person who'd blow someone off."

"She isn't. That's what concerns me." He headed out of Lincoln's office and to his car. He'd already packed all his gear this morning, knowing at some point he'd get tired of spreadsheets and distribution questions. He preferred the outdoors. He'd spent the past weekend helping a buddy from SAR paint the inside of the house he'd just bought with his new wife. They'd seemed so happy and in love and ready to start the next chapter of their life together and expand their family.

Maybe that's why he was thinking so much about Lucky and the note he'd left her last week. At the time, it felt right. But then he started second-guessing himself about how much he'd revealed by being so open and honest.

What if he'd crossed a line, and this was her way of letting him know he'd gone too far?

He slid into his car and connected his phone to the Bluetooth. "Call Happy Helpers Cleaning Service."

The phone rang twice before a woman answered. "Happy Helpers. How can I assist you?"

"I'm trying to get in touch with Lucky. She was supposed to clean my place yesterday but never showed up."

"Oh no. Is this Mr. Gunn?"

"Yes."

"I'm so sorry. I was supposed to call you."

"Is she sick?" He really hoped that's all it was, even though his gut was telling him something was wrong based on how the woman's voice filled with concern.

"Um. No. I don't think so. I really don't know. No one has been able to get ahold of her. As far as I can tell, she's been missing for a couple of days."

His stomach tightened with dread. "Did you call the police?"

"Yes, but they said we had to wait forty-eight hours. Adults are allowed to take off without telling anyone if they want to." That last part sounded like a quote from whoever she talked to at the police department. "We have to wait until tomorrow to file an official report."

"Okay, well, I know she was at Gunn Brothers Saturday night with a friend. My brother talked to her while she was there."

"Yes. We know. Her friend Desiree told us they'd gone out. Apparently Lucky had too much to drink and Desiree took her home, though I was surprised to hear that."

"Why?"

"Because Lucky's not really a drinker. She doesn't like to take anything that will alter her ability to think clearly. Not even an antihistamine when her allergies are bad, probably because of what happened to her family."

"What happened to them?" He had a vague memory about her parents dying years ago.

"They were all drugged and murdered by her boyfriend."

Holy fuck!

"Has someone been by her place?"

"All of us have checked everywhere we could think of to find her. Strange thing is, her car is at her place."

That did send up a huge red flag. If she wasn't there, that meant someone took her somewhere most likely. Otherwise, why wouldn't she drive herself?

He had to ask the hard question. "Is she seeing anyone now? Someone who'd know where she is, or be with her?"

"No. She doesn't date, though we've all tried to coax her to take a chance. But after what happened..."

Yeah, she probably didn't trust men.

"Okay. Well, would you ask her to call me when she shows up?" *If* she showed up. He didn't want to think that, but his gut just kept nudging him that something was terribly wrong. "I'd really like to know that she's all right."

"Of course. And what about your cleaning? Would you like me to send someone else over to do it."

"No." He didn't like strangers in his house. He only wanted Lucky. "Let's hope Lucky returns soon and I can reschedule with her then."

"Okay. Please let me know if you change your mind and we'll make arrangements to make this right."

"I understand. Sometimes people just need some space. Let's hope that's all this is and she comes back soon." He could relate to that. He'd done it enough times himself. He was about to get lost in the woods right now just to get his head straight again and blow off the excess energy building up in his system.

"Thank you for your patience, Mr. Gunn. I'll be in touch."

He ended the call and ten minutes later pulled into the hiking trail lot at one of the less popular trail heads. He climbed out and went to the back of his Range Rover, lifting the back, and pulling out his heavy gear. The SAR rucksack with all his supplies weighed about thirty pounds. He'd carry it and a few extra bottles of water, just in case. Last he grabbed the SAR baseball hat he wore for their softball games. Before he put on his rucksack, he did some stretching behind his car, loosening up his muscles. He'd learned with his extensive injuries, though recovered, he needed to take the time to warm up or he'd seize up later.

The sun was high. He'd get in a few miles of hiking before he had to head back to the bar to check in with the manager and go over inventory. Right now, he just wanted to get lost among the trees and nature, so he could let his muscles work and his mind rest.

He started down a trail that usually challenged him. Three miles in, he hit the fork and decided that he'd been going easy on himself a lot lately and needed to push himself with some rougher terrain to build up his stamina. He turned right down a lesser used trail, and really worked his legs as he traversed the winding hillside that brought him up to another plateau and around to another narrow gap between two hills. The trail was a little overgrown, but he could still navigate it. If he kept going, he should make it to another fork and yet another trail that wound back to his starting point.

The wind whispered through the valley and trees. He stopped at a large boulder and sat, taking out a bottle of water and downing all of it. He pulled off his ball cap, held it up, and wiped his brow on the crook of his elbow and arm.

"I'm here. Help me! I'm here. Help me!" The words were barely discernible, so much so that for a second he thought he'd imagined it as the wind's whispering picked up again.

But something in him wouldn't let him dismiss it as nothing. He pulled on his ball cap and headed deeper down the path, calling out, "Is someone there? Can you hear me?"

He waited, holding his breath, but didn't hear anything more. He kept moving forward, slowly scanning his surroundings, looking for anything, anyone, out here.

"Hello. Can you hear me?" He thought he heard a soft groan. More whispers.

Suddenly, a small rock landed five feet away and tumbled toward him. He turned his head to the hill up ahead of him. It took his eyes a second to register what he was seeing. Someone's bare feet. Whoever it was, he couldn't see the rest of them from his vantage point.

He ran to the slope where the trees grew out of the hill and jumped up to see if he could spot the person above him. All he caught was a glimpse of long blonde hair, dried blood matting some of it down as the breeze blew other strands, tangling them in a branch. "I see you. I'm coming up. Just hold on."

He didn't get a response and his gut knotted with dread. He studied the terrain leading up and figured out some handholds and footholds for him to haul himself up the seven foot rise. The second he braced himself at the top with the two trees as support, he gasped at the nearly naked woman lying face down, a thick stick sticking out of her shoulder, blood covering her back, her head, and dried and pooled beneath her.

Fuck!

He pulled off his pack and set it aside, then kneeled beside her, and gently brushed the hair away from her face.

"Help. Me." The words puffed out of her chapped and cracked lips so softly he'd barely heard them.

But then he pushed the last of her thick hair back, leaned down close, and really looked at her. Shock rocked him. "Lucky." It couldn't be. What was she doing way out here? How did she get here?

Why the fuck is she naked?

He looked up the hill from where she lay and could practically see the entire path she'd slid down by all the disturbed plants, dirt, and debris.

She didn't answer him, just groaned.

"Lucky. It's me. Hawk." His voice trembled. His heart thrashed in his chest. "I'm going to help you." He pulled out his phone and cursed. No signal. Of course not. And he hadn't brought his SAR satellite phone. Damn.

Stupid.

At least he was prepared to tend to her injuries and try to get her stable. First he needed to figure how bad she was hurt. Right after he called for help. "Lucky." He patted her cheek gently, trying to rouse her. "Hey. I need to head back down the trail a little ways so I can call for help."

"Staaayy." The word wheezed out of her.

He leaned down so he could hear her better, but he didn't like what she said at all.

"Don't. Want. To. Die." She sucked in a ragged breath and let out the next word on her exhale. "Alone."

"You're not dying. I'm going to get you to the hospital. But I need you to hold on. Can you do that for me? Please," he begged.

It was impulsive, out of character, and crossing a line, but he pressed his forehead to hers and kissed her cheek, feeling how cold she was. "You're not dying on me. Okay? I need you to live." He should have simply stopped at, I need you, by the way his heart pounded in his chest.

Damn. He really cared about her. More than he'd let himself admit or feel until now.

He dug into his pack and found the Mylar blanket, unwrapping it and spreading it over her, worried it wouldn't be enough to bring her body temperature up. He took her temp with a digital thermometer. Ninety-five. Too low. Knowing she'd last been seen Saturday night, he figured she'd been out here in the elements for nearly three days.

Fuck!

She was very close to dying. She needed fluids, heat, and a hospital. Not to mention he needed to stabilize any injuries she had from coming down the twenty-something foot drop from above.

He pulled out a saline bag and IV line. It only took him a minute to set it up and hook the bag above her on a tree limb. It took a hell of a lot longer to find a vein. He couldn't get to the inside of her arms, so he went through one in her hand. Took him three tries to find a good vein because of her dehydration. He squeezed the bag to get it going, hoping he wasn't too late.

He pulled out his stethoscope and listened to her heart through her back. Slow. Thready. Not good. He needed a helicopter evac if he was going to save her.

He leaned down close to her ear. "The fluids are going to help. I have to go make that call."

"Stay. Dying."

"No. You're not. You're going to fight. Promise me." A tear dropped onto her cheek. He hadn't even realized it slipped down his face. "Please, Lucky. Don't give up. Not now when you're so close to being saved."

"Promise. Try."

"That's my girl. Hold on. I'll be as fast as I can. A few minutes. Okay. Hold on." He didn't waste any more time and slid down the embankment he was on, hitting the trail at a dead run. He had to go back about half a mile to reach higher, open ground. His phone chirped with several incoming messages. He ignored them all and hit the speed dial for the SAR office.

The second Randy picked up, he started issuing orders. "I need the chopper up in the air immediately. I have a woman, twenty-four, hypothermic, stabbed through the right shoulder with a tree root, head and body injuries from a fall of about twenty to twenty-five feet down a hill. She's been out in the elements for approximately three days. Lucky Sinclair went missing as far back as possibly Saturday night. She's naked. Possible rape and dump." Those words coming out of his mouth about her nearly sent him to his knees. "I've got fluids started. I need to get back to tend to her wounds. I'm dropping you a pin now for my location, though she's north of me by half a mile on the hiking trail."

"Got it. I'll assemble the team and notify the sheriff's office. We'll be ready to airlift her out as soon as she's stable."

He hoped she wasn't dead by the time he got back to her.

"Hurry. There's no time to waste on this one. She's critical." He hung up and started running again. He'd never pushed himself so hard or so fast, but for her, where every second counted, he wouldn't quit. Not until she was safe and healthy again.

He climbed back up to her, relieved to see the metallic space blanket rise and fall as she breathed. "I'm back. The cavalry is on the way." He hunched down next to her again and started assessing her critically, starting with her head wounds. He found two large bumps, one with a laceration. He cleaned and bandaged it, then moved on to her neck.

She was lying at an odd angle.

"Lucky. Does your neck hurt?"

She tried to lift her head to answer him.

"Don't move. Just tell me."

"Head. Shoulder. Neck stiff. Back aches. Knee, thigh hurt." She moved her left hand. "Pinky."

Yeah, that was dislocated and turned sideways. He checked it out, wincing at the odd angle. Unfortunately that meant he needed to pop it back into place and splint it. "I'm really sorry about this. The last thing I want to do is hurt you. But your finger is dislocated and I need to fix it." He got the splint and tape ready, then took her hand, gripped the dislocated portion, pulled, and realigned the bones. She squeaked out what should have been a scream if she could manage it. He splinted the finger and taped it to her ring finger as well to keep it stable.

He checked the fluids, they were about half in her. "Are you feeling a little better?"

"No."

"I don't blame you. I honestly don't know how you survived this long. The temps at night had to get below fifty. You must have been freezing."

"So c-cold."

And she was partially lying on stone.

"Okay, here's the hard part. I need to get a look at your shoulder. If I can cut the limb stabbing you, maybe I can roll you over to assess your other injuries. There's blood by your thigh, face, neck, and upper body. You're covered in scrapes and bruises." He wanted to ask about the old, healed scars on her body. It looked like someone had taken a knife and sliced away at her. He'd suspect self-harm, except for the fact that they were all over her back and the back of her thighs. He wondered if her front looked the same.

"Hawk."

He brushed his fingers softly through her hair. "Yeah. I'm here."

"Don't want to be alone anymore."

"Me either. You and me, we're going to stick together. Okay. You promise me that."

"K."

"I need to hear you promise."

Her eyes opened for the first time.

He leaned in close, staring into the blue pools. "There you are. I got home yesterday and saw that you hadn't been there and..." He went for it. "I missed you."

She blinked back tears. A good sign the IV fluids were working. "Scared. So tired.

"I know. I won't leave your side. Now promise me you won't give up."

"Should have asked you out. I wanted to. So many times. Too late...now."

"No it's not. You just need to fight." He hoped she understood what he was asking for because he was having trouble finding the words. "You want a date. Done. Dinners. Movies. Sitting on the couch reading books together. Anything you want."

"Time. With. You."

"I want that, too. I have for a long time and I was stupid for thinking I didn't deserve someone like you. And look. I almost lost you, before I ever got the nerve to ask you out. Do you know how many times I wanted to come home early and find you in my house just so I could see you there?"

"Every time...I wished you were there." She sucked in a ragged breath. "Thought I was silly to dream you'd like me."

"I more than like you. You've been a really good friend."

"You. Too." She was having trouble staying awake.

He needed to put their personal stuff on hold and tend to her. First thing he did was take off his boots and socks. He slid the socks on her feet, hoping to help warm her up some more. He pulled on his boots, then tended to some of the deeper scrapes on her backside. He took a chance and gently shifted her left leg so he could see the long gash running down it in addition to a lot more of those scars. "This is going to need stitches. It's really deep. Right now, I'm going to clean and bandage it."

She didn't answer him, but he let her know he was there by giving her leg a soft squeeze, then he cleaned the wound, put a thick pad to staunch the new flow of blood, then wrapped her thigh in gauze to add pressure.

He didn't tell her about the maggots he'd brushed out of the wound.

"Panties wet. Couldn't hold it," she mumbled, shifting her hips like she was uncomfortable. With the wind blowing down the hill, he bet those wet panties were cold against her skin.

He grabbed a pair of scissors and cut them on both sides, then pulled them off and stuffed them into a plastic bag for evidence. Just in case. He didn't let his mind go there and took some comfort in the fact that she didn't seem afraid of him, or opposed to him touching her. Not that she could move all that much.

A new sound joined the whispering wind and he looked up. "I hear a truck coming. It's probably my guys." A few seconds later, a chopper hovered high above them, too. "Down here," he shouted up the hill, then grabbed the whistle out of his pack and blew it three times.

"Hawk?" Randy called over the ledge. "You down there?"

"What's up there?"

"Fire road."

That explained how she got here. Someone drove her and dumped her.

The rage that incited in him didn't bode well for the person who hurt her. He'd make them pay. One way or another.

But first he needed to get her out of here. Alive.

Chapter Three

Hawk wanted to breathe a sigh of relief that reinforcements were here, but Lucky was in too bad shape to think that she was out of the woods. He'd barely tended to her multiple wounds. She'd lost a lot of blood.

It had been a long time since he was this scared.

"I'm coming down to you," Randy called out, dropping a rappelling rope down the hill.

Hawk called up. "Take pictures as you come down. Sheriff will want them before we muck up all the evidence."

"On it."

The rest of the team spotted Randy on his descent and gathered all they'd need to get Lucky out of the ravine.

Hawk focused on splinting her grossly swollen knee, worrying the whole time about how quiet and still she was, despite him manipulating her injuries.

She had to be in so much pain.

It killed him to add to it. But he didn't dare give her any meds, not until they assessed her more thoroughly.

He couldn't see the front of her. That worried him, because she was lying in a lot of blood. Was it all from her thigh and shoulder wound? Or would he find something even more horrendous?

Randy made it down next to him. "How is she doing?"

"Not great. Did you bring a small saw to cut her away from the tree?" Just the thought of having to do it made his stomach turn and his heart clench. He didn't want to cause her any more pain.

Randy unsheathed the tiny saw with its ten inch blade. "Want me to do it while you hold her up so I can get under her?"

"I think we're going to have to dig some of the dirt out from under her to get to it."

Randy leaned over Lucky and tried to see underneath her, but her full breast was kind of in the way.

That's what worried him the most, that they might not be able to cut her loose and they'd have to lift her off the root stabbed through her. She could bleed out before they could do anything to save her.

Randy's face reflected his dire concerns. "This isn't going to be easy."

"We need to be able to see beneath her before we do anything."

Randy handed over a small gardening shovel. They had all kinds of things in their tool kits. "Let's do this a little at a time. Do you have leather gloves?"

Hawk pulled a pair out of his pack and slid them on. "I'll protect her skin, you dig toward the root and see if you can make a big enough hole to cut it."

"How the hell has she lain here like this for days? She's got to have a massive neck and back ache if not worse, the way she's bent."

Hawk knew if he'd been bowed like this for three days he'd be in major pain. "Focus on getting her free, then we can assess her better."

"How long has she been out?"

"Like ten minutes. Hurry." Hawk didn't want to feel like a perv, but he sort of did when he slid his hand under her armpit and wedged his fingers under her breast, pushing it so that Randy could shovel out dirt from beneath her. This was not how he wanted things to start between them.

He reminded himself this was all in the name of rescuing her.

They worked slowly. Carefully.

Three other SAR team members joined them around Lucky's limp body, watching and waiting until they could move her. They were all silent, like everyone was holding their breath to see if she'd make it.

She had to.

Hawk felt Randy jab the saw blade into his glove. "Watch it. You'll hit her."

"I need to just get this last little bit and then I think she'll be free, but I have to hit it at this angle to do it."

Hawk swore. "Fine. Just go slow. She's got enough fucking marks on her."

Randy sighed as he lay on his belly, arm outstretched as he pushed his arm back and forth and tried to see into the tiny space he had to work in.

Suddenly the pressure he kept on her breast loosened and he moved her several inches.

Lucky screamed with the shift in her body.

He stilled, soothing her with his voice. He hoped. "It's okay, sweetheart. I've got you now." He looked at the men around him. "Pete, get the backboard and neck brace. Theo, you hold her head. Kash, you take her legs. We'll roll her slowly and gently."

Randy got out of the way as they all braced her.

"Lucky, we're going to move you. Just be still. Let us do all the work. Okay?"

"K." She barely breathed out the reply.

"On three. One. Two. Three." Hawk stabilized her shoulders and used his hand on her chest to roll her with the guys.

She moaned in pain and shouted when the root protruding from her shoulder hit the backboard.

"Put some padding under her shoulder to stabilize it. We don't want to knock that thing loose. She's lost enough blood." He was standing in the evidence of it, now that they'd moved her.

"Head wound is bleeding through the bandage you put on it." Pete winced.

He nodded. "It's a deep gash. It's going to need stitches."

"What are we looking at here?" Kash stared down at the marks all over Lucky's body.

"Focus on what's new and needs attention." Hawk hated everyone staring at her naked body. "Where's the blanket? We need to get her warm."

Theo draped it over her and tucked it in around her, leaving her shoulder clear for them to pack gauze around the seeping wound.

Kash adjusted the knee splint, tightening it up. He cracked several ice packs and placed them around her knee to try to bring the swelling down.

Hawk took a second to assess her again. He was finally able to open her eyes and shine a light in them. Her pupils were even and reactive, though she squinted away from the bright light.

"You're doing great, Lucky. We're almost ready to get you out of here."

Her fingers brushed his leg. "Come with..."

"Yes. I'm coming with you. You and me. Remember. Promise?"

She tried to nod, but Pete had put the neck brace on her, keeping her from moving.

"Save your strength."

Randy put his hand on Hawk's shoulder. "Any idea how she got here?"

He shook his head, then stared down at the woman who'd captured his heart. "What happened?"

Her gorgeous blue eyes met his. "Drugged. I think."

He fumed. "What's the last thing you remember?"

"Linc. Nice t-to m-me."

Yeah, he bet his brother was. *It doesn't bother me one fucking bit,* he snarled in his head, lying to himself. "You missed your meeting with him. He's worried about you. So are your coworkers. They tried to file a missing person report."

"Where am I? No one h-here...until y-you."

"Chopper's coming in." Theo pointed to their right. "Let's get her down to the ravine. They'll drop down the basket and we'll get her loaded."

Things moved quickly now that she was free and they could move her. He and Theo dropped down between the two trees to the trail below. They each took a side of the board Lucky was strapped to and pulled her down to them as Randy and Kash dropped down and took her feet end.

The wind kicked up with the rotor wash and the helicopter dropped down, keeping above the trees, but making sure they didn't have to raise Lucky higher than necessary.

Hawk made sure the blanket was tucked against her and brushed the stray hair away from her face, not that it did much good with all the wind created by the chopper.

Theo caught the edge of the basket as it descended into the ravine.

They quickly secured Lucky. Hawk grabbed the rope and balanced himself on the edges of the basket, making sure he didn't touch any of Lucky's injuries.

"What the fuck are you doing?" Randy asked.

Normally, they'd send the victim up alone and whoever was in the chopper would tend to them on the ride back.

"I'm not leaving her. She's…" He didn't know how to say it. "We've had a thing for the past two years." That at least was true, even if he wanted a hell of a lot more now and was going to take it because you never knew when time would run out. He'd wasted enough keeping his distance from her the past two years.

His buddies all stared at him.

Theo spoke first. "I didn't know you were seeing anyone."

"Well, now you do. I am. She's…mine." He'd given her his word he wouldn't leave her and he wouldn't break that promise. He gave the bird above him a thumbs up and they started to rise to the open door on the chopper.

"What the fuck is this?" Bryce raised a brow at him hanging off the rope, no tether, standing over Lucky.

"I promised I wouldn't leave her and I won't. Get her in. Let's move. She needs surgery. ASAP," he shouted over the noise.

Bryce maneuvered them into the chopper, released the basket from the rope, closed the door, then leaned over Lucky. "Normally, he just grunts shit out. You've actually got him talking and making promises. Good for you." Then Bryce called over the radio to their pilot, Paloma, a veteran like himself. "Clear. Good to go."

Paloma took the chopper up and away.

"You got damn lucky finding her way out here." Bryce checked Lucky's IV line and her shoulder injury, making sure she wasn't bleeding any worse than she'd been when they loaded her up.

"I don't normally take that trail." He found Lucky's hand beneath the blanket and held it. A soft squeeze back eased his worry. He brushed her hair back, trying to give her what comfort he could, needing to touch her and let her know he was here. He wasn't going anywhere. Like he promised.

Bryce spent the flight keeping her stable.

As much as Hawk wished he was the one flying the chopper, because fast wasn't fast enough for him today, he appreciated all his buddies for doing their jobs and taking care of Lucky.

Bryce watched him as he continued to run his fingers through Lucky's oily, tangled hair. He didn't care that it was dirty and plucked out several leaves and twigs from it, tossing them to the floor.

"She means something to you."

It took him a second to shift his gaze to his friend. "Yeah. She does." How much, he was just starting to realize and accept.

And that's why he pulled out his phone and texted his brother.

HAWK: Found Lucky naked and dumped in a ditch.

HAWK: If she was last seen at the bar, WTF happened there?

BIG BRO: WTF Is she okay?

HAWK: Too fucking close of a call. SAR helped me get her out. Landing at hospital in 3 minutes.

BIG BRO: On my way.

BIG BRO: And I didn't see anything happen but we'll damn well check the video footage and find out. Want me to call Damon?

HAWK: No sense bringing him back early when there's nothing he can do.

BIG BRO: I've got you. In the car now headed your way.

Hawk tucked his phone away, then leaned down and kissed Lucky on the forehead.

Bryce gave him a look, one that hinted at envy. All the guys, except one, in the crew were single. They all dated. Hawk occasionally scratched that itch, but not since it felt like things between him and Lucky had turned into something meaningful, even if it was long distance. Sorta.

All he knew now was that he wanted them to stop keeping each other at arm's length and really try to see if what they shared could be even greater than what they'd built the last two years.

He felt close to her, closer than he did to most people. She knew things about him he didn't even share with his therapist. She was so damn easy to talk to.

Write to?

Whatever.

She couldn't hear him over the helicopter, so he didn't bother trying to talk to her. But he hoped she knew he was there. Beside her. Where he'd like to stay.

The second the chopper landed, he squeezed Paloma's arm, letting her know he appreciated her help.

They unloaded Lucky, still strapped to the backboard, onto the stretcher. Bryce smacked him on the back and yelled, "Call if you need anything!" before climbing back onto the chopper.

Hawk went with the emergency department team, calling out her vitals and injuries. The second they hit the triage room, Hawk breathed a sigh of relief to see Dr. Thad Meyer. "Hawk, you don't look like you're on today?"

He didn't have his usual SAR gear on. "I was out training and found my girl, Lucky. She's been missing nearly three days. Dehydrated, dumped from a fire road down a twenty to twenty-five foot steep embankment. She hit a lot of rocks, trees, and bushes on her way down. Knee looks bad, so does the cut to her thigh. She came to a stop at the bottom, getting stabbed in the shoulder by a tree root. We cut her loose. Head injuries look bad. I'm guessing she had a concussion that's gotten better over the last few days. Exposure to the elements left her hypothermic, though we've tried to warm her up. I stabilized her best I could in the field, but she needs surgery on that shoulder."

Dr. Meyer eyed him. "What aren't you telling me?"

Hawk used his free hand to pull his ball cap off and scratch his head. "She was last seen at the bar. I found her naked and dumped down that ravine. She was able to tell me that she thought she'd been drugged. So that makes me think that maybe..." He couldn't say it. He didn't want to even think it.

Dr. Meyer started belting out orders for x-rays, fluids, meds, and a bunch of tests he wanted performed, including a rape kit. "Does she have any family we can contact to get background on her and consent?"

Hawk squeezed her hand. "No. Her family was murdered."

Dr. Meyer winced. "Does she have anyone else?"

"She has me."

"Are you two…"

"It's new, but yes. I'm not leaving her. I promised her."

Dr. Meyer's eyes turned deadly serious. "You're going to be a pain in my ass, aren't you?"

"I won't break my promise to her."

Dr. Meyer rubbed his knuckles over Lucky's sternum, agitating her to wake up. "Lucky, I'm Dr. Meyer. You need surgery and a lot of other help."

Lucky's eyes didn't seem to focus, but when her gaze found Hawk's, she settled and stared up at him.

Dr. Meyer leaned close to her. "Do you authorize Hawk to make medical decisions for you if you're unable?"

Hawk saw her hesitate. "I'll take care of you. Promise."

Her gaze shifted to the doc. "Yes." And then her eyes rolled back and she started seizing.

Hawk swore.

Dr. Meyer sprang into action and the next twenty minutes were a blur until they whisked her away from him and up to surgery.

He found Lincoln in the waiting room and sat next to him, pulling out the gloves he'd stuffed in his back pocket. He hung his head and stared at the red stains on them.

"Is that her blood?"

Hawk tried to stay positive and reminded himself they'd gotten to her in time by some fucking miracle. "Yes. Randy accidentally cut her when we were trying to free her from the tree root she was impaled on."

"Fuck. Damn. That's..."

"Not even the worst thing that could have happened to her." He didn't know if some asshole had violated her. "Did you look at the surveillance footage?"

"Not yet. I wanted to be here with you. I know how much you like her."

"I more than like her. I told her we're going to do this thing right, now."

Lincoln turned and stared at him. "No shit. What did she say?"

"She wants me, too."

Lincoln draped his arm over Hawk's shoulders. "That's great, man. I'm happy for you. Both of you. She's going to make it. She'll be fine. You'll see."

He wasn't so sure about that second part.

She would definitely survive, but he didn't know if she'd be okay anytime soon.

No matter what, he'd be there to help her through her trauma, the way she'd helped him through his.

Chapter Four

The dark place she'd been in started to recede, slowly lightening to shades of gray. A kind of mist surrounded her. Then memories flashed, disjointed and disturbing. She heard his voice saying something about wanting to see her. Before the other visions overwhelmed her, she gasped for a breath and tried to run. Something held her down. The freezing cold she remembered from those nights in the forest chilled her bones as she tried to fight off whatever, whoever tried to hurt her again.

Sharp pain lanced through her chest and shoulder as she grabbed someone's wrist. That someone was saying something. It took her a second to really hear and comprehend it.

"You're safe. It's me. Hawk. You're safe."

Her eyes flew open and stared up into the most beautiful golden hazel eyes she'd ever seen, though they were filled with concern. "There you are. Welcome back," he said with a smile.

Her fingers clutched his wrist, though he was so big and strong they didn't make it all the way around. She immediately let go. "Sorry." Her voice was barely a rasp.

"Here. Try to drink some of this."

Her head snapped to the man on her other side. She glanced from one to the other, noting that the action made her stiff neck and shoulder hurt. "What are you two doing here?" She looked around the room. "What happened? Why am I in the hospital?" Her heart jackhammered in her chest. "What's wrong?"

Hawk sat on the edge of her bed and took her hand. "Breathe, Lucky. Slow down. We'll answer all your questions."

Lincoln held the glass close to her face with the straw at her lips. "Take a sip of this, it will help you feel better."

She obeyed, still eyeing both of them. "So this is heaven, right? Two gorgeous Gunn brothers. Here. With me." *Why did I say that out loud?*

Lincoln smirked.

Hawk squeezed her hand to get her attention. "Not heaven. And we're both more devils than angels."

"Speak for yourself," Lincoln teased his brother. "I can be wicked good."

The door to her room opened and a nurse and doctor walked in—along with someone she'd hoped never to see again.

Corporal Jase Kent from the sheriff's department. A guy she'd gone to more than a few times for help and gotten none. "Hello, Lucky. How are you feeling?"

"Confused," she confessed. The last thing she remembered was talking to Lincoln at the bar.

Jase nodded. "Well, Doc Meyer wants to get a look at you, then we'll talk and maybe together we can figure this out."

She eyed him. "It happened again, right?"

He nodded, his gaze grave.

"What are you two talking about?" Hawk hadn't let go of her hand, she realized.

It felt so good and strange at the same time that she just went with it, because his touch was the only thing grounding her at the moment. Inside, her emotions were all over the place even though she tried to hold it together as panic set in.

Jase didn't exactly clear things up for Hawk. "Lucky and I have a complicated relationship."

She didn't want anyone in the room, especially Hawk, to think they had something personal going on. "Yes. I report a crime and you do nothing about it." She sank back into the bed. "I don't know why you're even here."

"Because despite my lack of progress on your cases, I care about you. I want to help. I'm trying to find the person doing this to you so I can stop them."

Lincoln put his hand over her free one and she didn't even feel like pulling it away. Like Hawk's touch, it anchored her. "Has something like this happened before?"

Jase pressed his lips tight. "Not exactly like this, but other stuff. Weird things tend to happen around Lucky."

"To me. Not around me. They happen *to* me."

Jase acknowledged that with a nod, an apology in his eyes.

"Now will someone tell me what's going on?" Lucky looked to the doctor for some answers.

"Miss Sinclair."

"Lucky. Please."

"I'm Dr. Meyer. A friend of Hawk's. I usually work in the emergency department, but he asked me to watch over you. He brought you in yesterday. You have a mild concussion. As of this morning's scan, it seems to be getting better. You had surgery yesterday to remove a foreign object from a penetrating wound in your shoulder, just below your clavicle."

"What?"

Hawk leaned over her. "He took out a piece of a tree root that stabbed you."

Surprise shot through her at the same time pain throbbed in her chest and back.

Dr. Meyer went on. "We were able to repair some of the muscle. You were lucky. It missed your lung, though it was pressed right up against it, so you have some bruising. We stitched up a large gash on your thigh and splinted your leg to support the sprained knee you suffered during your fall. You've got multiple contusions all over your body. What's your pain level at the moment?"

She tried to absorb all the information. "Um. I'm sore. All over. I feel like I was hit by a truck."

Hawk brushed his fingers against her palm. "Try a twenty-five foot drop down a hill, where it appears you simply tumbled down, hitting trees and rocks and bushes on your way to a flat boulder where you cracked your head and landed on a tree root that impaled you." His light touch belied the intense fury in his gaze.

"Someone pushed me." She shook her head. "No. That's not quite right. I wasn't able to really stand. They had their arms around me from behind, then they just let me go." Flashes shot through her mind so fast she couldn't make any of them out. "I remember thinking I couldn't make anything work. I couldn't try to catch myself."

Hawk held up her hand and showed her the brace on her pinky finger. "You dislocated your finger and sustained a lot of other injuries on your way down. When I found you—"

Flashes of memory came back to her. "That's right. You found me." She scrunched her brow, trying to think clearly. "How did *you* find me?"

Hawk ran his fingers through his already disheveled hair. "Fucking luck. I was out training when I took a lesser known trail. I heard you call out to me."

"I saw something red flash through all the green. I knew I was dying. I called for you."

"Yes. And it's damn lucky I found you when I did, or you'd be dead."

Her hand contracted in his. She knew that to be absolutely true. "Th-thank you."

"I'm so damn glad I found you when I did. Another hour..." Hawk looked lost in the memory of finding her. The anguish on his face startled her. He really cared.

She squeezed his hand again. "I'm okay now, thanks to you. I really appreciate it."

Hawk tugged a lock of her hair. "We're going to talk about it later." He glanced at their audience, then back to her.

"Um. Okay." She had a feeling she was missing something important.

Dr. Meyer continued. "We're going to keep you one more night at least. The stitches in your leg, breast, and shoulder can come out in about seven to ten days. You'll need to keep them clean and dry. No baths, but a shower is fine as long as you pat them dry afterward." The doctor glanced at Jase, then back to her. "We've performed a series of tests. All of your bloodwork came back normal." He paused again. "Ah, because of the way you were found and that you'd indicated to Hawk that you'd been drugged..." He seemed to have a hard time saying the rest.

She spit it out for him. "You performed a rape kit, I take it."

"Yes. There were no signs of trauma," he said matter-of-fact. "Also no semen."

Jase added. "You were out there for several days. It's inconclusive. The guy could have used a condom." He winced after delivering that news.

She didn't know what to say or feel at the moment. "Okay." A flash of something...that voice rang in her head. "I was at the bar." She looked up at Lincoln. "I was supposed to meet you at your place."

Jase stepped toward Lincoln.

He held up both hands. "It wasn't like that. She's my brother's girl. I just asked if she'd clean my house and maybe make me some of her yummy food once in a while."

Jase backed off. "When was this?"

"Saturday night," Hawk volunteered and held up a flash drive. "Linc brought me the surveillance footage. We haven't had a chance to look at it yet."

Lincoln nodded. "We've been here watching over Lucky like Hawk promised he would."

Lucky remembered now. "You promised you wouldn't leave me alone."

"And I won't." He leaned over and kissed her forehead.

She blushed from her chest to the roots of her hair, but oh how she loved that sweet gesture. She wanted more. It had been so long since anyone had been affectionate with her.

Hawk eyed her. "You're really pretty when you're flustered."

She didn't know what to say to that, or make of this sudden development where Hawk was acting like they were more than housekeeper and client. "Um, yeah, I don't know what to do with that at the moment. But you should know I think I remember someone standing over me at the bar. I was lying down?" That didn't make sense. Where would she lie down in a bar?

Lincoln's eyes narrowed. "Lying down? Where?"

"I don't know. But I could still hear the music." She tried to pull the image into her mind but couldn't seem to find it. "Everything sounded...muffled. The wood beams in the ceiling were...collapsing?"

The nurse beside her finished taking her blood pressure and fiddling with the IV bag and line.

"It had to be the drugs making you hallucinate or something," Hawk supplied.

Dr. Meyer nodded for the nurse to go. "Do you have any questions or concerns?"

Lucky could barely take it all in. "Um, not at the moment. I'm still trying to wrap my head around waking up here." She glanced down at the hospital gown, her blanket covered legs, and Hawk sitting beside her. "Yeah. This doesn't seem real yet." She corrected herself a bit. "Except for the pain. That feels real."

"I can up your dose."

"No. I need to be alert. I need to figure this out."

Dr. Meyer nodded. "Okay. But hit the Call button next to you if you change your mind. A nurse will be in to check on you again soon." He glanced at Hawk, then back to her. "I'll be back to see you in the morning before your discharge, unless something else comes up and you need me."

"I hope I don't." She looked from him to Hawk and back again. "And thank you for taking care of me."

"You're welcome." He turned to his friend. "You have my number if you need me."

Hawk stretched his arm across the bed and shook the doctor's hand. "Thanks for letting me stay with her through everything."

"I know how you hate to break a promise." The look they shared told Lucky that Hawk had kept a promise to the doc at some point.

She waited for the doctor to leave before she asked Hawk. "What was that about? What promise?"

"Our promise. That we wouldn't leave each other alone. From the second I found you, until right now, except for a few minutes to update Lincoln, I haven't left your side. I was in the ER with you, took you up to the operating room, where I watched the surgery from an observation room, then to recovery, and now this room." When he promised something, he delivered.

She appreciated his dedication. "The hospital let you do that?"

"He wouldn't take no for an answer," Lincoln supplied with a prideful grin. "One thing about my brother...he means what he says."

"You must be tired of being here, staring at me. You should go home. Get something to eat. Sleep. Whatever. I'm fine."

Hawk shook his head. "First, you're not fine. Second, Lincoln brought me breakfast an hour ago. And last, there's nothing I like more than being with you."

"Man, you have it bad." Lincoln teased his brother.

"Get used to it."

She didn't know if Hawk meant that statement for her or his brother.

"Lucky." Jase leaned against the end of her bed and stared her down. "You need to tell me everything you remember. Even a small detail could help. Please. I know you don't trust me, but I am here to help."

She huffed out a breath. "The last thing I really remember is being at the bar with Desiree. Girls' night. I didn't really want to be there."

"Why?" Hawk asked.

If he liked honesty as much as he lived by it, then she owed him the truth. "Because you might be there."

He raised a brow. "You didn't want to see me."

She shook her head and winced at the pain in her neck and shoulders.

He brushed his hand down her arm. "Be still. Take things slow."

Good advice. So she sucked it up and did the hard thing and admitted. "I really like you." The blazing blush was back. "And we have this thing between us."

"Yeah," he encouraged.

"But it's been at a distance and I didn't know if you kept it that way for a reason. Like that's how you wanted it. I didn't want to go to the bar and mess things up by making you think I was crossing a line."

Hawk glanced at their spectators, then back to her. "Maybe I did because in the beginning, I was really fucked up. I still struggle sometimes, but I've worked really hard the last couple years to heal and rein in my emotions and deal with the things I can't control."

Lincoln pat her arm. "It's true. He used to just grunt a lot and go off unhinged in a rage. Even worse, he'd disappear, or just be silent for days. He'd get lost in a flashback and no one could pull him out until it was over. Now, he talks about what's bothering him. He has coping mechanisms so things don't go so bad."

Hawk patted her hand. "And I have you to remind me that there are good things in my life. You didn't have to do what you did the past two years for someone you didn't even know, but still you somehow saw me clearer than anyone else did." Hawk shrugged. "Well, maybe except for my psychiatrist."

She glanced at Jase, then back to him. "Maybe I understand because I've had some bad things happen to me, too, and I've not always handled it very well on my own. So I wanted you to know you weren't alone."

"You wanted me to know that it was possible to overcome my trauma and live again." He kissed her fingertips. "Every book you left me had a happy ending, even when things seemed dire for a while."

"Things change. We can change them."

His warm gaze made her insides mush. "You really believe that."

"I have to." Or why try at all?

Hawk nodded. "Me, too. And we're going to talk more about all that later. But first, answer Jase's questions. I need to know what happened and who did this to you."

She tried not to fidget when she looked Jase in the eye again. "He's out. You know that."

Jase wasn't part of the investigation of her family's death. He joined the sheriff's department years later and took on Lucky's many harassment cases. But he knew everything about the murders and how missing evidence kept Neil from serving time for the murders and her getting justice for her family.

She bit her lip. "I think he was there. At the bar." A yucky feeling creeped over her skin, like she could remember him touching her. She wanted to shower and scrub herself clean.

"Keep going," Jase coaxed.

"I remember talking to Lincoln about a job. Everything was fine then." She looked at him for confirmation.

Lincoln squeezed her arm again. "Yes. We agreed to meet on Sunday, so you could see the house and give me a price."

"Right. I gave you my card and Desiree and I walked away." She closed her eyes, trying to remember. "You made me a drink."

"Peach sangria. You loved it." Lincoln's gaze narrowed. "So did your friend. She kind of stole it from you for a second."

Jase studied Lincoln. "Did Desiree say anything, do anything?"

Lincoln shrugged. "She seemed..." He winced at Lucky. "Jealous of you."

"What? No." Desiree was her best friend. "She was sore that you didn't ask her out."

"I told you the truth that night. I'm not dating right now. Plus...I didn't like her vibe."

"She can be a lot," Lucky admitted. "After that, I don't know what happened. I have these flashes of memories. Hearing his voice. Seeing the stars. Smelling pine. Being dropped. Hearing critters in the bushes, crickets chirping. The cold." She shivered. "It was so cold. And then when I was finally more lucid, I just hurt everywhere. I felt trapped. I couldn't really move. I tried to call out for help. I didn't see anyone or hear anything. I tried to listen for a car. I felt...so alone. Lost."

"You were about two miles from the nearest road." Hawk pressed another kiss to her palm.

"Did anyone hit on you at the bar?" Jase asked.

"Not that I remember. But I'm not usually the one who gets hit on."

Lincoln chuckled. "Like ten guys were staring at her while we talked."

She shook her head. "You mean staring at Desiree. She's the pretty one."

All the men gawked at her.

"What?" They made her really nervous.

"You're gorgeous, sweetheart." Hawk nodded to reassure her. "Don't doubt it for a second."

The door swung open. "Well, aren't you a lucky duck to have all this man candy surrounding you?" Desiree swept into the room with a smile and flirtation in her eyes.

Lucky didn't realize she'd sunk her nails into Hawk's wrist until he tapped the back of her hand and brought her attention to where she'd gripped him so hard. She tried to let loose, but something had gone haywire inside her as she stared at her best friend.

Hawk stood and moved in close, his lips at her ear. "Relax. You're okay. No one is going to hurt you."

She loosened her grip, but didn't let him go.

"That's it." He kissed her forehead, staring into her eyes, grounding her in the here and now.

"I'm sorry."

Hawk brushed his fingers through her hair. "Nothing to be sorry about."

Jase caught her reaction and turned to her friend. "Desiree. Nice to see you again."

"Love the uniform." Desiree eye-fucked Jase, blatantly and shamelessly.

He seemed less than interested as his gaze turned stony. "Heard you and Lucky were at Gunn Brothers Bar Saturday night."

"We were. We ran into Lincoln. My girl landed a job with him. We danced. My lightweight friend had too much to drink—and not enough sleep as usual—so we called it a night kind of early."

Jase turned to Lucky. "Do you remember driving yourself home?"

She shook her head.

Desiree walked past Lincoln to her shoulder and dropped the overnight bag she carried on the floor at her feet. "Of course you don't. I drove you home because you were snockered. Tucked you into bed myself."

That doesn't feel right.

"What time was that?" Jase asked.

"We got to the bar early and left early. So maybe nine. Nine-thirty." Desiree shrugged. "I left her place before ten and got home a little later. My dad, your boss,"—Desiree unsubtly reminded Jase her father was the sheriff—"was asleep in front of the TV when I got home."

"What was he watching?"

She shrugged. "Don't know. Probably the news. I wasn't paying attention. I went to check on Krystal, then went to bed myself." Desiree turned to Lucky. "She wants to bake cookies with you again."

Lucky loved Desiree's little girl. Krystal called her auntie because she and Desiree were close as sisters.

So why did she have this odd feeling all of a sudden around Desiree? Why was her heart beating a mile a minute, like she needed to run away?

"I'm not up for having her at my place just yet. But soon. I need some time to recover."

"From what? What happened? All I know is they found you in the woods. No one will tell me anything more." Desiree waited for an answer.

No one filled her in.

Lucky didn't have an explanation. "I don't know what happened. I can't remember. I think I was drugged."

Jase asked her a question, but kept his gaze on Desiree. "You were found naked, except for a pair of pink and white polka dot panties that Hawk cut off you. Do you remember what you were wearing before your missing time?"

Her gaze shot to Hawk and she blushed again. "Uh. I guess you got an eyeful."

"I was more focused on keeping you alive." His fingers swept up and down her forearm. "Don't worry about it. You've got nothing to be embarrassed about."

She tried to focus on what happened. "I wore those panties that night, along with a blue maxi dress."

"Which is still on the floor in your room." Desiree volunteered. "I went by your place on the way here and picked up some clothes and things I thought you'd need when you leave here." That was really nice of her friend. And maybe a little out of character for her to do anything without being asked.

"How did you know I was here?"

Lincoln raised his hand. "I called your company to let them know Hawk had found you and that you were here. A few of the ladies stopped by last night, but Hawk told them to come back later, that you needed your rest more than anything. One of the ladies—Joellen, I think was her name—said she'd call Desiree and let her know you'd been found."

She put her hand over his on the bed. "Thank you."

Desiree noticed that she'd touched Lincoln and frowned, then stared hard at Lucky.

Lucky took her hand off Lincoln and stared at the sheet.

"They tried to file a missing person report for you," Jase explained.

"But there was some rule or whatever that you had to follow, so you didn't take the report," Lucky groused, knowing how these things went. She'd had nothing but trouble trying to get justice for all the things that happened to her. "You left me to fend for myself like always, because you could give a shit about me."

Jase folded his arms over his wide chest. "For all I knew, you'd decided to take a vacation and leave town for a few days."

"Yeah. Without telling anyone and ditching work. Because that sounds like me!"

Jase tensed, then sucked in a breath and reined in whatever argument he wanted to make. "Just because I didn't file the report doesn't mean I didn't look for you, because I was worried."

That caught her off guard. "Well…um…that's surprising."

Jase kept his defensive posture. "It shouldn't be. I do take you seriously. I just can't always find any evidence to back up what's happened. Like I couldn't find anything to prove you'd been kidnapped or whatever this was."

"Then how did she get out there where Hawk found her?" Desiree asked, a not so subtle hint of anger in her voice.

"That's what I'm investigating. We have some evidence to follow, but nothing that points to one person. So any and all details you can remember are helpful. Since your car is still at your home, someone else took you out there." But Jase obviously couldn't identify who.

Which meant, yet again, nothing would happen. Nothing was solved. The person hurting her would continue to harass her. Or worse. Because it felt very much like this time, they wanted her dead.

Was it Neil? Someone he'd sent?

Would she ever be free of this and her past?

"So basically we know nothing except that I was tossed down a hill?"

"Not exactly," Jase argued. "Based on your injuries, we know you went down the hill incapacitated like you've told us. There was plenty of stuff you could have grabbed or used to stop your fall, but you didn't. We'll test the blood we collected from the scene to confirm and determine what was used to drug you. Pictures from the scene show clearly that you rolled continuously, hitting your head, slicing your leg, and scraping your body along the way."

"Is that why my hip and back hurts?"

Hawk put his hand on her shoulder. "You hit some pretty big rock faces that tore up your skin. The nurse has been putting salve on them and changing the bandages regularly. They look better today than they did yesterday."

"Someone's getting a show," Desiree teased, but the room went silent. Neither Lucky, nor the men found it amusing or appropriate. But Desiree could be like that.

Jase finished writing some notes in his notepad. "So you don't remember getting home that night?"

"No. But if Desiree says she took me, then I'm sure that's what happened."

The skeptical frown on Jase's face spoke volumes. "Did Lucky say anything once you got her home about going out again or seeing someone?"

Desiree shook her head. "Not that I can remember." She tilted her head and tapped her lip with her index finger. "Come to think of it, there was the guy she danced with at the bar. He didn't seem to want to let her go. Maybe he followed us to her place." She shrugged like it could have happened that way.

Lucky couldn't even remember dancing with anyone. She usually liked to watch, instead of participate.

Desiree was the life of the party, not her.

"Okay. Well I have the surveillance footage, so I'll check it out and see if I can ID the guy and if he followed you out." Jase held up the thumb drive.

"Wow." Desiree's eyes went wide. "This is like a real life *Dateline* going on here." She seemed excited by the mystery.

Jase shook his head at Desiree. "Did anything seem out of place or disturbed at Lucky's place when you stopped by there earlier to pack her bag?"

"No. Well, come to think of it, the bed didn't look all that slept in. Lucky's a neat freak. I guess it goes with the job. Anyway, the cover was pulled back, but the bed wasn't messy like she'd slept in it."

"Anything broken or turned over, like there'd been a struggle?"

Desiree shook her head. "Not a thing."

Jase sighed. "I checked with your neighbors already. No one saw anything unusual since Saturday. Of course your place is kind of isolated. As far as I could see, no one broke in. The locks didn't look tampered with."

"You went out to my place?" Lucky couldn't believe Jase had already started investigating.

"I told you, just because I couldn't file an official missing person report didn't mean I wasn't looking for you."

"I appreciate that. I'll try to be more grateful and less agitating."

Jase put his hand over her ankle.

She twitched and he took it away.

He held up his hand. "Sorry."

She nodded, wishing she wasn't always pushing people away.

"I understand how frustrating this must be for you. How frightening. I'm going to do everything I can to figure this out. Okay?" Jase seemed genuinely determined to do something this time.

"Yes."

Jase turned to Hawk. "I know she's important to you, so don't bust my balls anymore. I'm working on it."

Hawk agreed with a nod. "Get it done. Someone out there tried to kill her. I want to know who and why. And I want them locked up for good."

"Me, too, man." Jase's gaze met hers. "It isn't right, what happened to you. What keeps happening to you. None of it. I really hope this time we catch whoever's doing this to you and stop them for good." Jase folded his notepad, tucked it into his pocket, then left the room.

It felt like he meant everything he'd said, and that eased her mind.

Lincoln headed for the door, too. "I'm going to the cafeteria. Anyone want anything? Hawk, I'll bring you some lunch." He looked at Desiree with a question in his eyes.

"I'm good. Not staying long. I need to pick up Krystal from daycare."

Lincoln left.

Desiree eyed Hawk. "Mind giving us some time alone?"

Lucky kept her hold on Hawk's arm, trying not to dig her nails into him again. The thought of him leaving made her feel desperate, like if he left he might not come back and she'd lose this chance with him.

Irrational? Yes.

But she'd earned a little bit of time to be out of her mind, hadn't she?

And for some reason, Desiree made her feel...unsettled.

Hawk stayed sitting by her side. "No can do. I made a promise. I'm not breaking it now."

"Okay." Desiree focused on her. "Lucky, I'm really sorry. I had no idea you were gone until Joellen called me, looking for you when you didn't show up to the office on Monday."

"It's okay. Thanks for filling in some of the missing time."

"You really can't remember?" Desiree stared her down, looking for cracks.

Lucky wished she knew what really happened. "Not really. Bits and pieces of the time when Hawk found me are starting to come back . Even that's scraps because I was so out of it."

Hawk laced his fingers with hers. "I'll fill you in from the time I found you to the helicopter ride to the hospital. You already know I haven't left your side since you got here."

"Helicopter ride?"

He winked at her. "I'll take you up some time, so you can enjoy it. You'll love it. A bird's eye view for miles."

She couldn't help her shy smile. "I'd love that."

He loved flying and she wanted to share that with him, even if flying in a helicopter seemed a little scary. He was experienced and wouldn't let anything happen to her.

Desiree pointed between them. "What's up with you two all of a sudden?"

Hawk kept his gaze on Lucky, but answered her friend. "We're together now. Isn't that right, sweetheart?"

"Unbelievably, yes." She hoped it wasn't wishful thinking or some delusion she'd had in the forest.

Hawk gave her an indulgent look. "It's real. Believe it."

"Wow." Desiree took a step back. "This seems awfully fast."

Hawk shook his head, his gaze locked on her. "It's been a long time coming. Right, Lucky?"

She nodded, a tear slipping from her watery eyes.

"Hey." Hawk stood and leaned over her. "What's this? Are you in pain? Want me to call for the nurse to get you more meds?"

"No." She grabbed his shirt and held on to him. "I'm happy. And a little overwhelmed."

"Me, too. But don't worry. Everything's going to be okay. You'll see." He brushed his thumb over her cheek, wiping her tears.

She wanted to believe him, but some instinct inside her told her this incident was different from the others. She'd nearly died. Was this just the beginning? It scared her to think they'd try again and this was just the beginning of the end.

Desiree's heavy stare made her look up. "What?"

"I never thought this would actually be a thing, but you did it. You actually got the guy. You must be really happy." Desiree sounded anything but excited for her.

She didn't seem jealous. More like annoyed, even though her voice remained neutral.

Maybe the pain meds were muddling her head and she was reading things wrong.

"I'm..." She didn't know what to say under the circumstances. "I'm trying to catch up to everything that's happened." Everything with Hawk seemed so new and fragile, but also absolute. Like he'd said, this felt like something a long time coming.

"You got the guy. What more do you want?"

"To know who hurt me and why?" *To stop them from doing it again. And succeeding.*

"Seems to me you might owe them a thank you for getting the two of you together."

What an odd thing to say.

Stunned, Lucky shook her head in disbelief, then glanced over to Hawk, who wore a similar expression. "I don't think I'll be thanking someone who tried to kill me."

Desiree seemed to catch herself. "Oh. Right. I'm just saying there's a silver lining here, that's all."

Lucky sank deeper into the covers. "I'm tired. I think I'll try to get some rest."

Hawk brushed his hand over her hair. "Close your eyes. I'll be right here the whole time, waiting for you to wake up."

She bit her bottom lip. "Um. Don't you have work or something?"

He bent close and looked her in the eyes. "I'm not leaving here without you. Especially when I don't know if you're safe."

"Looks like you've got everything you need." Desiree started for the door.

"Don't go. You just got here." She had questions for Desiree about that night.

"I have to run an errand before I pick up Krystal. I'll call you later and check on you. Your phone is in the bag." With that, Desiree opened the door, only to find Lincoln on his way back in. "Hey, if you change your mind about that date," she purred, "we could double." Desiree grinned at her and Hawk, then looked back to Lincoln, who looked flustered.

"Uh, I'll think about it." Lincoln's voice held little conviction.

Desiree knew he was just pacifying her, but kept her smile in place. "You know how to get in touch with me, since my bestie is your brother's new flame." Desiree sauntered out, leaving Lucky with the guys.

Lincoln handed a container to Hawk, along with a can of soda. "I don't know if you're allowed to eat anything yet, or I'd have brought you something, too."

The smell of pasta and garlic hit her nose and her stomach growled.

Hawk laughed. "I bet the nurse will bring you something soon."

Lincoln pulled a brownie out of his Gunn Brothers Distillery hoodie pocket and set it on the table beside her bed. "For later. You deserve a hell of lot more than dessert after what happened."

She blushed. "Thank you, Lincoln. I appreciate it."

They both took their seats and opened their containers, revealing a heaping pile of pasta Pomodoro, salad, and a chunk of garlic bread.

"Wow. They must have a really nice cafeteria here."

Lincoln shook his head. "They don't, so I ran across the street to a food truck."

"Well enjoy. I'm just going to close my eyes for a bit." She did just that and as she fell asleep she felt Hawk press a kiss to her forehead and whisper, "Sweet dreams. We'll talk more when you're feeling better."

She couldn't wait, because as dire as things felt, she had hope that with Hawk she might find some happiness.

Chapter Five

Lucky had been awake for more than an hour just staring at Hawk, asleep beside her. He couldn't be all that comfortable sitting in the chair, his head by her hip, face turned to her. One of his arms draped over her legs, his big hand wrapped around her thigh. The other hand rested on her stomach. She couldn't remember the last time she'd been held like this.

Had she ever felt this safe? This content?

She could lie here the rest of her life, watching him sleep so peacefully beside her.

He hadn't left her side since he brought her here.

It seemed so unreal that he'd put his whole life on hold for two days just to keep her company. It wasn't like she couldn't take care of herself.

Still, it was nice to have someone by her side.

Desiree had abruptly left yesterday and hadn't called, texted, or come by again. She was probably busy taking care of Krystal. Being a single mom wasn't easy.

The nurse came in bright and early that morning to remove her IV line and change her shoulder dressing.

Lucky made sure she didn't disturbed Hawk. He needed his rest.

She couldn't wait to be discharged later this morning. She wanted to be home where she felt comfortable. Where it was quiet and no one interrupted her sleep or her conversations with Hawk.

He'd kept their interactions light. They talked about their favorite movies, what they liked to do in their spare time, where she'd like to travel if she ever left this town, and what she liked to eat and drink.

She'd learned a lot about Hawk and his big family. Well, bigger than hers. She missed her brother. Not her abusive dad, though she did have a few good memories of him. Even monsters could be good sometimes. But she still had an aunt in Oregon who kept in touch on birthdays and holidays. She even had a set of grandparents in Arizona, though they were her father's parents and not very nice, as you could imagine. He was the way he was for a reason.

Beside her, Hawk stirred, his massive shoulders jerking as his hand gripped her thigh tighter. He didn't hurt her, but she could tell he was dreaming and in distress. "Lucky." He mumbled her name, then came awake, his eyes wide and staring straight at her.

"It's okay. I'm here. You're okay."

His gaze softened as the shock of coming awake so abruptly wore off. Looking to their joined hands, he picked hers up and brought her palm to his lips. He kissed her softly, his breath coming fast against her skin, and the scruff of his beard scratched against her palm.

She liked it, the contrast of his soft lips and the scrape of his golden beard.

"I thought I lost you."

She shook her head. "I'm right here."

He sat up and ran his gaze over her. "They took you off the IV and monitors."

"I'll be free to go soon."

"How are you feeling?"

"Lucky to be alive. Still a bit surprised, but grateful you're still here with me. Without you, I'd be climbing the walls by now."

He put her hand against his rough cheek. "I told you, I'm not going anywhere without you."

"I'm starting to believe you. I woke up and you were there and I…"

His gaze intensified. "What? Tell me."

"I was really happy to see you."

"I wish it hadn't taken this to bring us together."

A knock on the door made her jump.

"Come in," Hawk called, squeezing her leg to let her know he was there. Everything was fine. He wouldn't let anything happen to her.

An orderly walked in with her breakfast tray and set it on the table at her feet.

Hawk stood and hit the button on her bed to raise her head up. "Eat. You'll need your strength to get through being discharged."

The orderly lifted the lid on her tray. "Eggs, bacon, roasted potatoes, coffee and juice."

"Thank you." Her stomach rumbled the second the bacon smell hit her nose.

Hawk almost grinned beside her. "Go on. Eat it while it's hot."

"If you want to hit the cafeteria, I'll be okay."

He shook his head. "I'm not leaving you alone." He pulled out his phone and checked his messages. "Lincoln is on his way up with breakfast for me."

She bit her lip. "You guys are so close. It must be nice to have someone who has your back like that." It made her think about what she and her brother Danny would have been like now. As close as they used to be? Or even closer as adults, once they realized how much they needed each other?

Hawk squeezed her hand. "My brothers are always there for me. And you'll get used to us having your back, too."

While Hawk used the restroom, she dug into the bacon and downed half her coffee. It wasn't great, but the bacon made up for it. All in all, she was feeling fairly good, despite the pain in her shoulder that spiked every time she moved even the slightest bit.

Suddenly the door swung open without the knock that usually preceded it. Her heart sped up with a shot of adrenaline through her veins. The room morphed into the bar and she was lying on her back and her worst nightmare was looming over her.

Neil. Her ex. The one who killed her family.

A scream lodged in her throat.

She swore he was there the night she'd been drugged, abducted, and dumped in the middle of nowhere. Was he here to finish what he started with her family and kill her, too?

Terror had her scrambling off the bed, her arms up to ward him off. "No!" she screamed. This time, she wouldn't cower. She'd fight. She rushed him, slamming her fists into his chest, pushing him back. After one blow, the pain in her shoulder made her arm useless as she kept on hitting him with her good arm. "No. No. No. Stay away from me. I hate you. I hate you!"

Hawk burst out of the bathroom and hooked his arm across her waist and pulled her back from that piece of shit.

She hadn't realized that Neil had put up no resistance. He hadn't said anything. She didn't believe for a second he was here for any other reason than to taunt and hurt her again.

She tried to go after him again, but Hawk turned her toward him, picked her up, and pressed her back into the wall, his face right in hers. He cupped her jaw in one hand and forced her to look at him. "Do you see me?"

The haze of rage and terror washed away as she stared into his hazel eyes, gone dark gold with concern. "I won't let him hurt me again."

"Who?"

"Neil. He's going to kill me. You have to stop him."

"Okay. I believe you. Now look past me and tell me who is standing there."

She narrowed her gaze and wondered why he was asking that and not kicking Neil out, until she shifted her gaze and found Lincoln standing by the door, coffees in one hand, a bakery bag in the other. "Lincoln?"

"Hey, sweetheart. It's just me."

Tears welled in her eyes. "But?"

Hawk touched her chin with his finger, turning her face back to him. "It's okay. You're okay. You just imagined it was him." Hawk turned his face to his brother. "Give us a minute."

Lincoln left.

Hawk waited for the door to close before he turned back to her. "Flashbacks, waking nightmares, it's part of PTSD for some people. Trust me. I know exactly what you're going through because of my military service. You've been through a lot. It's natural that your brain is trying to make sense of everything and also trying to protect you. I get it."

She touched her forehead to his. "Of course you do. But...that's never happened to me before, seeing things that aren't there."

"I know. I'm sorry this is happening to you. But you don't need to be scared. I'm here. I won't let anything happen to you."

She kept her head dipped, trying to collect herself, then realized she had her legs wrapped around Hawk's waist, he had his huge hand on one of her ass cheeks, holding her up, and they were in a very intimate position. Her head shot up and their eyes locked. "Um." He was so very close to her. Closer than anyone had gotten in a long time. Too long.

"Yeah," Hawk breathed out. "You feel really good in my arms."

She didn't know what possessed her, but she closed the distance and hugged him like a monkey wrapped around a tree trunk.

His arms wrapped around her and tightened. "I've got you, Lucky."

"I'm really starting to believe that."

"Scared?"

"Hopeful."

Hawk rubbed his cheek against hers. "Me, too."

She sighed out her contentment, but that only punctuated how much her chest hurt from moving her shoulder.

The nurse was supposed to bring a brace for her to wear home and keep on for the next week or so.

"What's wrong?" Hawk leaned his head back, so he could look her in the eyes.

"Shoulder."

"You're supposed to be resting and not moving your arm, so that wound can heal." Hawk took the few steps to the bed and leaned over to deposit her back onto it. His hand slid from her ass along her thigh to her knee in a slow glide that made a thousand nerve ending light up like Christmas lights, warm and lively. Need danced along her skin and settled between her thighs.

"Um. Yeah." She blushed from her chest to the roots of her hair. "That was...nice."

Hawk brushed his fingers along her cheek. "You're even prettier when you blush."

Her face heated even more. "I look like I feel. Gross. I desperately need a shower. I don't know how you can stand being this close to me."

He gently took her calf and pulled her leg down flat on the bed, then smoothed her hospital gown down her legs. "I find myself unable to stay away. You're hurt, but you're alive. That's all that matters to me."

"I'm alive because of you. Thank you for finding me, for saving me."

"You saved me first."

She shook her head. "No. You did that all on your own."

"Not true. You helped in all those little ways you reminded me I wasn't alone even in the darkest part of the night when I was surrounded by ghosts and the things I couldn't change. I'd read one of your notes, the books you'd leave me with those happy endings, the mundane crosswords and word searches that gave my brain a break from the past. And always there was something tempting in the fridge that made me want to eat even when I had no appetite. For food or life."

"I just...know what it's like to feel like you're alone."

"I didn't realize you're more alone than I am. I'm sorry about that. As much as you gave to me and I gave to you, I should have done better at being your friend, because that's how I felt about you."

"And now?" She didn't mean to push, but she needed to know if he felt the way she felt.

"I want more. I want to give you more. If you'll let me. It's been a long time since I was serious about anyone, so I'm a bit rusty."

"Me, too."

"Then we're in it together."

A knock interrupted them. "Can I come in now?" Lincoln called through the door.

Hawk rolled his eyes. "You good?"

"Yeah. I am because you're here."

"I didn't want the first time I did this to be here, but I can't help myself." He leaned in and brushed a soft kiss against her lips.

The zing of electricity shot through her, making her want more.

But Hawk backed off with just that teaser of what was to come with a genuine smile on his lips. "I knew it."

"What?"

"That you could quickly become an addiction." He squeezed her hand, then shouted over his shoulder, "Come in."

"Finally," Lincoln grumbled, his gaze shooting right to her. "You good?"

"I am. Thanks. And I'm sorry for attacking you."

Lincoln held the cardboard coffee holder toward Hawk so he could take his cup. "No worries. I get it." His gaze briefly landed on Hawk before it came back to hers. "You didn't see me. But damn girl, you left a few bruises. I have no doubt you could hold your own if you needed to."

"Or if I wasn't drugged?"

Hawk sat on the edge of her bed. "Which means the person who did this knew they had to incapacitate you to get you out of that bar without a fight."

"So they could rape me? Or was it something else?" She kept her eyes fixed on the blue square pattern of her hospital gown.

Hawk put his hand over hers. "Which one of those things resonates with you? What do you feel inside you that happened?"

"It's all just jumbled flashes. But are they real? Or just my imagination conjuring my worst fears?"

"I can't answer that. What feels the most real to you?" Hawk's patience helped her to settle and think more clearly.

"It feels very personal, like someone I know really wants me to suffer. And maybe die." The weight of those nearly three days out in the woods prickled under her skin with all the fear and helplessness she'd endured over all those seconds, minutes, hours, and days.

A chill raced over her skin.

"We'll figure this out. Until then, you're coming to stay with me."

She gaped at Hawk. "What? No. You don't have to do that."

"How are you going to take care of yourself with one arm?"

"I'll manage." It would be hard, but she'd had to do everything for herself a long time now.

But wouldn't it be nice to have someone take care of me for once?

He shook his head. "Not happening. Besides, this is really about your safety. I won't be able to sleep, think, or do anything without being constantly worried that someone could take you again. I can't do it. So put me out of my misery and agree to stay with me, because one way or another, I'll convince you, even if I have to kidnap you myself."

"So what you're saying is I have no choice."

"Now you're catching on." He grinned.

She gave him her sternest face, even if she didn't really mean it. "I don't like being bossed around."

"I know. And I'll try not be such a brute about things in the future. But this...I need this."

She understood beneath the demand was genuine fear for her safety. "Fine. I need it, too," she admitted on a whisper.

He nearly grinned again.

Lincoln full on smiled and chuckled. "You two are adorable."

She stuck her tongue out at him, then turned to Hawk. "We'll have to stop at my place to pick up some of my stuff."

"No problem. We'll do it on the way home."

Home. That sounded so good, she tried to hide the way it warmed her heart and made her dream of a life she'd never let herself even contemplate before Hawk rescued her and changed everything.

Okay, maybe on the days she cleaned his house, she'd pretended that she lived there with him. Imagined that he was hers.

OMG! He was hers now, and he wanted her to be with him at his place.

Was she truly about to get everything she'd ever wanted?

Chapter Six

Hawk pulled into the driveway in front of Lucky's little cabin. He loved its simple design with the front porch tucked under the extended roof. He imagined walking into a living space with a small kitchen and the bedroom and bathroom at the back. The simple dark wood made it feel like it had sprung up from the forest floor. "How much land do you have here?"

"Just an acre. I wish the cabin was nestled in the trees out back."

"Is that why you've got a couple saplings planted on each side of the cabin?"

"I planted them last year. I can't wait to see them grow and surround the cabin."

"It'll be pretty." Crushed rock crunched under his boots as he made his way to the porch. The path was outlined in large river rock. The scent of lavender from the bushes outside the path reminded him of his mother's garden. The miniature pink wild roses growing along the porch added another splash of color.

"Let's get your stuff, secure your place, and head over to mine. You must be hungry." They'd left the hospital a couple hours after she'd finished her breakfast and the nurse fitted her with a shoulder brace to keep her arm immobile so her chest could heal.

She grabbed her mail from the box, then met him up at the porch. She didn't have her keys. Presumably they were in the house with her purse. She grabbed the spare she kept hidden beneath the bench in a metal hide-a-key she'd glued to the underside. She unlocked the door and stepped inside, halting a few steps in as he closed the door.

"What's wrong?"

"Nothing." It sounded more like a question.

He raised a brow. "You sure?"

"I don't remember coming home that night."

"Desiree said you were out of it. Drunk."

She squished her lips. "That's just it. I don't really drink a lot. Never have. I got drunk once and hated the feeling. Ever since, I slow down as soon as I'm feeling tipsy." Especially after she'd been drugged along with her family and woke up to them...dead. Yeah, no. She didn't like being even a little incapacitated.

Hawk's understanding gaze said she didn't need to spell it out. "Okay. Well, your car is here, so we know someone drove it." He glanced around the room. "Your purse is on the counter by the stove."

Her eyebrows shot up. "That's not right." She turned to the table by the doorway with a bowl filled with change and keys he assumed belonged to her clients, since they each had a tag with a last name on it, including his. Next to the bowl was a potted plant and a crystal dish filled with Hershey's Chocolate Nuggets. In the corner was a coat tree with a heavy coat, one lighter one, a sweater, and a couple of purses hanging from it.

He spotted a phone cable dangling over the table, too. "So you normally come in, drop your keys in the bowl, put your phone on the charger, hang up your coat or sweater and your purse."

"Exactly. So why is my purse all the way over there?"

"If Desiree brought you home, then she'd have just dumped your stuff on the way to taking you to the bedroom or bathroom at the back." The bathroom door was just past the dining area that was in the middle of the open space between the back rooms and the front living and kitchen space.

"I guess." She moved toward the bedroom. "Something still doesn't feel right."

He looked around the room, trying to pick out anything that felt or looked off even though this was his first time here. He loved the pictures on the walls. All were bright fields of wildflowers in bloom with the blue sky as the backdrop in some and the forest in others.

He spotted a couple pictures of Lucky when she was young, standing with a little boy. Her brother, he presumed. They had the same eyes, same nose. Lucky's hair was lighter than her brothers more light brown than blonde.

Lucky stopped at the door to the bedroom. "I never close this all the way." She put her hand on the knob. "Do you smell that?"

She turned the knob just as he yelled, "Wait!" She pushed the door open and a whooshing sound was the first thing that alerted him to danger, right as a bright fireball erupted, making Lucky stumble backward away from the heat and flames.

Hawk ran forward, wrapped his arms around her waist, picked her up, spun around, dropped her feet to the floor, then pushed her away. He spun back and ran into the room to put out the fire with the quilt from her bed.

Lucky braced herself with her hands on either side of the door frame, her eyes wide with fright and concern, even though the fire was out now. "What is that?" She notched her chin toward the glass bottle he pulled from beneath the charred blanket. "What happened?"

"Someone tried to burn down your house." *And maybe kill her, too.* He didn't say that last part out loud.

Lucky followed his stare to the back of the door where a piece of black duct tape held several burned up matchsticks and a partially burned matchbox taped to the floor.

When Lucky pushed the door open, the matchstick had scraped across the box, lighting it. She'd also knocked over a soda bottle filled with gasoline. As soon as the fumes hit the flame, it ignited and could have spread rapidly with the smeared gasoline spilling across the floor toward the bed. Everything would have gone up quickly.

He had to believe if he wasn't here, she'd have gotten out, run the second she saw the flames.

Her hand gripped his forearm. "Put that down. It's evidence. We need to call Jase."

He pulled out his phone and made the call. "Hey. It's Hawk. You need to come out to Lucky's place, maybe bring the fire department. Someone set a trap to start a fire when Lucky came home."

"What the...I'll be there soon. Don't touch anything. Get out of the house if you haven't already."

"We're headed out now." Hawk coughed alone with Lucky from the smoke and quickly put his hand to Lucky's back and ushered her out the door. Hawk pocketed his phone again and pulled Lucky into his chest on the porch. He held her close. "I'm sorry, sweetheart."

She buried her face in his chest. "You keep saying that but none of this is your fault."

He stared off behind her, wishing he could do something to make her feel better, or at least find this asshole and stop him. "What the hell is that?" He gently set Lucky aside and walked past her toward her car, parked next to his. The front left tire was completely flat. Squatting down for a better look, Hawk spotted a long slash in the sidewall—and a knife discarded just beneath the car.

"Are you kidding me?" Lucky leaned back against his Range Rover's fender and stared up at the sky. "Fuck my life."

He stood and took her by the shoulders. "Don't say that. We saved the house and I can change your tire."

"Yeah? And how long until you're tired of picking up the pieces of this mess and resent me for bringing all of this fucking baggage to your doorstep?"

He kissed her on the forehead. "We all have baggage. Mine's been a heavy load, which means I can certainly handle yours if it keeps you in my life so we can get to the good stuff."

"Not much of that the last few days," she grumbled.

"I know you're tired and sore and someone is messing with you, but I need you to hang on a little longer. Once we get to my place, you can rest and relax and let me take care of you."

She held her hand out wide. "Why would you want to do that?" She let her hand drop to her side and smack her thigh.

He cupped her beautiful face. "Because I care about you. You matter to me. And it pisses me off that someone is doing this to you, so I'm going to do everything I can to help you stop whoever this is, once and for all." He stared down into her tear-filled eyes. "Do you believe me?"

She put her hand on his chest over his heart. "Yes. I'm trying." Her gaze dropped to the ground behind him. "That knife was my father's. He used it—" The words abruptly cut off with her breathing.

"Lucky?"

"On me," she choked out.

The scars all over her.

She traced a long one down her arm. "I kept it to remind myself that he couldn't hurt me anymore."

This was some kind of psychological mind fuck someone was doing to her. "We'll figure this out." He held her trembling body close as they waited for Jase and the fire department to arrive.

It didn't take long for their cars and trucks to line the road and draw attention.

He and Lucky sat on the bench on the porch and answered Jase's questions, taking him through their arrival and going into the house.

Jase closed his notebook. "The fire inspector and I will collaborate on the arson report and investigation. I'll take the knife and send it for fingerprints. We can add vandalism to the list of charges stacking up."

"Did you speak to Neil?" Hawk wanted that guy back behind bars and far away from Lucky.

"I did. He has an alibi for the night Lucky went missing. It's a weak one. Said he was home with his parents. They corroborated."

"Doesn't mean he didn't sneak out," Hawk pointed out.

"Any other leads?" Lucky's solemn face held little hope.

"Not right now. I'm waiting on tests to come back, but they take weeks in some cases."

Lucky brushed her feet against the worn deck boards. "Can I go inside and pack a bag?"

"Yes. All the evidence has been collected. They should be done."

The wood floor, area rug, and her quilt were the only casualties of the fire. Her dresser and closet weren't affected, except for the smoke. It could have been a lot worse.

Lucky got up on unsteady legs and rubbed at her thigh that had the stitches in it and the knee brace. "I'll just be a few minutes." She hobbled inside, looking dejected and just plain worn out.

"Take your time. Let me know if you need help." Hawk called after her.

Despite her injuries, she turned back to him, reached out, and put her hand on his shoulder.

It felt so good to have her soft touch, to know she welcomed his in return. He wanted her to let her guard down with him. This small sign that she was bolstered him. They were getting closer.

He waited for her to go back inside before he spoke to Jase. "The knife."

"Yeah. That's personal. I wonder if the person who used it knows its significance."

"They could have taken a knife from the butcher block in the kitchen. It was right there. Instead, they took it from the drawer beside her bed." It creeped him out that they were in her room, by her bed, going through her personal things.

"I've always believed the person doing this was close to her."

"She thinks it's Neil."

"He's my lead suspect, even for the stuff that happened to her while he was behind bars, but I'll be talking to him about this. It had to have been done after Desiree came by to pick up her things to take to the hospital."

Hawk paused for a second. "So she has a key to get in. Neil doesn't. You said there's no forced entry."

"Whoever knows about the knife probably knows about the key under the bench?" Jase didn't sound sure, especially since Lucky had said only she and the crew who worked for her knew about the key, since Desiree had her own set.

"What about Desiree?"

Jase pursed his lips. "They've been friends forever. I've heard the sheriff say they're more like sisters, since they grew up across the street from each other.

Hawk didn't want to even entertain that her best friend would hurt her. Not when the guy who murdered her family was on the loose and probably looking to finish what he started after his jail stint. "So Desiree, the women who work for her, and anyone who got lucky while searching the porch could have gotten into the house." Every lead took them to a dead end.

Lucky appeared on the porch again with a rolling duffle bag and two totes stacked on top of it.

Hawk stood and took all the bags from her. "You're going to exacerbate your injuries."

"It's not that heavy with the wheels. Can we go?" Her tired eyes pleaded with him.

"Yeah. Is this all you want to bring?"

She bit her lip. "Um..."

He tilted his head. "What?"

"Can I bring my plant? I don't want it to die. Not that I'll be at your place that long. Right? I mean, it'll be fine. I'll be back here in a couple days when I'm feeling better."

Jase smacked him on the back. "I'll leave the two of you to figure this out."

Hawk caught the guy's smirk. "Thanks. Keep us posted."

"Will do."

With Jase driving off, Hawk focused on Lucky. "Sweetheart?"

"Yeah." She bit her bottom lip, her gaze on his black work boots.

"You're not coming back here until whoever is doing this is behind bars." *Or six feet under.* "So grab the plant and anything else you want.

We can fill up the back of the Range Rover and your car if that's what it takes."

She hesitated again. "I don't want to impose."

"I asked you to stay with me. I meant it. So tell me what else you want to take and I'll pack it up."

The last of the firefighters filed out of her house. "We'll be in touch," one of them said. "We cleaned up the gasoline and aired out the place. Did you know the window in your bedroom has a broken lock?"

Lucky's eyes went wide. "Uh. No. I'll have it fixed."

"I'll let Corporal Kent know about it. He'll probably want someone to print it just in case that's how they got in. The lock looks secure until you rattle the window and it comes loose."

Hawk frowned. "I'll make sure Jase takes a look at it before I fix it."

The firefighter nodded, then headed out with the rest of his crew, leaving them alone on the porch.

Hawk sent Jase a text with the details about the window. "Grab your plant and anything else you want." He took her bags to his car and loaded them in back.

She came out with her plant, a laptop bag, a blanket from her couch, and a wooden box.

"What's that?"

She smiled. "All my favorite recipes."

"Nice." He took the load from her and put it in his car. "You look tired. How about we come back for your car in a couple days? I'll change the tire then."

"Okay." She climbed into the passenger seat.

He met her in the driver's seat.

Before he started the car, she put her hand on his thigh. "Thank you."

"For what?"

"Everything." She laid her head on his shoulder, sending a wave of warmth and protectiveness through him.

All he wanted to do was keep her close and safe.

It had been a long time since he'd felt this close to a woman. No that wasn't true. He'd never felt this close to someone. This possessive and feral about keeping her safe.

He hoped he didn't scare her.

Because she was quickly becoming too important for him to lose.

Chapter Seven

Lucky couldn't believe she'd been so bold as to reach out and put her hand on Hawk's muscled thigh. Good god, he felt like steel beneath her hand. He didn't seem to mind her touch and she loved the warmth spreading from him up her arm. She imagined being a lot closer to him, wondering what it would feel like to have his hand on her thigh. Higher.

Butterflies and awareness fluttered through her.

He was just so...manly. Big. Imposing. But gentle with her. Patient.

And fierce about keeping her safe.

I'm falling so hard.

Actually, she'd fallen a long time ago.

Hawk stared at the rearview mirror. "Who's that coming up the road?"

She turned and spotted the silver sedan with the butterfly sticker in the corner of the windshield on the driver's side. She'd given the sticker to Desiree as part of her birthday present five years ago when Desiree's dad gifted her the car. "That's Desiree." She put her hand to her forehead, blocking out the sun from her eyes. "I wonder what she's doing here." She checked her watch. "School's out—she should be taking Krystal home."

Hawk slipped his hand around her neck, his fingers tangling in her hair. "Let's see what she wants." He let her loose, then climbed out of the car.

She did the same and met him at the back of his Range Rover.

"Are you sure there's nothing else you want from the house?" He took her hand and laced their fingers together.

She turned into his chest, his arm went around her, his big hand resting on her hip.

He hadn't stopped touching her since the fire exploded in the house.

"I've got everything I need."

His gaze intensified on her. "Is that right?"

She caught the double meaning of what she'd said and answered truthfully. "Yes. Amazingly. I still feel like pinching myself to make sure this is real."

He bent and lightly brushed his lips against hers. "Real enough?"

"Yes." The word came out breathy. Was that her?

Just looking at his handsome face made her catch her breath. He was so...sexy. And rugged. But soft with her.

He brushed his fingers along her cheek. "You look tired."

She leaned into his touch, amazed that with him, she wanted to be caressed. Craved it even. "I am."

"I'll take you home, tuck you into bed. You need to rest so you can heal."

"I'd like that. After a shower."

A glint lit his eyes. "I can help you with that." The heat in his eyes scorched her.

Desiree had already parked her car behind Lucky's, climbed out, took Krystal out of her car seat, and made it to them without Lucky even looking her way. Desiree grabbed her by the hips and pulled her around to face her.

Hawk's surprise and anger matched her own. "Hey. Be careful. She's hurt."

Lucky pressed her hand over her chest to ease the sting the sudden jarring caused. Not to mention the twist her knee took, making it throb in time to her heart.

Desiree rubbed her hand up and down Lucky's good arm. "Sorry. I came as soon as I heard." She pulled Lucky into a hug. "Are you okay? Did someone seriously rig your place to go up in flames?" She released Lucky and turned to the house. "Is it really bad? You can come stay with me until they rebuild whatever burned."

Overwhelmed, Lucky put her hand up to stop Desiree from saying anything more. "I'm fine. The house is fine. I'm a little sad I lost my mother's quilt to the fire when Hawk used it to put it out, but that's a small sacrifice. It could have been a lot worse."

"You put the fire out?" Desiree looked surprised.

Hawk shrugged like it was no big deal, then brushed his hand over Lucky's braid. "Sorry about the blanket. I didn't know. I just acted in the moment."

She gave him a soft smile. "I appreciate it. Really, I do. And I probably would have done the same thing if I hadn't been so shocked by it all."

"You've been through a lot. That's why you should be with someone familiar. With us." Desiree practically shoved Krystal into Lucky's legs.

Krystal wrapped her arms around Lucky in a hug. "Hi Auntie. You got a lot of ouchies?" Krystal's eyes held too much worry for someone so young.

Lucky couldn't squat down with the brace on her knee and she ignored the pain to her stitched thigh, because Krystal's hugs were the best medicine. "I'm okay, sweetie. Just some bumps and bruises and one broken pinky." She held up the appendage with the silver brace on it, her pinky taped to her ring finger.

"Does it hurt?" Her bottom lip trembled.

"A little bit." She didn't want to lie and say everything was fine. It definitely was not. She ached. Everywhere.

"I need to take her home." Hawk slid his hand to her lower back. "Come on, sweetheart. You need to get off that leg. The bright sun isn't good for your head injury either."

She wished she had sunglasses to block out the bright light piercing her eyes. "Do you still have the keys to my car?"

Hawk pulled them from his pocket.

"Would you mind grabbing my sunglasses from the visor?"

He went to retrieve them, while she turned to Desiree. "I appreciate you stopping by to check on me. It means a lot."

Her eyes narrowed. "You're just going to go stay with *him* instead of me?"

"Yes. It's my chance to see if there's more between us." She wanted so much more with Hawk. A real relationship. Time together. A deeper connection. Love.

"You barely know this guy." But Desiree knew how she felt about Hawk.

Lucky couldn't hide it, even if she'd kept a lot of the details to herself. "That's just it. It feels like I know him better than I know anyone else."

Desiree's eyes flashed with pain, then anger. "I've been by your side our whole lives."

"I didn't mean it like that." She pressed her thumb to the throbbing headache between her eyes. "The pain meds are wearing off. It's been a hell of a day. I misspoke." Not really though. She and Hawk had some kind of...chemistry, kismet between them.

Desiree sucked in a breath like she was trying to calm herself. "This isn't you. You don't go off with guys you barely know."

"I've been working for him for two years. We've been exchanging messages nearly that long. If nothing else, I know his reputation. People around town respect him, like him, admire him. He saves people. He saved me."

"That doesn't mean you owe him anything. And everyone also thinks he's a gruff asshole who might be crazy."

"He's not any of those things. Not anymore. He's changed. Healed. And the way he treats me...he cares." She glared at her friend as Hawk returned, probably overhearing Desiree.

"Ready," he asked, holding out her glasses.

She took them and slid them on. "Thank you. That's much better."

He kissed her on the head. "Anything for you."

"You're really big," Krystal blurted out, staring up at Hawk, her eyes wide and wondrous.

Hawk squatted in front of her. "I ate all my vegetables when I was a kid."

Krystal's pert nose squished into a yuck face.

Hawk poked her in the belly, making her giggle. "Don't you want to be big like me?"

"That's too big for a girl."

Hawk tilted his head like he was thinking about it. "Maybe you're right. Still. You should eat all the good-for-you stuff, then maybe you'll be as tall as your mom or auntie."

Krystal looked up at Lucky. "Is he your boyfriend now?"

Before she could come up with a way out of answering that question, Hawk simply replied, "Yes, I am," for her. Hawk stared at her, daring her to disagree.

After all this time wishing there was something more between them, she wasn't about to contradict him. And if he was willing to put it out there, the way he'd been doing since he found her nearly dead on that hill, then she could drop her own truth bomb. "I like him a whole lot." She said it for her niece, but held Hawk's gaze the whole time, so he knew how much she meant it.

Hawk stood and took her hand, lacing their fingers together again.

"Is there anything you need me to do for you?" Desiree asked.

It was harder than it should be to tear her gaze from Hawk. "Not right now."

"How long are you going to be at Hawk's place?"

"I'm not sure."

Hawk squeezed her hand. "You can stay as long as you like. At least until you're healed enough to do things on your own. And most definitely until they find and arrest whoever is fu—" He pressed his lips tight and changed the word to... "Messing with you." He dipped his head and whispered in her ear. "The longer the better."

She caught her breath, astounded that he'd say that when everything was so knew between them.

Desiree eyed them. "Keep me posted on how you're doing and what's going on with the investigation."

Lucky turned back to her friend. "You'll probably hear before me. Did your dad say anything about it?"

Desiree shook her head. "You know he likes to leave work at the office." Desiree's assertion that her father, the sheriff, hadn't said anything didn't ring true. When they were younger and Lucky spent time at Desiree's house, her father would often talk about things that happened at work, especially since in their small town everyone knew everything anyway.

The town had grown, but not so big that you didn't know your neighbors.

And she was Desiree's best friend. Surely her father would not only make sure Jase was following every lead but also ensure she and Desiree knew what was happening.

"Come on, sweetheart." Hawk waved his hand toward the car. "I want you off that leg, and your shoulder's got to be killing you. It's time for your meds again." Hawk used his hand at her back to steer her toward his car.

"Why aren't you taking yours?" Desiree asked.

"Someone slashed the tire," she called over her shoulder.

"What?" Desiree pulled Krystal toward their car by her hand. "I don't like this, Lucky. It feels like someone wants you dead."

Lucky stopped in her tracks, then turned her head to Desiree. "It's him. It's always been him. Or someone he sent. Just like the other times. But I'm not such an easy target now that I have Hawk watching my back."

"You're putting a lot of trust in him." Desiree buckled Krystal into her seat.

Hawk held the door of his car open for Lucky. "I won't let you down. I won't let anything happen to you."

"You better keep that promise," Desiree called out, then walked around her car and climbed into the driver's seat.

Hawk did the same after making sure she was secure in her seat. "She's very protective of you."

"She's been my friend since we were little. We lived across the street from each other, went to school together, did everything together."

He turned the key in the ignition, then glanced at her. "That's a long time." Something in his eyes told her he had more to say.

"What is it?"

"You two seem so different."

Lucky released a half laugh under her breath. "She can be a lot, but she's always been by my side."

"It's good to have someone who really knows you in your life."

"Like you have your brothers?"

"Yes." He backed out of her driveway and pulled onto the road. "It's how I want to know you and you to know me."

"Well, we're going to be in close quarters, so..."

He put his hand on her thigh. "It's going to be okay, Lucky. I know this is kind of fast, but it also feels inevitable."

She turned her head on the headrest and stared at him while he drove them home. "What took you so long, then?"

He glanced at her, surprise lighting his eyes. "All those rumors about me being gruff and difficult and that I had a short fuse...they were all true. I wasn't in a good headspace when I left the military. I'd seen too much, done too many horrific things in the name of democracy and freedom. Necessary things. And they left their mark and warped my mind for a while. There were times—still are times—when I lose myself in the nightmares. Awake and asleep. I've worked really hard the past couple of years with a therapist and by helping others to recover. But sometimes it all comes back to me. Not as often anymore. I know what to do to keep myself grounded."

She put her hand over his on the steering wheel he gripped so tightly his knuckles were white. "If you ever want to talk about it, I'm here to listen."

He reached out and dug his fingers into the hair at the back of her neck beneath her braid. "I appreciate that more than you know. And it goes both ways. I've watched you sleep in the hospital. I know you're plagued by nightmares of what happened to you. You call out in your sleep. All I can say is that it gets better as you process what happened. Therapy helps."

She cocked her brow at him. "You've been watching me sleep."

He shrugged. "I couldn't help myself. You were right there in front of me. Finally." He pulled into the long driveway to his family's land. "I couldn't concentrate on anything but you, thinking about all we might have lost."

"Everything we could have now?" she asked tentatively.

He stopped in front of his house, shut off the car, and turned to her. "I want you *here* with me more than anything."

Chapter Eight

Was it too presumptuous to say *welcome home* to her the second they walked in the door of his place? Probably. Did he want to say that? Yes. Absolutely. But he didn't want to scare her off. Even if it was what he wanted and how he felt.

His therapist would probably tell him to slow down and think first. He'd had two years to think about what he wanted. Her. Here. With him. Shared meals. Long talks. Movie nights. Kissing goodnight and good morning. Soft caresses and a lot of making love any way she wanted it.

Yeah, maybe he needed to slow his roll and let her settle in. She'd had a shit few days.

His phone chimed with a text.

MASON: We just hit town. Want to check on you and your girl.

MASON: How is she? We can't wait to meet her.

Shit. He didn't want to overwhelm Lucky with his cousin and best friend.

HAWK: Just walked in the door with her. She needs some rest.

HAWK: Give us a couple hours before you drop by.

MASON: See you then.

"Is everything okay? Do you need to go to work or something? You don't have to keep babysitting me."

He dropped her bag on the floor and took two steps to close the distance he hated between them. "I'm not babysitting you. I'm taking care of you. So tell me what you need right now?"

She let out a weary sigh. "It's all been too much. I'm...so damn tired." Her shoulders slumped and she looked ready to drop right there.

He cupped her face and stared into her sleep bruised eyes. "Okay. Here's where things get real. Do you want to sleep alone or with me?"

"I don't want to be alone anymore." She'd said that before.

He liked it a lot that she said what she meant. "Okay. You know the way to *our* bedroom." He picked up her bag and followed her down the short hallway past his office to the master bedroom. He had two spare rooms on the other side of the house, past the kitchen and dining room. He'd hate to have her so far away, even if she was still in the same house. This way, he could be close and they could settle into this new intimacy between them.

It wasn't like he was going to pull any moves on her. She was hurt and in need of patience and care. He wished his body got that message, because having her here made his dick remember how long it had been since he'd been with a woman and how much he'd fantasized about being with Lucky.

She stepped into the room and stared at the rumpled sheets he'd left behind the morning he'd gone for his hike. He'd intended to make the bed after he got home and showered.

"Let me change the sheets while you put on something more comfortable to sleep in. If you want, I can give you one of my shirts."

"Are you going to sleep with me?"

He rubbed his hand over the tight muscles at the back of his neck. "Yeah. I'm beat. Sleeping in a chair for days was not great on my back. I can't wait to lie down with you and let everything go for a while."

"Then leave the sheets and give me your shirt."

He eyed her. "The one I'm wearing."

She nodded, giving him a shy smile.

Oh, that would never do. He didn't want her to be nervous with him at all. And if she wanted the shirt off his back, she could have it. So he pulled it over his head and draped it over his shoulder as he carefully took the sling off her arm and set it on the edge of the bed. "I'll help you get undressed like we did at the hospital. You tell me if anything hurts and I'll stop. Okay?"

She turned her back to him. He gently took the hem of her shirt and pulled it up her body. She pulled her good arm out first, then he lifted the shirt sideways over her head toward her injured arm, and drew the shirt down without her having to lift it. Next he undid her bra clasp and slid the straps down both her arms. It landed on the end of the bed. He bunched up his t-shirt and slid it up her injured arm, then over her head, and down her body in the reverse way he'd taken hers off. With her back to him, she kept some modesty as their relationship hadn't gotten that intimate. Yet.

She was going to need him to help her take a shower. No way could she do that on her own.

He was both eager for it and dreading the torture it would be to have his hands on her, but not in the way he wanted or needed. Still, he loved having this chance to take care of her, for them to get closer and build trust and intimacy.

"Okay, sweetheart, let's get the rest off." He slipped his hands up under his t-shirt on her and over her hips. He tugged her soft yoga pants down her legs. She'd kicked out of her shoes so all he had to do was pull off one leg at a time, including her socks. "Keep the underwear or ditch them? Do you prefer to sleep naked or..." He let that hang.

"I'm good like this. For now."

He rubbed her arms. "Okay. Do you want the sling on while you sleep?"

"No. I don't think so. Um, is it okay if I take the left side of the bed? I like to sleep on my side and I'd rather be facing you. Plus that will mean I'm not on my hurt side."

"Whatever you want, sweetheart. Do you need the bathroom before you crawl in?" He went to the drapes and closed them, so they'd sleep better.

"Um. I'm okay."

He checked the time on the clock by the bed. "Do you want something to eat or drink before you crash?"

"No. I'm good. Thank you. But could you get my meds and a glass of water?"

He dug through her bag and pulled out the meds. He popped the top on one, poured out a pill, then did the same with the other, closing the bottles and leaving them on the nightstand. He handed her the pills, then went into the bathroom and came back with a glass of water.

Lucky popped the pills and downed half the glass of water.

He pulled back the covers. "Come on, then. Crawl in." He waited for her to settle, then tucked the sheets around her. "You good?"

"Yes." She inhaled, then sighed. "It smells like you." A soft smile tilted her pink lips as her eyes drooped closed.

He couldn't help but kiss her on the forehead. "Is that why you wanted my shirt?"

"Yes." The grin made his stomach feel like it was floating.

His heart felt too big for his chest. How did she do this to him in such a short time? He was absolutely falling hard and fast for her.

He used the bathroom, brushed his teeth, washed his face, then pulled off his shoes, socks, and jeans and climbed in beside her in nothing but his black boxer briefs.

She lay facing him, her eyes closed, face soft.

He gently brushed a strand of her golden hair away from her face, thinking of how he'd done the same when he'd found her lying face down in the woods. He couldn't believe she was here with him in his bed.

It had been too close a call. Another hour without help and she'd have been dead.

I saved her.

And she saved me.

He scooted as close to her as possible without disturbing her, then slipped his hand beneath the covers and over her side where he knew she didn't have any scrapes or bruises. He wanted her to know he was there with her.

She let out a dreamy little sigh and shifted another couple inches closer to him before she settled back into sleep.

He drifted off without having to use any of his relaxation techniques or meditations to clear his mind. He was too damn happy to have her here to think of anything else and too exhausted not to fall into a deep sleep.

Three hours later, he woke to the doorbell ringing. He pulled on his jeans and a clean tee, reluctantly left Lucky sleeping in his bed where he wanted to stay, then opened the front door to his cousin and his wife.

Lyric was round with their first child and looking positively radiant. She wrapped him in a hug and held on. "Are you okay? It had to be traumatic to find someone you know under such terrible circumstances."

Mason stepped in behind Lyric and closed the door, grinning indulgently at his wife hugging another man—his cousin knew Hawk adored Lyric like he would a sister. "Sorry if we woke you."

"It's all good. Lucky's still sleeping."

Lyric stepped back, but kept one hand on his shoulder. "Tell us. Is she really okay?"

"She will be. There's a lot we don't know. Things we can't know for sure because she was drugged and can't remember."

Mason had his FBI face on. "What do the cops suspect?"

"She was drugged at the bar. My bar. Right in front of everyone." He couldn't help the rage in his voice.

Mason's eyes went wide. "So they saw who did it?"

"No. She was with a friend. It happened after they had a chat with Lincoln at the bar about Lucky working for Linc. Desiree, her friend, said Lucky got really drunk, so they left early. The odd thing is that

Lucky told me she doesn't ever overindulge, not after being drugged and waking to find her family killed."

"Holy shit." Mason's face grew even more intense.

"That was several years ago. Desiree took Lucky home and put her to bed. But based on how close Lucky was to death when I found her, she had to have been taken and..." It was hard for him to think about what happened to Lucky, let alone say it out loud. "Someone dumped her naked down a very steep embankment off a fire road in the middle of nowhere."

Mason winced. "What about the surveillance footage?"

"Jase with the sheriff's department has a copy. I haven't seen it yet. I've got a meeting with him tomorrow."

"She's going to be okay now." Lyric squeezed his shoulder, offering him comfort.

"What else?" Mason asked.

"Lucky has flashes of that night and she swears her ex, the guy who killed her family, was there. I don't know if it's real or he's just the boogeyman in all her nightmares. Of course you could add in her abusive asshole father who liked to slice her skin with a fucking six inch blade for shits and giggles, then maybe he's her true nightmare, because she calls out, 'No, Dad' in her sleep a lot, too."

Lyric wrapped him in a hug. "Breathe, Hawk. Slow it down."

He gently set her away from him and paced. "Sorry. It's been hell the last few days. From finding her, to thinking she was dead, that I'd lost her and missed my chance." He pulled at his hair. "Fuck. She doesn't deserve this. Any of it. And yet some asshole is taunting her, trying to kill her. He even tried to burn her place to the ground today."

"What?" Mason and Lyric said in unison.

"Someone rigged matched and a bottle of gasoline to light the place up the second Lucky walked into her bedroom."

"What?" Mason's concern etched lines in his forehead. "Like a booby trap?"

"Yeah. I got lucky and put the fire out with the bed quilt before it got too out of control." Shame washed over him. "It was something her mom had hand made. Now it's ruined."

Lyric frowned. "She must be devastated to lose something so precious."

He wiped his hand over his face. "I didn't mean to destroy it."

"Of course you didn't," Lyric and Mason both said in unison.

They'd been together long enough to finish each other's sentences, too. It was adorable. And eye-roll-inducing sometimes, but it showed how close they were and how much they loved each other.

He wanted that with Lucky. Now. But he had to be patient. Even though he wanted to barrel on ahead full steam.

He raked his fingers through his hair. "I'll make it up to her. Somehow. Some way."

"It's not as important as the fact that you saved her and her home," Lyric pointed out.

He held out his hands to his sides. "Yeah. I'm kind of hoping she makes this place her home now."

Lyric's smile was bright and filled with mirth. "Oh yeah? So it's like that now."

"I told her I want a real relationship with her. One like you and this dumbass have together."

Mason smacked him on the shoulder with the back of his hand. "Watch it, asshole. I drove all the way from Wyoming just to see how you're doing."

"And I appreciate it. I really do. It's just, I've got a lot on my mind. I don't know how to help her, because I don't know exactly what happened to her. There's a real chance that someone violated her. And I'm not talking about her being drugged."

"Was there any evidence she was sexually assaulted?" Mason pulled Lyric close, like just the thought of that happening to her made him want to protect her.

He felt the same way. But he hadn't been there to protect Lucky because he'd been a dumbass and kept her at arm's length.

What if he'd stepped up sooner?

He couldn't let his mind spiral like that.

"It wasn't your fault." Lyric held his gaze, hers earnest.

"I know. I just hate that this happened to her."

"Well, with you by her side, I'm sure she'll be feeling better soon." Lyric was always so positive.

"As much as I think I know her, there's still so much I don't know *about* her."

"Now you have all the time in the world to get to know her." Lyric headed for his kitchen. "I bet she'll be hungry when she wakes up. Let's make something."

"By *we* I hope you mean *you*." Hawk got by in the kitchen, but Lyric was magic with food.

Lyric rolled her eyes. "Definitely."

"Thank God. I'm starving."

While Lyric rooted through his freezer and fridge, he and Mason grabbed beers and sat at the bar, catching up while he kept one ear out for any sign that Lucky was awake and needed him.

Chapter Nine

Lucky knew she was dreaming, but couldn't seem to pull herself out of the loop that kept playing out. She'd open her eyes in the dream, and he'd be coming straight for her. Neil stared her down with those brown sugar eyes, his baby face set stern as he prowled closer, looking threatening despite his youthful appearance. Heart racing, her mind screaming for her to run, her limbs wouldn't obey. She gasped awake, the sheets tangled around her. Staring at the empty side of the unfamiliar bed, she felt utterly alone.

Except she wasn't. Not really. She was in *his* bed. Hawk.

She inhaled deeply and smelled him on the sheets. She buried her nose in the pillow. She could get used to this. Him.

Except she'd rather wake up to him in the bed with her.

Where is he?

She untangled her legs from the sheet and slowly rolled to her back, trying not to disturb her shoulder or pull on the stitches in her thigh. She loved the exposed wood beams overhead. She'd imagined herself in this room with him a thousand times since she started working for him. This room felt the most like him. Masculine. Strong. Sturdy, like those beams. And cozy with the river rock fireplace.

She knew the view was spectacular from the floor to ceiling windows, though the dark blue drapes were closed right now.

Where was he?

How long had she been asleep?

She peeked at the clock on the nightstand. Nearly dinner time. She'd slept for four hours. She needed it. The hospital was noisy and the nurses were in every few hours to check on her.

It took her a few seconds to muster the strength and wherewithal to sit up, setting off all her many aches and pains. She could really use a shower, but she'd need Hawk's help.

That set off a flush to her cheeks and thoughts about him and her in the shower. Naked. Together.

She stopped that train of thought before it headed to Dirty Town—it just made her frustrated and needy when she could barely move.

It took far too much effort to get out of bed, but she made it to her feet. The sling she needed to support her shoulder slid on relatively easily, relieving her of the worst of the pain. One glance at her shirt—Hawk's shirt—revealed that she hadn't bled through her bandages. Good. She hadn't torn anything while she slept.

For the first time, she noticed the hushed voices coming from the other room.

Hawk had company.

She walked to the door and glanced down the hallway and her heart sank.

As much as she thought she knew about Hawk, she didn't know everything. And she certainly hadn't imagined that he had a pregnant...friend?

"I love you. You know that," the woman standing in his kitchen professed.

Lucky's stomach dropped. Maybe she was an ex.

"I'm just thanking you for coming and supporting me. It means a lot, considering your condition and how messy this is."

That didn't sound good. Did the woman want him back?

"I want to see you happy." She had to be an ex. There was no one else in the room.

Hawk wouldn't ask Lucky to be with him, say all the things he'd said to her if he was still together with that woman. Right?

But she couldn't stand to be the person between him and the woman carrying his child. They deserved a chance to be a loving family. If it was her, she'd do anything to give her child that kind of stability. Something she never had growing up.

She couldn't stay here.

She couldn't be the reason a family split up, even if it had already happened. The baby would come and they'd realize they wanted to be together for their child.

It took some doing, but she managed to pull on her leggings, knee brace, and socks and shoes.

By the time she made it out of the room, rolling her bags behind her, Hawk and the woman were hugging.

He stepped back the second he saw her. "Lucky? What are you doing?"

"Leaving. I don't belong here. You've obviously got a lot on your plate. You don't need me messing this up." She lifted her chin toward the gorgeous brunette.

Hawk looked from her to the woman and back again. "This isn't what it looks like."

"Maybe not right now. But you seem like a guy who'd be a really good dad and want to be there for his kid. I don't want to get in the way of that."

She pulled her phone out of her pocket. "I'll call Desiree and wait out front for her to pick me up. Thank you for everything you did to help me. You have no idea how much it means to me." *Or how disappointed I am that this won't work out.*

She choked back tears and put her hand on the knob and opened the door a mere couple of inches before his hands landed on the wood and slammed it shut.

"You're not going anywhere, sweetheart."

She turned and stared up at him as he leaned in so close she could see the flecks of gold in his hazel eyes.

"Everything I said to you was the truth. I want you here with me. I want a relationship with you. So before you walk out that door, maybe give me the benefit of the doubt and listen." He brushed his thumb over her cheek and she leaned into his touch without thinking, then caught herself. "That's right. You feel this crazy deep connection between us. The one I can't deny anymore and won't. I want you to know me and my whole family, including my best friend, Lyric, over there. She's visiting from Wyoming with her *husband*, my cousin, Mason, who stepped out to take a work call. They're expecting their first baby in a few months. And while I love her like a sister, my feelings for you go a hell of a lot deeper."

He leaned in and put his lips right next to her ear, whispering, "I'm sorry you woke up alone. I wanted to stay in bed, right beside you so bad, but then they showed up. I didn't wake you because you needed your sleep and maybe some time to get used to being here with me before things get really intimate between us. So drop the bag and kiss me like you missed me, because I've been missing you."

Lucky didn't know what to say. She'd read the situation all wrong. But here Hawk was giving her the truth and letting her know he wanted her to settle in here and with him. He made it very clear he was hers. So she dropped the bag, took him by the t-shirt fisted in her hand, went up on tiptoe, and kissed him with all the longing she'd stored up over the last two years.

He kept his hands on the door on either side of her head, but leaned in, his chest pressed to hers, softly so they were connected, but not so he hurt her injuries.

The kiss was all passion and need as his tongue dove into her mouth and tangled with hers, until she felt the earth move.

Oh, wait, that was someone trying to open the door at her back.

Hawk shoved it closed and tore his mouth from hers. "I'm kissing my woman, hold your horses."

"Let me the fuck in, asshole."

"Wait a minute." Hawk dove back in and the woman in the kitchen laughed.

Lucky couldn't concentrate on anything but the man in front of her and the way he made her knees weak.

"How long is this going to take? Send my woman out so I can make out with her at least." He sounded so forlorn.

She couldn't help it, she chuckled against Hawk's lips, then reluctantly pulled away. "Maybe we should let him in."

"I didn't invite him here, so he can wait." The grumble was back in his voice.

"I'm family. I don't need an invitation. Though I would like to meet your girl."

Hawk turned to Lyric. "Are you sure you want to keep him?"

Lyric grinned. "I'm sure."

Hawk pulled Lucky away from the door by the hips and shook his head. "I'm sorry about this. He's going to kiss you on the head to piss me off. Are you okay with that?"

Lyric called out, "Hawk and his brothers do it to me to make Mason upset, because he's possessive, but the guys are just being sweet."

Hawk pulled the door open and shook his head at his cousin. "She's hurt and doesn't like being touched by anyone but me. Be careful with her." Hawk turned to her. "Lucky, this is my cousin, Mason. He's got a brother, Nick, you'll meet another time, along with his wife and adopted daughter."

Mason and Hawk definitely looked like they were related. "Are all of you drop-dead gorgeous?"

"They are," Lyric confirmed. "That one's mine."

Lucky grinned. "Apparently Hawk's decided to be mine."

"Damn straight." Hawk reached out to wrap his arm around her, but Mason got to her first and drew her a step away and kissed her on the forehead. "It's nice to meet you, Lucky." He released her immediately, taking into account Hawk's warning about her sensitivity to being touched. "Are you sure you want to keep him? He's a bit feral at times."

She stared up at Hawk. "I think he's perfectly imperfect like the rest of us."

Hawk moved in and wrapped her in a hug, kissing her head like his cousin had done. "Thanks, sweetheart." He pulled back just enough to look her in the eye. "Are you hungry? Lyric put together an amazing beef stew and even made some fresh baked rolls."

Her stomach rumbled. Loudly.

Everyone chuckled.

"You're starving." Hawk's eyes filled with guilt. "I should have fed you before I put you to bed."

"I was too tired to care or eat."

Lyric pulled bowls out of the cabinet.

Mason joined her in the kitchen and uncorked a bottle of red wine.

Hawk picked up her bag. "Where are your meds? You should take them after you eat."

"In the bag." She went to get them, but he beat her to it and handed her the two bottles.

"Go sit at the table and rest." Hawk took her bags back to their room. It seemed so strange to think of it like that already, but she went with it because she wanted this to be her life so badly.

Lyric and Mason were already at the table and had placed two bowls at the empty seats across from them.

Lucky took her seat.

Lyric smiled from across the table. "Is Lucky your real name or a nickname?"

"Real. My father was Irish and loved to tell stories about leprechauns and fairies and say he had the luck of the Irish. He called me his lucky charm."

"Sounds like he had a good spirit and whimsical side."

"The only side I can remember was the back of his hand across my face and the point of his blade across my skin." She didn't have to hold up her arms for them to see her scars. They were visible all over her exposed skin. She couldn't hide her past, so why not be real about it.

Hawk took the seat beside her and dropped his hand on her knee. "He can't hurt you anymore and no one else will ever again."

"Any updates on the case?" She asked, even though she didn't really want to know.

Hawk shook his head. "No. I'm meeting Jase tomorrow morning to get an update. Tonight you sleep, knowing you're safe here and not alone anymore."

Lyric reached across the table and put her hand over Lucky's.

She checked the impulse to pull her hand back.

"I'm sorry I said that. I didn't know about your father."

"It's okay. Turns out, I'm not lucky at all."

Hawk brushed his fingers down the back of her head. "I am, because you're here. And you are because you survived." Hawk kissed the side of her head. "Eat, sweetheart. You'll feel better. Later, I'll help you take a shower."

She ducked her head. "Yeah. I haven't made the best first impression." She pushed her oily braid over her back.

"You may not be at your best, but you're still gorgeous." Hawk squeezed her thigh. He was always touching her.

She hadn't known how good it felt to be caressed and held the way Hawk loved on her.

Lyric passed her a roll. "I'd kill to have hair as thick as yours."

"It's so long it gets in the way a lot. I usually keep it in a ponytail, but with my shoulder...Hawk braided it for me at the hospital." She touched the bandage on her head. "I haven't actually looked in a mirror, but I imagine I'm black and blue and scraped up."

"It's really not as bad as you think," Lyric consoled her. "You're alive. That's what's important."

"Any new memories come back to you?" Mason asked.

Hawk pointed his fork at his cousin. "Let her eat in peace. You can interrogate her later."

"I just asked a question." Mason frowned back at Hawk.

Hawk turned to her. "Mason is FBI. He's not being nosy, he just wants to help."

"I appreciate that." She smiled at the man across the table, wondering if he or anyone else would be able to figure out what really happened. "I woke up with the same image repeated in my head. Neil coming toward me."

Mason perked up. "He's the ex-boyfriend who killed your family."

"Yes." A wave of grief hit her when she thought of her little brother, the blood running from his slit throat and down his small chest.

"Mason." Hawk put a warning in his voice.

She put her hand on Hawk's thigh beside hers. "I brought him up."

Hawk's gaze dropped to her hand on him, then his lips widened to a smile and he put his hand over hers. "You don't have to talk about it if you don't want to."

"There's not much I can remember of that night at the bar. I just know I saw him."

Mason leaned in. "In your mind, is he young or older?"

She tilted her head. "Do you mean like he was a teen when he killed my parents or an adult who just got out of prison?"

"Yes. Which version do you see?"

"Huh. I hadn't really thought about it because I was so shocked to see him. I hadn't seen him in so long and he'd changed so much, but not enough that I didn't recognize his voice and his face."

"What did he say to you?"

"Something like, are you finally going to let me see her?"

Mason and Hawk shared a concerned look.

"Who was he talking to?" Lyric asked.

She turned to her. "I'm not sure. It's kind of a blur. I was with my best friend, Desiree, so my inclination is to say her. But that can't be right. I'm really not sure what happened. And she'd never betray me like that. He killed my little brother. I won't ever forgive him for that."

"And your parents?" Mason studied her.

"My father terrorized all of us, me especially, because I tried my hardest to shield my brother. My mother...is complicated."

"She didn't save you," Hawk said simply. "She should have saved you." Hawk swept in, taking her face in his hands, and kissing her so gently it ached with longing for more. Then his lips were all over her cheeks, kissing away her tears.

She hooked her hands over his wrists and held him tight as she looked him deep in the eyes. "You saved me. I've been drowning in loneliness for so long I didn't see a way out of it, except one." She choked back more tears. "Because of you...the letters...I held on. Hoping beyond hope."

"Why the fuck did I wait so long when I've known for a while now that you were everything I wanted but didn't think I deserved?"

She laid her chin on his shoulder and stared into his eyes. "You showed up at exactly the right moment."

His eyes turned dark and stormy. "I was almost too late."

"But you weren't. And I'm still here. And you're here."

"And you're not leaving. Ever. We'll figure this out, eliminate the threat, and it'll be you and me from now on." Hawk kissed her like he'd never get to kiss her again.

She wrapped her good arm around his neck, pressing into him as much as she could because close wasn't close enough.

They both forgot about their captive audience until a soft sob came from across the table.

They broke apart and stared at Lyric in Mason's arms, her head on his shoulder. "You guys! You're so perfect for each other. I'm so happy for you." Her smile was wide and genuine despite the tears. "You deserve so much love."

Lucky didn't know if that sentiment was for Hawk, or both of them, but she took it to heart. She'd endured a lot of heartache and abuse in her young life. Now she wanted the good stuff.

And he was sitting beside her with her hand in his, their fingers laced together like he never wanted to let her go.

Lyric picked up her water glass with one hand and wiped her tears with the other as she recovered from the swell of emotion her pregnancy hormones had unleashed. Mason followed her lead and raised his bottle of beer, but it was Lyric who gave the toast. "To the saviors in our lives, the ones who show up when we need them most."

Hawk and Lucky picked up their drinks, her wine only a quarter full because she was taking pain meds. "To saviors." She clinked her glass to Hawk's first, then Mason and Lyric's.

"So how long are you in town?" Lucky asked, wanting to get to know Hawk's family better.

Lyric buttered another roll. "We head back tomorrow. Mason has a case. But you'll hear from me often, since I'm Hawk's best friend."

She looked from Lyric to Hawk, then back again. "Yeah. How did that come about? And aren't you a bit jealous?" she asked Mason.

Hawk spoke up right away. "You don't need to be jealous. Most of our calls she's got Mason on speaker. We're not telling each other our secrets or anything like that."

Lyric grinned. "We share a lot of recipes. I'm the chef at the Dark Horse Dive Bar I own with my family. That's where Mason and I met. And when I learned about his cousin who'd withdrawn from everyone in the family because of what he'd experienced during his military service, well, I decided maybe he just needed a friend. So I called him. The first few conversations were mostly just me talking. But I wore him down."

Hawk shook his head. "I couldn't resist her. Not the way Mason can't. It's just, she's usually so happy and it didn't matter if all I did was grunt at her those first few calls. She made me get to know her and I liked her. I especially liked her for Mason, who also needed some sunshine in his life."

Mason held his beer up again and the two clinked bottles over that.

She turned to Hawk. "So you've basically had two women who saw you needed someone in your life and forced their way in."

"I guess you could put it that way. I was trying to spare everyone my bad temper and the trauma I couldn't process. It started with you, and I guess you could say it opened the door for her to sneak in, too."

She picked up her wine glass. Lyric followed suit with her water, and they clinked them together.

For the first time Lucky felt like she was making new friends and connections with people who thought she mattered.

"So you own a bar?" She wanted to know more about Lyric.

"She's also an amazing singer-songwriter. If you like country music, you might have heard a couple of her songs on the radio." Hawk's pride in his best friend showed in his eyes.

"Really? Do you tour?"

Lyric shook her head. "No. I write the songs and sell them to other artists. I sing at the bar a lot, but I love being home with my family. I want to hear my songs on the radio or live at a concert, but family is what's really important to me." She rubbed her hand over her baby bump. "We're happy in Wyoming with my family. And Mason loves his new job. He's left undercover work behind and loves having more regular hours."

"That's nice. I always wished my family was different. Nicer. I thought about taking my brother when I turned eighteen and just leaving with him. I couldn't imagine going off to college and leaving him behind at my father's mercy. But then they were gone and I was truly alone. My mother ran the cleaning service I took over and own now."

"The one she's tripled in size." How did Hawk know that?

"That's impressive." Mason studied her.

"Not really. When I took over, there was twelve of us. Now, we're thirty-seven. I expanded the business out of necessity. I inherited what my family left behind, including their debt. I needed to put a roof over my head once I realized I couldn't afford to keep the house."

Lyric looked impressed. "I know what it's like to run a business. I hope you have help."

"I have one full-time office person. Everyone else is in the field, so to speak."

Hawk squeezed her hand. "Why do you still clean houses instead of running the office?"

"Because the office is boring. Endless paperwork. My mom put me to work when I turned fifteen. I spent time after school and on weekends cleaning other people's houses and businesses. It kept me away from my father. Not that my mother did it to help me. I was free labor. And my dad waited for me to come home so he could let off some steam and play with his prey." It felt so easy to open up to Hawk, she didn't care that his family heard the truth about her past, too.

Hawk's whole body went tense next to her. "That sounds ominous."

"Imagine walking into it night after night." Since he had her hand, she went to use the other one without thinking and pulled at her sore shoulder. She winced through the pain. "Some nights, he was just a jerk, pushing my buttons, putting me down. Other nights he was worse."

"You didn't get paid to work because he wanted to keep you under his thumb. He wanted to make sure you didn't have a way out," Hawk guessed correctly.

"His favorite thing to say to me was, don't be too smart for your own good. Or your brother's."

Lyric gasped. "He threatened you and your brother? If you tried to leave, he'd hurt him?"

"He hurt us anyway. But I knew despite Desiree's father being the sheriff that I was never getting out. If I told anyone what was happening, he'd have killed me. I believed that from the time I was seven and he choked me out the first time, that no matter what, he'd always win. I wasn't strong enough to beat him, only to endure him."

"The cops would have helped you," Lyric pointed out.

She caught the disbelief in Mason's eyes and confirmed what he must know, having presumably seen a lot on the job as an FBI agent. "My best friend's father was the sheriff, but the sheriff's best friend was my dad. All he ever said about bruises or cuts on me was that I should stay out of the kitchen if I was that clumsy with a knife, or that my father should take it easy on me when I screwed up. In his mind, it was my fault because that's what my father made him believe. He was a guy's guy. Everyone loved him. He made sure to the outside world we looked like a happy family. And I cooperated, wearing long sleeves and hiding my wounds from everyone. After they were gone, I didn't care anymore who saw them. I didn't care about anything anymore. I simply existed."

"Did you and your ex talk about what was going on at home?" Mason asked.

"Sometimes. If he saw my injuries, he'd ask. I mostly didn't want to talk about it."

"How did he feel about it?" Lyric asked.

"Like I felt. Helpless. Oh, he talked a good game about wanting to take my father out for hurting me, but I never believed he'd actually do it. My father liked Neil."

"I'd think the last thing he'd want is someone knowing he was abusing you," Hawk pointed out.

"He threatened Neil the first time I introduced him as my boyfriend. I'd tried to hide it for a few weeks, because I wanted to keep the one good thing I had mine. I knew it would eventually get out, but I craved Neil's attention."

"Something good," Hawk guessed.

"Yes. My one rebellion. But my father got wind of it from other parents. I thought he'd order me to stop seeing him. Instead, he invited Neil to dinner. Right there at the table where they were all killed, he casually told Neil that if he ever said anything that put me or my family in a bad light, he'd have me accuse Neil of rape. Didn't matter if it was true, it would ruin Neil's life."

"Damn. That's diabolical." Mason sat back heavily in his chair.

"I tried to break up with Neil that night, but he wouldn't let me. He said I mattered to him and having him around might make my dad stop. He was wrong on both counts. If I mattered to him, then why did he kill my innocent little brother? He knew how protective I was over Danny. And my father never stopped hurting me. The night before he was killed, he'd come to the dinner table and asked why I hadn't fixed my hair or put on a clean shirt. I hadn't noticed I'd spilled soda on it. Like one tiny drop on the front. But he saw it and I got a fist to the side of my head that rang my bell. He pushed me out of my chair and dragged me by my hair to my room and ordered me to fix myself and present myself to him once I was dressed and cleaned up properly for dinner. When I did, I was swaying on my feet, dizzy from the blow. My ears rang for like an hour. He asked if I was drunk and had stolen his booze."

Mason's hands fisted on the table. "He had to know you were hurt."

"He didn't care. He just wanted an excuse to keep piling on the pain."

"What did he do?" Hawk didn't look like he really wanted the answer.

"He took out his knife and cut me." She tilted her chin back and showed him the scar along her jaw. "I don't know if he was going for my throat or what. My mom screamed when she saw how much blood was pouring out. I just stood there, dead inside, wishing he'd have aimed better and put me out of my misery."

Lyric reached her hand across the table toward her. "Oh, Lucky. I'm so sorry you felt that way. And I'm so glad you survived."

Hawk scooped her out of her chair and into his lap. His huge arms wrapped around her and held her tight, his lips pressed to her ear. "I hate that you ever felt that way and that he made you feel like that was the only way out. I know what it's like to feel trapped. To feel like there's no way to make it stop. That's not your life anymore." He said the last louder for the others to hear.

"But it is. Sorta. Someone, most likely Neil, is still hurting me."

"Why?" Lyric asked. "If he loved you and took out your family to make you safe, why keep hurting you?"

"Because I was angry he killed my brother. Because I refused to go along with his denial that he did it just to help his case. He swore he was framed and I called bullshit. Because I refused to speak to him at all after he was arrested."

"You didn't want to know what he had to say for himself?" Mason asked.

"No. At the time, I was in a fog. I woke up to..." She swallowed back the bile and scream that had been in her throat even then. "It was horrible. All the blood. The utter silence." She leaned into Hawk even more. "I felt so guilty. Why was I alive and he was dead? He was just a little boy. He'd never done anything in his whole life to deserve that."

Hawk held her close and kissed her head. "Neither of you deserved what happened to you. You're so strong and resilient. I don't know how you do it."

"Yes, you do. You've had to overcome a lot after your service. You probably don't want to talk about it, and that's fine, but know that I'm here if you ever need me to listen."

Lyric leaned on her forearms on the table. "I worried that maybe this wouldn't work between you because she's so much younger than you."

Lucky was twenty-four but felt much older.

Hawk had to be in his early thirties.

To her, it didn't seem like a huge age-gap.

Lyric went on. "But you've both endured so much trauma and found your way out of it. You're exactly what each other needs."

Hawk rubbed his nose into her hair. "All I know is that now that I have you, I'm not letting you go."

She wrapped her arm around his neck. "I don't want to be anywhere else."

"I really like you two together." Lyric's bright smile could blind them.

"Let's have dessert," Hawk suggested. "Lyric made some killer brownies."

"My favorite."

Hawk met her gaze. "Yeah? Me, too."

She loved that they were finding things in common.

Hawk gave her a soft peck on the lips then nudged her up to take her own seat, while he headed to the kitchen counter to retrieve the pan and plates.

Lyric got up to clear the dishes. Lucky stood to help, but Lyric waved her back down into her seat. "I'll do it. You sit and rest or Hawk will have a heart attack that you're overdoing it."

"She just got out of the hospital." He set the pan on the table along with the plates.

"I'm fine."

"You wince every time you move." Mason gave her a *don't argue* look that Hawk nodded agreement to.

So she sat and let Lyric clear the dishes while Hawk doled out the brownies, and Mason refilled everyone's water glasses.

She and Lyric talked about owning their own businesses. Lyric loved some of her stories about the weirdest things she'd discovered in people's houses while she cleaned. Lucky laughed at some of the dumbass things drunks had done at the bar. One guy had passed out face first on the pool table in the middle of trying to convince some woman to come home with him so he could show her how he could fuck all night.

"He probably couldn't get it up if he was that drunk." Hawk shook his head. "Dumbass."

Lucky found herself smiling and laughing again. How long had it been since she'd felt this light and carefree. Sure they'd talked about some heavy stuff tonight, but somehow she still felt light. Because of him.

He made her feel safe here.

"We better get going. We're leaving early in the morning," Mason announced. "And I'm no dumbass, so Lyric will be up even later." He winked at his wife.

She rubbed her hand over her baby bump. "My name might not be Lucky, but I'm getting lucky tonight. Yay me!"

Hawk's big hand landed on Lucky's thigh again. "You must be beat."

She let her tired gaze answer for her. "I still desperately want a shower."

He nodded. "We need to change your bandages, too."

Mason and Lyric stood. Lyric picked up the rest of the plates and forks. "I'll put these up, then we'll let you two get ready for bed. It was really nice to meet you, Lucky. I haven't seen Hawk smile or talk this much ever. I hope they catch whoever hurt you. I'll call and check on you in a few days."

"I'd really like that. If you'll excuse me. I'm going to use the restroom and let you say goodbye to Hawk." She walked out of the room, overhearing Mason say, "She's everything you said she was. She's perfect for you."

"I really like her for you," was the last thing she caught before ducking into the bathroom, desperate to be clean, so she could sleep comfortably tonight, hopefully with Hawk right beside her again.

Chapter Ten

H awk knocked lightly on the bathroom door, which Lucky had left slightly ajar. An invitation? He hoped. "Can I come in?"

"Um. Yes." The hesitation in her voice made him cautious.

He opened the door slowly, revealing a stunningly beautiful, half-naked Lucky in front of him. She was still in her bra and panties, the plain white cotton just as sexy on her as lace.

She'd managed to get the rest of her clothes off without his help. The sling lay discarded on the double vanity, along with her knee brace and the used wrap and bandage from her thigh. She was currently pulling the bandage off her chest, her gaze darting to him and away as her cheeks flamed pink with embarrassment.

"Want some help?" He tried to put her at ease by seeming nonchalant about her near nakedness and all her scars on display.

"Do you know where the ointment is that we brought home from the hospital?"

That *home* in her sentence did all kinds of things to his head and heart. It made him hope that she really felt like this could be home. Here. With him. "It's on the dresser. I'll get it." It only took half a minute to grab it from the other room and return.

She turned away from him. "I can't reach the one on my back."

He set the ointment and new bandages and gauze on the counter and carefully pulled the tape on all four sides of the large square covering. The stitches were still intact and the wound looked good. "No signs of infection on this one. Turn and let me see your chest."

She turned with a shy grin. "So you're a boob man?"

He met her gaze, even though her spectacular breasts were right there. "I'm a Lucky man. I like everything about you." He brushed his knuckles down her cheek. "Thank you for tonight. It meant a lot to have you here with my cousin and best friend. I know it's unconventional to have a female best friend."

"But she wouldn't take no for an answer." Lucky didn't show an ounce of jealousy. "You told me. And I like her—them—a lot. I've never seen a couple so in love."

"They're the real deal. Nothing can tear them apart. Not after how hard they fought to be together."

"I believe that. It's been a long time since I made new friends. I'm usually too quiet and standoffish to try."

"I get that. I spent way too long pushing everyone away after I returned home. Lyric helped me break that habit."

Her head tilted as she studied him. "Were you ready for it?"

"I'd done a lot of therapy by then to address my PTSD." He put it out there, so she'd know he wasn't whole. Probably never would be again. But he wasn't as broken as he used to be. He'd mended the pieces he could put back together. "What I hadn't done was open myself up to others. Not even my family. I don't know what it was about her. Maybe her direct, take-no-excuses way she came at me did it. But her kindness and joy was infectious. I couldn't be brash with her. Mason deserved to be happy after all he'd been through being undercover with the FBI and away from his family. She was good for him and I didn't want to mess that up for him in any way."

"You love him like a brother." Sadness filled her eyes, like she was thinking of the brother she'd lost.

He couldn't imagine losing either of his brothers or cousins. They were so close.

And now Lucky was alone.

Whoever did that to her and claimed it was to protect her didn't understand Lucky and the depths she'd gone to protect Danny. Killing him for no reason made all she'd sacrificed and suffered meaningless.

"I think of Mason and Nick as brothers. We've been close since we were kids. I'd do anything for them. I know they'd do anything for me. I'm ashamed I pushed them away so long when all they wanted to do was help."

"You needed time. They understood that."

"I knew they would and that's why it made it worse, because I counted on the fact that no matter how much of an asshole I was, they'd never stop trying, and I felt worse for lashing out every time they held a hand out to reach me."

"Sometimes we hurt the ones closest to us because we want them to feel our pain. To understand. I'm sure you've made it up to them."

"I try. Mom says I don't have to do anything but be happy. That's all they want for me."

"That's got to feel really nice, to know no matter what, they have your back."

He tipped his forehead to hers. "I know you don't know what that's like, but you have it now. I won't let anything happen to you. I want you to be happy. I'll do everything I can to make you feel that way."

She cupped his cheek and brushed her thumb against his skin. "Why?"

He stood tall and stared down at her. "Because I care about you. You know that, right?"

"I'm standing here half naked, trying not to be completely self-conscious in front of the second guy to see me naked, wondering what this is between us."

He tilted his head, trying not to get too caught up in the fact she'd only been with one guy. Years ago. How was that even possible? Did guys just turn mute and stupid when they met her? Their loss. His good fortune.

But he understood that after what happened with her ex and her family, trusting anyone didn't come easy.

He'd prove to her she could count on him, even if he was a more deadly motherfucker than her ex. That was a different him. A different life.

Except sometimes his mind took him back there.

Not as often anymore. Thank god.

And now he had her to focus on and keep him grounded. Because he wanted to be with her, in her light, in her warmth, and in her arms desperately.

What was she asking him?

Oh, yeah. "Do you want a label for us?" Would that help her feel secure?

"I just...I haven't done this...and I just want to be clear about what it is. What we are. What you expect."

"You can use boyfriend for now."

There went that head tilt again. "For now?"

"Yeah." He gripped her hips and pulled her to his body, her thighs to his. Her belly to his. Chest to chest. "Because that's not as permanent as I want us to be."

"Oh. Oh!" Her eyes went wide. "You want us to be more."

"You're everything to me." He swooped in and kissed her to make his point, hooking one arm around her hips and pulling her flush against his achingly hard cock. He couldn't help it. She was nearly naked and so close he could smell her. Sure she needed a shower, but there was still and underlying sweetness about her.

And she didn't seem to mind the kiss. Her tongue tangled with his with just as much passion and need as he poured into her.

She tried to move her arm up his shoulder and winced against his lips.

He stopped kissing her long enough to ask, "Are you okay?"

"Sorry. Moved my arm. Hurt my shoulder."

"Damn. I'm taking this too fast. You need time to heal. Sorry." It took a second for his mind to catch up and for him to throttle back his need for her.

The hand at the back of his neck fisted his hair. "Don't be. I like it."

He could see it in her eyes. It had been a long time since someone made her feel good. "Okay, sweetheart. Let's get you cleaned up."

"Okay. But I'll feel a little less exposed if you're as naked as me."

He couldn't help the grin that spread across his face. "Okay, just know that my cock gets really hard and happy when you're around. I can't help it. Ignore it."

"What if I want to see it?"

He groaned. "Oh baby, you're not going to be able to miss it." He brushed his fingers through the sides of her hair. "But know that nothing's going to happen until you're better."

The disappointment in her eyes gave him hope that she wanted him as much as he wanted her.

He couldn't help it when his gaze roamed over her, landing on one scar after another, but also appreciating her long lithe legs, the curves that made him want to touch her everywhere.

"Do they bother you?" She crossed her arm over her chest and put her other hand over a particularly gnarly scar on her thigh.

He didn't like her trying to hide from him.

"Your scars are a badge of strength and survival. They are the mark of all you've endured, the pain you suffered, the endurance it took to keep on living. They're part of what makes you beautiful."

To make her more comfortable, and to show her he didn't come out of his past unscathed either, he pulled off his shirt and tossed it on the vanity.

Her gorgeous green eyes took him in. The smile on her lips showed her appreciation of all his muscles but slowly died on her face as she took in his scars.

Normally, he'd dismiss the stare and not say anything, but he wanted to let her in, so he pointed to his chest near his shoulder. "Gunshot wound from my first tour." He went through the other scars. "Shrapnel from an IED. Knife." He traced his finger along the long scar across his belly and another on his forearm. He pushed his pants down his hips and turned his back to her, showing off the other bullet wound just above his right butt cheek.

"There are more scars on my legs from a chopper crash." He brushed away some of the hair from the side of his head, showing her a long scar. "Really bad concussion, cracked skull, and thirty-two stitches."

"Hawk, how did you survive all this?"

"I got lucky. Just like when I found you. I had good surgeons and the will to live, because I had people I loved back home waiting for me. And I'm stubborn. I didn't want to leave my brothers in arms. I wanted to win with them. I believed in what we were doing. I saved a lot of people." Even if he'd had to kill to save others. To keep his brothers in arms safe. For his country. For the people he loved.

"And you keep saving them. You saved me."

He cupped her face again. "Best thing I ever did." He kissed her because he needed it more than his next breath, then held her close, his mouth at the shell of her ear. "I don't ever want to lose you, especially now that I have you. I lost too many people during my time away. Good soldiers. Friends. Brothers. I can't lose anyone else. Especially not you."

She pressed into him even closer.

His cock got excited, but he kept his cool and his hands at her back, holding her close the way she needed him to for now. "You don't have to hide your scars from me or anyone else. Wear them proudly. They tell people who you are. A survivor."

Tears glistened in her eyes. "Thank you for saving me and giving me this."

"What do you mean?"

"This. Acceptance. Comfort. Safety. Affection. A place beside you."

What he was giving her was all his love, she just wasn't ready to say it. He'd give her time. Soon she'd believe it.

"You belong with me." He hugged her as tightly as he dared without hurting her, then kissed her on the head and set her gently away from him. He pivoted toward the shower and turned on the tap, adjusting the temp until it was just right. He didn't want to burn any of her scrapes or cuts, but she needed some heat to loosen her sore muscles. "Okay, sweetheart, get in." He turned and gulped when he got a look at her fully naked.

Pale pink nipples hardened into tight buds at the tips of her creamy breasts. Her flat stomach had a nasty bruise and some scrapes across it. Her hip bone on one side had another dark bruise, the other side a mass of scrapes. And her mound had a dusting of trimmed golden hair, avoiding her stitches.

God how he wanted to get his hands on her, his fingers and tongue inside her. "You're so beautiful. And tempting. You're killing me."

That bashful lopsided smile came back. "Do you have a razor I could use? It's...ah...been a while."

He pulled a disposable blade out of the cupboard under the sink.

She ducked into the shower while he finished undressing. He walked in behind her, closing the glass door. She'd already gotten under the spray and was rinsing her oily hair thoroughly.

He'd put her shampoo and conditioner in the shower before she went to sleep. He should have helped her get clean before they had company, but she'd been so tired.

He squirted a healthy dollop of shampoo in his hand. "Turn for me. I'll do your hair."

She turned her back to him and let the water run down her chest.

He pulled all her hair into his hand and on top of her head, then massaged the shampoo into her scalp, sliding his fingers through the thick golden strands.

"Oh, that feels good. So does the hot water. My whole body is super tense."

He could think of a dozen ways to loosen her up, and all of them ended in orgasms. His cock got excited again, but he messaged her scalp and neck, enjoying how much she loved it. "The way you were stuck lying on that hill had to have hurt your back and strained your muscles."

"Tell me about it. But your bed was super comfy."

"*Our* bed," he corrected her. "I spared no expense on the mattress. Rinse."

She turned and dipped her head back into the stream of water.

He helped get the soap out by combing his fingers through the strands, even if he was sneaking peeks at those stunning breasts again. They'd be the perfect handful. "Turn again."

He picked up the bottle of conditioner and squeezed out a generous portion. Her hair was long and thick and he worked the conditioner in carefully.

"Let me shave while the conditioner sets in." She grabbed the bar soap and lathered it under her arm, then shaved it. But when it came to the other side, there was no way for her to lift her arm without pain.

He took her wrist. "Let your muscles go loose. I'll hold your arm up and shave it for you."

"Seriously?" Her whole face flamed red.

"I don't mind. It's not a big deal and you'll be more comfortable." He did the job in a matter of seconds and gently lowered her arm.

"This is kind of embarrassing." A blush flushed her cheeks.

"When I was shot, a nurse had to literally hold my junk and help me pee into a container. Sometimes, you gotta do what you gotta do."

She pressed a kiss to his sternum over his heart. "I ache thinking of you going through something so traumatic. It scares me that you came that close to death, even though I know you're here. Alive." She put her hand over his heart. "I think about how you found me... What if I lost this chance?"

He cupped her face and looked deep into her gorgeous green eyes. "But we didn't. I'm here. You're here. Like it was meant to be, our two worlds intersecting."

She looked up at him, a soft smile tilting her pink lips. "Thank you for helping me."

"You don't have to be embarrassed about anything with me. Soon, I'm going to have my hands and tongue all over you, up in all your business." He gave her a wicked grin.

She shocked him by taking his hard length into her soapy hands and stroking him. "Let me say thank you and relieve some of your tension."

He tried to hold back the moan of pleasure that shot through him with her small hand encircling him at the base of his rock hard cock. "Sweetheart, you don't have to do that." But oh, how he loved the feel of her hand gripped around his shaft.

Her eyes sparkled with delight. "What if I want to?" She stroked him up and down, her fingers wrapped around him, sliding easily along his length thanks to the soap.

"There's something you should know." He barely got the words out, he was so focused on her beautiful face and her hand giving him more pleasure than he could ever give himself.

Her hand stilled right over his cockhead, her thumb brushing the slit. "What's that?"

"I'll never say no to sex of any kind with you." He loved her smile and the confidence his words gave her.

"Good to know. So if I wake you up with my mouth around your dick, you won't mind?"

That sounded like heaven. "Will you mind waking up to my tongue in your pussy?" He wanted to taste her so badly.

"That sounds like a very good morning to me." Her smile dimmed a bit. "I don't have a lot of practice with...any of this, so be patient and tell me what you like and don't like. I want this to be good for you."

He stared down at her hand working up and down his length and thought if she was trying to please him, it was damn good to him. "Go with your instincts. Your hands on me always feel good."

She slid her hand down his shaft, her fingers squeezing tight. "I'm...eager to be a good lover. I've read some racy romances, so I know the basics, but I want you to be able to tell me what you want."

"Faster and harder if your aim is to get me off with your hand."

Her smile lit up his heart and her hand doing exactly what he said got him even harder. "That's it. It's so good."

She kissed his chest, right over his bullet scar. "When I'm feeling better and can move more easily, I'll be able to do more."

He didn't like the disappointment in her eyes. "You're doing spectacular." He wanted to thrust into her hand but held back, letting her be in charge, so she'd be more comfortable with him.

She was staring at her hand sliding up and down his length.

He tipped her chin up with his fingertip. "Look at me. Watch what you do to me. See how much I want you?"

Her gaze met his and he let her see how she riled him up and made him burn. It revved something up in her, too, because she squeezed a little tighter and jacked him faster.

His balls tightened and his lower spine tingled with his impending orgasm. "That's it. Keep doing that. I'm going to come." He couldn't help it, he grabbed her hand and held it still while he thrust toward her, spraying ropes of cum over her belly as she wrung him out. "Fuck, that was fantastic." He swooped in and kissed her deep, needing her taste on his tongue as much as he needed her body pressed to his.

When he ended the kiss, he stared down into her dazed gaze. "You okay?"

"So good. But tired."

He turned her under the spray and cleaned her up, though he loved seeing her marked with his cum. He dropped to his knees, lathered her legs and shaved them for her, trying not to notice how close he was to her wet pussy. Her energy was fading, he could tell, and she steadied herself with one hand on the wall.

The soft grin never left her lips as she stared down at him taking care of her.

At last he rose, turned off the water, wrapped a towel around her and dried her softly. He quickly dried himself with another towel, then used it to squeeze the water out of her long hair. He grabbed her brush off the counter and ran it through the slick strands. With every minute that passed, she became more relaxed. "Do you want a shirt or something to sleep in?"

"If it's yours and smells like you, yes."

He pulled her into his arms. "You make me think dirty thoughts and want to hold you close all night."

"Hmm. That sounds nice. I forgot how nice it feels to be close. But I never felt it this strongly until you."

He brushed his thumb over a particularly puckered scar on her shoulder. The gash had to have been deep.

Who hurts their child like this?

He kissed her forehead. "I'm here for all the cuddles you want." Nothing felt better than having her skin against his.

While he'd pushed everyone away for a long time, it felt so good, so right to keep her close.

He put ointment on her shoulder wounds and thigh, then re-bandaged them. It took a bit longer to treat all her scrapes, especially since he kissed above every injury, hoping to ease her pain and build the intimacy between them. "The head wound looks better. Less swollen." He kissed her forehead, brushing her soft cheek with his thumb.

He thought about her plummeting down into that ravine and the callous person who sent her plunging to her death. He wanted to find them and beat them bloody.

He tamped down his rising anger and grabbed the shirt he'd worn today and slipped it up her arm on her injured side, then over her head, and pulled it down so she could put her other arm through the hole.

"Thank you."

"You're welcome. Now you look like you're done in, so go climb into bed. I'll be there in a second." She walked away, leaving him to clean up the bathroom.

He needed a minute to cool off. He'd never wanted a woman the way he wanted her. That hand job in the shower wasn't nearly enough to satisfy him. He wanted to be balls deep inside her.

Soon.

He wanted her safe.

Right now, she needed comfort and his protection. He'd give her both. Everything she needed and more. Because she belonged to him and he belonged to her. Once she believed it, they'd grow closer together. They'd build a life. And neither of them would ever feel alone again.

And whoever was out there plotting to hurt her again, they'd get what's coming to them.

He wouldn't stop until they were found and neutralized.

Chapter Eleven

Hawk woke to Lucky mumbling in her sleep, her body twitching. It took him a second to realize what she was saying.

"Don't Desiree. No, no, no."

She kicked him in the leg and pushed at his chest, her nails biting into his skin.

The nightmare made her restless. Nearly panicked.

"Des, stop."

He wondered what her best friend was doing or saying in the dream.

The two had a long history. They'd grown up together. They seemed close in real life, though their personalities were like night and day. They probably bickered often, their opinions clashing. Still, the friendship lasted this long. They were probably used to each other and knew that any dispute would blow over with time.

He imagined Lucky needed a friend so badly growing up with her sadistic father always tormenting her that anyone who was halfway decent would seem like a saint compared to him.

Maybe Desiree's brash personality didn't really matter to Lucky, because her friend had always been there for her in the best way she knew how.

Lucky mumbled and moaned in her sleep, then yelped, like she wanted to scream but couldn't get it out, her arms flailing again.

Her whole body twitched and moved.

Hawk couldn't take it anymore. He needed to wake her, but didn't want to startle her out of whatever nightmare plagued her.

"Desiree!"

Why was she calling out her best friend's name in distress?

Desiree was at the bar with her that night, but it was her ex's face she kept remembering.

He wished he knew what really happened that night.

He'd keep fishing for answers, but right now he needed to bring Lucky out of her nightmare and into the dream of what he wanted their life to be together.

The sheet slowly slid down her body. Then the shirt Hawk had put her in last night inched up. With every new patch of skin uncovered, Lucky felt Hawk's warm lips laying a trail up her belly to her nipple. He took it into his mouth and sucked it to a peak, making her back arch off the bed and offer her breasts up for him to feast.

"Mm." She sank her fingers into his soft light brown hair and held him to her. "Morning." Light was barely making its way through the crack in the drapes. It had to be early.

Hawk licked a circle around her other nipple, then sucked it into his mouth. "You taste so good." He raised his head and met her gaze, sliding his hand into hers, silently reminding her that moving that arm would hurt her shoulder. Always taking care of her. "I love that smile.

Waking up beside you this morning…nothing better." He nuzzled his nose against the underside of her breast. "I left you hanging last night after our shower."

"I fell asleep before you even got in the bed. I'm sorry."

He swept his hands up her sides and over her breasts. "I wanted to taste you so bad, but I knew you needed your sleep. Time to recover. So let me do all the work this morning before I have to head into the office for a few hours."

She didn't want him to go. She loved spending time with him. It felt like every moment she had with him drew them a little bit closer together. "I'll miss you," she confessed. When had she ever missed anyone?

Well, except her little brother.

But this was different. This was Hawk, and he was here, trying so hard to make her feel better, safe, and connected to him.

His gaze turned possessive. "I'll miss you, too. And if I could blow off the meeting, I would."

She brushed her fingers through his hair because she could. He wanted her touch. And that was so amazing. "I don't want you to put work off for me. You've done so much already, staying with me at the hospital all that time. I know how important working with your brothers is to you. You told me how they keep you grounded and sane in your letters. Gunn Brothers and Search and Rescue gives you a purpose. Everyone needs that."

"What if I want to make you part of my purpose? You feel more important than anything." He kissed her chest, right over her heart.

"I can be that for you while you take care of business. I'll be here, waiting for you."

He growled and nipped her bottom lip. "You have no idea how good that sounds to me."

"Probably as good as it feels to know you're coming back to me later." Tears welled in her eyes. "As good as it felt every time I opened my eyes in the hospital and you were still there. I can't believe you didn't leave me there." A tear spilled over her lashes and down her cheek.

Hawk pressed a kiss to her skin, soaking it up. "I couldn't leave you. Not when you needed me."

"I didn't know how much I needed you. So much that I'm afraid it's too much and you'll pull away and I won't ever feel like this again. The way only you make me feel."

"What do you feel?"

"I think this is what it feels like to be happy. It's been so long, I hardly remember ever feeling this way. Waking up to you wanting me...I can't even explain it." Her heart felt too full.

"You don't need to. I know exactly how you feel, because I feel it, too. Now let me make you feel even better." He trailed kisses back to her nipple, continuing where he left off, making her skin burn and her body writhe.

He went from one breast to the other, giving each equal attention as he slid down her body, kissing her belly, licking her belly button, then placing his mouth over her clit and licking her again, waking up her body even more.

He looked up at her. "You okay?"

"Don't stop."

He didn't. He ramped things up, tracing her slit with his finger, spreading her juices over her skin, then sinking his finger deep inside her. "You're so tight." He pumped his finger in once, twice, then again before adding a second finger, stretching her. His tongue played with her clit, amping up her arousal and need. He made her feel so much, like her body was filled with sparks bursting, ready to be set free.

He replaced his fingers with his tongue and circled her clit with his wet fingers.

God, that tongue.

He fucked her with it until she was holding his head to her pussy, grinding on his mouth and tongue.

She went off like a rocket and he kept pumping his fingers into her, helping her ride out the orgasm, prolonging it until the ultimate finish.

As she came down, her heart racing, lungs panting out heavy breaths, Hawk kissed her inner thighs from knee to hip, up both sides. "That's my girl." He wiped the back of his hand over his mouth and grinned up at her. "Good morning, sweetheart."

"It is now." She giggled. When was the last time she did that?

She pressed her hand to her sore shoulder. Breathing heavy set off shockwaves of pain.

He kissed the back of her hand over her wound. "Sorry about that."

"I'm not. Not even a little bit."

Worry still clouded his eyes. "Did you sleep well?"

"Next to you...yes."

"You were talking in your sleep. Dreaming. Do you remember about what?"

She tried to bring it into focus. "Not really." It seemed fuzzy. Like she remembered dreaming but couldn't bring it back to mind. "What did I say?"

"You were saying Desiree's name a lot."

"Huh. It kind of makes sense. She's my best friend. We talk all the time. She's the one I call anytime I need someone to talk to, or I need help with something."

"Do you trust her?"

She raised a brow. "Most of the time. Why?"

Hawk's gaze narrowed. "Do you think she had anything to do with what happened to you?"

"Do I think my best friend tried to kill me? No. Why would she do that? We were out having fun. She took me home. She brought me clothes to the hospital. Why would she hurt me?"

"I don't know. You seemed upset in your dream. Scared. I didn't like it. And if she upsets you, I want to know why."

Unsettled, Lucky tried to explain her complicated relationship with Desiree. "We've always had a lopsided relationship, mostly because our personalities clash. She wants to be in charge. She wants the focus on her. When it's not, she gets upset and says things she doesn't really mean."

"And you take it because she's your friend and you don't want to make things worse."

She loved that he understood. "Yes. After my family was murdered by someone so close to me, it was hard to trust anyone. Desiree has always been by my side. She's always been consistently true. I know what to expect from her and there's comfort in that." She wanted to lighten things up. "Do you really want to talk about my friend while we're in bed together? Naked.

"I like where your mind is going, but...stay here. I'll be right back." He hopped out of bed wearing just a pair of black boxer briefs, his impressive hard-on pressed against his belly.

"I can help you with that." She held her hand out to him, hoping he'd come back to bed. She'd gone so long without someone's touch, now she wanted to explore all the things she'd missed over the past several years. And because it was Hawk, she wanted to show him how much she appreciated and needed him.

Hawk stroked himself once, like he was trying to ease the ache she saw on his face. "Can't. No time. Just stay right there. I have something for you." He rushed out of the room.

She laid back and enjoyed the post orgasm bliss, wondering how she ended up here. In Hawk's bed. In his house. And his heart.

I'm his girlfriend. That seemed so wild.

Hawk walked in carrying a mug and plate. "Breakfast in bed." He waited for her to sit up, then handed her the coffee with milk, just the way she liked it, and a cheese, green onion, and bacon omelet. "How did you remember how I like my coffee?"

"I think it was the third time you cleaned for me, you left me a bag of the coffee you like best and said that if I was going to drink coffee at all hours of the day and night, I should at least drink *good* coffee. You said you liked yours with a dollop of milk. I still don't know how you knew I drank it at all hours."

"You weren't as neat as you are now. I'd find mugs left out on the back deck table, in the bathroom, and on the coffee table, and next to your dinner and dessert plates."

"Only because you left me dessert."

"I wanted to sweeten up your life." She sipped her coffee and sighed. "It's perfect. Thank you." She took a forkful of the omelet but didn't get to try it because Hawk swooped in and kissed her, long and deep, like he had all the time in the world to tell her what she'd said and done mattered.

"You did sweeten my life. You're still doing it. Now we get to be there for each other. I really, really want this to work."

"So far, it feels like we should have done this a lot sooner."

"Then you understand why I don't want to waste any more time. I know this is all fast, you being here, what we did in the shower and this morning without us really dating."

"And yet it feels like I've known you a long time. It was at a distance, but it still felt real and deep. I know you better than some of the people I work with and see every day."

"I just don't want to come on too strong and push you away."

She had the same concern. "I think we're both worried about the same thing when we both simply want more of each other. Right?" Hope bloomed in her heart, even though she was so scared he'd change his mind and want his space now that she'd been here overnight.

"Yes. I want more nights like last night and more mornings like this."

"Then let's just go with it and remember to communicate if it's too much."

"Or not enough," he quickly added. "You can ask for more. I want to be everything you need."

She held up her mug. "Can I have more coffee?"

He took it with a grin. "Yes. But eat your food so you can take your meds. Doc said you need to eat to get your strength back after you lost so much blood."

It was going to take a couple of weeks at least for her to feel back to normal. So she dug into the omelet while he fetched her coffee, then showered.

When he came out with just a towel around his waist, his hair damp but combed, she moaned, making him give her a wicked grin.

"Not now, sweetheart. I've got to get to work. But later..." The promise in his words and eyes said he'd deliver.

She watched him get dressed, caressing his skin with her gaze as it ran over every dip and valley, all those glorious muscles. "What time do you think you'll be home?"

"I'm hoping I can check in, attend the meeting, then leave, so maybe two to three hours. I'll text if I'm going to be later. You can text me if you need something while I'm out." He studied her. "You feel okay? If you'd rather I stay…"

"No. I'm good. Mind if I crash on your couch and watch TV?"

"Make yourself at home. Do whatever you want. Use whatever you want. Eat whatever you want. Treat this place like it's yours." He leaned over, his slacks unzipped and unbuttoned, his gorgeous chest on display, and kissed her. "I mean it. I want you to feel comfortable here." He brushed his hand over her hair. "You're so beautiful."

She rolled her eyes. "I must look a mess."

"A loved-up mess, maybe, but still beautiful." He kissed her forehead. "You need help with anything before I leave?"

"I think I'll be okay." She'd do her best with the use of only one arm.

He pointed a finger at her. "Don't overdo it today."

She loved that he worried about her. "I won't. Go. You don't want to be late, and I want you back as soon as possible."

He finished buttoning his blue dress shirt, tucked it in, then kissed her like he had all the time in the world. "Text me if you need me."

"I will. But I won't. I'm fine." She thought about what she could do to occupy her time. "I'll probably call into work and have Joellen catch me up."

"Okay. I'll set the alarm when I leave. You should be safe here. If it goes off, lock yourself in the bathroom and call me. The alarm will notify the police of an intruder."

That made her feel better about being left alone. "Maybe Desiree will want to stop by to keep me company."

Something flickered in his eyes for just a moment.

"Would you rather I didn't invite her over?"

"No. It's not that. I just want you to rest." It sounded like more.

"I will. Promise."

He kissed her again.

"You're never going to get out of here if you keep doing that."

"I like kissing you. Which is new, because I never really liked kissing. Now, I'm addicted." The glint in his eyes confirmed it.

Her heart swelled. "Well, I'd appreciate it if you reserved that for me."

"You're the only one I want to kiss. And more."

She gave him a gentle push. "More later. Work now." She shooed him away with one hand.

He backed away toward the door. "Are you getting up?"

"I'm going to lay in bed smelling you on the sheets while I check my email."

He growled low in his throat. "You make it really hard to leave."

She glanced at the thick, long rod pressing against the zipper of his slacks. "I can see that." She licked her lips, thinking about tasting him, since he'd been so nice waking her up this morning.

"I'm going to enjoy making you come over and over again when I get home for teasing me with that mouth of yours."

"Threaten me with a good time, why don't you."

He growled again and left the room as she giggled some more.

How had this become her life? When had she ever felt this light?

She'd nearly died and now she was happier than she'd ever been.

She wouldn't take this for granted. She'd appreciate it and him.

And hope that whatever trouble was coming her way, she'd stop it before it affected her and Hawk's relationship. She wouldn't let anyone come between them. Not now. Not ever.

All she had to do was figure out how to take down her conniving ex once and for all. So she could breathe. So she'd be safe. And she and Hawk could be like this every day for the rest of their lives.

Chapter Twelve

Hawk walked out of the Gunn Brothers Distillery conference room, checking his watch and wincing that the meeting had taken so long. But they had a lot to cover, and he and Lincoln had missed several days to be with Lucky at the hospital.

Lincoln followed him into his office. "How is she?"

"Better than I expected after she had another rough night." His thoughts turned to the disturbing things she said in her sleep, even if they were disjointed and hard to put into context.

"Is she still in pain?"

"Some. But her mind is trying to figure out what happened and replaying things over and over again." He'd had enough therapy and long nights of his own with his PTSD to recognize her symptoms.

"It's fucked up what someone did to her. And we don't even know if it's the worst case scenario or what."

It ate at Hawk, the not knowing. But... "She's not afraid of me. While she doesn't like being touched in general, she never shies away from me." He thought about it a bit more. "She was nervous around Mason at first, but she quickly relaxed around him."

Lincoln grinned. "He's a big, ruthless looking dude. I wouldn't blame her for being apprehensive around him."

"Yeah. But she saw him with Lyric. In fact, she studied them like they were some science experiment."

Lincoln nodded. "She's probably never seen that kind of love."

"Her parents were abusive. Her ex killed her family. Yeah, I'm guessing she's never seen love like that."

"Except you've shown her you care. You'll help her. You'll be kind. Gentle. Patient." Lincoln dropped his hand on Hawk's shoulder and squeezed. "You're different with her." He squeezed again. "Not that you weren't nice to the other women who came and went from your life. But there's something about *her* that makes you so careful."

"I don't want to fuck this up." *I need her so much.*

"You won't."

"How do you know that?" What if he didn't live up to the man she'd made him out to be in her head these last two years?

"Because you love her. You've never loved anyone the way you love her. I can see it. Anyone who sees you two together can see it."

"I just...she's...I can't lose her." Just the thought made his chest tight, his stomach drop.

Lincoln smacked him on the back. "Then go home and take care of her. We've got you covered here."

"Lincoln's right. We can cover for you." Mercy stepped up to the side of Lincoln.

He could swear his brother leaned in closer to her. *Interesting.*

He and his brothers owned Gunn Brothers Distillery, but Mercy was the beating heart of the place. She kept every department running smoothly. Smart, organized, knowledgeable about their products and processes, and gorgeous—not that it mattered for her to do her job. On top of all that, she had an attention to detail that had saved their asses on many occasions.

Lincoln could do a hell of a lot worse.

And maybe she was the reason he hadn't seen his older brother out with anyone lately.

He didn't have time to dive into that now. Lucky was at home and hurting and probably wanted some lunch right about now.

"I'm leaving distribution in your capable hands and going home to take care of what's really important."

"Say hi to Lucky for me." Lincoln smirked.

Mercy stepped forward. "I heard about what happened to her. I hope she's okay."

"She will be once I put the fucker who did this to her in the ground." He clenched his fists at his sides.

"I hope you get him." With that, Mercy headed down the hall toward her office.

Lincoln couldn't take his eyes off her.

Hawk grinned, happy to see his brother pining for someone for once. Usually he was the one being chased by women. "You should ask her out."

"I did. She turned me down." Lincoln's gaze fell to the floor.

Hawk dropped his hand on Lincoln's shoulder. "When have you ever taken no for an answer?"

Lincoln's gaze turned tortured. "She doesn't want to mix business and pleasure. She likes working here and thinks dating me would mean the end of that."

"Prove her wrong. Because I'd fire your ass before I'd fire her. She's a huge asset to this company. If you remind her of that, and how this place wouldn't be the company it is without her, maybe she'll give you a chance. Convince her it's real, not some dalliance."

Lincoln's eyes turned thoughtful. "I want her like I've never wanted anyone, or anything else."

"If you mean that, and it's more than just getting into her panties, then I'm sure you'll figure out a way to make her see it."

"And if I fuck it up and she decides to leave Gunn Brothers?"

"I'll fucking kick your ass and make you beg her on your knees to get her back."

"I'd happily drop to my knees for her any minute of the day or night."

Hawk smirked. "Damn, you've got it bad."

"Keep it to yourself. If she finds out anyone at the company knows, she'll be really pissed."

"My lips are sealed." His phone chimed with a text.

JASE: I've got an update. You coming or what???

"Fuck. I forgot I'm supposed to meet with Jase about the case."

"Go. We've got you covered here."

"Thanks, man." Hawk hauled ass out to his car and drove over to the sheriff's department. Before he went inside, he texted Lucky.

HAWK: Finished my meeting at work. Meeting Jase for an update on the case. I'll fill you in when I get home.

HAWK: How are you? Need anything?

He waited but got no answer. Maybe she'd fallen asleep, or was in the bathroom. Maybe she simply couldn't get to her phone. He didn't know and it worried him.

He climbed out of his car and walked into the station. He spotted Jase in a cubicle and headed over to him.

"Take a seat." Jase looked all business.

Hawk sat but couldn't relax. "What do you know?"

Jase turned in his swivel chair and pointed to his computer screen. "I've looked through all the security footage and I think I found something, but I want you to watch and tell me what you see."

Hawk narrowed his gaze, but nodded for Jase to play it. He watched two guys approach Lucky and Desiree at a table by the dancefloor. They chatted for a little while, then one of the guys asked Lucky to dance. A few minutes later, they were back at the table with Desiree and the guy she'd stayed with while Lucky and the other guy danced.

He kept watching as Lucky took several sips of her drink, then seemed to lose her balance. Desiree took her by the arm and walked her to the bathroom.

Jase paused the recording. "So, what do you think?"

"Lucky looks perfectly fine, not drunk, until after she finished her drink. Neither of those guys drugged the drink. Their hands are in plain sight the whole time. It doesn't make sense."

"And yet, we know it was spiked. That's why I zeroed in on when the guys approached them. So if they didn't spike the drink—"

"Then it had to have been done before the guys showed up." Hawk didn't like what he was thinking.

Jase rewound the footage. "So I went back to when Lucky and Desiree went to the bar to order their drinks and spoke to Lincoln." Jase met his gaze. "Just so you know, I've cleared Lincoln. He and

Lucky talk while he makes her drink. There's no indication he drugged her."

"Of course he didn't fucking drug her!" Hawk had never suspected his brother.

Jase held up a hand. "He had the opportunity."

"That doesn't mean he'd do something so vile." No way. Never. Lincoln was a standup guy.

"I agree. Lincoln loves the ladies, but he's never been accused of hurting anyone. But it's my job to suspect everyone involved and rule them out." He pushed play on the video. "So instead of watching Lincoln and Lucky, watch Desiree."

"What? No." But he had felt a lot of her behavior was odd.

"Watch."

Hawk couldn't take his eyes off her. Every move she made seemed so innocent, except for the look in her eyes as she watched Lucky talking to Lincoln. Her hands fisted in her lap. Her eyes and lips narrowed with anger. She knocked back a double shot. It didn't seem to improve her attitude.

She slipped her hands into her purse. It looked like she was trying to feel for something inside the bag.

Why didn't she just open it and look inside?

Finally, she pulled her phone out, checked the black screen, then set it face down on the bar. A second later, Lincoln slid Lucky's sangria across the bar. Desiree snatched it up and took a sip.

"What the fuck?"

"Yeah. Seemed rude to me, too."

"What was she rummaging in her purse for? The phone seems like something easy to find in a small purse like that."

"You caught it, too." Jase seemed pleased.

"Go back to her taking the drink from Lucky."

They watched the footage again.

Hawk seethed. "She could have spiked the drink when she grabbed it by the top. If the drug was in her hand, it would have dropped right into the drink. She takes a sip with the straw, the bottom of the drink couldn't have anything in it. Not until it was stirred up a bit more. It isn't obvious, but she could have done it. It's much more likely her than Lincoln or the two guys they met."

"My thoughts exactly."

"Why would Desiree want to hurt her best friend like that?" It didn't make sense to him, even if Desiree seemed abrupt with Lucky most of the time. He didn't know her well enough to assume that she was simply like that with everyone.

Though she had come off as a flirt with Lincoln.

But in the hospital, she never asked Lucky about what happened. Never asked if she was okay like a best friend would. In fact, she didn't seem overly concerned about her friend's mental and physical wellbeing at all.

Jase pulled him out of his head. "I've been looking into the ex. Neil. I wasn't around when he was arrested for killing her parents, so I asked some of the other officers about the case." Jase held his gaze. "Did you know there was a rumor going around that Neil was cheating on Lucky?"

"No. She hasn't mentioned anything like that. The thing that seems to hit her the hardest is that he killed her little brother, Danny. She misses him."

"Yeah. Seems like the not-so-secret secret was that Mr. Sinclair liked to get rough with his family."

"Mostly Lucky, from what I've learned. And it isn't much of a secret when you look at the scars marring half her body."

"I asked her about them every time something happened to her. She shut me down each and every time, saying that it was the past."

"Tell me about these other incidents. What happened to her?"

"The day after Neil was sentenced, someone egged her car and spray painted *die bitch* on her front door."

"I assume Neil's family and friends who still supported him might have taken out their anger on her. He did swear he didn't do it, right?"

"Yes. His alibi was that he was home sleeping after drinking some beer and smoking some pot."

Hawk rolled his eyes. "Alone. I presume."

"His parents were home. They swore he hadn't left the house."

"As far as they knew. He could have snuck out a window."

"I assume he did, or the parents were so distracted they didn't notice him sneak out a door. Police found a backpack in his closet with the bloody knife in it, along with a stash of ketamine. He says he can't remember some of that night."

"Convenient."

"Ketamine can cause amnesia with a high enough dose."

"So, what? He was high, decided Lucky's family had to die to keep her safe, including a kid who'd never done anything to anyone, someone she loved so much she put herself in a monster's path time and time again?"

"Killing the kid doesn't make sense."

"Unless he didn't want to have to raise the kid with Lucky." Hawk hated the idea.

"In Neil's mind, he was saving her. He probably thought she'd be so grateful they'd live happily ever after on whatever her parents left behind."

"Except the family was in debt and Lucky had to use whatever money there was to pay off bills. She couldn't even keep the house."

"So you two have talked about the past." Jase gave him a knowing grin. "You are getting close."

"Yes. She's staying at my place. If I have my way, she'll never leave."

Jase settled back in his chair, a knowing grin on his smug face. "So it's like that."

"I want it to be. I'm trying not to rush her, but it's hard not to want everything all at once with her."

"Word is going to spread that she's with you. That could put a target on your back."

"Whoever is doing this seems hell bent on making *her* life miserable."

"Yeah. After the egg and graffiti incident there were a few other things."

"Like what?"

"Someone pushed her down a flight of stairs at a house she was cleaning. No one else was home at the time."

"So someone knew she was there, broke in, and tried to kill her?"

"That's what she claims. She had bruises and a busted lip from where she hit the hardwood stair treads, but there was no evidence anyone had been in the house, except her word."

"She wouldn't throw herself down the stairs for attention."

"I never said she did."

Hawk fumed. "It was implied."

Jase gave him an evil look. "That's what she accused me of, too, and I'll tell you what I told her. I believed her, I just couldn't prove it."

Hawk relaxed a bit. "Okay. What else?"

"Stupid shit. Leaving the gas stove on but unlit, filling the cabin up with gas. Breaking into her house and moving shit around, so she knows someone's been there, but not who. The first year that her family was gone, someone left her notes on the tenth of the month, every month."

"What did it say?"

"*You're the reason they're dead.*"

"Fuck." He ran his hand through his hair. "That's fucking harsh."

"Someone started a rumor that Lucky was offering more than housecleaning services to her clients. Her business got dozens and dozens of calls from men wanting to hire her. She got propositioned just about everywhere she went. Some guy even pushed her up against the glass ice cream case in the supermarket, stuffed a fifty in her pocket, along with his phone number, and kissed her. She kneed him in the nuts and clocked him with a bottle of juice. Dude was covered in mango peach."

He'd have to remember that she liked that and pick some up on his next grocery run.

"Those last few things were more nuisance than harmful. Though the guys going after her could have turned out a lot worse."

"And she thinks these things were set in motion by her ex?"

"That's her theory. And I agree that it could have been someone in his family, friends of his, or even some cellmates who owed him a favor. The thing is, there's no proof." Jase smacked his hand on the thick folder in front of him. "Complaint after complaint and I have nothing. She asks for my help and I can't find anything that will make this stop." Jase hung his head. "Even worse. She's been drugged two other times. Once at a different bar. She woke up in her car in her driveway with no clue how she got there. Receipts from the bar showed she'd had a single drink, so she wasn't drunk."

"Was she there with Desiree that time, too?"

"Technically. She'd taken her whole crew out for drinks after work. Desiree was there on a date. A couple of the ladies said that Desiree and her date had an argument and he left. Lucky went over to console her friend, then the ladies all left and Desiree said she left before Lucky, who stayed behind to pay the tab."

"So someone still in the bar could have connected with Lucky and drugged her."

"Maybe. There were no cameras in the bar, so all I could go on was what people reported to me."

"And of course, no one copped to drugging her or seeing anything."

"People were there to have a good time. They were drinking themselves." Jase shrugged.

"Fuck. I'm as frustrated as you now." It made no sense. Why do all these things to her and not confront her head on? Just to torment and torture her?

"Here's what's even weirder. The last time she was drugged—before you found her in the ravine—she hadn't been drinking. She'd cooked some beef stroganoff with some dehydrated mushrooms she'd bought at the store. It was a large bag and she'd used half in another meal."

"So the bag was previously open."

"You got it. And about ten minutes after she ate, she started tripping and called 911."

Hawk's anger skyrocketed. "Someone dosed her with magic mushrooms."

"Yep. Because I doubt the manufacturer made that kind of mistake. Not where there are so many kinds of mushrooms that are poisonous."

"Lucky is nice. Kind. Caring. Quiet. She'd never hurt someone on purpose. So why is someone fucking with her like this? It doesn't feel like the work of an ex who loved her so much he killed for her. After doing something like that out of misguided love, why start actively making her life a living hell? Because he got caught? Because she was angry that he killed her little brother? It seems like he'd understand why that would upset her. Hell, he'd know before he did it that she'd be furious and hurt. It makes no sense."

"Exactly. I spoke to Neil. He knows what happened to her. Want to know what he said to me?"

"What?"

"He said, 'You need to stop the person doing this to her.' "

Hawk leaned forward, his forearms on his knees. "Did he sound sincere?"

"Very."

"Was he talking about you stopping him, or someone else?"

"He didn't say and I couldn't tell. The guy spent years in prison and he's not the same kid who went in. He's hardened. Careful. He doesn't want to go back, but he's also not willing to jeopardize his freedom either."

"I get that. But we need answers. Because Lucky believes he was there the night she was drugged."

"Maybe he was. Maybe he wasn't. She could just be putting this all on the guy who wrecked her world."

Hawk shook his head. "I don't think so. She talks in her sleep. Over and over again she wants to know why he's there. And she doesn't see him as he was years ago. She says he's older now. Different."

"I can't arrest the guy because of a dream."

"I know. But we can't rule him out either. And if he was there, but isn't the one who hurt her, then maybe he knows something he's not telling you."

"I've spoken to him twice now. His story is the same every time I ask about that night. He sticks to the same details."

"There's got to be a way to figure this out."

"At this time, I'm looking more toward Desiree than Neil."

Hawk thought about everything he knew and what he didn't understand. "How did Lucky's car end up at her house?"

Jase sat up straighter. "Desiree said she took Lucky home that night."

"Right. So Lucky's car should have still been in the Gunn Brothers parking lot."

Jase turned pensive for a moment. "The video we have shows them going into the back room where there are no cameras. When the video didn't show them leaving through the main entrance, I called Lincoln to ask about the banquet room. He said there's a side exit in there that leads to the parking lot."

"There is. But there are no cameras out there." Hawk's frustration rose. Initially, they wanted the cameras to watch over the registers and customers in the bar. He needed to talk to Lincoln about putting some cameras outside, too. Hawk tried to piece things together. "So Desiree would have had to take Lucky home, drive back to the bar, driven Lucky's car to her place, then gotten a rideshare back to the bar, then gone home herself?" It seemed a lot to do in one night when Lucky could have simply gotten a ride to the bar the next day.

Jase shrugged. "It's definitely something I need to investigate further."

"But will it really get us closer to figuring out who is behind all this?"

"I'm doing the best I can with the evidence I have, and it's not a lot to go on." Jase's frustration showed in the lines on his forehead.

"I know. I'm frustrated, too. I hate what's happening to her."

"Me, too. Like I told her, it's not that I don't believe her, it's that I can't prove anything."

"I need to change the locks on her place. I don't like that someone keeps getting in so easily." Hawk would make it a priority.

"I did follow up with the busted window lock after the fire department flagged it. I had it dusted for prints. Nothing. It was clean—like, no prints at all. Someone covered their tracks."

"Of course they did."

Jase tapped the thick file folder. "I'll call Desiree and ask about the car."

"I'm headed home. Let me know if you get an answer that points to whoever is doing this."

"I want to end this for her just as much as you do."

Hawk hoped he did it soon. "I appreciate it." Hawk headed out, anxious to check on Lucky, especially since she hadn't answered his earlier text.

He needed to talk to Lucky and figure out a plan to keep her safe. No one was above his suspicion now. Not even her best friend. Because sometimes the people closest to you knew how to hurt you the most.

He hoped for her sake there was some other explanation.

She'd been betrayed enough.

Chapter Thirteen

Lucky lost herself in the *Marked Men: Rule + Shaw* movie on one of the many streaming services Hawk's TV was set up for. She loved the movie just as much as the book by her favorite author. It was the perfect distraction and guaranteed a happy ending, one she never thought she'd get herself, until Hawk saved her. The determination and caring she saw in his eyes every time he looked at her let her know that he truly, deeply wanted her.

Can my luck finally be changing?

She hoped so, because it had been a long time, if ever, that she'd felt this kind of happiness.

She glanced at the clock on her phone.

He's late.

He probably got caught up at the office.

Rule and Shaw were kissing on screen and it was hot and passionate, reminding her of the steamy kiss Hawk laid on her when she tried to leave. He'd made it perfectly clear that he wanted her to stay. And he simply wanted her. It still seemed so amazing and surreal to get what she'd wanted after so long. Her heart didn't know what to do with all the emotions being with Hawk stirred up. Love. Joy. Acceptance. Hope for the future.

That was certainly a new one for her.

Instead of endless days working and wishing, now she dreamed of a life with a man who truly knew her in a way no one else did. They could be a family, not like the one she'd lost, but the one she craved.

Did he want children?

He'd be an amazing father.

She wanted to be a mother. She would love her child with everything she had. They would never fear her or think she was mean. Not the way her father had been cruel. She'd build her children up instead of tearing down their self-esteem, turning their love to hate.

She knew she wouldn't be perfect, but she'd try. She'd dole out hugs and kisses and praise with smiles and gratitude to be a part of a family who cared about each other and raised each other up, instead of tearing them down.

The doorbell rang just as she noticed a text from Hawk, making her heart race.

Who would come over when Hawk was at work?

It took some effort to get herself off the couch. Once she'd settled in, her body simply wanted to rest. Her sore muscles protested being asked to carry her to the door.

Maybe she'd try out the soaker tub in Hawk's amazing bathroom once her stitches came out.

She checked through the peephole and frowned.

"Open up, or I'll huff and puff and bang on the door until you...Let. Me. In." Those words were punctuated by more knocks.

Lucky punched in the alarm code and opened the door. Standing in the opening, staring at Desiree, she wondered why she was so reluctant to let her in Hawk's house, or near her.

The instinct confused her and made her wary.

Is it because I don't want anything to burst the bubble of contentment I've felt since arriving here? Do I fear Desiree somehow belittling or sabotaging what Hawk and I are just starting to build together?

I'm being ridiculous.

Desiree was her best friend. She wanted Lucky to be happy.

"Aren't you going to invite me in?"

She didn't answer verbally, just opened the door wider, her gut tightening with apprehension.

Desiree stepped into the open living room and kitchen area, turning as she took in the cozy but spacious space. "Damn, girl, you hit the jackpot. This place is amazing."

Lucky closed the door and wrapped her free arm around her waist, her other arm was strapped in the brace that kept her shoulder from moving too much. "Hawk has incredible taste." The room was somehow elegant but comfortable with the light gray sectional anchored by a beautiful and plush sky blue rug. Brushed nickel glass-topped end tables and a coffee table filled out the space. The end tables had beautiful lamps, their bases had stacked four inch balls of blue glass with pristine white shades on top. Family photos in silver frames lined the gorgeous redwood fireplace mantel. The TV hung over a dark wood cabinet across from the sofa. Two glass and black metal lanterns sat on either side with a tall, fat candle in each. In between was a lovely green plant that matched the one sitting in the middle of the coffee table. She didn't know plants that well, but she loved their variegated leaves of green and almost white.

A terrarium filled with different kinds of moss sat on the dining room table.

The drapes on the huge windows and sliding glass door to the back deck matched the blue glass on the lamps.

The kitchen bar was in the same blue with white quartz countertops. The cabinets along the back wall were dark wood that matched the bar stools.

The place was perfect. Lovely. Not too masculine and dark, but a balance. A few colorful throw pillows, maybe a blanket, some fresh flowers would give it a feminine touch.

Then again, the lavender blanket she'd brought from home complimented his couch and other décor rather well.

"You like it here," Desiree announced, bringing her out of her fresh look at Hawk's place as she tried to see it as not just Hawk's place but theirs.

"It was very nice of Hawk to let me stay while I recover. He's been really sweet about taking care of me."

Desiree's eyes lit up. "Oh, I bet he has." She glanced at the paused TV screen. "Speaking of Marked Men, does Hawk have tattoos? I've never seen any on him, but I bet you got an up close and full naked view of him by now."

A blush swept up her neck and face. "Just the one across the inside of his bicep that says, *If you want it, go after it Gunns blazing.*" And a lot of scars and yummy sculpted muscles.

Desiree's smile widened. "You dirty girl. You hit that, didn't you?"

She didn't want to talk about it. What happened between her and Hawk was...private. Precious. Meaningful. Hers.

It wasn't some hookup.

It was real and deep and theirs.

"Hawk and I have grown closer."

Desiree rolled her eyes. "Come on. Details. That man is hot. I bet he's a beast in bed."

He was passionate. Attentive. Considerate because of her injuries. Even though he was holding back, the feelings and intent behind every kiss, caress, lick, and orgasm were focused on bringing as much pleasure as both of them could give and take.

"Hawk takes very good care of me. That's all I'm going to say." She glanced at the time again. "What are you doing here? Shouldn't you be at work?"

Desiree worked as an administrative assistant at the courthouse, a job her father had gotten her when Krystal started preschool, giving Desiree a few hours each day to work and earn some money of her own.

Lucky thought about that wad of cash Desiree had flashed in the bar. Had she made all of that at work? Maybe she had a side gig she hadn't mentioned. Or maybe she was just frugal and saving everything she made for Krystal.

When Desiree got pregnant in high school, two months before Lucky's family had been killed, Desiree had kept it a secret until she couldn't hide it anymore. She refused to name the father. To this day, it was a secret Desiree hadn't shared with anyone, including her best friend.

It made Lucky feel like Desiree didn't trust her, or that she felt like Lucky would judge her for whoever she'd slept with. It didn't matter to Lucky. She loved Krystal. And she knew Desiree could be reckless sometimes and impulsive—she often wondered if Desiree hadn't gone after some older, married man. Lucky wouldn't put it past her. She liked to cross boundaries. It gave her some kind of thrill to be doing something she shouldn't.

While Lucky was her best friend, her father's punishments were enough of a deterrent to keep her on the straight and narrow. It often caused friction between her and Desiree, but their friendship some-how survived Lucky not giving in to every one of Desiree's whims and wild schemes.

"You're not going to give me any dirty details. Come on. This is the first guy you've been into since—"

"Don't say his name. I don't want to hear it. Not in this house. He's dead to me. And if he's the one doing this stuff to me, I hope they put him back in jail." She fumed, her hands shaking.

Desiree's eyes narrowed. "Whoa, girl. Take a chill pill."

"No. I'm sick of this! All this shit happening all the time. Maybe I should just confront his ass. Take a stand, because this can't go on. What the fuck did I ever do to him to deserve this?" Lucky waved her hand down her body, indicating all the bruises, bumps, scrapes, stitches, and sore muscles.

"It got you the guy you wanted." The way Desiree said it didn't sound like she was happy for Lucky.

Then again, Desiree preferred being the center of attention. She liked it best when she had everything someone else wanted.

"Hawk and I were inevitable. It was going to happen one way or another. We'd been circling each other for a long time. One of us would have finally made a move." She had a feeling it would have been her. Some grand gesture to get his attention. Or maybe simply finding the courage to ask him on a date.

Maybe he'd finally follow that urge to come home while she was here and start up a real conversation.

Didn't matter now.

"Inevitable? Wow. You really think that." Desiree sneered at such a notion.

I know it. "You don't know what we've shared the last two years."

"Maybe he's just caught up being the guy who rescued you, you know? Like now that you're safe all the urgency and emotions will settle and you'll just go back to being the girl who cleans his house."

"Thanks for the support and understanding and thinking that he could really love me." It hurt with an ache in her heart to hear her friend not believe that someone like Hawk could really care about her.

"That's not what I mean at all. I just don't want you to get your hopes up too high when everything is so new between you two."

"That's just it. You haven't seen the way he treats me. It's...special. It's like we've known each other forever."

"I think you've watched too many Hallmark movies and read too many books where everything ends in a happy ever after."

"What's wrong with that? It happens. There are happy couples out there, who are in love and care about each other and build a relationship on trust. I met Hawk's cousin Mason and his wife Lyric. They were so in love and in tune with each other. They never stopped looking at each other with so much love in their eyes. I could tell how much he cherished her, adored her. The way he touched her baby bump with reverence and a kiss for her to let her know he loved that she was growing their baby, protecting and nurturing it. I want that."

"You can have that and more." Hawk's deep voice and words soothed her like nothing else.

She turned to him. "You're home."

He walked toward her. "Miss me?"

"Yes," she managed to get out before he wrapped her gently in his arms and kissed her, long and slow, his lips pressed to hers, his hand on her face, thumb brushing against her cheek.

He broke the kiss and looked deep into her eyes. "You're supposed to be on the couch resting."

"I was, until Desiree showed up a few minutes ago."

Hawk turned to her friend without letting her go. "Nice to see you again. Thanks for checking on my girl."

Desiree planted her hand on her cocked hip. "She was mine long before she was yours."

Hawk's gaze sharpened. "Guess I didn't get the best friend stamp of approval."

Desiree gave him a flirty smile. "Oh, I don't know. You're certainly handsome enough. You've got the whole badass vibe. You fly helicopters and save people."

"Saving Lucky didn't win me enough brownie points?" He eyed Desiree like he was trying to figure her out.

Good luck. Lucky had been friends with her forever and still couldn't keep up with the way Desiree ran hot and cold all the time.

Desiree's smile slipped. "Lucky deserves the best. I want to be sure she gets it."

"I think we're off to a good start." Hawk fixed his gorgeous hazel gaze on her. "Don't you think, sweetheart?"

"I seem to remember you and me starting off the morning with a bang."

The heat in his eyes matched her own. "Happy to repeat it every day for the rest of our lives."

Desiree fanned her face. "I didn't think you had it in you."

The comment stung. Lucky had kept most everyone, men especially, at arm's length. But that didn't mean she didn't want intimacy and sex, or couldn't enjoy it and let loose with the right person. "I need to use the restroom. I'll be back in a minute." Before she stepped away, Hawk pulled her into another kiss.

"I'll make you something to eat when you get back."

"There's Tuscan chicken and vegetables in the crock pot. It will be ready in an hour."

Hawk's smile made her heart float. "Is that the amazing smell?"

"I thought you might be hungry after work."

He brushed some loose strands of her long hair behind her ear. "I'm supposed to be taking care of you."

"I literally dumped everything into the crock pot and turned it on. No big deal."

"It is. And I appreciate it. You're an amazing cook."

"Thank you." This time, she initiated the kiss and saw in Hawk's surprised eyes how much he liked it.

"That's better."

She knew what he meant. He wanted her to feel comfortable enough to touch and kiss him without hesitation. It felt right. It felt good. Really, really good to have the connection and trust between them. It made it so easy to just be herself, the one she was with him. The woman she had always wanted to be. The one she got to be with him.

Chapter Fourteen

Hawk waited for Lucky to walk into their bedroom before he focused on Desiree and the way she was looking at him. Like she was picturing him in bed with her.

That didn't sit right with him. Neither did the way she treated Lucky. It wasn't like his relationship with his brothers. Close. Respectful, even with the ribbing and joking they did with each other.

Something seemed off.

"How was she when you arrived?" He wanted her take on Lucky's mental health. He needed to know she was okay. Healing. Feeling Safe.

Lucky had been through a lot and he hoped that she was coping okay. He hated to leave her this morning, but he had obligations and he'd gotten back home as soon as he could to spend the rest of the day making sure she was pampered and recuperating.

"She seems fine. Stiff. Sore, I imagine." Desiree pointed to the TV. "She's watching another happy ending, hoping she gets hers someday."

"She will. I'll make sure of it." He'd do anything and everything to make her happy and keep her with him.

Desiree gave him a coy smile. "Come on. You can't tell me this isn't about the fact that you saved her and now you feel somehow obligated to help her."

"Obligated." He studied her face and realized she was serious. "I'm relieved that I found her in time. She's been a beacon of hope for me for the last two years. Her kindness and caring helped me through more hard nights than I care to count. I can't imagine my life without her."

"That's our Miss Goody Two Shoes."

"Why do you talk about her like that? I thought you were best friends."

"We are. Have been forever. But we aren't exactly alike in a lot of ways. She's...adorably broken."

Everything inside him rejected that statement.

Desiree's snide comment and dismissal of Lucky's endurance and strength frustrated and angered him. "Men can't help but want to help her. Love her. Even if she keeps them all at arm's length." Desiree took a step closer. "Until you. I imagine the interactions you've had passing notes gave her some courage to try with you. But she's not ready to jump into whatever you think you'll have with her. She's too good and sweet and kind to let go and really satisfy a man like you."

He let her speak, giving her space to show who she really was, because it didn't seem like she was really Lucky's friend. More like a frenemy.

"You don't seem like a guy who wants some passive lover."

Lucky wasn't passive last night when she took him in hand in the shower. She was lost in the moment with him this morning, writhing and moaning and tugging his hair as Hawk ate her pussy and brought her to an explosive orgasm.

She'd been beautiful, flying free beneath his hands and lips and on his tongue.

Desiree didn't know Lucky the way he knew her.

And if Lucky was like that while injured, he couldn't wait to see her when she was well and whole.

She'd probably kill him. And he'd die a happy man.

Desiree's hand landed on his chest.

He immediately stepped back. "Don't do that."

"What? Touch you? I could do a hell of a lot better at making you burn than she ever could. You can't possibly be satisfied with those soft kisses. You need someone wild, free, uninhibited. Someone who can take you and handle you. Someone who isn't afraid of your rough side." She purred out the last, an invitation in her eyes.

He did have a rough side. Not that he'd ever hurt Lucky, or any woman for that matter. He could be gentle like he'd been with Lucky so far in consideration of her injuries. But he liked getting lost in passion with a lover. He knew he and Lucky would get there when she was feeling better. And he knew it would be better with her than anyone else because of their connection, because it was built on all those tender feelings Desiree seemed to think made Lucky weak, or something. They didn't. They made her care. Deeply. And that added a layer of intimacy and trust and understanding that allowed for walls to come crumbling down to expose all the raw emotions and feelings that made it possible to truly let go.

He couldn't wait.

But he could be patient. For her.

"I don't know what you think you're doing, but I'm going to choose to believe that you're not actually trying to steal me away from your best friend. Because that would be a really shitty thing to do. And it will never happen. I'm not a cheater, or so fickle to drop her for you because you think you're hotter in the sack than she is. What we have is special. A once in a lifetime kind of thing. So I'm going to believe that this is some sort of bait you think I'll take and prove that I'm not good enough for your friend." He didn't believe that for a second. Desiree had a selfish side that made her mean. He didn't like it. And he'd protect Lucky from it from now on. "I am a hundred percent dedicated to Lucky. She's mine. I'm hers. From now on, it's *us*, so get used to it. No amount of flirting is going to change it. And if you try to sabotage what we have again, I won't be nice, because I'll do anything to keep her and make her happy."

"That's all I needed to hear." She played off the whole thing, but she didn't look happy about his rejection, or even relieved for her friend. Anger lit her eyes before she banked it. She didn't like to lose.

He dropped it. "Good. Now I have a question for you. How did you get Lucky's car to her place after you drove her home from the bar?"

The calculation in Desiree's eyes didn't surprise him. "I have a friend at the courthouse who did me a favor and drove her car to her place. Why?"

"Who was the friend?"

That coy smile came back. "Just a guy I know."

"Who?"

She pressed her lips tight. "Someone who has someone who wouldn't like hearing that he did me a favor."

He imagined some guy with a girlfriend or wife that was fucking Desiree on the side. She didn't seem to care about people crossing boundaries and betraying others, so long as she got what she wanted.

She flipped her hair back. "What's the big deal about the car?"

"It just seemed odd that it was at the house and you'd go through all the trouble to get the car there when you could have just picked up Lucky the next day and driven her to the bar to get her car."

"Well, I am her best friend, so it was no trouble at all. And I drop off Krystal at school early in the morning, then have to be at work. Lucky gets an early start as well and I wanted to be sure she had her car because she'd agreed to go out with me that night and I know it's not really her thing. You know. Drinking. Dancing. Having fun. She's such a boring homebody."

"Nothing wrong with that."

"Says the guy who owns a bar."

"Maybe Lucky will be more comfortable going out with me." He hoped so. But if not, they could have fun at home.

"Sure she will." The tone of her voice said she didn't believe it for a second. "Is that all you needed to know?"

"For now. Jase is still looking into everything."

"I'm sure one of those guys we were with will probably be arrested soon then."

He shook his head. "There's no evidence they spiked her drink. In fact, I've watched the footage. There's no indication either of them came close enough to her glass to spike it. So it must have happened earlier that night. Like right after Lincoln made her the drink."

"I don't see how. There was no one close enough to her then."

He took a chance. "Except you."

"What?" Lucky stood in the opening to the hallway, her eyes wide with shock by his statement. "Desiree would never do something like that to me."

Hawk kept his gaze steady on Desiree's, his heart telling him she might.

Desiree didn't bat an eye. "Of course I wouldn't. I love you. You're my bestie. My ride or die." That seemed to be laying it on thick.

Even Lucky seemed to think so when she raised a brow at Desiree. "It's probably going to turn into another one of those things we never get an answer to."

Hawk hooked his arm around Lucky's shoulders and drew her into his body. He loved the feel of her against him. "You ready to veg?"

"Yes. Please."

Desiree headed for the door. "I'm off to pick up Krystal from school. You're looking better, Lucky," she called over her shoulder, then opened the door and turned back to Hawk. "Be good to her."

"Always." It was an easy promise to make. One he'd keep no matter what.

Desiree sailed out, closing the solid wood door with a sharp thunk.

He held Lucky close and dove in for the kiss he'd really wanted to lay on her when he got home. He slid his tongue along hers, tasting the peppermint tea he kept on hand for Lyric now that she was pregnant and needed it to keep her nausea at bay in the early months of her pregnancy.

Lucky pulled him close, matching the intensity and need he poured into their kiss. She felt so good in his arms. So responsive. So giving. He couldn't get enough. It would never be enough.

"I missed you," he confessed again, then kissed her like he'd never get to kiss her again.

Lucky broke the kiss panting. "Missed you, too. You made my head spin." She held on to his biceps, a pretty grin on her lips. "What were you and Desiree talking about?"

"Your car. She said someone from work helped her get it to your house."

"That's nice."

"You don't think it's odd that she called someone up, someone who's not her boyfriend or family, late at night to move a car?

Lucky grinned. "You've seen Desiree. You've seen her flirt with your brother. Do I think she could call up someone and sweet-talk them into doing her bidding? Yes. I absolutely do believe it."

Hawk's frustration rose. "I feel like she has an agenda."

"No doubt. She always wants to get her way."

"And when she doesn't?"

"She acts out. She gets angry. The therapist I saw after my family was murdered called her emotionally immature. She needs to be the center of attention and acts out when things don't go her way."

"Why did you talk to your therapist about her?"

"Because I couldn't understand why she couldn't sympathize with me and what I'd been through. She wanted me to just snap out of it and embrace my new carefree life."

"She's jealous of you."

Lucky shook her head. "She thinks she's better than me. And I really don't care that she feels that way. My life hasn't been that great. Most of the time, it really sucks. But I know I didn't do anything to deserve all the bad shit that's happened to me. I'm a good person. I treat people with kindness, even if they don't always deserve it. And I like who I am."

"You're amazing."

"I'm glad you think so, because I feel the same way about you. Now...enough about her. How was your day?"

"Better now that I'm home with you."

Her smile widened as she tapped her hand against his arm. "Come on. Tell me. How did the meeting go?"

"Fine. We got a big new order from an Amsterdam group that owns several bars in a chain of hotels."

"That's fantastic." She beamed with pride for him.

"Yeah. We're really happy about it. I've got to set up the distribution schedule and figure out the best way to ship to them, but it's going to a new market for us."

"Well hopefully you can expand throughout that country."

"That's the plan."

She yawned, pressed the back of her hand to her mouth. "Sorry. I'm not at a hundred percent yet."

He nudged her back toward the couch. "Sit. Watch your movie. Tell me what you need and I'll get it."

"You."

"What?"

"I want to cuddle with you."

He loved that he was what she wanted when she wasn't feeling well. "Let me change into something more comfortable and we'll spend the rest of the day on the couch. Together."

"Perfect."

He waited for her to get settled and start her show, then headed down to their bedroom. Her bag was sitting inside the huge walk in closet. He pulled her clothes out and put them away in the drawers, on the shelves, and on hangers. He loved seeing her things with his.

He unlaced and kicked off his boots, pulled off his slacks and dress shirt, then pulled on a pair of old black sweatpants and a gray tee, then headed back to the living room where Lucky was lying on her left side staring at the quiet TV.

"I restarted the movie, so you could watch with me. It's one of my favorites, based on a book by an amazing author."

"Really. Cool. Let's watch it."

She gave him a sheepish look. "Uh. It's a romance. I hope you don't mind."

"Not at all. Whatever you want to watch." He pressed his knee into the cushion near her feet. "Skootch forward, so I can lay behind you." He slid into place as she moved forward on the wide cushion. He slid his arm beneath her neck, put his other hand on her hip and pulled her back to his front. "That's better. You good?"

She nodded, then pushed play on the remote.

He slid his hand up her hip and under her shirt, laying his palm spread across her warm abdomen. "It feels so good to have you close and my hand on your skin."

She squirmed, her ass brushing his dick, making him hard.

"Be still, sweetheart, or we're going to miss the movie."

She rolled her hips again. "I'm feeling kind of...restless."

This time he thrust his hard cock against the seam of her ass. "Do you mean empty?"

"Yes. All I've thought about is you coming home and the things we did last night, this morning. What we could do again."

He growled in her ear. "Do you want me to make you come again?" He'd make her come as many times as she could handle it. He loved the sounds she made, the way her whole body bowed then relaxed. The way her lips parted, her tongue darting out to swipe across her bottom lip before she bit it.

She was so damn sexy, he was nearly ready to blow just thinking of her coming apart for him this morning.

She rubbed her ass against his thick cock. "I want you inside me." She tried to turn, but ended up shifting her sore shoulder, hissing out her pain.

"Be still. Let me do all the work."

"But I want—"

"You'll get it. Every inch. I promise. But we're going to do it my way. I don't want to hurt you. I can't handle hurting you. So be still and let me do this." With one arm under her shoulders, he lifted her enough for him to slide under her, settling her head on his shoulder, her back to his chest. He used his feet to get her legs on top of his. It took a little maneuvering and her help to slide her leggings and panties past her hips. He used his foot to push them to her ankles. He shimmied out of his sweats, using the same maneuver with his foot, but kicked his sweats off. "Drop your feet on the outside of my legs."

She did what she was told.

He spread his legs, making hers open, leaving her pussy open and bare, ready for his touch. So he slid his hands down both sides of her, over her hips and part of her thighs, making sure not to touch her bruises or stitches.

"Hawk, that feels so good." She squirmed, needing more.

He loved touching her. "Are you wet for me?" His aching cock was pressed along the seam of her ass, begging to dive deep into her welcoming warmth.

"Yes. Please. I need you. I missed you so much today." The softly whispered confession made his heart flutter and swell with a feeling that he'd never felt for any other woman. Not like this.

He lightly traced circles over her skin, bringing his hand closer to her core and the heaven it promised. He slid his fingers over her mound, dipping lower over her soft lips, then sliding up her slit. Her juices coated his fingertips and he brushed them over her clit, making her sigh and moan with every little touch. "You like that."

"More." With her on her back on top of him, she couldn't really touch him, but her fingertips skimmed his forearms up and down before she slid her hand to her side and ran it up and down his waist and hip. Her bare skin against his set off electrical pulses through his system, revving him up.

But she needed to be ready, so he plunged one finger, then two into her tight channel. "You squeeze me so good." She'd be a tight fit.

He'd have to go slow, work his way in. But first he'd make her come to make it easier on her.

He pumped his fingers inside her as she rocked against his hand, using him to get herself off. He loved the wild and free way she was with him, not waiting for him to do the job, but letting herself go and reveling in the pleasure he brought her.

"That's it, baby. Take what you need." He circled her clit with his other hand, starting slow and letting things build as he applied more pressure.

"Yes. Like that. God, that feels so good. I've never orgasmed without a vibrator before."

He'd gotten her off this morning with his mouth and fingers. She'd come on his hand again, then he'd fuck her to orgasm, too. No way he left her hanging. Not ever.

She. Goes. First. Every. Damn. Time. He punctuated that thought with his fingers driving into her. She came, screaming out her release on a high pitched shriek that was too fucking sexy. Something he wanted to hear again and again. Her juices gushed over his fingers.

He brought them to his lips and sucked them clean. "Are you still with me?"

Her panting breaths had slowed. "Yes. So good." She took his wrist and wrapped his arm across her belly, kind of hugging him to her. "I wish we hadn't waited so long for this."

He kissed the side of her head. "It's only going to get better." He hugged her to him, then took her by the hips and raised her up enough so he could set his aching cock free between her spread thighs. "You ready for me, or do you need another minute."

"I need you now." To prove it, she reached for him, taking his cock in hand and guiding him to her entrance.

He rubbed the head against her soft, wet folds.

"Now," she begged.

He liked that, and didn't keep her waiting. He slowly sank the head past her soft folds.

"You're so big."

He could feel the stretch. "You can take me." He pushed in a little at a time, giving her body time to accommodate him. This wasn't the easiest position, but it kept all her injuries from hurting worse. "You good?" He was halfway in.

"Yes. I want you. All of you." She widened her legs.

He sank in deeper, trying to go slow, but she felt so damn good that he thrust in the last few inches and let out a ragged breath. "Damn, sweetheart, you feel better than anything."

She squirmed on him, making him hit deeper. Her moan said she liked it as he bottomed out, his balls aching for release.

He wanted to make this last, make her feel good.

"Hawk?"

"Yeah, sweetheart." He wrapped her in his arms, her body tight to his. Right here, right now, she was safe and happy in his arms. One with him.

"I don't know how to explain what I'm feeling right now connected to you. It's so...overwhelming and amazing. I don't ever want to lose this. You."

"I'm sorry, sweetheart. I really wanted to do this nice and sweet for you, but when you say things like that and my heart is about to burst with all the feelings I have for you...well, you brought this on yourself." He unleashed himself, holding her close, pumping into her, fucking her hard and deep, so she'd always feel him and what he did to her. He couldn't help it. Couldn't stop.

The sounds she made were music to his ears, a cadence that he followed as he sank into her deep again and again. He held her to him with one arm and used his other hand to slide his fingers down over her mound, past her clit, to where they were joined. He brushed two fingers along her stretched lips on either side of his dick, collecting her juices.

She clenched around him.

"You like that."

Not a question, but she answered him anyway. "Yes."

He did it again and again with every stroke in and out of her until she was writhing, one moan rolling into another.

His balls drew up tight. He was about to unload, but she needed to go first. He slid his soaking wet fingers up to her clit and rubbed tiny circles over it until she was panting, her pussy squeezing him tight. He pressed down on her clit and she went off like a rocket. Her body convulsed with the force of her orgasm as she yelled her satisfaction to the room.

He thrust into her hard and deep, once, twice, then stayed buried in her as his dick pumped every last drop of his seed into her.

He had a fleeting thought about it taking root and seeing her round with their child. A child who would grow up with Mason and Lyric's baby.

Too soon. But someday. He hoped.

For right now, he was content to have her in his arms. In his house. In his life.

All he had to do was figure out a way to make her want to stay.

Forever.

Chapter Fifteen

Hawk couldn't tell if he was awake or dreaming. All he knew was that he was in a nightmare. Waking or dreaming, didn't matter when the flashbacks took hold and turned his world into chaos, because it felt so real. Like he was right back in the war. The fight.

This time, he heard the incessant sounds of beeping, along with the rat-a-tat-tat of gunfire pinging the helicopter. He was going down and he had three other people on board. Soldiers he'd picked up right out of a firefight, saving their lives and taking them to safety.

Except, they weren't going to make it. They were going down in enemy territory.

One of them screamed, "Robinson took two to the chest!"

Fuck.

Brown dropped next, a hit to his thigh as the helicopter suddenly listed to the right. No matter how hard he tried to control it, the helo was going down.

"Brace for impact!" He hoped they heard his warning over the screeching engine and blades whapping. "Mayday, mayday, mayday. Call sign Hawk. Taking heavy fire. Four on board, two soldiers shot." He gave his coordinates. "Going down. Mayday, mayday, mayday."

He saw the ground coming up fast, knew it was going to hurt like hell and probably kill him, but he tried with all his might to control their erratic decent.

He wanted so desperately to save them all.

The moment of impact brought him out of his flashback and to reality as he struggled with the tangled sheets. Everything was quiet for a moment, then the buzzing sound started up again.

He wasn't thinking straight when he rushed out of the room to the kitchen and grabbed Lucky by her biceps and shook her. "Make it stop."

Her eyes went wide with fear and she struggled to free herself from his punishing grip. "Let. Me. Go." She leaned in, her gaze direct and demanding, showing him she meant business even with the terror in her eyes.

Suddenly, he realized what he was doing and let her go, putting his hands to his ears, trying to block out the incessant sound before he fell into another nightmare.

Lucky smacked the blender button, the noise ceased, and she stood before him, her chest heaving with her own distress as she stared wide-eyed at him, her hands shaking at her sides. "What's happening? Why are you sweating so much? Are you sick? What's wrong?" All the questions ran over each other as she quickly spit them out and he tried to keep up. But his mind was split between here and there. Her and them. Life and death. Sorrow overcoming him for the ones he lost, even though he tried so hard.

He fell back against the counter and sank to his ass on the hardwood floor, knees up, his fists in his eye sockets as he breathed even heavier than her and tried to clear the bloody memory from his mind, while also silently chastising himself for grabbing her like that. "I'm sorry. I'm so sorry." He rocked back and forth, but it didn't soothe him. He just got more agitated. "I didn't mean to grab you like that. I should have never touched you like that. It wasn't you. I was just trying to find my way out. I needed to get out. To make it stop."

Her warm, trembling hands slid over his hands and into his hair as she crouched in front of him. "You startled me. I wasn't expecting you to come at me that way. I'm okay." It sounded like she was trying to convince herself. "You didn't hurt me. Everything is okay."

He wondered if she was telling herself that or him.

"Ssh. You're okay. Everything is fine. You're safe." She kept brushing her fingers through his hair, her body snuggled up against his up drawn legs.

He didn't know if he could ever look at her again and not see the fear he'd put on her face. "I'm sorry."

She pressed her cheek to the top of his head. "Was it a flashback?"

"Yes."

She wrapped him in an awkward hug. "Do you want to talk about it?"

No. He didn't. But he owed her some kind of explanation. "I." He swallowed back the bile still rising in his throat from the flashback and from treating her so badly. "I told you I'd been in a helicopter crash."

"I remember. The shrapnel wounds you have are from that accident."

"It was no accident. We were shot down. Of the four of us on board, only two of us made it."

Her hands stilled on his head. It felt good to feel her holding onto him. "I'm so sorry that happened. I can't imagine how horrifying and devastating that must have been."

"Sometimes, I'm right back in the helo seat watching the ground coming at me, hearing the guys yelling, the bullets hitting the chopper. I can smell Robinson and Brown's blood, the smoke from the engine, and hear the grinding of the engine gears as the blades whap, whap, whap so loud it's like I'll never hear anything else."

"The blender." She breathed out the words. "No more smoothies. Got it." She wrapped her arms around him again, her cheek on his forehead. "What can I do to help you?"

"You're doing it. Your voice. Your touch. I need them to ground me in the here and now."

"Well, then, I'll talk and hold you as long as you need." She settled in between his legs and leaned into his chest. "You're not the only one who woke up from a nightmare today. I'm sorry I wasn't in bed with you. I'm sorry my breakfast gave you the flashback."

He kissed her on the head. "Not your fault. I never know what will trigger me. I haven't had a flashback in nearly a year."

Her chin fell to her chest. "Oh God. Definitely no more smooth-ies." She held him tighter.

He actually almost smiled at that and her kindness and acceptance. He brushed his hands over her arms where he'd grabbed her. "Are you really okay? Did I hurt you? Your shoulder? Your knee?"

She shook her head, her long hair catching on the stubble on his chin. He loved feeling the silky strands against his skin. "I was more surprised than anything."

Everything had been going so well for the last five days. She was getting better. They were getting closer. She was even back to working in the office doing paperwork and billing, while the others still covered the houses she cleaned.

She no longer needed the brace on her arm. She had about three quarters of her range of motion back in her shoulder. She was due to get her stitches out tomorrow. And she'd swapped her knee brace for a compresion sleeve, which gave her support and some range of motion.

Hopefully, she'd get a clean bill of health, too.

Not that he didn't think she was well. She seemed to be happy living with him. They had breakfast and dinner together every day. Their sex life was off the charts. The second he woke up, he wanted her skin to skin. As soon as he came through the door each night, she was reaching for him. They were like horny teenagers and he loved it.

But it was more than just great sex. They talked about their days together. They spent time learning about what each of them liked and disliked. They cooked together. They sat out under the stars and talked about their pasts.

He felt closer to her than anyone he'd ever dated.

That feeling of falling all those months leading up to them finally being together...well, he finally had to admit to himself that he hadn't been falling, he'd well and truly fallen the second he'd found her in the woods.

He loved her. More than anything.

And he couldn't believe how he'd treated her this morning. Even if he'd not been in his right mind. There was no excuse. "Please don't be afraid of me."

She'd talked about her father with him. How he'd terrorized and traumatized her over the years. He didn't want to be someone who frightened or hurt her.

"You've taken such good care of me. You're never mean or scary. But honestly, this morning did frighten me. I didn't know what was wrong with you. I understand you can't control your flashbacks and how you react, that you're in soldier mode and that means in your mind it's life or death and you need to protect yourself. I would never hold that against you. You've been through enough. But like you, I can't help my reactions. They're born of the trauma I suffered, too."

"I'm not like him. I will prove that to you. I really haven't had an episode in months."

"I believe you, and I'll be more cautious about loud noises like the belnder."

He squeezed her hand. "Please don't leave me."

"I'm exactly where I want to be. I will always be your safe place to fall."

He leaned his head back against the cabinet and stared up at the ceiling. "You mean fall apart."

Her hold on him tightened. "I fell apart on you. You showed me compassion and let me cry it out because that's what I needed. I will give you what you need, whenever you need it."

He wrapped her up close and buried his nose in her hair, smelling her sweet, sunshine scent. "I know. I'm sorry. I just don't like you seeing me like this. Out of control. Out of my mind."

"Hawk, it's okay because I know the real you." She went quiet and still. "And I..."

He held his breath waiting for her to finish that sentence.

"Love you. You're the strongest person I know. Inside and out. I know you've worked really hard to overcome your past. It must be frustrating and disappointing to feel like it will never end. Maybe it will. Maybe it won't. No matter what, I'll be here to help you through it."

He turned her in his arms and cupped her face in both hands. "You love me."

She nodded despite it not being a question. "Very much. With my whole heart." She bit her bottom lip and stared deep into his eyes, probably hoping he said it back. Her parents were horrible to her. Her little brother depended on her. Did anyone ever tell her they loved her?

"I've been wanting to say it for so long. I love you, too. I don't know how it happened, but it feels like it's always been there now."

"I was just waiting for you, too."

It felt very much like his whole life had been headed in her direction and he'd finally landed in the right spot to make her his.

He kissed her like his life depended on it and that made him hard for her. He was always hard for her whenever he thought about her or she was in close proximity.

He broke the kiss and met her hungry gaze. "You know how much I love it when you're wearing nothing but my shirt."

She bit that bottom lip again. "Uh huh."

"I think I want my shirt back." He stood, pulling her up with him, then he dipped his shoulder and hauled her over it. With his hand on her very fine ass, he walked out of the kitchen toward their bedroom.

"What are you doing?"

"I want my shirt and you naked beneath me. You ready?" He dumped her on the bed with her back hitting the mattress with a bounce and her giggling. "Damn, I love that smile." He ran his hands up both her legs. "Take off my shirt."

She did and threw it at him.

He caught it, inhaled her scent and his mixed into the fabric, and grinned himself. "You have no idea what you do to me."

She pulled her knees up and let them fall wide. Her pussy glistened, beckoning him to fill her up. "Show me."

He shoved his boxer briefs down his legs, kicked them off, then practically dove for her, covering her body with his, kissing her senseless, as he thrust his aching cock deep inside her. She felt so good. So tight. So right. So his.

He got lost in her scent, the kiss, the rhythm of their bodies moving together. He loved her nails raking down his back and sinking into his ass as she pulled him in deeper.

Her moans, the soft gasps she made when he hit that spot inside her, all of it drove him on to make her feel as good as she made him feel.

More than that, it was the way she looked at him. So much love in her eyes and heart pouring out to him. He hoped he'd earned it. No matter what, he'd keep loving and making her happy for as long as he lived.

That thought made him think about the future and making her his wife. And the thought of that sent him to the edge. But she had to come first, so he thrust deep, knowing she was right on the verge of ecstasy as her pussy squeezed around his cock. He took her nipple in his mouth, laved it with his tongue, loving the moan that rose out of her. He did the same to her other nipple and slid his hand between them and pressed his thumb to her swollen clit, then circled it as she went over the edge, taking him with her. He went stiff as his cock pumped his seed into her, filling her up.

Her orgasm subsided and she relaxed into the mattress as he laid a trail of kisses down her neck, across her chest, and up the other side of her throat to her ear where he whispered, "I love you so damn much." He wrapped his arm around her and rolled with her until he was on his back and she was lying on top of him, smiling down into his eyes.

She snuggled into him, their bodies still connected, with her head on his shoulder.

"Do you want to have kids?" He hadn't really thought about it until recently, but the idea was growing on him, becoming something he wanted with her.

"Yes. I've always seen myself as a mom someday. You?"

"I see you as a mom. You're kind. Caring. Fun to be around. You'd be the kind of mom who bakes cookies and finger paints with the kids."

She giggled. "I would do those things. But I meant, do you want to be a dad?"

"Not until I started thinking about a life with you, seeing all the good things I could have if I just took a chance. Seeing Mason and Lyric so happy together...it gave me ideas. I can totally see Mason holding a baby, chasing after a toddler, being a dad like his and mine. I love my family. We're close. I want what I was a part of growing up."

"I can't wait to meet Damon and your parents. Lyric and I caught up yesterday on the phone. I really like her."

That made him so damn happy. "My parents are dying to meet you."

She brought her head up and stared down at him. "They are?"

He brushed his fingers through her hair. "Yes. I've been putting them off."

"Why?"

He didn't like her frown. "Because I wanted you to have time to settle in here with me. I wanted you to have the space you needed to heal without the pressure of meeting my parents."

She rested her chin on her stacked hands on his chest. "I bet they're lovely people."

He tilted his head. "Why do you think that? Not that they're not. They are."

"I know because I've seen you and Lincoln together. You respect each other. You like each other. You're close. I imagine the qualities I see in you—loyalty, honor, integrity, trustworthiness—come from how you were raised."

He pressed his forehead to hers. "They're going to love you."

"I hope so. I want to be good for you in every way I can. I'd never want to be a burden or someone who causes a rift in your family. They're important to you."

"I'm sorry you didn't have that kind of family."

"Me, too. But maybe I'll have that with you."

"No maybe about it. You're a part of me and a part of them now."

Her eyes glassed over. "Thank you."

He raised a brow, confused. "For what?"

"Saving me again. In so many ways. I've never known kindness and caring the way you wrap it around me with your words and actions and how you share yourself with me."

"You do the same for me." He held her close and kissed her on top of her head. "You and me, sweetheart. Forever."

"You and me. Forever."

He'd take that promise and give it back to her as long as they lived.

Chapter Sixteen

Neil stared down Desiree, standing on her front porch, Desiree acting like a sentinel, keeping him out. "I want to see her."

She stepped out onto the small porch and closed the door behind her. "You are a convict. You're accused of killing Lucky's family. They found the bloody knife in your room. Your prints were on it."

"I didn't fucking kill her family. I loved her. I would never hurt her. I wouldn't hurt anyone."

Desiree eyed him. "Except you did. You killed that guy in prison."

He fisted his hands at his sides. "He tried to fucking stab me in the back because I wouldn't join his fucking gang. I defended myself." He practically spit the words out.

"You stabbed him seven times." Her accusing gaze held a note of admiration.

Or was that just a figment of his imagination?

Desiree had always had a twisted sense of right and wrong. She loved to push people's buttons, and she was good at it.

"The guy wouldn't quit. He kept coming at me, others egging him on. I had no choice. That place is not for the faint of heart." You lose yourself in there. And he'd been everyone's target. So he'd learned to toughen up. Stand his ground. Push back when someone pushed him.

It was the only way to survive in a cage with all the other wild things locked up with him.

Either you fought or you endured the punishing abuse, hoping you didn't end up dead. Either way, every second in that place took a piece of his soul.

But he was out and all he wanted to do was see *her*. "I need to see her."

Desiree's eyes gleamed with scorn. "If you know what's good for you, you'll stay away from us." She turned and stormed into the house, slamming the door and punctuating the threat he couldn't heed.

This was too important.

She was his life. He needed her.

Suddenly, he realized he didn't need Desiree's permission. He could find another way.

He just had to find the right moment to steal some time with her.

Chapter Seventeen

The buttery soft leather beneath Lucky cradled her in comfort as she drove Hawk's way too expensive Range Rover to his office. Damon had picked him up this morning, so she could use his car to get to work. She'd managed a six hour day in her office, updating schedules, paying bills, finalizing payroll for the week, and checking in with all of her employees, without being too tired. Her strength and stamina were getting better.

And yay! No more stitches. Though her scars still gave her chills and reminded her of the ordeal she'd been through.

Hawk suggested she talk to his psychiatrist. She had an appointment with him next week. She wanted to be the best version of herself for Hawk. And she wanted to finally put the past behind her, even though Neil was still out there, taunting her, trying to kill her. Her frustration and anger had to go somewhere and maybe talking about how unfair and maddening it was that no one seemed to be able to stop him would help.

Well, maybe she'd get some answers today.

Jase had asked her to come down to the station—he had some information about Neil and the case. She hoped it was good news, that they finally had some evidence to put him away again.

Her heart sank a little as her doomsday brain taunted her with thoughts of how long this had been going on and how he kept getting away with it.

Would today finally be the day he was caught?

She hoped so. But first she was stopping by Hawk's office to see if he'd go with her.

He always said, anything she needed, he'd be there. Well, she was going to try to lean on him. It wasn't her way. She'd been alone a long time. She'd never really counted on anyone. But she knew Hawk wanted to be a part of stopping Neil and making her safe.

She just wanted him by her side.

She pulled into the lot outside of Gunn Brothers Distillery and parked the car several spaces away from any other cars. It made her nervous that she'd ding the door, or someone would scratch it trying to get into their car.

I'm being ridiculous. It's just a car. He won't dump me if I scratch it. Right?

Her stomach knotted. "Hawk loves you more than the car," she reminded herself.

Holding onto that thought, she remembered to lock the door and headed toward the building, hoping she'd see him right away and she wouldn't have to talk to anyone else.

She opened the door to the building and stared at the Gunn Brothers Distillery logo above the reception desk along with their motto. "If you want it, go after it Gunns blazing!"

"It's the family motto," the perky receptionist with the wavy blonde hair, pouty lips, a sophisticated blazer over her ample chest replied.

The motto seemed to suit the brothers—at least Hawk and Lincoln. She had yet to meet Damon, but his reputation as a go-getter, party boy, and ladies' man preceded him.

Hawk hadn't gone after her like that, until he'd found her in the woods and made up his mind that she wasn't getting away. Then he'd been all in.

He loves me.

It still felt so amazing, surreal, and too good to be true.

"Can I help you?" The receptionist stared, her gaze impatient, making Lucky nervous.

"Um. Can you tell me where Hawk's office is?"

"Do you have an appointment?"

"No. I need to ask him something."

"I can take a message."

"I need to see him."

"Last I heard, he was in the warehouse. Non-employees are not allowed back there. If you'd like to leave your number, I'll have him contact you."

"I can wait in his office for him to come back." He probably wouldn't be that long. She could send him a text and let him know she was here. But first she'd give this one more shot. "Um. Yeah. I'm Lucky."

"Good for you. I hope some will rub off on me."

"No. My name is Lucky."

"Lucky!" someone called from down the hallway. Another woman. "Yes?"

The click of heels sounded, coming quickly down the hallway and echoing off the polished cement floor. The most gorgeous auburn haired woman stepped into the lobby and smiled at her. "I've been dying to meet you."

"Ah. Okay. Hello." She bit her lip. "Who are you?"

The woman came forward, hand extended. "Mercy Matlock. Head of Operations. I run this place with the guys. Hawk is gaga over you."

A sudden blush burned her cheeks and ears.

"Who are you?" the receptionist asked again.

Mercy turned to the woman. "She's Lucky, Hawk's girlfriend. She can go anywhere she likes on the premises." Mercy waved Lucky forward. "Come. I'll show you to his office."

"I didn't know Hawk had a girlfriend," the receptionist said under her breath, a look of confusion and disappointment on her face.

Lucky could relate. She'd wanted Hawk for a long time and imagined him with other women, feeling like he was way out of her league.

She never thought she'd be the woman by his side, but here she was, living in his house, driving his car, and walking into his business to see him while at work.

He's mine.

The thought made her heart swell.

"That's the same lovey-dovey look he gets when he's talking or thinking about you." Mercy knocked her elbow against Lucky's arm. "He is one hundred percent in love with you."

"I know. It's kind of crazy."

Mercy laughed and waved her hand down the hallway she'd come from. "No it's not. You're gorgeous. Smart. Funny. Kind. And you make him happy."

"How do you know that?"

"Well, Hawk's not a big talker. Most of that came from Lincoln. He likes you, too. Said you're the best thing to happen to Hawk."

"He said that?" Her heart soared with joy.

"Yes." Mercy stopped in front of a closed dark wood office door with *Hawk Gunn* printed on it and knocked. "I saw him return from the warehouse a few minutes ago."

"Come in," Hawk called out.

Mercy didn't open the door right away, but turned to her. "I would really like to get to know you better. Would you like to grab drinks at Gunn Brothers one night this week?"

"Only if Lincoln or Hawk are pouring the drinks for me."

Mercy's eyes filled with sympathy. "I'm sorry about what happened to you. We were all angry about you being drugged in the bar. I hope it will help that the guys amped up security, adding more cameras inside and out of the building. I promise if you're with me or the them, you'll be safe."

The door opened and Hawk stared from Mercy to her, then back again. "What's going on? Why isn't Lucky safe?"

Mercy rolled her eyes. "Down, boy. She is. I asked her out for drinks and reassured her that with me and you guys, she definitely won't have to worry about anything."

"Oh." Hawk brushed his hand down Lucky's arm and took her hand. "I think you and Mercy would get along great. You're both so dedicated to your jobs that you don't make time for anything else. I think you'd have a lot in common."

If this was someone important to Hawk, and she must be if they trusted her to run the business with them, then Lucky definitely wanted to be friends with her. "I'm sure Hawk has your number. I'll text you and we'll work out a day and time to meet up."

"Great." Mercy beamed, joy and expectation in her eyes. "I'll leave you two and get back to work."

"Lincoln was looking for you earlier. He wanted to take you to lunch."

Mercy tried to hide her smile, but a hint of it peeked through before she caught herself. "Uh, thank you for telling me."

"You might say yes to him once in a while," Hawk suggested, a hint of humor in his voice.

"Yes. Well. Back to business." With that, Mercy hurried down the hall to the open door three down from Hawk's.

"What brings you by, sweetheart? Did you miss me?"

"I hope it's okay I just dropped in."

He pulled her into his spacious office. His desk was to the left, a credenza and bookshelves behind it. He had a laptop open on the desk, along with a phone and pen holder, otherwise there was no clutter. A couch and coffee table to the right of the door provided another seating area. And on the far wall were low file cabinets beneath a wall of windows that looked out toward the warehouse next door, mountains in the background.

"You can drop in whenever you want. Is everything okay?"

"Yes. I think so." Before she could explain further, Lincoln rushed into the room, stopping short when he spotted her.

"Hey, Lucky. Good to see you." He looked at Hawk. "Have you seen Mercy?"

Lucky didn't know what came over her, but she backed away, the room feeling like it was getting smaller and smaller. She couldn't breathe. There wasn't enough air.

Hawk hadn't taken his eyes off her and noticed immediately. "Sweetheart, what's wrong?"

She stared from him to the door, Lincoln in front of it. No way out. She couldn't get out. Her ass hit the filing cabinet by the window as Hawk stalked closer to her, his hand out to her.

"You're okay. Just breathe. No one is going to hurt you. You're okay."

She shook her head, her eyes glued to the door behind Lincoln.

Hawk followed her line of sight. "Lincoln, get the fuck away from the door."

Lincoln moved without question, walking toward Hawk's desk. "I'm sorry, honey. I didn't mean to block you in."

"Breathe, Lucky. Do it with me," Hawk implored. "Deep breath in. Hold it for four, then blow it out for four." He did it with her, inching his way closer to her until he had his hands on her cheeks.

Her heart slowed and she could breathe again. She put her hands on his wrists and sighed. "I'm sorry. I don't know what happened." She sagged into Hawk's chest and he wrapped his arms around her.

"It's okay. You had a panic attack."

"I'm really sorry," Lincoln said again with so much feeling.

"You didn't do anything wrong. It's just me." She met Hawk's worried gaze. "I'm okay now."

"Why did you come? Were you upset? Did something happen?"

"Aside from my fucked up life?"

Hawk held her face. "Talk to me."

"Jase called. He wants to talk to me. I thought maybe you'd come with me if you had time."

"Yeah. Sure. No problem."

"Just like that?" She couldn't believe how caring he was, or how he'd drop everything for her.

"Yes. Just like that. All you have to do is ask."

"Um, I need to find Mercy. I'm going to leave you two now," Lincoln interrupted, heading for the door. "Lucky, I hope you get good news."

Probably not. She didn't have that kind of luck. "Thank you. And I'm sorry I made you feel bad for walking in here."

"No apology necessary. I get it. You've been through a lot."

"Tell Mercy I'm looking forward to that drink."

Lincoln's eyes lit up. "You guys are going out together?"

She nodded.

"That's great." He dashed down the hallway.

She didn't know why he cared if they had drinks but didn't question it. "Is it me, or is he acting oddly today?"

"I don't know what's gotten into him the last few days." He rubbed his hands up and down her arms. "You good?"

"Yes. Thanks to you. You always make me feel safe."

"You do the same for me." He leaned in and kissed her softly. "I'm so glad you came. I wouldn't want you meeting with the sheriff's office without me there with you."

"It's not like they're going to arrest me."

"I know. But you don't have to go through this alone. I'm here for you. Always."

She loved hearing that and knowing he meant it. "I don't want to do it alone. I need you."

Hawk pressed his forehead to hers and linked their fingers in both hands. "Need you, too, sweetheart." He kissed her again, this time longer and deeper, until she melted into him. "Let's go see what Jase has to say."

Chapter Eighteen

You know those sayings? Actions speak louder than words. The way people treat you shows you who they really are and how they really feel about you. But also...when someone tells you who they are, believe them.

Well, Hawk was everything he seemed to be and more. Sweet. Kind. Caring. Incredibly sexy. The man looked amazing in black jeans, a dark red button down with the sleeves rolled up, and a pair of heavy black work boots. The chrome watch with the dark blue face probably cost three to four times her monthly mortgage. Well, she didn't know watches all that well, so it could cost even more. It looked like it could be more expensive than her car with all the tiny dials and gears inside it. She definitely didn't own anything to wear that expensive.

But it wasn't the way he looked, the expensive car he drove, the gorgeous home, the nice clothes, or the money he had. Nope. It was the way he held her hand on the drive to the sheriff's department. It was the way he looked at her, checking in to be sure she wasn't getting too nervous or having another panic attack. It was the way he turned off the car in the parking lot, brought her hand to his lips, kissed her palm, then told her, "Let me get the door for you."

He opened the door, took her hand again, linking their fingers, then pulled her close and kissed her on the head. "Everything's going to be all right."

She believed him, even though there was no evidence to support that except his promise that he'd find a way to end this.

"Thank you for coming with me."

He hooked his arm over her shoulders and walked with her toward the building. "Nowhere I'd rather be than with you."

She looked up at him, catching his eye. "Me, too."

He kissed her softly, then opened the door for her and let her lead the way inside.

"There you are," Jase called out from a large open space, cubicles marking out several desk areas. Jase waved them over, grabbing an extra chair from a nearby cubicle. He sat in his chair, then waved for them to do the same.

She took the chair closest to Jase so she could see the file opened in front of him. "What did you want to talk about?"

Hawk didn't sit. He stood behind her and put his hand on her shoulder. Support. Comfort. He offered her everything she needed and more.

Jase rubbed his fingers over his brow. "I have nothing but you telling me that you saw Neil at the bar that night. His alibi is shit. I know it. You know it. But I can't place him at the bar. Have you remembered anything else about that night?"

She shook her head. "Not really. I just see the same thing. Him coming toward me asking, 'Are you going to let me see her now?'"

Jase perked up, a knowing look in his eyes. "Why would he say it like that to you?"

She shrugged. "I don't know. Things are really hazy after that. It's all in and out of consciousness."

Jase leaned in close. "I don't think he was talking to you."

"Same," Hawk interjected. "It doesn't make sense. You were there with Desiree. You saw him coming, then he asked that. Why would he ask if he could see you? He had to be asking Desiree if he could see someone else."

Lucky shook her head. That didn't make sense to her at all. He'd sent her countless letters. She never read them, but she could guess he wanted to speak to her about what happened. "If he wanted to see me now that he's out of jail, he could simply show up at my door. He knows where I live and work."

Jase tapped his finger straight up and down on the folder on his desk. "True. I couldn't figure it out, so that must mean I'm missing a piece of the puzzle. So I thought about when all this first happened. Lucky's family being murdered was the catalyst. Right?"

Lucky found herself thinking back. "Well. Sorta."

Hawk squatted beside her. He was so tall, they looked at each other nearly eye to eye. "What do you mean, sweetheart?"

"I got picked on a lot at school. I wasn't popular. Desiree was the outgoing one. I was more on the fringe of her group. They let me tag along, mostly without incident."

"Explain that to us." Jase leaned in like Hawk.

"I thought most of the girls liked me, but sometimes they'd leave me behind. Someone wrote bitch on my locker once. I'd find something gross smeared on it. A few times someone would *accidentally* spill something on me."

Hawk put both his hands on her thighs. "I'm really sorry you were bullied like that."

She brushed her fingers over his jaw. "You were probably the most popular boy in school. Always."

He smirked. "I did okay."

She bet he did. And he probably didn't pick on others. He was too much a protector.

She shook her head and rolled her eyes at how he downplayed his popularity. "When I meet your parents, are they going to tell me all about the sports you played, the top grades you made?"

He gave her a sheepish look. "Maybe. But what's really important is that I'm the luckiest bastard on the planet because the most beautiful woman, inside and out, that I've ever known decided I'm hers. No one compares to you. High school flings included."

"Flings?"

"I've never really been a relationship guy. I was too busy with sports, school, then the military. You're the only one I ever saw myself with forever." He leaned in and kissed her like Jase wasn't their captive audience.

Jase sighed. "Okay, that's all great. And super sweet. My teeth ache. But we're missing the point I'm trying to make. Lucky, when you think back on that time and around the time your family was murdered, what was Desiree like? Supportive? Kind? Distant? Were you getting along?"

Lucky had to really think about it. "She was...smug. Self-assured. Maybe a little too cocky sometimes and it irritated people. Like she is now. But worse back then. She thought the world revolved around her. She acted out, but there were no consequences. It used to make me really mad that she got away with everything and I..." She deflated in the chair, hanging her head.

Hawk pressed his hand to her cheek. "You were being abused. Cut. Degraded at home. You were sticking up for your brother. Probably your mother, too. You couldn't get away with anything. You couldn't escape." Hawk squeezed her thighs again, trying to get her attention. To look at him.

"Yes," she answered on a whisper. "It seemed like everyone liked her. Covered for her. Went along with her. And I felt invisible most of the time, like nobody saw my pain."

Hawk kissed her temple. "They saw it. They were just dealing with their own shit and didn't know how to help you."

Jase leaned on his forearms on his knees. "Teenagers are selfish and trying to figure out who they are and where they fit in. Everyone's just jockeying for the best position, worried about if everyone likes them. So were those other girls really Desiree's friends? Or were they just using her, or vice versa?"

"Yes." The immediate response didn't actually feel true.

"Really?" Jase raised a brow.

"Well...I was truly her friend. I had been since we were little. *I* was always there for *her*. We lived right across the street from each other." She thought about the other girls. "Desiree runs hot and cold. One day she's super sweet, protective, on your side. Everyone loves to be around her when she's like that. She can be so charismatic. But then she can be a real bitch, picking at you, saying things she apologizes for the next day. She's always been...moody. She gets fixated on things."

"Like what?" Hawk asked.

"If someone was mean to someone she cared about, she wouldn't let it go. She wanted to get even. If she felt there was some injustice, she'd desperately find a way to make things right. If she did something wrong, she'd go overboard trying to fix it. If someone was an asshole, she'd be a bigger asshole back. I benefitted from that a lot. I knew she cared, even if she didn't always show it. It made it easier for me to dismiss the times when she was mean. Sometimes she could be a bully. I think to make herself feel better, bigger, stronger. It was an act. Sometimes, I think she feels too much and doesn't know what to do with all of it. She wants everyone to pay attention to her, but she doesn't realize she's pushing them away at the same time."

"How did she react to you being hurt by your father?"

She didn't like to think about that time in her life. "I hid a lot of it for a long time, even from her. But once she knew it was happening, she kept pushing me to do something. Fight back. Run. Go to the police, even though we both knew her father would side with my dad."

"Did she tell you that?" Jase held her gaze, like he anticipated her answer to be something that would help him solve all this.

"She didn't have to. I knew my father and Bob's relationship was tight. Desiree told me he did all kinds of favors for his friends, looking out for them."

"So you took that to mean he wouldn't help you?" Jase seemed to hold his breath.

They were talking about his boss after all.

"Desiree wouldn't hurt me. Not like that."

Jase suddenly sat up straight.

Hawk cupped her face. "Why would you say that?"

"He wants me to say that Desiree wasn't actually trying to help. That because we had a rocky relationship, she wasn't always on my side."

"Had? Or Have? Jase asked pointedly.

She stared into Hawk's steady gaze, her thoughts about Desiree all mixed up in her head. "We *have* a rocky relationship." The admission was hard to take because that night at the bar was still so fresh in her mind. At least the parts she could remember. Desiree getting upset about her trying to help hook her up with Lincoln. The way she spoke to her. The way she stole her sangria. The drink that drugged her.

She thought about her relationship with her father. How he controlled her. How he degraded her. How he hurt her. How he sometimes made it seem like he cared, then turned around and did something to hurt her. With his words. With his actions. With his knife.

They seemed so similar at times.

Tears filled her eyes as she stared at the floor, unable to look at Hawk any longer with the revelation filling her mind. "I'm in an abusive relationship with Desiree. She controls what we do and when we see each other. She puts me down, making it seem like she's just trying to "help" me. She wants me to drop everything for her when she needs something, but she doesn't reciprocate when it's inconvenient for her." She finally met Hawk's gaze. "She's not a good friend at all. You've treated me better in the little while we've been together than she has in years. It's all about her. I just go along because she's all I have. Or had."

Lucky sat with that for a second. "When she invites me over, she always asks me to help her clean up while I'm there and she spills her guts about whatever is bothering her. She asks me to watch Krystal so she can run an errand, go on a date, or whatever. I don't mind watching Krystal. I love her. But now it all feels...calculated."

Jase tapped the folder with his fingertip again. "I think Desiree likes having you around because you defend her. You make her look like someone who is helpful and nice. I think you want Desiree to be that kind friend. The one you've thought you had all these years."

"She's changed," she admitted. "Back then, I really thought she wanted to help me."

"When did she change?"

"After my family's murders, Neil's court hearings, then finding out she was pregnant. It was a lot all at once. I understood why she was so out of sorts about it all. I was a wreck, too, trying to figure out life without my parents and dealing with finishing school and settling their estate. I was so lost in my grief and survival I wasn't really there for her like she needed me. I think it broke something between us that we haven't been able to fully mend."

"When she talked about you being hurt and wanting to do something about it, did she say *she* wanted to do something, or *you* should do something?"

"Both, I guess. She wanted us to run away, hit the road and travel. Be wherever we wanted to be. Do whatever we wanted to do."

"Did you want to do that?" Jase studied her.

"I wanted out, but I couldn't just go. Sure, we could take her car, but I didn't have any money. How would we get by? And I had to think about Danny. I couldn't leave him behind. I couldn't just leave him with a monster."

"How did she take that?"

"She tried to tell me that we could find jobs and camp and live like gypsies. She didn't want to think about practical things or the fact that we were minors who'd be missed and probably have an APB out on us by her father, especially if we took Danny with us."

"Is there another reason you didn't want to go with her?" Jase waited out her silence, until she broke and finally spoke.

"She talked about how things would be so much better if my parents were dead. Neil would agree with her and say something had to be done." She thought about those conversations, how they confused her back then because while she wanted her father out of her life, she didn't want any of them dead. "After everything happened, Desiree said something to me that I can never get out of my head."

"What?" Hawk asked, compassion and sympathy in his eyes.

"You should thank the person who did it. Now you're free." It wasn't just what she said, it was the way she said it with a smile. It was disturbing.

She said "the person who did it." Shouldn't she have told me to thank Neil?

"You're afraid of her," Jase blurted out.

She tilted her head. "How do you know that?" It was true. Sometimes Desiree looked at her a certain way and it sent a chill up her spine.

Jase didn't answer her, but asked, "Has she checked up on you since you got out of the hospital?"

"She stopped by a few days ago."

Hawk rolled his eyes. "Yeah, and flirted with me when you left the room."

Her head snapped around to him. "What? No."

Hawk nodded. "Yes. I didn't like it. Especially when she made it clear that she was far more...adventurous, open, and appropriate to have on my arm than you." He brushed his hand over her head. "It's bullshit. You're the most beautiful woman I've ever seen. You're everything I need and want. Especially since I'm pretty sure my wallet appealed to her a lot more than I did."

She brushed her fingers down his cheek. "Look in a mirror, honey. Every woman wants you."

His grin lit up his whole face. "I am loving that honey."

She'd have to call him that more often. "I'm sorry she acted that way."

Hawk shook his head. "Don't apologize for her. Not when she tried to steal your boyfriend away from you."

Oh. I love that boyfriend. Even if it didn't seem quite enough.

She was loving having him so close, so connected to her.

Jase shifted in his seat. "You two are so into each other. I'm happy for you. But can we get back to this case and Desiree's contradictions?"

"What is it you're trying to tell me?" Lucky asked, tired of doing this in some roundabout way.

"You were at the bar with Desiree. You somehow got drugged, even though it appears that the guys you were with never went near your glass."

She sat up straighter. "Is that what the video showed? You're sure?"

"Yes," both men answered.

Jase went on. "After you came out of the bathroom together, she led you to the banquet room. You remember seeing Neil in there."

"Yes." They'd gone over this already.

"What was Desiree doing?"

She tried to picture it but couldn't. "I don't know. That part's really fuzzy."

"Now put Neil's question into context," Jase prompted.

It finally dawned on her. "He wasn't talking about me."

"You were right there. She must have contacted him and told him to meet her there. So why ask?"

She sagged in the chair. "I don't understand. Who did he want to see?"

Hawk swore under his breath. "He was asking about the kid."

Lucky gasped. "Why would he ask about Krystal?"

Jase's eyes softened. "When I hit a dead end with the video, I went back to when I thought this all started. I asked some of the guys who have been here the longest about your family's murders. I wanted to know what wasn't in the reports."

"What did you find out?" This time, she was the one leaning in to Jase.

"Did you know there was a rumor going around that Desiree and Neil were hooking up behind your back?"

"What?" She sprang up out of her chair, then fell back into it in shock.

Instead of answering her, he asked another question. "What were they like together?"

Lucky had to wrap her head around what that rumor meant if it was true. "Um. They got along. We hung out, the three of us, a lot. It wasn't unusual for me to see them walking together between classes or talking in the halls." She frowned, thinking about how often she spotted them together, Desiree's hand on his arm. She smiled at him all the time. She complimented him. She flirted.

Just like she did with Hawk apparently.

Lucky covered her face with both hands, then dragged them down until they fell back into her lap. "How could I be so stupid?"

Hawk took her hand and kissed her palm. "Hey. None of that. You're not stupid. They were hiding it from you."

"Not that well, now that I think about all the times I saw them together. They were so...chummy." She stared at the floor, feeling sick and betrayed.

Jase nudged her knee with his. "Did you know Desiree had been...detained multiple times by us, since the time she was thirteen?"

"No."

Jase nodded. "There's nothing officially on record, but the guys I talked to said she'd been brought in for all kinds of things--shoplifting, drunk and disorderly, possession, joyriding, speeding tickets and a bunch of other petty stuff. They'd catch her and haul her into her father's office. The last offense was just a couple of months ago. Some guy pissed her off and she slashed his tires."

"Sounds familiar." Hawk glared daggers at the room.

"And she gets away with all of it?" Lucky's stomach soured.

Jase's steady gaze dared her to think otherwise. "Let's play this out with the added information that Desiree has a history of breaking the law and getting away with it, and she and Neil were...having an affair."

She cringed. "If Desiree was hooking up with Neil behind my back, then I suppose they were also talking about me, too. Things were getting really bad at home. Both of them had talked to me about running away. I couldn't. Not yet. Not without Danny. Not until I graduated. I'd need my diploma to have any kind of chance of getting a job."

Jase went back to the past. "Desiree probably met up with Neil at his house, so no one would see them and out them. Right?"

Her stomach tied into a knot. "That seems the most logical place. His parents worked, so the house was empty until six weeknights. I would tell my parents I was studying with a friend, but I'd go to his place for a couple hours. I couldn't take the chance of sneaking out at night, but Desiree did it all the time." She thought about all the trouble she'd gotten into while Lucky was at home fending off her father's abuse. "It would have been easy enough for her to meet up with him behind my back, maybe sneak into his room through his window. They had a lot more freedom than I did." Her heart hurt just thinking about them talking about her, laughing that she didn't know what was going on between them.

It hurt even more to think that those nights she was being hurt by her father, they were snuggled up all cozy in his bed, fucking and carrying on like they didn't know exactly what was happening to her.

At the time, the only good thing she had in her life was Neil and Desiree. The two people who seemed to care about her. Neil even said he loved her.

But none of it was true.

They lied.

He cheated.

They had a baby together!

Oh. My. God!

She didn't mean anything to them.

And if that was true, then... "Why kill my parents if he was cheating on me with Desiree? Why put himself at risk for me? He obviously didn't care about me if he was sleeping with her." She gasped as the answer to Jase's early prompt came to her.

Jase very quietly said what she was thinking. "I don't think Neil killed your family. I think Desiree knew about Neil's side business selling drugs, stole some from his house during one of their trysts, drugged your family, killed them because she maybe felt guilty for sleeping with your boyfriend and also wanted to save you from your father and punish your mother for allowing you to be hurt and not protecting you."

"And then what? Set up her lover to take the fall?"

"Yes." Jase nodded. "To make sure no one suspected her."

"But that meant Neil went to prison for a crime he didn't commit."

Jase shook his head. "He wasn't tried for the murder, remember, because the evidence disappeared from lockup. He was convicted on the drug charges."

The light bulb went on in her head. "Without the knife that had his prints, they had no evidence against him." She lost focus, staring at nothing as it all fell into place. "She stole the evidence from here. No one would have suspected anything if she just walked into the office. They'd think she was visiting her dad. She knows everyone here. They wouldn't bat an eye if she was walking around talking to everyone she knows."

Jase smacked his hand on the desk. "And that's how she got away with murder and made sure Neil didn't go down for it either."

"Except she didn't steal back the drugs they found in his closet." She pinned Jase in her gaze. "Why'd she let him go down for that?"

"I think because he loved you and wouldn't leave you for her." He shrugged. "It's the only thing that makes sense."

"But they were having a baby together."

"She didn't know that at the time."

Lucky thought about it. "Right, she found out after Neil was in prison." That really hit her. "I bet she was upset that he wasn't there for her. She played it off at the time that she didn't want the father involved at all. But I think secretly she was kicking herself for not getting him off on all the charges so he could be with her."

She thought about what he said in her memory. "He wants to see his daughter. He's still covering for Desiree because she won't let him see Krystal. With his rap sheet, no way he'd get visitation. Not unsupervised. Especially with the murders of three people hanging over his head."

She sat back and stared off into space. "Holy fuck. She got away with everything. She sat there consoling me about my family. She told me how lucky I was to have someone who would go to such lengths to keep me safe." She scrubbed her hands over her face. "She was talking about *herself*. She wanted me to be grateful. She kept saying whoever killed them did me a favor!"

She slammed her hand down on the chair arm. "Fucking bitch!"

They'd kept their conversation low, not wanting to disturb the officers working around them. Now, every head turned in her direction. But she only saw one person. The one standing in his office, looking right at her, guilt and shame in his eyes.

Sheriff Bob Collins.

She stood so abruptly her chair tipped back and hit the cubicle wall.

Hawk tugged on her hand. "What are you doing?"

"I'm going to get some answers."

"I'll come with you." He didn't let her go.

She finally took her eyes off her target and met Hawk's worried gaze. "He won't talk if either of you come with me. He's got too much to lose if he does. He'll protect her like he's been doing since the day she was born. He can't help himself, even if he knows who and what she is."

"What if he decides to silence you before you can out his daughter?"

"That's a chance I'm willing to take, because I don't believe he'd go that far. He always told me I was like a second daughter to him." She rolled her eyes. *Who let's a daughter be abused?* "He said I tempered Desiree. My friendship with her gave her stability, especially after her mother died. I was the one who held Desiree's hand through the funeral. I was always her best friend, even if she wasn't mine." A tear slipped down her cheek.

Hawk brushed it away with his thumb. "I'm so sorry, sweetheart."

"Seconds before you found me in that ravine, I truly thought I was at my lowest point, and I didn't even know that it was my best friend who'd dropped me down that hill." A flash of memory came back, but it was Hawk who made it all too real.

"No, Desiree. Don't." Hawk pulled her into his chest. "You say it over and over again in your sleep." He held her tighter and kissed the top of her head. "I want to kill her."

"Whoa, buddy. Let's just keep that to yourself." Jase looked around the room, making sure no one else had heard.

"I didn't know how truly alone I was when you found me." This time, she swiped the tears away. "I can't lose you," she whispered, trying to get the words out for him to hear and understand how necessary he was to her.

"You'll never lose me. Ever."

She hugged him as hard as she could. "I desperately need you to mean that."

"I do. A thousand percent. You're never getting rid of me."

"Okay," she choked out. "But I need you to let me go so I can do what I have to do. I need the whole truth."

Hawk didn't let loose his hold around her shoulders for a good ten seconds, and even then, he simply pushed back enough to kiss her on the forehead. "I wish I could do this for you."

"I can do it because I know I have you to come back to when I'm done."

Hawk kissed her, resting his lips against hers for a long moment, pouring his love into her. "So fucking strong and fierce. Go get your answers. I'll be waiting right here for you."

Chapter Nineteen

Lucky walked into the sheriff's office and stared at the man who'd known her since she was little. She'd been in his house a thousand times, walking in without even a knock. She slept over countless times over the years. She'd eaten at his table. Hugged him on his birthday and Christmas and at his wife's funeral.

She knew him.

He knew her.

But there was a line between them. A lot known but unspoken.

They didn't discuss the abuse her father inflicted on her. They didn't talk about Desiree's erratic behavior.

They kept their secrets. The silences between them spoke volumes.

He knew more than he'd ever say.

She knew he'd turned a blind eye to what had been happening to her because he loved his daughter.

He'd do anything for Desiree and let Lucky suffer.

Jealousy rose up.

Why didn't she have that with her father?

Why did Desiree get all that love and devotion?

She stared into his gray eyes, so filled with everything unsaid and the apology he'd never offer.

Desiree was so lucky to have someone in her corner, willing to overlook the bad and always trying to find the good in her. He'd never let her fall.

Lucky had never had someone like that in her life.

Her brother might have grown up to be that person for her.

She'd never know. He didn't get the chance to grow up at all.

Someone took him from her.

Was it at Neil's hand? Or Desiree's?

Did they do it together?

She didn't know which one was worse. The lying, cheating, drug dealing boyfriend, or the best friend, who wasn't really a friend at all?

Tears threatened but she choked them back as the stare-off continued.

She broke the unbearable silence. "Did Neil kill my family?"

Bob looked like he aged ten years in the time it took for his shoulders to sag, his face to turn weary, and his eyes to fill with resignation. He hung his head and finally answered. "I don't know."

She challenged him. "His prints were on the knife."

"Yes." That wasn't enough to convince him, which meant there was something that didn't add up about the case for him either.

She went at him from another direction. "I hid what was happening at home for a long time."

His exhausted eyes met hers. "I didn't know it was happening until you were in high school." Shame hunched his shoulders even more. He couldn't even look at her.

"Even then, you didn't do anything about it. You never asked me about it. Why?"

He raked his hand over his head, the dark brown strands mixed with threads of silver now. "Because I didn't want to have to arrest my friend, someone who got me through the worst time in my life."

Her heart clenched just thinking about Gayle, his wife, who died in a car accident. "He helped you move past your grief."

"He was the only one who'd talk to me about Gayle. I warned him, more than once, to stop hurting you. I told him if he did it again, I'd have to do something about it."

"But he didn't heed your empty threat. Did he? No. He just got more clever about how he'd hurt me."

"You always seemed fine."

She seethed inside. "Yes. I suppose I would seem fine with a death threat looming over my head while the bruises and cuts were hidden beneath my clothes. I suppose that made it easy for you to bury your head in the sand and leave me to face a monster every day!" She tried to catch her breath after shouting there at the end.

"I didn't know it was that bad!" His outburst didn't sway her.

"You're lying! Desiree knew everything in middle school, which means you knew, because she would have asked you for help."

His face said it all. He knew. He just didn't do anything about it. His reputation was on the line. People would ask, how could he miss the abuse when he saw her nearly every day? He knew the signs.

"If you considered me a daughter, didn't I deserve better?" She fisted her hands at her sides, wanting so badly to lash out, even knowing it would only get her in trouble. He had too much power. His position protected him. Insulated him.

This conversation was futile.

Still, she needed to try to get the truth out of him.

His shoulders slumped again. "You do deserve better. But there's nothing I can do now. They're gone. You've moved on."

"Moved on? Seriously? You think I've moved on. I've been stuck in a loop, just surviving each day, wondering when the next shoe is going to drop. And all this time, you knew I was still being taunted by someone, hurt, and Neil wasn't the one behind it. He didn't kill my family."

"I don't know any of that." His face lied for him. He did know. He just didn't want to admit it. Because if he admitted it to himself, he'd have to look at someone else as the killer. And he couldn't bring himself to do that. Not yet.

But she'd make him see beyond a shadow of a doubt and he wouldn't be able to hide it anymore. "You *do* know it. You've spent your life working here. You've honed your cop instincts. But it's more than that. For months leading up to my family's death, I was being bombarded by pleas to turn my father in, to make you do your fucking job before he fucking killed me!" She tried to rein herself in. She could feel Hawk just outside the office, watching, waiting for any sign that she needed his help.

"Lucky..." Bob's eyes pleaded with her to understand. To not go down this road.

"Don't Lucky me, Bob. Desiree had to have asked for your help. *You*, who would do anything for *her*."

"I told her to leave it alone. You'd graduate soon and leave for college. You just had to get to college."

"And leave my brother with *him*?"

"He was different with Danny."

She shook her head. "You are so delusional. *I* kept him from Danny. Most of the time, but not all of it." And it killed her every time her father put his hands on her little brother. "You were right across the street. You had to hear the shouting, my screams. You had to see my pain. You *knew*!"

"I had my own pain to deal with, along with Desiree's and reining her in from doing something stupid and self-destructive. She was out of control. You know what she was like at that time."

"I thought I did, but I didn't know the half of it, because you're a good dad. You take care of her. Always. Even when she gets into trouble. You smooth it over. You make it go away. Speeding tickets. Shoplifting. Bar fights. DUI's." She held his gaze. "Murder."

"No." He shook his head emphatically and waved his finger back and forth in her face. "No." That finger stopped and pointed straight at her. "You don't have any proof."

"How about drugging someone? Because I was drugged before I remember seeing Neil in the bar."

Bob dropped his hand and swallowed hard.

Well that was telling.

"She's the only one who had the motive and proximity to do it. Does she hate me that much?"

"Sometimes," he conceded. "The spotlight always has to shine brightest on her."

Lucky nodded. "It always felt like anything good that happened to me, she wanted to take away. Danny, because I spent time with him, time she wanted me to spend with her. Neil, because he loved me. She wanted to be the only one I turned to for everything. She wanted the love I so desperately needed."

"She loves you, even when she hates you."

Desiree treated him the same way. They'd had some epic arguments over the years.

"Right. It's a twisted kind of love. One where she needs to be in control, where she gets everything she wants and I have nothing."

He held his head in both hands. "I don't know what happened to her."

"Her mother died and she didn't want to lose anyone else."

Something changed on his face, so fast she almost missed it. Grief mixed with pure fury.

"Wait a second." She held her hand up, pointing her finger at his chest. "You. She loved *you* so much. Such a daddy's girl. She'd get upset when Gayle got between you two. She always wanted your attention. You spoiled her. But Gayle...she was the one who doled out the rules and consequences and pushing Desiree to be kinder, to think before she speaks, to get better grades, be polite, get a job, think about her future."

"Like you," he whispered.

It all made so much sense now. "Gayle compared her to me."

"All the time. She thought you were something special. So studious and willing to help. You even worked with your mom, you had a plan for college. You wanted to be a nurse. Desiree lived so in the moment, she didn't think about consequences or the future, just having fun and getting whatever she wanted. You were the only one who could see through Desiree's insecurities and shake off her meanness and just be her friend."

"You didn't do anything about my father because you knew my mother would have taken me and Danny to be closer to her family. She'd wanted to move for years, but my father wouldn't hear of it. He needed to keep us away from anyone who would challenge him and what he was doing to us. You needed me to be Desiree's friend."

His chin hit his chest. "Yes. She needs you."

"Even though she spends half her time making herself feel better by taking little swipes at me?" She held up her scarred arm. "They don't make me bleed like my father's cuts, but they still hurt."

His eyes pleaded with her to understand. "She's gotten better."

"She tried to kill me! She drugged me, stripped me, then dumped me down a hill and left me to die!" She raked her fingers through her hair and paced back and forth. "No wonder you didn't come to see me in the hospital." Her eyes went wide with the revelations popping into her mind. "No. You sent Jase. I'm your daughter's best friend, *like a daughter to you*, and this is how you treat me." She stopped pacing and glared at him. "You knew it was her."

He shook his head rigorously. "No. I don't know that at all. From what you reported, they were both there. If your memory is even correct." He was gaslighting her, making it seem like she didn't know what was going on. It made her even angrier.

"You don't want to believe that she's capable of all this. But you have to wonder how your wife died in that car crash and Desiree walked away without a mark on her. Desiree was driving. She lost control of the car. But she was on a road with a speed limit of forty miles an hour. Yet the car hit that tree on the side, smashing it in so hard that Gayle died." More revelations hit her. "She must have been speeding recklessly. Or more accurately, purposefully to hit that turn and slide into that tree, crushing her mother."

His gaze dropped away again, tears sliding down his cheeks.

"Oh my god. She did it. She killed her mother."

"I wasn't there. I don't know what really happened." He bit out the words, a world of rage in them.

"But you had your guys on the case investigating. You saw the photos and evidence. They'd covered up so many other things she'd done. You had them by the balls. So they did what they expected you wanted them to do and they declared it an accident."

The fact that he couldn't meet her gaze spoke volumes.

"I just spent two minutes thinking about it and the answer is so obvious now—you think your whole department was stumped for years? Please. We can't all be blind and stupid."

"You don't know anything. The accident reports are clear. It was an accident."

"Bullshit. You let her get away with murder. Literally. She killed your wife. Her own mother. And then she killed my family and tried to kill me."

He didn't say anything for a long time, then his head came up and he looked her right in the eye and confessed, "Gayle was gone. The only person I could try to save was my daughter. She's all I have left."

"No. You have a granddaughter who needs you. Because Desiree is never going to stop being who she is. I've been thinking about all those reports in my file. The things that have happened to me over the years. They were all preceded by some kind of argument or perceived slight with Desiree. At the time I never saw it. I never suspected her. I thought she was my friend. But you're right, she doesn't want me to be happy. She wants me clinging to her. My only friend. The only one who's stood beside me through everything. She likes to smack me down, then pull me close. It's a twisted game with her. Except this time, she tried to kill me, steal my boyfriend, and pin it on Neil. Again. Who does that to the father of their child?"

Bob's eyes went wide. "She told you."

"She didn't have to." She tapped her finger to her temple. "I remember seeing him that night, asking someone. *'Are you going to let me see her now?'* He wasn't talking to me. He was talking to Desiree, asking if he could see Krystal."

"Yes. Think about Krystal. If you blow this all up, Krystal won't have a mother."

"Good. Desiree doesn't deserve that little girl. She'll corrupt her, or worse, treat her the way she's treated me. No. I won't let that happen. She's not going to stop." Another revelation came to her. "You know why she tried to kill me that night?"

"Lucky, please."

"She wanted me to help set her up with Lincoln Gunn at the bar. She thought he was sexy and had a lot of money. The perfect guy, even if she knew absolutely nothing about him. But I knew Hawk, so Desiree thought I could somehow make it happen. When I tried, Lincoln shut me down, saying politely that he's not dating right now. It wasn't a cut to Desiree. I'm sure he had his reasons, but it had nothing to do with her. She was furious with me. I can only imagine how even more irate she was when she walked into my hospital room and found not only Hawk there, but Lincoln, too." And more pieces fell into place. "That's probably why she set up my place to burn and slashed my tire, then tried to flirt her way into Hawk's heart and me out of it."

Rage built inside her. "I'm going to take her down. She will not get away with this anymore. The question is, are you going to stop me? Because I know you're not going to help."

He fell back, leaning on his desk. "There's no evidence linking her to her mother's death, your family's murders, or anything else that she's done to you. Neil's claims that he didn't do it aren't enough. I won't help you hurt my daughter. I can't."

"Will you help save your granddaughter before Desiree turns on her?"

The silence in the room could be cut with a knife, it felt so thick and heavy.

She pushed. "Desiree needs to be stopped before she kills anyone else you love." She drove the first nail into his coffin. "Jase has already figured out that Desiree is the most likely suspect. Will you fire him to protect Desiree? Will you let this go on until she hurts someone else? Me? Hawk, because he dares to love me? Lincoln because he turned her down for a date? What does she have to do before you do something, even if it's simply letting me take her down?"

"The knife is gone and probably didn't have her prints on it anyway. You have no memory of that night before Hawk found you. What is it that you think you can do to prove anything?"

"Leave that to me. I know how to handle her. I've had years of experience. But it will only work if you don't tell her I'm coming after her."

He planted his hands on his hips and stared up at the ceiling. "I want Krystal safe. I want her to feel loved."

"Maybe what she needs are grandparents who put her first." Between Bob and Neil's parents, maybe Krystal had a chance to grow up loved like she deserved.

A knock sounded on the glass in the door.

Lucky turned to find Hawk pointing down the hallway as he mouthed *Desiree.*

A few seconds later, Desiree stood in front of Hawk and walked her fingers up his chest as she purred, "Hello again. Miss me?"

Hawk's face remained void of emotion as he stepped out of reach. "I'm just waiting for my girlfriend." His gaze turned to Lucky and he smiled. The kind of smile he only gave her. One filled with love and an *I want you* attached to it.

Desiree opened the door and stepped in, her gaze shifting from me to her father and back again. "Hey," she said to Lucky. "I heard you were in the building. I thought I'd run over and see if you were okay? Is everything all right?" Her gaze shot to her dad, then back again.

"Everything is fine," Bob assured her. "Lucky came in to answer some questions for Jase about her case. She just wanted to say hi and let me know she was on the mend."

"Yes," she rushed to say. "Your dad just wanted a few minutes to find out how I am and what I've been up to since we haven't seen each other in a while." She bumped her shoulder against Desiree's. "I think he also wanted to find out if Hawk is treating me right."

"He better be." Bob stared down Hawk, who was leaning against the doorframe now.

Hawk held his hand out. Lucky took it without hesitation and leaned into his side, his arm wrapped around her waist. "Hawk loves me. I'm happier than I've ever been."

Which should make my best friend happy for me.

Except Desiree's smile didn't reach her eyes and her face tightened, like it was a strain to hold her smile. "You kept him a secret for a good long while." Desiree shifted her gaze to Hawk, her sultry glance rude and inappropriate, especially right in front of Lucky. "I look forward to getting to know you better."

Hawk kissed Lucky on the head and asked her, "Did you get what you needed?"

Not yet. "I guess we'll never know what really happened that night, with my memory wiped."

"Still no leads?" Desiree stared at her father.

"Jase is heading up the case. He's hit a dead end."

Desiree chuckled. "Just like Lucky almost did." No one except Desiree found that funny in the slightest.

"You ready to go?" Hawk asked. "I thought we could head over to Lincoln's place and you can finally give him that quote and get him on your schedule."

"Sounds good." It was a way out of here without looking suspicious.

"Can I come?" Desiree chimed in. "I'd love to see his place and maybe get another shot at a date."

Lucky frowned. "Um, this is business, and I would only feel comfortable doing that if I had Lincoln's permission. Sorry. You understand, right?"

Desiree stared daggers at her. "Fine. Whatever." She didn't deserve a man like Lincoln.

"We should get going. I want to ask Lincoln if he knows a good time to meet Mercy for drinks, since he seems to know her so well."

"Drinks?" Desiree eyed her.

"Yeah. Mercy works with the Gunn brothers. She's close to Hawk and I want to be part of his world, so when Mercy asked me out for drinks, I thought it was a great way to make a new friend."

Bob's gaze narrowed. He was catching on to her baiting Desiree, making herself a target. She was allowed to make new friends, even if it did make Desiree feel threatened.

She set the trap. All she had to do was wait for Desiree to retaliate.

"I'm surprised you want to go out drinking after what happened last time." Desiree tried to look sympathetic but it was just another fake mask.

"Mercy promised Lincoln or Hawk would pour for us and no one else."

Hawk grinned. "So I'm invited to this girls' night?"

"It is your bar. And you're buying, right?" she teased.

"Anything you want, it's yours."

"You. That's all I want."

He kissed her right there in front of the two people she had left from her past, who should have been the ones she could count on to have her back. Neither of them did and it left her feeling like everything they'd shared over her whole life was a lie.

Hawk drew her out of the office before he ended the kiss, making her laugh.

She was smiling so big, it was hard to stop when she turned to Desiree. "Let's catch up soon. I'll call you. Kiss Krystal for me. I love that little girl. I'd do anything for her." She looked past Desiree to Bob. "Thank you for the talk and helping me see things clearly."

"It's the least I can do."

Yes, it was. The very least. He should have done so much more.

He could have saved her family. Danny.

As she and Hawk made their way down the hall, she heard Desiree ask her father, "What did she mean?"

His answer assured her that he'd keep quiet about what she knew. "She was upset and ranting about the injustice of the case. I promised I wouldn't tell anyone about her outburst, then laid out the very few pieces of evidence we've found. I promised her we'd keep investigating and that she has every right to be angry we haven't caught the person who nearly killed her."

Lucky hoped he choked on those words and really took them to heart. Because that's what Desiree had intended.

She left me there, naked and alone.

Some friend.

She's going down.

Chapter Twenty

Hawk didn't know how it happened. One minute he was sitting in Lincoln's kitchen while Lucky toured the house and she figured out a bid for weekly housekeeping services, and the next...his parents showed up to meet Lucky.

Lincoln had to have texted them that she was here. He was always trying to score points with Mom, so she'd drop off a casserole or pot of chili for him.

Hawk hoped he choked on it for surprising Lucky like this. Not really. He loved his brother. But he'd wanted to prepare Lucky, not ambush her.

After what she'd been through, he couldn't fault her for her caution around new people, even if they'd figured out that Desiree was responsible for all of her heartache and pain.

He had no idea how she handled it so well, being betrayed by the person closest to her. If one of his brothers betrayed him like that, he'd be devastated. He wouldn't trust anyone ever again. Because if the person who was supposed to be the one person you could count on hurt you like that...how could you ever trust anyone.

But Lucky trusted him. Right?

He'd just have to keep on proving himself to her. He had no intention of ever letting her down, let alone hurting her. She was quickly becoming his whole world.

He wanted forever.

He needed to come up with a plan to make her his.

First, they needed Desiree behind bars where she belonged.

They were going to need some help with that because local law enforcement couldn't be trusted—and he knew the perfect person, besides Jase. Someone who could take down everyone who'd betrayed Lucky.

He'd have to invite his cousin for dinner. Soon. Because he didn't want Desiree to have another chance to hurt Lucky.

Hawk tuned back into the impromptu introductions going on in front of him.

"We're so pleased to finally meet you." His mom looked over Lucky's shoulder at him and winked.

Lucky looked a little shell-shocked to find his parents waiting for her when she came downstairs with Lincoln on her tail. As usual, she stepped back, giving herself some space. "It's lovely to meet you, too. Uh, Hawk talks about you a lot."

He hoped Lincoln had warned his parents about Lucky's aversion to being touched. Though she seemed to handle it with him and Lincoln. Mason had kept his affection short and sweet when he'd kissed her forehead during his visit, and it helped that Hawk had warned her it was coming.

His mom, Donna, beamed, looking very much like she was already planning a wedding in her head. "Really? I can barely get two words out of him most of the time."

"Mom." He gave her a look she read all too easily.

She put her hand to his cheek. "I'm just saying that you're the strong, silent type."

Lucky tipped her head to the side. "Really? We've had some really great long talks."

"Then you must be magic," his dad said, extending his hand to her.

Lucky only hesitated for a second before she shook it. "I think Hawk's got some kind of magic. He found me in the middle of nowhere."

Mac put his free hand over their joined ones. "And wasn't that lucky for both your sakes." His dad released Lucky and shared a look with him.

Hawk had confided in his dad about Lucky and the pseudo relationship they'd formed over the last two years. His father hadn't pushed him to turn it into something more formal and intimate. Instead, he'd encouraged Hawk to take his time to get to know her, to go at his own pace while he healed and focused on himself, so he'd be a better version of himself for her, too. He told Hawk if it was meant to be, she'd still be waiting for him when he was ready.

He'd needed that time to get his head on straight and figure out if he still had enough of the pieces of his heart to share with someone else. He hadn't been hurt by others, more like his heart had taken a beating watching so many atrocities play out. It made him wonder if there was anything good left in the world where he'd somehow survived as he watched others perish.

And the answer seemed so easy when he'd come home to find a note, a book, a meal, whatever it was she left behind in his home, something that made him feel like someone cared. Something that made him want to smile and believe in good things again.

Little by little, she'd helped him rebuild his heart, and begin to want something more than surviving.

And now, seeing her chatting with his parents about the ranch they'd built and she'd barely gotten a glimpse of, he saw it. She fit. Him. His family.

She was everything he wanted and more.

And if she needed to hold his hand while she opened her sweet heart to his parents, well, that just meant they were a team, supporting each other.

"How are you healing?" Donna asked. "You're so beautiful, I'd never guess you're still recovering from your injuries."

Lucky immediately covered the worst scars on her arm with her hand, her teeth digging into her bottom lip. "Um. All the stitches are out. My ankle and knee are better, so long as I don't overdo it. Otherwise, it's just the mental stuff. You know."

He slipped his arm around her back, planted his hand on her hip, and pulled her into his side, kissing her on the head. Her wild mane clung to the scruff on his jaw. He brushed it away, tucking the long golden strands behind her ear. "You're tough, sweetheart. You've been dealt a heavy blow. But you're stronger every day, and I know you're going to handle Desiree like a champ."

Her gorgeous green gaze met his. "I won't let her get away with everything. Not anymore."

His dad narrowed his gaze and stepped closer to them.

Hawk felt Lucky check the impulse to step back. He rubbed his hand over her hip, reminding her he was right there. She was safe.

Mac caught her instinctive reaction but didn't comment on it. "Who is Desiree? I thought it was your ex who hurt you."

Hawk tried not to let his anger show, but it came out in his voice anyway. "We believe it was all a setup for him to take the fall. In reality, it looks like her best friend Desiree has been messing with Lucky for years. It all seems to come down to Desiree wanting Lucky to depend on her, and only her.

"Desiree had an affair with Lucky's ex and we believe they share a child. Desiree's daughter Krystal is the right age, and Desiree found out she was pregnant only a couple months after Neil went to prison. Desiree also tried to come on to me. I shut that down immediately."

"Of course you did," his mother defended him. "You're a good man. You'd never do something like that. None of my boys would, or I'd have something to say about it." She'd taught them all to respect women and relationships. To always tell the truth, even if it meant hurting someone's feelings. Better to break up than hurt someone worse by betraying their trust.

Lucky kissed his cheek. "Desiree knows a good thing when she sees it."

"I thought she was into me," Lincoln complained.

"You dodged a bullet there, brother." Hawk nuzzled his nose into Lucky's sweet-smelling hair. What was that? Strawberries and flowers? Whatever it was, he was addicted. "Anyway. Desiree is going to get what's coming to her. I'm just sorry it will come at her daughter's expense."

Lucky turned into him, seeking even more comfort. "Desiree killed her mother. I don't want to give her a chance to turn on her own child."

Hawk couldn't believe what he'd heard. "What? She killed her mom? How do you know that?"

"I started putting all these pieces together during my talk with Bob. If she could do all those things to me, what else was she capable of? She framed the father of her child, not once, but twice to keep suspicion off of her. It made me think that maybe all of this was because she'd lost her mother. But then I thought about my relationship with her and the one that she has with her father. We enabled her by always trying to see the best in her. Her mother was the one who disciplined her, pushed her, and apparently compared her to me."

"I bet that didn't go over well," Lincoln chimed in.

"No. And it ended in Desiree driving her right into a tree." Lucky pressed her palm over her heart, rubbing hard. "She soaked up the sympathy like she couldn't get enough. She loved the attention. She'd bring up her mother's death around others so everyone was paying attention to her. I didn't see it that way back then, but now..."

"Now that you know what she's capable of, the past looks different."

"I really thought we were friends. I thought she cared about me. After my family was gone, she was there, hugging me, encouraging me to live the life I wanted now. All the while, she'd taken the one person I loved more than anything away from me. Why Danny? He was just a little boy. He'd never done anything to her. To anyone."

He wrapped her in a tight hug. "I don't know, sweetheart, but we are going to get that answer from her. Soon. She won't get away with it."

Lucky wiped the tears from her cheeks and looked up at him. "Sorry. This is not how I intended meeting your parents would go."

His mom stepped up and put her hand on Lucky's shoulder. "You've been through a lot, dear. We know that. And we're family. You don't have to be anything but yourself with us."

Tears gathered in her eyes again as she stared up at Hawk. "Wow. I don't think I've ever had that."

"You do now." He kissed her, right there in the foyer with his family looking on.

"Hey," Lincoln grumbled, "I have a bet to win."

That got his attention. He reluctantly broke the kiss, not just because of what Lincoln said, but also because he didn't want his family watching him with Lucky. He'd show her how much she belonged with him later tonight. "What bet?"

Lucky found her smile again. "He bet that I couldn't make a meal out of whatever he's got in his kitchen."

"The cupboards are bare. Mostly." Lincoln rubbed his hands together. "I'm so winning this bet."

Hawk knew for a fact that Lucky could make something edible out of just about anything. And he knew that look in his brother's eyes. Even if he lost to Lucky, which he would, he'd still win because he'd be eating something good tonight.

His mom got in on the fun. "Let's go see what's in the kitchen."

An hour later, he was having a family dinner with Lucky. She'd turned a package of boneless chicken thighs, leftover rice from Chinese takeout that Lincoln had hardly touched, a bag of frozen broccoli, a can of condensed cream of chicken soup, and a jar of nacho cheese sauce into a cheesy chicken divan casserole. It was delicious, even if Lucky insisted real cheddar cheese would have been better.

Lincoln lost the bet and paid up by making her a pitcher of peach sangria, which she shared with everyone.

Even better was the way his mom, dad, and Lincoln spent the whole dinner asking about Lucky's life and sharing stories about him. He didn't mind that most were embarrassing. He just loved having her sitting next to him, her hand in his on top of the table for all of them to see.

He was so damn happy. Happier than he could ever remember.

When his parents headed for the front door, they turned back and gave him a look, one he hadn't seen in a long time. They were proud of him. They were happy for him. All the worry they'd carried since he joined the military and came home a broken man had disappeared, leaving only the joy of seeing their son finally content.

Lucky had given him that moment. She made all the difference.

He was finally settled. Safe. Home. Maybe not whole, but as close as he'd get.

All he had to do was hold on to Lucky and keep her safe.

Chapter Twenty-One

Hawk pulled into his driveway and stared up at his house lit up inside and out. *Lucky's home.* The warm glow welcomed him and made him feel like the house was more than just the walls and roof. It felt like their place. A place filled with warmth, conversations, togetherness, and laughter.

He loved having her in his house. He loved coming home to her. *I love her.*

And he wanted more.

Dinner with his family last night had gone so well. His mom and dad both called him at work today to tell him how much they liked her. They thought she was good for him. More than that, they wanted him to know they were happy to see him so happy.

It had been a long time coming. He'd spent a lot of sleepless nights wondering if he'd ever truly be happy again and if he even deserved it.

She made him want it. He'd become a better man for her. Because of her.

They needed to have a talk about the future. He didn't want to wait for the dreams he was having. He wanted everything now.

He hoped she did, too.

It seemed the more time he spent with her, the more impatient he became.

The second he walked in the door, he smiled at the soft music playing, the smell of something cheesy, and the sight of his woman standing in the kitchen humming and stirring something in a pot, a plate of chocolate cupcakes on the counter beside her.

"Honey, I'm home," he called out with a grin and a chuckle, loving having someone to come home to.

Her gaze shot to his, her smile blooming, brightening her gorgeous green eyes.

He wished he'd brought her flowers or something. He needed to do better, showing her how much he appreciated her, especially since they hadn't done the traditional dating things.

"Hey. I was just thinking about you."

He walked up behind her, kissed her neck, and stared down into the pot of homemade cheesy mac and cheese with chicken, bacon, and green onions. "That smells delicious." He rubbed his nose up her neck and into her hair. "And so do you." Strawberries and flowers. She went straight to his head, heart, and cock.

God, he wanted her. He slipped his hands around her waist and pulled her back to his chest, letting her feel the steel length of him against her amazing ass.

She rubbed her cheek against his jaw and pressed her hands to his forearms. "How was your day, honey?"

"Busy. One of the shipments went out late. Another had several cases stolen while it was being unloaded outside a posh bar in New York."

"I bet your customer was upset."

"Not really. I promised to replace what was stolen and add a case to keep him happy. The driver's the one who got reprimanded for leaving the truck unlocked."

"I bet he'll never do it again."

"If it happens again, he'll be out of a job." He hugged her hard, loving the feel of her in his arms.

She turned into him and rose up on tiptoes, kissing him softly. Sweetly. Temptingly.

Damn, she was potent. He took the kiss deeper, needing her close, so he could fill himself up with all her sunshine and goodness. All the tension from today melted away.

The mac and cheese started to bubble.

Lucky bit his bottom lip, then sucked it into her mouth, her eyes alight with mischief before she released him and turned in his arms, stirring dinner once again before it burned. "This is ready. Wash up and let's eat." She spooned the food into two deep bowls while he washed his hands at the sink. She pulled two plates out of the fridge, piled high with a fresh green salad.

The dinner table was set with silverware and two glasses of water.

He pulled a bottle of wine from the fridge and a bottle of beer. She loved the same Moscato Lyric liked when she visited.

He joined her at the table with the drinks while she set the dinner bowls at their places.

She stood next to her chair, looking up at him. "I hope you don't mind I didn't ask what you wanted for dinner."

He sat and stared at her seated next to him. "Why would I mind you making whatever you want for dinner? If you're cooking, it should be your choice. And you know I love everything you make." He glanced down at his bowl, took a big bite, and moaned. "So good. This is the best mac and cheese ever!"

She chuckled, taking a much smaller bite than his next one. "I used cheddar, like most people do, but I added some Gruyère and a little cream cheese to make it creamier. I added the chicken for protein, and bacon because...bacon."

He agreed. "What did you do today?"

"Cleaned one of my houses, then went back to the office to pay bills, check schedules, and talk to a very picky client who keeps asking for additional services while Julie is at the house, but doesn't want to pay for them."

"Did you straighten her out?"

"I told her if she wanted extra work done, she needed to notify us at least two days in advance. It also gives me a chance to let her know up front what the additional charge will be. It's all in her contract. She knows this. She's just persistent and stingy—never even gives a holiday bonus, which almost all our clients do."

He loaded his fork again. "For all you do...I should pay more." He stuffed the decadent goodness into his mouth and grinned at her.

"Well, I don't do that stuff for all my clients. You're special." The blush on her cheeks made her even more beautiful and endearing.

"Special, huh?" He covered her hand with his on the table. "Well, I think you're amazing. Strong. Independent. Smart. Kind." He stuffed another bite into his mouth. "The best cook ever," he said around the mouthful, making her giggle again.

"Slow down."

"Can't. It's too good."

"Eat your salad, too. It's good for you."

He swallowed and stared at her until the blush was back and she squirmed under his scrutiny.

"What? Why are you looking at me like that?"

He couldn't help the heat that flared between them. It happened whenever he thought about her, or was near her. "Because I love you. And I'm so happy you're finally here."

"Finally? I'd think by now you'd wonder when I'm going back to my place."

"Why?"

"Because I'm better. I'm not a hundred percent, but I'm close. I can take care of myself."

He shook his head. "No. Why would you want to go back to your place? Don't you like it here?"

"Yes. But this wasn't permanent. You just wanted to help when I was too hurt to do things on my own."

"No. That's not why I wanted you here." He raked his fingers over his head. "Well, it was an excuse to get you here, so you'd get to know me better, so you'd stay."

"Stay?"

"Yes." His frustration made the word come out clipped.

"I need to go home."

"It's not safe. You're staying here."

Her brow went up and he knew he'd made a mistake. "I know you're not making decisions for me, because I'm perfectly capable of doing that for myself. I've been on my own since I was seventeen and I've gotten by just fine."

He held back his desperate need to make her stay and shot from his heart. "I want you to stay. Please."

Her gaze softened on him. "Don't you think this is a little fast? Shouldn't we date first?"

"No. I like the way things are now. I thought you did, too."

She opened her mouth to say something, then closed it.

"You want to be with me, right?"

"Yes. It's just...this is too important to screw up."

"Is that what you're afraid of?"

Her eyes pleaded with him to understand. "Losing you? Yes."

He shook his head. "Never going to happen."

"Look at my life. It's a mess. I don't want it touching you anymore than it has. For all I know, Desiree could be plotting to take you out, just to make me suffer. And I would, because you're—" she choked up, "—everything good I ever wanted. If something happened to you..." She trailed off, tears in her eyes at the thought. "I wouldn't survive."

He cupped her cheek in his palm. "First, Desiree isn't coming after me. I'm too hard a target. She will not win that. Second, do you really think I'd let you go back to your place alone? Unprotected? Not a chance."

"I know she's coming. But it's not going to be easy for her to hurt me anymore. I'll be prepared."

"You can't even guess how she's going to come at you. It's better that we stick together. You want to stick it to her, show her how happy we are together. Let her see that there's no way she'll ever break us apart."

"You seriously want me to stay. Here. With you. Like move in?"

"This place is bigger than yours. We'll need room if you want to have kids. I do. I hope you do, too." There. He'd laid it all out there.

Her fork fell from her fingers and clanked on the bowl before tumbling onto the table, smearing cheese on the wood. Her shocked gaze never left his. "Hawk."

"Yes?"

"Are you serious? Like really serious?"

He sat back and smiled at her. "One hundred percent."

"Don't you think it's too soon?"

He leaned in to her. "Don't you think it's been a long time coming? I love you. You love me. I want to be with you all the time. I drove up to the house tonight, saw the lights on, knew you were home, and I was just so damn happy to see you. I want that every day."

"But we just started dating."

"Is that what we're doing? Because I thought it was more than that. I thought we were sharing our lives, working toward something much more permanent."

"Like babies."

His smile was back. He hadn't smiled this much in forever. "As many as you want."

Her face softened, her eyes filling with hope.

Yeah, he had her now. "You said you didn't want to be lonely anymore. I promised I'd be with you. So be with me. Let me take care of you. Let's have everything we ever wanted."

"A family." She'd lost hers and wanted to be part of another.

He could give her a new one. They could build one of their own. "Yes. Just say you'll stay." He held his breath, desperate for her to say yes.

"Your house *is* bigger than mine."

"*Our* house."

"And you're ready for me to bring my stuff here, to move in? To make this place my home."

"*Our* home. Because it's only that if you're here."

She picked up her fork. "Two. Maybe three." She lost him.

"What?"

"Kids." She stuffed a big bite into her mouth and chewed, a smile tugging at her lips and lighting her eyes.

His whole body sizzled with excitement. "Really? When?"

"How about we take care of Desiree, I move in for real, we spend some time really getting to know each other and learning to live together, then we go from there to having kids."

I need a ring, Hawk realized.

She deserved a kickass proposal.

She deserved a happy life. And he'd give it to her, or die trying.

"How about we celebrate you moving in with those amazing cupcakes you made?"

"After."

He raised a brow. "After what?"

"You take me to bed." She wiped her lips on her napkin, pushed her chair back, and started walking toward their room.

He jumped up, toppling his chair, picked her up bridal style and carried her into the bedroom. He tossed her onto the bed. She bounced with a laugh and he dove for her, locking his lips with hers, devouring her while joy lit him up inside because this beautiful woman loved him, broken pieces and all.

And didn't that make them a perfect match?

He took his time undressing her, kissing, licking, worshipping every patch of skin he uncovered. He kissed his way down her belly, thinking about her growing round with his child, then dove deeper to her mound, pressing a kiss there before lapping at her clit with his tongue.

"Hawk."

Oh, how he loved the way she moaned his name.

His impatient woman didn't let him linger too long as he tongue fucked her, loving the feel of her thighs pressing against his head as she held him by the hair, pulling him closer to her pussy as she ground against his mouth and went off like a rocket. He loved watching her come apart beneath him. But she was desperate for more and attacked his button and zipper on his slacks, her hand diving into his boxer briefs to clamp around his stiff cock.

"You look too damn good dressed up. It's like the best kind of porn seeing your sleeves rolled up over those defined forearms."

He chuckled. "You like my arms?"

"You have no idea." She pumped his cock and licked her lips like she wanted to devour him whole.

"I'll remember that." He shucked off his clothes, spread her thighs wide, and settled between them, the crown of his cock nudged right at her silky smooth, wet entrance. "You want me?"

"Yes. Please."

"You'll stay?"

"Promise."

"I'm going to hold you to it." He drove into her, hard and deep.

She was so wet, he slid home in one stroke, loving the feel of her wrapped around him. And then he lost himself, making love to her, kissing her, showing her with his body and whispered words that she was everything to him, too. He couldn't get enough. He wanted her every second of the day.

He wouldn't let anything or anyone come between them.

She deserved the family she wanted, the peace she'd been robbed of, the happiness and love she'd finally found with him.

No one would take that away from her.

He kissed her again and again, his tongue tangling with hers as she welcomed him into her body. Her heart. Her life.

He made love to her like it might be the last time, pouring his soul into her, hoping it was enough to make her feel safe and loved and cherished, because that's how she made him feel.

There was nothing he couldn't do with her by his side.

"Hawk," she gasped as her body tightened around his.

"Give it to me. Come."

Her channel quaked around him, and he followed her over the edge, pumping hard and deep to help extend her orgasm as he spilled his seed deep inside her. Maybe one day soon she'd stop her birth control and it would take root and they'd welcome a little girl or boy into their lives.

He wanted that as much as she did.

With one last kiss, he rolled over, taking her with him and settled on his back, Lucky tucked into his side, her head on his shoulder. "That was amazing."

She kissed his heated skin. "Yes. It was. Now I just need one more thing."

"What?" He couldn't imagine what she wanted from him after all the love he'd showered on her.

"Cupcakes." Her smile was contagious.

Chapter Twenty-Two

Seeing her ex shouldn't make her nervous, since she believed now that he hadn't killed her parents. Still...it had been a long time since they'd seen each other. She didn't know him anymore. He didn't know her.

Did he help Desiree dump her in that ravine?

He'd never been mean or vindictive. The only time she'd heard him threaten anyone was when he got angry about what her parents were doing to her. He'd only ever been kind to her.

Well, except when he cheated on her.

It just went to show that you never really knew someone.

Except Hawk seemed to be exactly who she'd always thought him to be. And so much more. He truly cared about her.

Which was why she was sitting on a purple couch in the children's section of a bookstore a half hour from closing halfway between her place and Neil's a town over. The place was practically empty. Which made it easy for her to spot Neil walking in the door, his head on a swivel as he clocked the clerk at the register and the three other customers roaming the stacks.

The second his eyes landed on her, he stopped in his tracks, his gaze sweeping over her from her long hair, down her simple sky blue tank dress with her cropped denim jacket over it, to her nude wedge sandals.

Hawk got one look at her after work, practically gaped at her before his eyes filled with heat and he asked if he could spin her toward the wall, press her hands against it, flip up her skirt, and fuck her into tomorrow. She'd given him a saucy smile, fought the heat welling inside her and the wetness dampening her panties, and simply told him, "Later."

He made her promise she meant it.

Right now, she dismissed the lust in Neil's eyes as he stared way too long for it not to be obvious that he still wanted her. Like he had any chance after betraying her.

She'd wasted all her efforts being a good girlfriend, loving him with her whole heart, only to be deceived by someone who swore they loved her back all while sleeping with someone she thought was her best friend.

It really hit her. The people closest to her always seemed to break her heart.

She felt Hawk's presence at her back, hidden by the stacks, where he kept out of Neil's sight. A sentry guarding her. Calm. Steady. But ready to help if Neil stepped out of line.

His devotion solidified the absolute faith she had in him that he truly loved her. He'd never hurt her. He'd never betray her. Instead, he took every opportunity to beg her to stay with him and showed her how much he meant it in his every word and deed.

She especially loved the dirty deeds she'd woken up to this morning. The things he'd do to her tonight when they got home.

It was almost like she could feel the love coming off him from his hiding spot.

She wanted to turn to him, go to him, let him wrap her in his arms and hold her and the world at bay. But she had to do this, to know that she was strong enough to put the past behind her and end this once and for all.

Neil snapped out of the trance he'd fallen into and walked the last few steps to her. She didn't stand to greet him. She didn't offer a smile. She simply said, "Sit," waving to the open seat beside her.

He sat too close.

She slid a good foot down the couch, keeping him in front of her.

"I repel you that much?" His voice had gotten deeper. His face had more lines. A scar slashed across his cheek to his temple. He'd filled out with more muscle, though he was still lean. The look in his eyes was one of want. "Man, I've missed you so damn much. I think about you every day."

Everything inside her buzzed with anxiety. "Then why did you help Desiree try to kill me?"

His eyes narrowed and his lips pressed into a deep frown. "Is that what she told you? Fucking bitch." He scrubbed both hands over his face. "That's not what happened."

"I remember seeing you at the bar. I was out of it, but I remember you coming in the back door and asking if you would get to see *her* now."

"I wasn't talking about you. I thought you were drunk off your ass."

"When have you ever seen me drunk like that?"

He leaned in. "I don't know you anymore. After all you've been through, I wouldn't blame you for checking out whenever the fuck you want. So, yeah, when I saw you, I just thought you'd had too much to drink and Desiree had, too. She called me that night and said she needed a ride home. I wanted to see…" He caught himself before revealing too much.

She already knew what he was going to say. "Krystal. Your daughter. Yeah. I know you were fucking Desiree behind my back and you got her pregnant."

He raked his fingers through the side of his hair. "I came here hoping we could put the past behind us and…I don't know…find a way to be friends again."

"After you dumped me naked down a ravine and left me for dead, asshole!"

He leaned in close. "I did not do that. She did. All I did was drive your car back to your place. I thought she took you inside and put you to bed, even though I was the one who wanted to take care of you that night and hopefully get a chance to apologize in the morning."

"Apologize! You killed my parents and Danny." She knew he hadn't but wanted to see what he said about it.

"I was never convicted of that." His gaze dropped to the floor.

"That's all you have to say after you sent me letters for months and tried to call me dozens of times from prison?"

His gaze met hers. "There are things you don't know."

"I know Krystal is yours. I know that you're a fucking liar and a cheat and you betrayed me again and again. How many times did you fuck her, then come to me acting like you loved me, like nothing happened?"

"It wasn't like that. I wasn't her willing partner. She fucking figured out I was stealing the drugs from the vet office where I worked and selling them. She threatened to turn me into her dad if I didn't cut her in on the business. So I paid her. Then, that wasn't enough. She hated how happy you and I were together. She wanted me and I told her no. I loved you. But she wouldn't fucking stop with the threats to turn me in or to tell you what I was doing. I didn't want you to know."

"Why? Why were you selling drugs? That didn't seem like something you'd do. At least that's what I thought at the time."

"I was doing it for us! It was quick cash. And a lot of it. I was saving up to take you away, to keep you safe."

"What?" She'd never once thought he'd been doing it to help her. "You put yourself and your future at risk for me?"

"Worth it to keep that motherfucker's hands off you."

"Even after I told you I couldn't leave without Danny?"

"I intended to take him with us. We'd find a small town somewhere in a distant state and we'd make a life, far away from your parents."

"We'd be fugitives."

He shrugged that off. "Who would blame us for saving Danny the same fate you'd suffered? I was happy to pay the price to save you both."

"Did Desiree know about your plan?"

"I had to tell her when she demanded I pay her off. I told her the money was for you and Danny. She didn't care. She said it would never happen, that you'd never leave her behind."

Lucky pressed her palms to her knees, reeling. "She hates me but she can't let me go."

"You're the only one who's stood by her all these years. I never understood why. She's such a bitch sometimes."

"It's a defense mechanism. *I'll hurt you before you ever get the chance to hurt me.*"

"Yeah, well, she fucked my life and has kept me from my daughter."

"Then help me take her down. I know the drugs that knocked me and my family out were most likely yours. I know Desiree was the one who killed them. I know she framed you, but you never threw her under the bus."

He shook his head. "Every time I thought I had the upper hand, she put me in my place."

"She got rid of the knife with your prints on it."

"Exactly. She set me up, then at the last minute saved me, but still let me go to jail for the drugs to keep me away from you."

"Did she steal the drugs from you that night, or before?"

Neil didn't look like he wanted to talk about it at all, but with her steady glare on him, he relented. "She showed up at my house after school around four and snuck in through my window like she always did...."

Neil was lying on his bed listening to music and reading The Great Gatsby. *He had to write a paper on it next week but couldn't get into the story. He heard the tap on his window and cringed. She was back and it pissed him off. He'd told her the last time, it was over. She didn't listen the time before that, or the one before that, or any other time he told her how much he hated deceiving Lucky.*

He loved Lucky. He wanted to be with her and only her. And every time Desiree showed up and coerced him into cheating on Lucky, he felt another piece of his heart break, his self-loathing rise, and the anger and frustration that built had nowhere to go because she had him by the balls.

"Hello, lover."

He hated when she called him that. There was no love between them. He didn't fuck her to make some kind of connection or because he wanted her. He did it to keep his secrets, so he could save his girl.

Lucky needed out. Now. She couldn't take much more of the abuse her father inflicted on her. Every bruise and cut, every putdown, every push and shove was tearing her broken pieces into pieces. She was always so sad and lost and desperate to keep her brother safe, fuck herself. He didn't like that. But he admired it.

Since the cops wouldn't help, he'd have to take matters into his own hands.

"I see you're brooding over Miss Perfect again."

"I'm not doing this with you anymore. It's not right. If she finds out, she'll be heartbroken. Not just because of what I've done, but because you did this to her, too." The argument was the same, and so was her answer.

"Then do what I want and she'll never find out." She crawled up the bed toward him, a smile on her lips that only revolted him. Her hands planted on his shins, then his thighs as she moved up his body.

"You're the fucking worst friend. All you do is fuck with people."

"Exactly. It's fun. And I want to have some fun with you." She palmed his flaccid dick, rubbing it up and down, trying to get a response from him. Though his brain and heart said, never going to fucking happen, *his dick rose to the occasion, happy to be pet.*

His stomach rolled as his own body betrayed him. Exactly what he deserved for doing this to the girl who stole his heart and loved him like no one else ever had.

She was so kind and pure.

He was an asshole with good intentions.

But that wouldn't matter if she found out. He could only hope she never learned what he'd done to save her.

Just a few more months until they graduated and he could take her away from here.

The second his dick was hard, she undid his button and zipper, pulling him free of the confines and putting her mouth on him. In normal circumstances, he'd be all for enjoying a girl's lips wrapped around his cock. But not this manipulative bitch.

He took her by the shoulders, and shoved her back. "Stop. I don't want this." He pulled his pants together, covering himself.

"Don't be like that. You know you want it. You're so hard, it's throbbing."

"A physical reaction doesn't mean I want it."

She sat back on his legs and stared at him for a few seconds, then stood and pulled her panties down her legs, kicking them off and right into his face.

He snatched the lace trimmed black cotton and tossed it right back at her. "Take those and leave. I'm not in the mood."

"I don't give a fuck. You know what I want and what will happen if you don't give it to me."

"Why are you doing this when you know I don't care about you, let alone like you?"

"You lie. Your dick tells me everything I need to know. The way you fuck me tells me you like it."

He hate fucked her every time. At some point, she'd push him to the breaking point and he'd slam into her, punishing her for making him cheat. For making him hate himself for giving in again and again. It had nothing to do with wanting to be with her. He hated her with every cell in his body.

"I only do this to save her *and you know it."*

Something dark came over her, like it always did when he pissed her off. "Why do you even bother? She's never going to leave without

Danny. And what? You're going to take him, too. Be a family? Raise him together? You think she'd really be happy stuck raising a kid, you two looking over your shoulders, living paycheck to paycheck?"

"It's better than watching her sink deeper and deeper into depression and despair. I hate the guilt I see in her eyes every time her dad manages to get past her to Danny. I hate seeing the defeat in her eyes when her dad hurts her again. I hate the way she can't look at me when I give her a compliment because her mother keeps tearing her down, one insult and gaslighting at a time. And instead of you trying to help me save her, you're here betraying her and forcing me to do something I don't want to do. It's fucking rape and you know it."

"And yet you can't help fucking my brains out on the regular. Complain all you want, but you love it. You want it. You just don't want to admit it."

"You are fucking delusional."

"Then go to the cops. Tell them I've been raping you. See if they'll do anything about it. See if they'll believe I could make you do anything against your will. You want this to stop, all you have to do is say no and mean it."

"And then you'll turn me in."

"I can't let you tarnish my reputation, now can I? I won't go down without taking you with me. You'll lose her. You'll lose everything. Your parents think you're the golden boy. What will they think when they find out you're just a low-life drug dealer, peddling that shit to kids?"

"I don't deal to kids." He still had some scruples.

"Whatever! You're ruining my plans for tonight."

"I'm sure you've got someone else on your hook. Go fuck with him and leave me alone."

"You're not being very smart about this."

"I'm tired of feeling like a fucking whore because of you. I don't want to touch you. I don't want you to touch me." He gripped his hair in both hands and tugged on it until it hurt and the pain replaced the ache in his chest.

Suddenly, something jabbed him in the thigh, pinching. He raised his head and stared as Desiree pushed the plunger on the syringe. Within seconds he felt the rush as the ketamine entered his system.

"Fuck. What did you do?"

"Just a little something to remind you I'm in charge. You don't get to play the white knight. You don't get her."

She backed up off the end of the bed. He tried to make a grab for her, but she shuffled out of his reach, then pushed him back onto his back and pillow as the drugs really took hold and sent him flying into euphoria.

He had a vague notion that she was in his closet, in his stash, but he couldn't do anything about it. He was too high. He vaguely hoped she hadn't administered an overdose or he'd be really fucked.

And that was the last truly coherent thought he had until he was shaken awake by the cops, being handcuffed, read his rights, and wondering what the fuck happened.

Lucky didn't know what to say and the silence between them stretched.

"I know you hate me. You have every reason to, but I want you to know it wasn't my choice to be with her. I never wanted her. She is so repulsive to me that even thinking about her, makes me want to vomit or punch something. I did what I did because I wanted to save you. All I did was fuck everything up."

"How many times did you have to…you know?"

"Nearly every fucking day for three months." He hung his head and put his hands over it, looking completely dejected and pissed with the stiff set of his shoulders and tightly laced fingers. Then his head came up and he met her gaze. "You know what really sucks?"

"All of it."

"Yes. But when I found out she was pregnant, I raged. Mostly because I didn't want my kid to have a mother like her. But also because I always wore a condom. Every damn time. I needed that barrier between us, thin as it was. It helped me mentally have some sort of distance, even though I was…intimately close to her. But about a week before the murders, she crawled through my window and I'd already worked myself into a good mad. I wanted to rage, but my parents were home and I didn't want them to find out what was going on.

"She gave me that damn smug smile and called me lover and I just lost it. I shoved her up against the wall, pulled down her leggings and panties, and I fucked her from behind, barely any of me touching her. It was punishing, without any kind of finesse. I just wanted to get it done fast without all the vitriol we went through every time she came over. I finished in a couple of minutes, not caring that she didn't get off. I never cared. Even though it often lit her up to know she was fucking your boyfriend." He scrubbed his face with his hands again. "That was how my daughter was conceived. It makes me so angry that she wasn't born out of love and that I hate her mother with a passion so strong that I don't know if she'll be able to see it on my face and know it's in my heart. But still, I want to see her. I need to see her. I can't stand the thought that she thinks I've abandoned her the way I abandoned you."

"You didn't really have a choice."

"I could have gone to her father. I could have found one of the cops she wasn't blackmailing."

"What? How do you know that?"

"She bragged about it. She had like four or five guys on the force under her thumb. How do you think she got away with so much shit?"

"Damn. Are they still in the department?"

"I'm sure they are, or she's got more of them on the hook."

Lucky needed time to think about that later. Right now, she needed to get the details on how her family was killed. "So she drugged you that night and left you in your room."

"Yes. The cops picked me up the next morning. I presume she gave her father some version of what my plan was to save you and used that against me."

"So she left your house, came to mine, drugged the glasses on the table my mother had set, waited for everyone to pass out, then slit their throats."

"And probably walked out smiling, a job well done. She'd saved her friend from being hurt ever again or from having to raise a kid."

"Something that sounds like she didn't want herself, but ended up doing anyway."

Neil shrugged. "I was surprised she kept the baby, to tell you the truth. Though now I see how much enjoyment she gets from keeping Krystal away from me."

"Can't you file for visitation?"

"I did, but she works in the courthouse and has the judge under her thumb. He keeps moving the court date. I don't think I'll ever get my case heard."

What the fuck!

Desiree had all the bases covered. She got away with everything, because she had connections in the sheriff's department, the courthouse, even a damn judge in her pocket. She wondered what Desiree had on the judge.

No wonder she always had money.

"How would you like to take her down with me?"

"You're never going to get her. There's no evidence. And even if there was, she'd just walk into the evidence locker and get rid of it like she did with the knife. Or worse, she'll plant evidence, send in one of the cops she owns to arrest me again. Or you."

"She tried to kill me."

"I had nothing to do with that. I wanted to come and see you when you were in the hospital, but I didn't think you'd want to see me. I was so worried. Are you okay now?"

"Yes."

"I hated to think about you alone in there."

"I wasn't alone. Hawk was with me."

"Hawk?"

"My...boyfriend. I'm living with him now after Desiree tried to burn down my cabin with me in it."

"What?"

"Yeah. It happened right after I got out of the hospital. I know she drugged me at the bar, then you came. What happened after that?"

"I demanded to see my daughter. She refused just like all the other times."

"What did she want you to do?" Lucky figured there was always some angle Desiree was playing with everyone.

"What she always wanted. For me and her to raise Krystal together. To show you that she took me from you and we had some happy life together."

Lucky couldn't even fathom her making that proposition to the man she'd blackmailed and raped. "Saying she has a screw loose doesn't even cover half the crazy she's got going on."

"Tell me about it. Which is why you're never going to prove she did anything."

"I don't need to prove it. I'm going to get her to confess."

Neil shook his head. "She's too smart for that."

"I think she wants to brag about what she's done to me. How she got away with it. How nothing and no one can touch her."

"She'll be suspicious as fuck. And a recording won't be admissible. Montana is a two party state. You'd be breaking the law if you recorded her without consent."

"I don't plan to record her, just to get her to confess in front of the right witness."

"You'll only get one shot at it. If she figures it out, you'll never get another chance."

"I know. But it's worth the risk. Either way, I'm going to get all of this out in the open between us. No more lies and manipulations. No more attempts on my life. I'll know she's coming and she'll know I'm expecting it and looking for any evidence to take her down."

"I'm happy to help in any way I can without breaking the terms of my parole. I can't go back. Not ever again." Pain and fear flashed in his eyes.

She couldn't imagine prison had been anything other than a nightmare for him. "Maybe we can use that to our advantage as well."

"I just want to end her reign of terror and have a real chance to be a part of my daughter's life."

"We're owed some real justice and I plan to get it one way or another."

Neil rested his forearms on his thighs and looked her in the eyes. "Are you happy?"

Her smile came so easily when she thought about Hawk. "Very. And it's all because I found someone who really cares about me."

Hawk and Lincoln stepped out from opposite sides of the shelves and closed in on her and Neil.

She smiled up at Hawk as he stood beside her, his hand on her shoulder. "This is Hawk, and his brother Lincoln."

"Watching her back, I see." Neil stood and held his hand out to Hawk. "I'm glad she has someone who puts her first."

"Always." Hawk shook his hand. "I thought you were the bad guy. Now I see you were trying your best to save her in a shitty situation."

"I put myself in that position. I was so focused on saving her, I didn't reach out to her to help save me." He looked down at her. "If I'd told you what Desiree was doing, we could have maybe stopped her together. At least then, you would have known what a terrible friend she was to you. It wouldn't have gotten you out of your situation, but maybe if we'd both gone to the sheriff's department, we could have found someone who would help."

"Her father knows I'm going to take her down. He's agreed to stay out of it and let me handle it. He has his own reasons for not doing it himself, but he won't stand in our way."

Lincoln closed their circle. "Are you sure you're really in? Because things could get dicey if she figures out what we're doing."

"She needs to be stopped. And I want her away from Krystal before my little girl starts acting like her mother, or worse, becomes her target."

Lucky couldn't let that go. "She's been really good with Krystal. Maybe not as lovey dovey as some moms, but she provides everything she needs. I've never seen her be mean or aggressive toward her. It's more that she does what needs to be done and not much else."

"Desiree is too self-centered to offer hugs and kisses and praise." Neil looked sick with worry for his daughter. "She needs more than the basics. She needs to know someone cares and loves her above all else."

"You can do that for her once we take down Desiree." Hawk brushed his hand down Lucky's hair, giving her comfort.

Neil caught the affectionate caress. His eyes filled with regret. "And how are we going to get one over on her? Desiree is one of the most manipulative people I've ever met. And I've been to prison."

Hawk rubbed his hands together. "We have a plan."

They all sat quietly on the purple couch in the children's reading section of the book store until closing. They talked through the basic plan, then went through every conceivable variable until they had everything worked out. At least they hoped so.

In the parking lot, Neil turned to her before heading to his car. "Thank you for giving me a chance to explain."

"I'm sorry I didn't give it to you sooner. If I'd opened one of your letters or taken one of your calls, I would have known how deceitful Desiree truly is and maybe I wouldn't have ended up nearly dead in a ravine."

Neil hung his head again. "If I'd told you back at the beginning the first time she pressured me into sleeping with her..."

She reached out and took his hand.

He gasped at the contact, his gaze coming up to meet hers, then look at their joined hands again. "I don't deserve this." He covered her hand with his free one and squeezed.

"I understand why you did what you did. I should have saved myself and Danny long before you were put in that position. I should have made the sheriff listen to me. I should have made him do his job. And if he wouldn't, I should have found someone who would. I don't know why Desiree took it on herself."

"To be your hero. To keep you close. I think the more people she had under her thumb, the more she realized how alone she was. She made everyone around her hate her because she used them up and spit them out."

"She deserves to be alone," Hawk added.

Lucky squeezed Neil's hand. "I just want you to know that you and I are square and I believe with my whole heart that you deserve to be with Krystal and she'll be lucky to have you for a dad."

"I really don't deserve your forgiveness."

"You have it anyway. Now forgive yourself for what you did, because your heart was in the right place."

"I tried, I really did, to get it right. I really wanted to keep you safe."

"I know."

Neil hooked his arm around her shoulders and pulled her into a hug. "I hope you have nothing but happiness from now on," he whispered in her ear. "Love you."

She squeezed him back. "Thank you for trying and loving me when no one else did." Well, except for her brother. But that was different.

Neil released her, avoided Hawk's death stare, and headed for his car.

Hawk pulled her close. "You okay, sweetheart?"

"I will be." She went up on tiptoe and kissed him.

Lincoln groaned. "If you two are going to be all kissy face, then I'm leaving. Catch you later."

Hawk broke the kiss and called out, "Thanks for coming."

"Always," his brother called back.

She smiled up at her man. "I love you."

"Love you more, sweetheart. Always. And I'll keep you safe and make sure you know every day that you're loved. Desiree's time in your life is just about up. Then you'll be free to be happy."

"That sounds like a plan, and I can't wait."

Chapter Twenty-Three

Lucky opened the door to her so-called best friend with a smile she hoped looked genuine and a heart that broke at the sight of the little girl she thought of as a niece.

"Aunty Lucky!" Krystal barreled into her legs and wrapped her little arms around Lucky's thighs.

Lucky choked back tears and hugged the little girl to her, kissing her on the head. "I've missed you so much, munchkin."

"Did you make bow-nies?" So cute.

Desiree walked in and looked around the room. "Where's your hunky man?"

"Getting ready to leave for work at search and rescue."

"He's leaving you home alone on a Saturday?"

"He loves his job."

Hawk needed it. It gave him a sense of satisfaction and purpose. She wouldn't take that away from him.

"I'd think you two lovebirds would want to stay cuddled up in bed on a Saturday morning."

They'd made love practically all night into the early morning. She was concerned Hawk hadn't gotten enough sleep to fly his helicopter. He woke up assuring her he was fine and last night had invigorated him. He'd kissed her before his shower with the same passion he'd shown all night. The man was insatiable and she loved it.

"By the look on your face, I'd say you two are getting along well."

Lucky turned Krystal toward the dining room table where crayons and a coloring book awaited her. Krystal ran for them, giving her and Desiree a chance to talk more privately. "We are. He asked me to move in permanently." She didn't much feel like confiding anything in Desiree, knowing what she knew now, but that was something she'd share with a best friend.

"Of course you're going to do it. You can't pass up an offer like that! It's the best one you'll ever get."

She took offense, tired of Desiree always putting her down. "What does that mean?"

Desiree gave her a look that rang with stupid. "The man loves you. What better offer could you get?" Nice save. "Mind if I use the restroom before I go? It's a long drive."

"Where are you going? You never said. Hot date?" She waggled her eyebrows.

"I wish. You never did get me that date with the other hot Gunn brother, even though you have the inside track."

"He meant it when he said he wasn't dating right now. He's stuck on someone else. And you don't want someone who loves someone else." Like Neil had loved her while Desiree had manipulated and coerced him into doing things she was sure he'd never get over. "It would be heartbreaking to be someone's second choice." Okay, maybe she was being a little mean. And obvious. But she'd earned it.

Desiree couldn't hide the moment of hatred that flashed in her eyes before she banked it. "I always get what I want eventually. And when I don't..." She shrugged. "You know me. I don't wait around for something to happen. I make it happen."

She made others miserable. She used people, blackmailed them, coerced, and corrupted. Everything was about her and what she wanted. It made Lucky enraged and sick. She wouldn't stand for it ever again.

"And what are you making happen today?"

"Nothing really. Just a few overtime hours at the office. It's hard being a single parent. Krystal is growing like a weed and needs new clothes, plus her daycare went up. Again."

"Has the father stepped up to help you at all? Maybe it's time to reach out to him and make him pay his fair share."

Desire stepped closer. "That will never happen. She's mine. No one is taking her from me."

Lucky put on her most sympathetic face and played devil's advocate. "Maybe Krystal would benefit from having her father in her life. You're so close to your dad. Maybe she'd like being with her dad, too, having that sense of security that he's looking out for her. And you."

Poor Krystal. She deserved a chance to know the man who really wanted to be a part of her life. And probably would be soon. Especially if Lucky could get the evidence and confession she needed from Desiree.

"There's nothing between us anymore. I don't want anything to do with him." Desiree wrinkled her nose.

Because he doesn't want anything to do with you either?

"Anyway, the restroom is the second door on the left down that hall." Lucky pointed to the hallway between the kitchen and dining area.

She waited until Desiree closed the door, then dug through the purse she'd left on the console table behind the couch, keeping an eye on the hallway and Krystal at the table. Desiree's phone was locked and Lucky didn't know the passcode. She rifled through receipts, two candy bars, a makeup bag that didn't have anything damning in it, and a small black notebook with a strap holding it closed.

She opened the book, but didn't understand the letters and numbers and dates. It didn't matter right now. She held up her phone and started taking pictures as fast as she could. Page after page.

Hawk caught her in the act. "What are you doing?" he whispered.

She tried not to get distracted by the dark gray t-shirt stretched across his chest and around his biceps, or the way his thighs pressed against his pants. Not to mention that package behind his fly. No. She clicked away.

"She's coming," he whispered.

One last click, then she closed the book, secured the strap around it, stuffed it in the purse, then went up on tiptoe to kiss Hawk, saying against his lips, "Push the purse off the table."

Hawk didn't waste time and hooked one hand around her waist, palming her ass. The other moved to do the same, but he "accidentally" hooked his hand through the strap and made it fall, spilling all its contents at their feet. Hawk didn't stop kissing her for a second, just pressed his hand to her lower back and pulled her in closer.

She got lost in the kiss, until Desiree squatted behind her and slapped the back of her thigh. "Do you mind?"

It wasn't hard to fake her surprise or the sting she inflicted when Desiree pushed her aside. "Hey. Oh. Sorry. I didn't realize that happened. Let me help you." She sank to her knees and grabbed the book off the floor.

Desiree snatched it out of her hands. "I've got it." She shoved the book, her wallet, and phone into her bag. "I need to get going. Be back in a couple of hours." Desiree headed to the door without even saying goodbye to Krystal. She opened the front door and gasped.

Standing on the threshold, Neil's hand was raised as if he'd been about to knock.

Right on time. "Neil." His name came out with a made up hint of anger and surprise. She had to play this just right. Like they hadn't seen each other since the night before he'd been arrested. "What are you doing here? How did you know I live here?"

His gaze shifted from her back to Desiree. "I followed you here. I didn't know whose house it was. I want to see my daughter."

Desiree froze, then slowly looked at Lucky.

"What is he talking about?" she asked her so-called friend. "Why would he say that to you?"

Desiree rolled her eyes. "You were always so oblivious."

Lucky narrowed her gaze, cool calculation filling her heart. "You slept with my boyfriend?"

Desiree seethed. "I don't have time for this. Yes. We fucked. A lot. He's going to tell you some bullshit that he didn't want it, but the truth is he did, otherwise he wouldn't have done it over and over and over again." She glared at Neil, then turned back to her. "I did you a favor. He could have been your forever, instead he cheated and ended up in jail, nothing but a drug dealer and murderer."

Neil defended himself. "That guy came at me. It was self-defense. I didn't want to hurt anyone. I had no choice. I wasn't even charged."

Desiree rolled her eyes. "Always an excuse for his bad behavior. You don't need that in your life. You've got Captain America now. Helicopter pilot, hero, successful business owner. He's not just gorgeous, he's rich. You hit the jackpot. Be happy. Stirring up shit in the past will only make things worse. Let it go."

"Forget that you stabbed me in the back, that you got pregnant with Neil, and I'm just supposed to drop it, just like that?"

"I'm telling you not to go down this road. It won't end well for you."

"Did you just threaten her?" Hawk moved in front of Lucky, blocking her from Desiree.

"See. That right there. Everyone's always trying to protect you, while I'm scrambling to hold on to what little I have."

This was Lucky's opening. "You want help? Then ask your baby-daddy to step up and do his share. Let him take some of the responsibility."

"Krystal is *mine*."

"She's mine, too," Neil snapped. "I deserve a chance to prove I can be a good father."

Desiree cocked her hip and planted her hand on it. "You couldn't even be faithful to your girlfriend. How do I know you won't run out on your daughter?"

"I would never abandon my child."

"No. Just her mother. For another woman."

Neil threw up his hands and let them drop back to his sides. "We're not even together anymore, thanks to you."

"You mean you," Desiree shot back.

Neil leaned into her face. "How about I tell her the real story?"

Desiree didn't back down. "You want visitation. You know what you need to do." Desiree turned back to her. "He is not allowed near Krystal. I have full custody and need to be somewhere."

"And you expect me to watch her after the bomb you dropped on me?"

"Yes. Because you love her like she's yours. And no matter what's happened, I'm still the best friend you ever had."

"With friends like you, I don't need enemies. You knock me down enough."

Desiree fisted her hands. "I can't do this with you right now."

Lucky caught Krystal staring at them wide-eyed and pale at the table. This wasn't the time to finish this. "Fine. Then you and Neil will meet back here tomorrow at two and we'll hash this out."

Neil folded his arms in front of him, blocking the exit even more. "Fine. Maybe you can talk some sense into her, so she'll let me see my daughter."

Desiree huffed. "I'm leaving and so are you. Tomorrow we'll talk about the dirty little secret you kept from the woman you supposedly loved more than anything, including me." Desiree shoved Neil out the door and slammed it behind her.

Suddenly, Lucky felt tiny hands wrap around her leg from behind. She turned and put a hand on Krystal's back.

"Is he really my dad?"

She couldn't lie, or leave Krystal in the dark. Her mother lied and withheld the truth long enough. "Yes, honey. His name is Neil and he very much wants to see you."

"But Mommy said no."

"She did. But I'm going to fix that tomorrow. I promise." She hoped nothing kept her from keeping that promise.

Hawk squatted next to Krystal. "In the kitchen you'll find a cupboard door next to the dishwasher. Open it and you'll find something special."

"Really?"

"Yes." Lucky brushed back Krystal's hair and kissed her on the forehead. "Uncle Hawk picked up some treats just for you."

"Thank you, Uncle Hawk."

He smiled at the little girl. "You're welcome. I'll keep it stocked for when you come visit. That will be your special cupboard."

Krystal ran to the kitchen.

Hawk cupped Lucky's cheek. "I hate to rush off after all that, but I'm due at work in half an hour and it's a twenty-five-minute drive."

"It's fine. We got what we wanted. A meeting tomorrow."

"What about that book?"

"I'm going to send the pics to Mason and see what he thinks. I'm hoping it's proof of her blackmail."

"We'll see if Jase discovers anything today while he tails Desiree."

"I hope so. Do you think the scene with her, me, and Neil made her suspicious?"

"It didn't seem that way, but we'll find out either tonight when she picks up Krystal or tomorrow when she shows up to talk about the past."

"Nothing she can say is going to make what she did any better. But if she confesses to nearly killing me, I'll be happy to see her behind bars."

Hawk kissed her like he'd never get to do it again. "I don't think she'll do anything with Krystal here, but keep sharp. Don't let her get you alone. Don't let her out of your sight. I'll try to be back before she gets here."

"Until then, I'll set the alarm and be anxiously awaiting your return."

Hawk kissed her one more time, then squatted again to say goodbye to Krystal, who'd found a berry applesauce fruit pouch and a bag of fish crackers. "Be good for Auntie Lucky. I'll see you later."

"Bye, Unc." Krystal slurped up more berry applesauce.

Hawk stopped in his tracks and stared at the little girl, his heart in his eyes as he turned to her. "Wow. That was…" He didn't have to say it. She could see it in his eyes. He was so humbled to be someone Krystal called family. "Are we doing the right thing?"

"Yes. Or do we give her another shot at me?"

Hawk shook himself out of the love bomb Krystal dropped on him, his gaze narrowing. "Sorry. I got caught up in how sweet Krystal is."

"I don't blame you. I want that little girl to have the best of everything. But there's one person in her life who may not always see her as innocent and untouchable." And it broke Lucky's heart to think that, let alone say it out loud.

Hawk kissed her one last time, the look in his eyes telling her he loved her and hated to leave her. Then he walked out the door, ready to rescue someone else when the call came in that someone needed him.

Her hero.

And then Lucky was alone with her niece, her simmering rage, and a plot to take down Desiree once and for all.

Chapter Twenty-Four

Hawk was doing a preflight check on the helicopter, making sure it was ready if the search and rescue team got a call today. With the weather getting warmer, there were more hikers, climbers, and mountain bikers out on the trails. Anything could happen, from a fall, to someone getting lost.

His phone buzzed with an incoming text. He pulled it out and glanced at the picture of the district attorney standing in front of what looked like an open motel room door meeting a young blonde, who had to be at least a decade younger than the married man.

He'd bet every penny in his bank account that wasn't his wife.

His phone rang with Jase's name and number on the caller ID. "Someone's being naughty today."

Jase chuckled under his breath. "So I followed Desiree from your place to this motel. She went to the front desk, had a brief conversation with the clerk, handed over some cash, got the key, then went into the room with what looked like a gift bag and stayed for less than five minutes before she came out with the bag. When she went in, the bag was pristine. Coming out, a little less so. Then she got in her car at the back of the lot and waited. Half hour later, the blonde showed up, got a key from the clerk, then went into the same room. I thought maybe Desiree was going to meet her. Maybe they had something going, but Desiree stayed in her car. Ten minutes later, I see a man crossing the busy road between the sports park and the motel. As he crossed the lot headed straight for room 108, I got a good look at him."

"I wonder if his wife knows he's cheating on her."

"I wonder if the twelve-year-old daughter he dropped off at softball knows he's not watching her play and instead is getting his willie wet across the street with a woman who's probably her babysitter."

Hawk shook his head and tried to think. "So Desiree is there to blackmail the asshole district attorney, so she'll have him in her pocket along with the judge she's already squeezing."

"That's my guess. My other guess is that the bag she carried in held some sort of recording devices."

Hawk rubbed his hand over the back of his neck. "Damn. How'd she know about the guy meeting up with the woman?"

"I'm guessing this isn't the first time. She probably tailed him a couple of times, figured out he's cheating, and set this up today."

"She's resourceful, that's for damn sure."

"Exactly. I'll bet she's watching them from in her car, recording everything."

"He's going to get the surprise of his life when she confronts him. He'll lose his wife and career if she decides to out him."

"Which means he'll pay whatever she wants to keep her quiet."

"Depends on how ruthless and motivated he is to shut her up."

"She's been doing this long enough to know how to stay one step ahead of her targets. Her father is the sheriff. That alone gives her some leverage."

"Are you going to stay on her today?"

"Yep. I can't wait to see what she does next. This shit is mind-blowing. After all she's done to her best friend...I wouldn't put anything past her at this point. She meant to kill Lucky by dumping her in the middle of nowhere."

"She's ruthless." Hawk secured his pack in the back of the helicopter and waved his teammates over so they could do some last minute prep. "She's not getting Lucky alone ever again."

"I've got eyes on her now. I'll call Damon once I follow her back to your place when she picks up her kid."

Hawk was happy to have his younger brother home, and that he and Lucky would finally meet. "Damon will stay with her until I get home. Tomorrow, we end this."

"I can't wait. I hope it goes to plan."

"You and me both. Thanks for helping like this. I know it's your job, but it still means a lot. She's strong, but enduring this is taking a toll, especially now that she knows Desiree betrayed her with Neil. Lucky's a good friend to have on your side. Desiree never appreciated that."

"There's something not quite right with that girl."

"Understatement of the year." Hawk held up a finger to let Kash, Pete, and Bryce know he'd be ready to go on patrol in just a minute.

They loaded their gear and got strapped in, ready to do some training maneuvers.

"Call if anything comes up. I'll be flying some, so I may not be able to respond. Cell coverage is spotty out here. Anything urgent, you can use the SAR dispatch to get me."

"Got it. Are you going to update Lucky?"

"Yeah, as soon as I get home. I don't want to keep anything from her. She needs to know everything, including what kind of person

Desiree truly is. She'd hate what Desiree is doing to other people just as much as what she's done to her."

"I've never met anyone as truly nice as Lucky is, even after what she's endured. I'm glad she has you."

Hawk savored the knowledge that Lucky was his. Now and forever. "We let this thing between us grow over the last couple of years. Now...I can't imagine my life without her in it. Tomorrow can't come soon enough. We'll end this once and for all and she'll be free to live her life without looking over her shoulder."

Chapter Twenty-Five

Lucky answered the doorbell with Krystal by her side and Damon at her back. He'd been such a big help today, keeping her and Krystal company, playing with her pseudo niece, and making her feel safe, knowing she'd have to face her nemesis again, while she pretended not to know everything she knew now. She'd enjoyed his company and getting to know Hawk's brother. He was definitely the easy-going one, ready with a smile and one humorous or disastrous story about his travels after another.

Hawk would be home in another hour for dinner with them. He couldn't wait to see Damon, too.

Jase had texted that Desiree was on her way back about ten minutes ago after she'd finished gathering her blackmail on the district attorney.

Lucky's stomach turned at the thought of her going out of her way to ruin people's lives like it was nothing but an errand.

She opened the door and held up Krystal's backpack. "I fed her lunch. She's ready for dinner."

"I have my own snack cupboard," Krystal announced.

Desiree didn't respond to her child. Her eyes were glued on the Gunn brother behind Lucky. "Well, well, well, looks like the wandering Gunn is back. And looking really fine."

Damon's gaze shot to Lucky's. "You were right."

Lucky smirked at her new friend. "Told you."

"What the hell is going on?" Desiree planted her hands on her hips and glared at both of them.

Lucky stared down her "friend." "I told Damen when you saw him here he'd be the only thing you focused on and that you'd flirt with him, shamelessly, even though you pretend to be only interested in Lincoln. Or Hawk. Really it's any of them because you don't really care as long as you get the guy, even if he's with someone else."

"Jealous?"

"No. Furious that my friend"—she made air quotes—"betrayed me."

"What's going on?" Krystal stared up at all the adults.

Lucky reined in her fury. "Sorry, sweetheart. Your mom and I had a disagreement. We're going to talk about it tomorrow and sort everything out."

Damon squatted next to Krystal and kissed her on the head. "Thanks for hanging out with me and kicking my butt at Candy Land. I haven't had that much fun in a long time."

"I could fix that for you." Desiree had no shame, even after what she'd just said about them being in an argument.

"Mama, when can I see my dad again?"

Desiree lost her smile and glared at Lucky. "I don't know. I need to work some things out with him and your aunt tomorrow. Then, we'll see."

"I want to see him and talk to him. Maybe he'll play games with me, like Damon. Maybe he's nice, too." Krystal looked up at Damon. "You'd be a really great dad."

Stunned, Damon's eyes went wide, and then a huge smile broke on his face. He picked up Krystal and held her to his chest, so they were eye to eye. "That's the nicest thing anyone has ever said about me, munchkin. I would be the happiest dad on the planet to have a little girl like you."

Krystal beamed, wrapping her arms around Damon's neck and hugging him tight.

Damon's eyes shined with unshed tears before he blinked them away and set Krystal back on her feet. "You're really special. Never forget that."

"Can I come back and play tomorrow, Aunt Lucky?"

"No," Desiree cut in. "You're with grandpa tomorrow while Lucky and I figure some things out."

"You never let me do what I want to do. Everything always has to be your way."

Lucky understood Krystal's frustration and the absolute truth in her words.

Desiree took Krystal's hand. "Come on." She pulled Krystal out the door, calling over her shoulder, "We'll hash it out tomorrow, and then let it go."

Not this time.

Lucky closed the door, hoping everything went as planned.

Krystal deserved better.

Desiree deserved to get what was coming to her.

And Lucky wanted to be free from Desiree's brand of friendship, so she could fully embrace her new life. With Hawk. His family. Soon to be her family, she hoped.

Chapter Twenty-Six

Lucky opened the door and the knots in her stomach loosened just a little at the sight of the big man standing in front of her with his arm wrapped around his pregnant wife. "Mason. Lyric. So good to see you both again. Please come in. Hawk will be out in just a moment."

Mason walked in, hooked his free arm around her neck and pulled her close so he could hug and kiss her on the forehead.

She kind of loved their little ritual of riling each other up by kissing each other's women. "You know Hawk's going to get you back for that."

"Like he hasn't already kissed my wife a thousand times."

Lyric rolled her eyes and came in close to hug Lucky. Lyric's even bigger baby bump pressed to her stomach and Lucky felt a pang of envy.

Maybe someday she and Hawk would hold their baby, too. Soon. Ish.

They still needed time to settle into life together, though there was no doubt she loved him like crazy and wanted to be his forever.

One thing at a time, even if she wanted it all at once. With him.

Today was about letting go of the past and exposing all the secrets that had kept Lucky afraid and Desiree in control too long.

"I'm sorry for the reason we're here, but I'm so happy to see you again." Lyric pulled out of the hug. "How are you holding up?"

"I'm okay. Even if I can't get Desiree to confess to trying to kill me, we have enough evidence of her blackmail scheme to put her in jail. At least that's something."

Mason put his hand on her shoulder, and she was proud of herself for not flinching.

Mason squeezed, letting her know he was offering comfort. "With the information Jase sent me yesterday, I was able to secure warrants for Desiree's devices. I'm betting there's even more incriminating evidence on them."

Lucky felt even surer that Desiree would pay for her crimes and treachery. "Thank you for helping with this."

"My pleasure. You're family. And besides, she has a judge, the DA, and who knows how many others in law enforcement in her pocket. You need federal help, since the locals are compromised."

"Do you think the plan will work?"

"Since I don't spend a lot of time here, and the family doesn't talk about me or my job, she won't know I'm FBI unless someone tells her. All you have to do is goad her into bragging about how she did it and got away with it."

"I think she really hates me and wants me to know everything she's done that makes her smarter and better than me."

"Sometimes the people we let close turn out to be the people who hurt us the worst. She's resentful, jealous, and has a sense that you have what she wants. Instead of being happy for you, she wants to knock you down so that she feels better about herself."

"There's nothing I have that she can't have herself."

"Really?" Lyric asked. "Because you have a really great guy who loves you. She doesn't have that. In fact, she tried to steal that from you with Neil, but instead of him loving her more, he doubled down that he'd never stop loving you."

"I think that's what sent her over the edge and why she killed my family."

Mason's eyes filled with sympathy. "I'm surprised she didn't kill Neil that night, too."

Lucky hadn't considered that. "I think she really cared about him. At least enough to let him live, even if she did make sure he went to prison."

"Right. But not for killing your family," Lyric pointed out. "She wanted him to get out. Maybe she hoped they'd finally be a family with their little girl."

"She refused to let him see her."

"Maybe she's been waiting for him to make a move on her, to prove he's not just there for their child, but her, too."

Lucky didn't know what was in Desiree's twisted mind anymore.

Hawk came out of the bedroom looking yummy in a pair of worn black jeans, a black tee stretched across his shoulders and biceps, and a smile for her and their company. His hair was still damp, his feet bare. He had big, manly feet to match his hands, the nails clipped short.

Like always, he kissed her with a sweet brush of his lips against hers. "You doing okay?"

"I'm fine," Lucky assured him again. "I'm ready for anything today."

He cupped her cheek. "I know you are. That doesn't mean it's going to be easy."

"Nothing in my life has been easy. Except you."

"That's because he wants to be your sex slave," Mason teased.

Lucky laughed when Hawk glared at his cousin, then looked at her like she was his everything and nodded his agreement. She reassured him, "You're more than that to me and you know it."

"I'll be whatever you need me to be." He kissed her again like no one was watching, right in front of his family.

"I could use a drink," Mason announced. "Let's leave the lovebirds alone for a few, angel."

Lucky heard Lyric giggle as Mason led her away.

Hawk let her up for air and brushed his nose against hers. "I love you. Everything is going to work out today. And even if it doesn't, Desiree will face the consequences of her actions. At least the ones we can prove."

"I know. It's going to be fine and I'll finally be free."

"Lunch?" he asked to distract her.

"I've got it all ready and in the fridge."

They joined Mason and Lyric in the kitchen. Lucky set out the chicken pesto pasta and crusty bread. Everyone served themselves a bowl, then took a seat at the table. Hawk had prepared a strawberry peach cocktail that was light and refreshing, and a glass of limeade for Lyric.

They chatted about life since they'd all seen each other last. She and Lyric talked about her upcoming baby shower while the guys talked about the game they caught last night.

It was wonderfully normal, even though they were all just killing time until Neil and Desiree arrived.

Hawk got the text from Jase right after they finished eating a slice from the double chocolate cake she'd made this morning just to keep busy. He held up his phone so she could see it.

JASE: Desiree ETA 10. I'll stick close in case you need back-up.

Lucky's heart sped up. "She'll be here soon."

Like he'd heard her, Neil rang the bell.

"I'll get it." Lucky hadn't even gotten out of her seat when Hawk rose and put his hand on her shoulder to keep her in place.

"I'll get it just in case."

"In case of what?" she asked.

"I don't know. But I'm not putting you in harm's way any more than I have to."

She wanted to roll her eyes, but maybe he had a point.

Hawk checked the peep hole, turned off the alarm, then opened the door. "Open your jacket and turn in a circle so I know you're not armed."

"Armed," Neil scoffed. "Dude. You're paranoid. I'm on parole."

"Just do it," Hawk instructed again.

Neil must have complied because a moment later, Hawk opened the door wide enough for him to come inside. The second Neil spotted her, he walked forward. "Lucky." Her name sounded like a prayer. "I can't believe this could all be over today."

"We'll see." She rose and met him by the table.

He looked like he wanted to hug her, but held himself back.

Hawk had no trouble hooking his arm around her waist and planting his hand on her hip. "Did your parole officer agree to come?"

"Yes. He said he'll leave his car down the road a bit, then walk in and wait out back like you instructed."

Hawk let her go and opened the window closest to the deck out back. "Are you going to be able to keep your cool?"

Neil nodded. "I know what I have to do. For Lucky. For me. For my daughter."

"Good." Hawk stared toward the front of the house. "Because she's here." Hawk checked his phone as a text pinged again. Had to be Jase alerting them to Desiree's arrival.

Lucky turned to Mason. "You ready?"

"Do your thing," he encouraged her.

Lucky headed for the door to answer the bell. Hawk was right behind her.

Desiree stood on the porch, her hands behind her back, face a mask of composure.

Lucky waved her in. "I'm glad you came. It's in Krystal's best interest to have her father in her life."

"Why? It wasn't in your best interest to be with your father," Desiree shot back.

"Neil is nothing like my father."

"He betrayed you. Again and again and again." Her voice grew breathy, like she was remembering their intimate time together. Or simply trying to stick it to Lucky.

Lucky's stomach churned.

Desiree zeroed in on Mason and Lyric canoodling in the kitchen. "Who are they?"

Hawk chimed in. "That's my cousin and his wife. They just arrived for a family visit. Kind of a babymoon before the baby arrives. Don't worry about them. They're always in their own little world."

Lucky held her arm out toward the couch. "Sit. Let's talk about the bomb that got dropped yesterday and about Neil seeing his daughter."

Desiree sauntered past Neil, a gleam in her eyes. "He's not her father. He's the deadbeat drug dealer who knocked me up. That's all."

Lucky snagged Desiree's wrist and halted her. "Don't be like that. We can have a civilized conversation. Can't we?"

"I don't think you're going to like what comes to light. Like how your boyfriend used to fuck me hard and deep, like he couldn't get enough."

Neil brushed past Desiree and took a seat on the couch furthest away from the window. "How about you tell her that you had to blackmail me into sleeping with you at all and how every time I begged to get out of it." He gave her an insincere smile. "Every. Time. Because I didn't want you. I loved *her*."

Lucky and Hawk took the chairs across from the couch, leaving Desiree the far spot on the couch with her back to the kitchen and dining area where Mason and Lyric were still pretending no one else existed but them. Not that Desiree could see them now. She was too focused on her and Neil.

Lucky steered the conversation. "Why won't you let Neil see Krystal, spend time with her?"

"Because she's mine. He doesn't deserve to see her after he left us."

Neil scoffed. "Left you? Seriously? I went to jail because you set me up."

Desiree laughed. "Are you still high on what you stole?"

Neil leaned toward her. "I never used the drugs I stole. But you did."

Desiree sneered, keeping the bravado going. "I did not."

"You had access to them every time you came to my house and crawled through my window, looking to fuck me and fuck over your best friend. That night, I turned you down. For good. I wasn't going to take it anymore. *You* drugged *me*, because I hated you and wanted her."

Desiree exploded. "You deserved it! You pissed me off. We had something good and you had to mess it all up. Why couldn't you see that?"

Lucky couldn't believe this was actually working.

Neil's eyes glowed with victory. "Right. You drugged me. So how did I kill Lucky's family? How did my fingerprints get on the knife?"

Desiree seemed to catch herself and clammed up.

Lucky came in for the kill. "Desiree, answer the question. If you drugged him...Did you do it for me?" She tried to make it sound like she'd appreciate it, but feared her revulsion leaked through.

"Of course I had to do it! This lame-ass didn't have the balls. He kept stalling, making excuses. You were going to be dead at your father's hand before he did anything to stop it."

"So you did it to save me?" Lucky wanted there to be something good inside Desiree.

Desiree shook her head. "You are so much like *him*. Always wanting to help. Always nice. Always wanting me to be good, be better. That's what my mother wanted. For me to be like *you*. Like *him*. I wasn't supposed to know. But I overheard them talking. Mom heard you screaming. Again. *He* wanted to do something. *He* couldn't stand it anymore. Knowing and doing nothing about it, because you were *his*."

Lucky couldn't seem to process what Desiree was saying. It couldn't be. Desiree was lying again.

"Mom warned him that if he went over there and interfered, it could all come out. Then your dad would really want you dead, because my father was your father."

The whole room seemed to freeze in silence.

Lucky's heart pounded against her ribs, making it hard to catch her breath. *Oh God.* This was so much worse than she thought.

Desiree looked so pleased to drop that bomb and distract them from what she'd done. "You're so stupid. Didn't you ever wonder why our parents pushed us to be friends so hard? We're sisters. Once you know, it's not that hard to see it either. We both take after our moms, for the most part, but we both have his nose and chin and the arch of our eyebrows."

Lucky stared at Desiree's face, trying to see the similarities but her mind just wanted to shut that down. It couldn't be true.

Sheriff Collins was her father.

And he abandoned her to a monster.

Desiree shrugged and kept spilling her guts. "I don't know how it happened. I just know it did. So when he caught me in your house that night..." Her gaze sharpened and filled with rage. "He wouldn't let me finish the job. Because he loved *you*. Because *you* were his. He told me that once he was gone, all I'd have left is my dear sister. You'd be the one to stick by my side like you always had. I didn't want to give Neil back to you. I didn't want to share him with you anymore. But we were sisters and that meant I had to choose you. And then when I found out about Krystal, I realized Daddy was right. I did need you. And if something ever happened to me, Krystal would need her aunt. So I let go of my anger and I tried to be your friend. But you make it so infuriating! You can't do anything right. Look at how you botched getting me and Lincoln together."

"He doesn't want to date anyone right now," Lucky said, because that was the truth and not her fault and her brain knew that for sure when everything else felt like a scrambled mess in her head.

"Right. He's got it bad for someone else. Story of my life. Neil wants you. Guys in the bar are always looking past me at you. Hawk, a guy who's so far out of your league...you show him those puppy dog eyes all filled with tears, boo-hooing that your life is so hard, and he falls at your feet."

Hawk leaned forward, his forearms on his thighs. "Watch it. I won't let you disrespect Lucky in her own home."

Desiree rolled her eyes. "I guess you like the pathetic ones."

"You're the one desperate for attention. She stayed your friend all these years, trying to make your life a little bit better along the way. But you...you just tear her down because you know you'll never be even half as good as her." Hawk's words touched Lucky so deeply her heart overflowed with the love she had for him.

Lucky met her sister's hostile gaze. "Why did you kill Danny?"

"Daddy always said I should be a helper. Do good things. Putting you all out of your misery was a mercy killing. I wasn't sure I could do it, but after your parents, it was so damn easy."

"And not the first time."

Desiree grinned. "You think you know all my secrets, don't you?"

"Why not get it all out in the open?" Lucky taunted. "You said it yourself. Your mother always compared you to me. That had to infuriate you."

"I hated it! Why did I have to be like you? We are who we are. I just wanted her to see *me*, instead of always worrying about *you. Poor Lucky has it so bad. She doesn't deserve that.*" Desiree fisted her hands and let out a frustrated huff. "*She* didn't do anything about it. She kept Daddy from doing anything about it, because she was afraid your crazy ass father would retaliate against them. Your own mother refused to leave the bastard, afraid that if he found out you weren't his, he'd kill her. And you."

Lucky's heart sank. "That was definitely a possibility."

Desiree seethed. "I could only take so much. Mom kept saying how strong you were. How independent. But she worried you were so sad and all alone and needed someone who really cared and protected you. We were driving together when she confessed what I already knew. She wanted to take you in with us."

"You didn't want that." Lucky already knew. That would have set Desiree off to have her in her house, right under her nose, the focus off her, their attention divided.

"I wasn't going to share my mom and dad with you. Bad enough I had to share your boyfriend."

"You didn't have to kill Danny. He was mine. And you took him from me."

Desiree's head fell. "I will admit, after I calmed down and the adrenaline wore off, I was sorry for killing him. He was a cute kid. Too bad he probably would have grown up to be like your father."

"Not if I'd gotten the chance to take him away, the way Neil and I had planned."

"Yeah, you two were never going to live happily ever after. Not after he cheated on you. He was so mired in guilt, he was going to spill that secret soon enough. That would have been the end of you two and possibly the end of you and me. Which is why I made sure he never told you."

Lucky wouldn't let her get away with anything. "And to keep your mother from bringing me into your family, you rammed your car into a tree?"

"She just never stopped talking about you. Like you were the daughter she always wanted. I couldn't let her have that. Daddy is the one who truly loves me. He protects me. He cares about me. He doesn't look at me and wish I was you. He always put *me* first."

Lucky nodded. "Yes. He did. And left me to fend for myself against a monster. It must have made you really happy that he abandoned me."

She smacked both hands flat on her thighs. "I was enough for him. He didn't need you. And I don't need you either. Krystal will be fine without you."

"You mean, without you." Lucky stared down her sister. "As of today, since I'm her closest living relative, I'll be taking custody of her, because like you, your dad isn't going to be around."

"What? You can't do that."

"I can. And I will. Until Neil is able to have a judge who isn't being blackmailed by you hear his case for custody of her, I will take care of her."

"You can't do that. You have no proof I did anything."

Lucky stood. "You just confessed to everything! You even threw your dad under the bus as someone who was there the night you murdered my family. He convinced you not to kill me."

"You can't prove it."

"I don't have to. I have witnesses."

"Neil is an ex-con with an agenda to get his daughter from me. And Hawk is your lover. Hardly credible, since he's in love with you and would lie for you."

"Don't forget the FBI agent and his wife sitting behind you. Oh, and Neil's probation officer sitting by the open window. They heard everything."

Mason stood just as Desiree jumped up and turned to him.

"No!" She shook her head. "This is entrapment. You tricked me."

Lucky shook her head. "You knew Mason and Lyric were in the room. You had no reason to think our conversation was private. You didn't ask them to leave."

"You set me up." Desiree's gaze bounced around the room and landed on the big man coming through the back door, tattoos peeking out of the collar of his shirt and wrapping around his forearms.

The parole officer's gaze went from Desiree to Neil. "Now I know why you asked me to meet you here for our check-in." He turned to Desiree. "You may have some powerful people under your thumb, but I'm not one of them." He focused on Neil again. "I'm sorry I believed her when she came to me with stories of you harassing her, backing that up with the judge's ruling that you were unfit for even supervised visitation. I'll report what I heard here today and let the new powers that be know that you've done everything I've asked of you, and you should be reevaluated for custody of your daughter."

"No!" Desiree shrieked. "She's mine. No one is taking her from me."

Mason moved in behind her.

Hawk stepped passed Lucky and glowered down at Desiree. "You've hurt Lucky for the last time. You're going away and soon, she won't think of you at all, because she'll be so happy with me, her real friends, and her niece that she won't even spare you a thought. You'll be all alone in a cell, locked away where you belong, so you can't hurt anyone ever again."

"That's not happening. My father won't let it. I know people."

Mason took her by the arm. "They're all going down with you. Your father aided and abetted the murders of Lucky's family. And if I find the real reports on your mother's so-called accidental death, he'll go down for that, too, because covering for you only helped hurt others.

Maybe he loves you, or maybe he was just too afraid of what you'd do to him if you turned on him."

A mischievous smile made her look even more deranged. "I have dirt on everyone. No one can touch me." She turned to Lucky. "Not even you, little sister." Desiree yanked her arm free from Mason's hold, grabbed the silver candle holder on the coffee table, and swung it at Lucky's head.

Hawk swept his arm out to move Lucky out of harm's way and grabbed Desiree's wrist with his other hand, pulling it up behind Desiree's back.

Desiree screamed. "You're going to break my fucking arm."

"Don't tempt me."

"Huh," Lyric chimed in. "I didn't have death by candlestick in the living room on my Clue card." She grinned up at her husband. "Slap the cuffs on her, baby, and get her out of here. She's had enough attention. It's time she rots in a cell and thinks about all she threw away by being petty."

"You don't know anything, bitch!"

Lucky got in Desiree's face, covering her mouth with a punishing grip on her jaw. "Shut up. You don't get to talk to her like that. The only thing that should come out of your mouth right now is a *please*, begging me to take care of your daughter, and *thank you* because you know I'll make sure she's happy and well and grows up to be a better woman than her mother could ever hope to be."

"Fuck you!" Desiree winced when Mason secured the cuffs on her wrists.

"Yeah. That's what I thought. Even now, you treat me like the enemy when all I ever did was try to be your friend."

"If only you could have been happy to be free, then maybe I'd have left you alone. You never appreciated what I did for you."

Lucky stared up at Hawk's solemn face. "She still thinks she did me a favor."

Hawk saw all her pain and frowned, brushing his knuckles over her cheek, making her realize she was crying.

She met Desiree's truth with one of her own. "Do you have any idea what it's like to be happy that your father is dead, your mother, and feel so guilty at the same time because your freedom came at a cost you weren't willing to pay? Do you know what it's like to know that your little brother will never grow up to be the man you saw in your head? Smart. Caring. Fiercely protective, even when the odds were against him. Danny never did anything to anyone. He was a jokester, the one person who always tried to make me smile. The one who always hugged me with all his strength."

Desiree deflated. "I said I was sorry about him."

"But. You. Aren't. Sorry!" Her hands fisted at her sides. "You don't care about anyone but yourself. You twist up your convoluted feelings and lash out at even the smallest affront to your heart. You want love, so you try to force it from Neil and steal it away from me. You want me to yourself, so you kill my family. Not because you love me, but because you want to control and hurt me. You don't even tell me I'm your sister. You don't give me a chance to be that to you before you try to kill me. You're so busy blaming me for your own misery, you can't even be happy that I found the love of my life."

"You don't deserve it."

"Right. Because I have it and you don't."

"Because you go around making everyone feel sorry for the sad girl."

"Up until recently, my life *was* really fucking sad. Look at all the things I've endured. Hawk is the one thing I have that means everything to me. I'm taking you down to have a happy life with him. I would die for him."

Desiree tried to come at her again. "Then die already." She kicked out, trying to strike Lucky but Mason held her back. "I hate you!"

"Good. I hate you, too." She let out a deep sigh. "Get out of my home. You're not welcome here anymore. You can picture me here from your cell. Think of me with Krystal, with Hawk, with the kids we're going to have, the life we'll live, the happiness we'll share. You wanted me to be free? With you gone, I finally will be."

Mason pulled Desiree to the door.

"You should thank me, then," Desiree bellowed.

"I thank Hawk for rescuing me from you. He saved me. He loves me. He's all I need."

Lyric slammed the door in Desiree's face before she could spew anymore hate.

Hawk pulled Lucky into his arms. "You did it."

"She did it. All of it. And now she'll suffer the consequences."

"Do you want to be there when Mason locks up Sheriff Collins?"

"No. But I would like to talk to him once he's behind bars. I think it would be better if I can't get my hands on him."

Hawk's fury showed all over his face. "I'd like five minutes alone with him, myself."

She fisted his shirt at his waist in both hands. "He let it all happen. All of it. I suffered and he just stood back and did nothing. Oh, he gave my dad a warning, but that was too little, too late. That didn't stop anything. He knew I was his and he just turned his back on me to save his own ass from the fallout of revealing that secret. All he had to do was arrest my father. To do his fucking job!" Tears streamed down her cheeks, even though she was so, so numb inside.

Hawk simply held her, letting her take whatever time she needed to settle her head and heart.

"I'm going to go down to the station and give my statement to Jase." Neil put his hand on her shoulder.

Hawk stiffened, but didn't bark at Neil to keep his hands to himself like he probably wanted to.

She managed to lift her gaze to Neil. "I hope you get a chance to finally spend some quality time with your daughter. She's an amazing kid."

"Yeah, well, she's got a kickass aunt who loves her. Whatever happens next, I hope you'll stay in her life, even if I'm in it."

"I'm not mad at you. You did what you thought you needed to do at the time. You've paid the price for it. More than you should have by missing all these years with Krystal. I know you can't get them back, but you deserve a chance to be the father she needs and deserves. I think you'll be great."

The parole officer smacked Neil on the back. "Come on. I'll follow you to the station and make a statement on your behalf."

Neil squeezed her shoulder. "I missed you like crazy." He glanced at Hawk. "And I know that ship has sailed, but I'd really like it if we could be friends again as well as being family for Krystal's sake."

"I'd like that."

Neil looked like he might lean in and kiss her on the cheek, but thought better of it when Hawk let out a little growl. Then he left with the parole officer and she was left with Hawk and Lyric.

"Can I get you something?" Lyric asked. "A shot? A cupcake? A whole sheet cake maybe?" She snapped her fingers. "Ice cream?"

Lucky found half a grin. "I've got everything I need right here." She hugged Hawk closer.

He tightened his arms around her. "I'm not going anywhere."

"I think I'll leave you two alone. Mason can drop me at our cabin before he hauls in your sister and throws the book at her."

Lucky reluctantly stepped out of Hawk's arms. "Thank you for coming. I know it's a lot when you're carrying that baby."

Lyric rubbed her hands over her baby bump. "I'm good. And I wouldn't have missed this for the world. That was an epic takedown. I never saw some of that coming."

"You and me both." Lucky raked her fingers through her hair. "I still can't wrap my head around it all."

"She's probably the most ruthless woman I've ever met." Rage rolled off Hawk in waves.

She felt the same way. The second it receded, she'd think about something else she'd learned today and it would boil again.

They saw Lyric to the door.

Hawk stepped out to talk to Jase and Mason before they left.

She stayed in the quiet house staring out the back windows at the green pastures, tall trees, and fat clouds floating in a sky so blue it didn't seem real.

Her heart ached with sadness for a sister she'd thought was a friend, for a niece who lost her mother, for an ex who'd done the wrong thing for the right reasons, and for herself. A girl who had one father who abused her and another who let it happen. She had a mother who enabled and ridiculed and a stepmom who unknowingly pitted one daughter against the other.

She hadn't heard Hawk walk in, but she knew it was him the second he touched her, wrapping his arms around her from behind and pressing his hands to her belly. "Did you mean it when you said you want to have kids?"

"Yes. You said you wanted them, too."

"I do. I want it all with you."

She let her head fall back on his shoulder. "Sounds perfect." She turned in his arms and looked up at him. "Is everyone gone?"

He nodded.

"Good. Then take me to bed and make me forget everything except the way I feel when you love me."

"I love you every second of the day."

"I know. Show me."

Hawk picked her up bridal style. "Whatever you need, sweetheart."

He set her down in the middle of the bed before he peeled off her shoes and socks, then attacked her jeans and panties.

She'd barely taken a breath when he pulled her shirt over her head and let it sail over his shoulder, while his free hand undid her bra and pulled that off, too. She had no idea where it landed because he leaned forward, licked her nipple, then took the tight bud into his mouth. He sucked and laved at it until she was moaning before switching to her other breast, giving it the same attention while he fondled the other, pinching it between his warm fingers.

She slid her hands down over his shoulders and back up, raking her fingers through his dirty blond hair, then grabbing his shirt and bringing it up and over his head.

He pressed kisses down the center of her chest, placing one long kiss over her heart before he sank lower, kissing her down to her mound, then licking her clit.

"You make me feel so good." She wasn't thinking about anything but him and the way he made her feel. Everything else could wait. She needed this. Him.

"Love you so much." He drove his tongue into her. "You taste so good." He hooked his arms around her thighs and pulled her closer to his mouth so his tongue could dive deeper. He thrust again and again, taking her higher and higher until he replaced his tongue with one finger, then two filling her up. He sucked her clit, starting off softly, then ramping it up the way he pushed and pulled his fingers inside her, hitting that bundle of nerves that sent her over the edge.

He kissed his way back up her body to her mouth and devoured her with so much passion he stole her breath. He reared back and undid his pants, letting loose his long, thick cock.

She took hold of it and stroked him, once, twice. He shucked off the rest of his clothes and crawled back to her, but when she put her hand on his shoulder and lightly nudged, he fell onto his back beside her and pulled her over him.

She straddled his hips, her hands planted on his chest, and stared down at him. "I meant what I said. I want a really happy life with you."

"Anything you want, it's yours."

"I just want you." She sank back onto his cock, taking him into herself and loving him with everything she had to give.

He took her nipple into his mouth, licking it, while he held her other breast, brushing his thumb over the pebbled peak.

She rode him slow and sultry at first, loving the feel of him filling her up, stroking her most sensitive flesh. Pleasure rippled through her, swelling along with the tempo she set, igniting shared moans and desperate kisses as the crescendo crashed over them and ecstasy had them wrapped up in each other's arms, panting out their breaths and whispered words of love and devotion.

Hawk held her in his protective embrace like he'd cocooned her in his love. Exhausted from all the drama and revelations, she fell into sleep, safe in his arms. Every time she stirred awake, her mind swamped with the past and what would become of all of them in the future, Hawk was there to distract her yet again. He made love to her like it had been days, not mere hours since the last time. He lavished her with pleasure and promised that everything was going to be all right, so long as they faced it together.

When the morning dawned, crisp and fresh, she found herself warm and sated in her lovers arms, ready to face whatever came their way.

Hawk made her coffee and breakfast while she showered and dressed for the day. When she emerged into the kitchen, he was a sight, standing by the stove, flipping an omelet for her, bare chested, hair tousled by her fingers all night, a pair of black joggers barely hanging on to his hips. Gorgeous.

"How did I get so lucky?"

He hooked his arm around her shoulders, drew her close, kissed her lips like he had all morning to do it, then replied, "That's my line. I don't think I could be any happier having you here with me."

"And I'm never going anywhere. You're stuck with me."

"Good. Because I'm never letting you go."

She went up on tiptoe, kissing him on the tip of his nose. "We missed dinner. I'm starving."

Hawk plated their food and led her to the dining table.

She took her seat and looked up at him. "Tell me." She could see he had something on his mind.

"Mason and Jase want us to come down to the station to give our statements. The sheriff wants to see you before he's transferred." Hawk cupped her cheek. "You don't have to see him if you don't want to."

"I think I do, one last time, otherwise I'll have all this stuff locked up inside me. I never got to tell my dad off for what he did to me. This time I have a chance to unload and I'm going to take it."

Hawk gave her a firm nod, then sat and ate his breakfast while she plotted what she wanted to say and how she wanted the visit to go, fortifying her resolve that she wouldn't let sentiment get in the way of the justice she deserved.

Chapter
Twenty-Seven

Lucky walked into the station and all heads turned her way. The place was abuzz with activity, but it seemed everyone had a spare second to stare at her. Then the applause started with one officer and spread to all of them clapping for her.

She didn't know what to say or do and just looked at Hawk, wondering if he knew what was happening.

"I think they're happy that the corruption has been exposed."

Jase came forward and everyone went silent. "Because you never gave up trying to figure out who was always taunting and hurting you, you forced me and others to look at what was happening in this office. How was someone getting away with what happened to you? That led us to Desiree and the blackmail scheme she had orchestrated that encompassed seven officers, two judges, the district attorney, and the sheriff. We have proof of all of it, thanks to the little black book you found in her purse, the files we found on her phone and computer, and the safe deposit box we found this morning with over one hundred and fifty thousand dollars in cash and a stash of incriminating evidence against her victims. This alone would be enough to put her away for a long time. But in addition to all that, we found digital recordings on her phone that prove she killed her mother, coerced Neil into a sexual relationship he didn't want, along with recordings of your father threatening you before his death."

"She had the evidence to put him away, to get me and Danny away from him, and she didn't use it?" Lucky wasn't surprised just sorely disheartened and feeling betrayed again. She should be used to it by now, but it still stung.

Mason stepped forward. "We think she was building a case, hoping to get enough incriminating evidence—but then she stopped. We think around the time you started seeing Neil, based on what Sheriff Collins remembered. Then Desiree either got jealous, or simply changed her plan and went after your family."

"Both," Lucky suggested.

Jase nodded. "Because of you, we unraveled all her plans and misdeeds." Jase hung his head, then met her gaze again. "I'm just sorry it took so damn long and so many fell prey to her blackmail instead of helping to put a stop to it."

Lucky was feeling charitable this morning. "You did what you could with the information you had at the time."

"Not good enough. It was never good enough in my book. That's why I always kept trying." Jase's eyes were as apologetic as his words.

"I appreciate that. Thank you to everyone who's been working to close out this case. I appreciate it. And now I can hopefully lead a normal, boring life." She found a smile for everyone and hoped the spotlight fell away from her now.

Mason waved her over to the desk he seemed to have commandeered. "Jase will take Hawk's statement. I'll take yours. Since I had to write up my own report about what happened, I've taken the liberty of putting yours and Hawk's together, too. Just read through it. Make any additions or modifications you want, then we'll print it out and you can sign it."

She took a seat and read through the report, making changes and additions so that everything was clear and what she wanted to say. She wanted every detail spelled out so that Desiree had to account for every misdeed.

Mason went over some of the new evidence with her, letting her listen to some of the recordings Desiree had made.

It disturbed Lucky on a deep level, the lengths Desiree had sunk to, all because she wanted the attention on her and Lucky to suffer.

She and Hawk signed their statements together, then she turned to Jase. "Where is he?"

Mason frowned. "In holding. Desiree is back there, too. They're being transferred later today. Are you sure you want to do this? You can always visit him in jail later."

"I'm thinking this is going to be a one and done kind of thing." Maybe she'd change her mind later, but right now it was all she could do to face the man who lied to her every day of her life, turned his back on her when he knew she was being abused, and who chose her sister over her at every turn.

Jase gestured for her to precede him down a hallway, where he unlocked another door that led into a reception area where several officers in uniform watched over three men and one woman, all in handcuffs waiting to be processed.

Hawk squeezed her hand. "You sure you want to do this?"

"Yes. He can't hurt me anymore. Neither of them can. And once I finish this, nothing but happiness for me and you."

Hawk stared at her, his gaze direct and filled with love. "So damn strong. So optimistic even when you're facing betrayal. I don't know how you do it."

"You're a thousand times better than what they've put me through. I can face this because I'm going home with you. I can fall apart because I know you'll be there to hold me while I put myself back together. I can imagine the wonderful future I have waiting for me because I know you're a man of his word and will build it beside me. For the first time in my life, I feel loved. Nothing can touch that. They can't take that away from me." She squeezed his hand back and kissed him softly. "Now, I'm going to say what I came here to say."

"Go get 'em, sweetheart."

She walked through the door Jase help open and spotted the cells running along the wall with a wide walkway along the other side of the expansive room. Desiree was in the cell furthest away. Sheriff Collins was in the closest one to her.

Hawk stopped next to her, brought her hand up to his lips for a kiss, then let her go. He stepped back and leaned against the wall.

She stood facing the sheriff, for the first time knowing he was her biological father.

He stood up and met her sharp gaze. "I never wanted you to find out this way. I had no idea Desiree knew the truth about the affair I had with your mother."

"How did it happen?"

"Desiree overheard Gayle and me talking."

She shook her head. "No. How did the affair happen?"

"Oh. Well." He rubbed his hand over the back of his neck. "We lived across the street when your parents moved in. Newlyweds like us. Gayle had just found out she was pregnant with Desiree. I'd be-friended Marty, your mother and Gayle were like peas in a pod. One night about three weeks after they moved in, your mother showed up on our doorstep, bloody lip, swollen eye, and bruises on her arms. She swore he'd never hurt her before, that his rage came out of the blue. She was shaken and upset. I asked her to come inside so I could get her some ice and take her statement. I was just starting out in the sheriff's department at the time. She refused to press charges, no matter how much I tried to persuade her that men like him were dangerous. If he hit her once, more than likely he'd do it again."

The sheriff paced the small cell. "You have to understand, I didn't mean for anything to happen. Gayle was away visiting her sister. I was missing her. I didn't like being on my own. Joy was...nice."

She hadn't heard her mom and dad's names in a long time. It wasn't lost on her that the unhappiest wife and mother was named Joy.

"Your mother was a good woman."

"Until she wasn't," Lucky snapped.

The sheriff nodded, acknowledging that her mother had turned just as hard and hurtful as her father. "I wanted to help her. I cleaned her up, made her tea while she iced her wounds and held her hand to offer her some comfort. I felt sorry for her as she confessed that she'd thought Marty was different. She couldn't understand the man who'd been so sweet and swept her off her feet could turn on her like that."

She couldn't get past one thing. "Different how? From other men she'd dated?"

"No. Her father had apparently been very strict. She was used to being punished for stepping out of line. I think Marty lulled her into a false sense of security when he was dating her and his true colors only came out after they were married."

"So in the course of taking care of her after her husband beat her, you took advantage of her because you were lonely for your pregnant wife who'd been away a few days?"

The sheriff's eyes filled with anger. "It wasn't like that."

"It sounds exactly like that," she snapped back.

Hawk put his hand on her shoulder. Just that simple touch to let her know he was there and she was all right.

"She called herself stupid for falling for his lies and getting caught up in their whirlwind affair and marrying him so quickly. I told her she was smart and funny and that it wasn't her fault. She hugged me, thanking me for helping her and being so kind. She said she wished she'd met a man like me." He stopped his pacing and stared at the wall like he was lost in the memories of her. Them. A soft smile tugged at his lips. "She kissed me. I didn't respond at first. And then she said she just wanted to feel like she mattered again. I looked into her sad eyes and told her she did matter. That I would help her leave him. She threw her arms around me and kissed me again and I...I don't know what happened after that but we found ourselves tangled up on the couch, her in my arms, her head on my chest, the two of us out of breath and holding each other in the quiet." He got lost in his memories again.

"She suddenly scrambled up, fixed herself, then said she'd made a terrible mistake and had to go. She was sorry for disturbing me and dumping her problems on me. She was out the door in a flash before I even thought to say anything. And then reality crashed down on me. I'd cheated on my wife, a woman I loved more than anything. I couldn't let her find out. I didn't know if your mother would tell her. And for the next month, I didn't see Joy. She avoided coming to our house when I was there. I barely caught glimpses of her at your place. I thought it was over, never to be spoken of again."

"And then she was pregnant. How did you find out you were the father?"

"I didn't know, didn't even suspect when she and Gayle resumed their friendship like nothing was different weeks later. They bonded over the fact both of them were pregnant. I was eventually able to corner Joy and ask if the baby could be mine. She swore that she and Marty had been trying since they got married and more than likely it was his. I let it go. I had a pregnant wife and then a baby to take care of, so I focused on them and tried to put that night out of my mind. And then one day Joy brought over her six week old baby girl to show off to Gayle and to make friends with Desiree. I don't know how Gayle knew, but she did. She took one look at the girls side by side and she looked up at me and I saw it in her eyes. Since she'd gotten home from her sister's she'd looked at me differently. Like she knew something happened while she was gone. Not necessarily with Joy, but something. I didn't think I'd changed in any way, but she'd sensed it, or I'd acted off and she noticed."

"Did she confront you when she saw Desiree and I together that day?"

"No. She didn't say a thing. She didn't accuse me or Joy. She simply acted like it never happened."

Lucky could understand. "Gayle had a newborn of her own. If she'd said anything, she'd jeopardize her marriage, her security, her ability to care for Desiree on her own."

The sheriff agreed with a nod. "I figured she knew she had every advantage staying with me. And I made sure she knew that when we went to bed that night and I told her that she was the only woman I loved and I would spend the rest of my life proving it to her. She must have believed me enough to stay and I made sure every day that she knew how special and important she was to me."

"And then you realized, or she did, that I was being abused."

"Desiree brought it to our attention with an innocent statement. 'Lucky seems to get hurt an awful lot.' My blood ran cold and I locked eyes with Gayle, who'd seen bruises on your mother. We couldn't pretend anymore that there wasn't this not-so-secret secret between us. She told me I needed to do something. It couldn't go on. Someone was going to get really hurt or die and it was on my head if it happened. But I was afraid of making things worse."

"You were afraid that if the secret came out, you'd lose your wife. She'd be humiliated. My father would be furious and probably take some kind of revenge."

"I was afraid he'd take it out on you and your mother. I didn't want that on my conscience."

"So you did nothing and let me suffer."

"I was running for sheriff. The scandal would have cost me the job. I needed to support my family. I couldn't help you if I was kicked off the force."

"So you won the position and turned your back on me completely. Because you never lifted one finger to help."

"I spoke to your father many times, warned him what would happen."

"To no avail. He never stopped hurting me. Ever. You gave him a free pass."

"No. I hated what was happening to you, but I had other problems to deal with, namely Desiree and her penchant for getting into trouble. She was out of control."

"Yes. And you had no problem asking me to help you with that."

"She listened to you."

"Really? When? Because it seems like she was plotting shit behind our backs and getting away with murder." She held up her hand. "Oh wait. I didn't die. So I guess it must be okay."

The sheriff gripped the bars and tried to shake them but they didn't budge. "Damnit, Lucky, I didn't mean for any of this to happen!"

"You didn't do anything to stop it!" And nothing he said was going to change that. He couldn't come up with a logical excuse for leaving her in the hands of a monster when he had the power and authority to remove her from that house and her parents. "Do you know why my mother named me Lucky?"

He sighed. "Because when you were born and she looked into your eyes and saw pieces of me in your face and not his, she said the first thing that came to mind. Lucky."

"As in, I was Lucky not to be his. But that wasn't true, because I remained his from day one until Desiree freed me from them."

"Yes," he bit out.

"You're welcome!" came from the other end of the room.

She didn't give Desiree the time of day. "You are a disgrace as a husband, a father, a man of the law, and a man in general. You let others suffer so you could keep the peace in your home. So you could keep your secret and not be shamed for what you did to your wife, my mother, Danny, me. How did that work out for you when Desiree killed her own mother, your precious Gayle, who stood by you even after you betrayed her?"

His face tightened with conviction. "Desiree would never do that."

"She did. Tell him, Desiree." Lucky kept her gaze on the sheriff.

Silence came from the other end of the room.

Lucky guessed her sister was all out of confessions. "No? I'll tell him, then. The daughter you loved instead of me not only planned to kill her mother, your wife, she recorded it on her phone. According to the transcript I read, Desiree taunted Gayle while she struggled to take her last breaths that no way was Gayle going to call child protective services and get me removed from my home and placed into yours. She wasn't going to share you with me. Ever."

Bob's face paled and she feared he might actually faint from shock.

"I was supposed to die, too, the night she killed my family, but you showed up and apparently said enough to get her to spare my life. I suppose I should thank you for that, except you could have stopped all of it from happening in the first place."

He leaned into the bars. "I love you. I never wanted to see you hurt or dead. Desiree needed her sister. I needed you."

"Yes, to keep her in line, because you couldn't. And you *love* me? Bullshit. You haven't shown me an ounce of love, not in the way I needed it. It's too little, too late now. The time to save me was the moment I was born and you knew I was going home to an abusive man. He broke my mother and she hated me for not being her ticket out of that man's clutches. If you'd done the right thing, Danny would be alive today. Do you ever think about *him* and what he suffered?"

The sheriff's head dropped. "Yes. I do."

"Then you must not have a heart, because you didn't care even enough to make a phone call to CPS. You didn't have to blow up your life. All you had to do was remove us from that hell. That's all. That would have been enough. I would have been so grateful to be free." She swiped the tears from her cheeks. "Now you will have all the time in the world to think about your choices and the lives they cost. You can think about Danny, the way I do every day, wondering what his life would have been like if he'd been given just a tiny bit of your time. One phone call. One act of kindness. One good thing you did for the daughter you made suffer. I could have lived my whole life without knowing you were my father, and I'd have been okay with that if Danny and I were together. You could have kept your family. I could have had mine. One call."

"I'm sorry." Tears streamed down his face, shame in his eyes, regret pulling his mouth into a mask of pain. "Please, Lucky. Let me make it up to you."

She pressed her lips tight and shook her head. "What is a life worth? You can't give him back to me." She rubbed her hands up her exposed arms. "You can't take away a thousand cuts and all the vile words my father used to tear me down. You can't change the fact Desiree wants me dead."

"I don't," she called out. "You'll take good care of Krystal for me. Won't you, sis?"

The sheriff's tears poured down his cheeks again. "What I wouldn't give to see her grow up under your influence. What I wouldn't give to go back and make that call."

"You had the power and you didn't use it to save me. You betrayed me every day you knew what was happening and you didn't stop it. So this is it for us. I do not want to hear from you. I will not contact you. Let this be the end of our sad story."

"But I want to make things right. I want to know what happens to you, to Krystal."

"We will be happy and better off without you. I will love her enough, so that she never goes looking for love disguised as whatever kind of crazy Desiree is or the kind of neglect you inflicted on me. She'll have a good man to show her what true love and protection looks like." She glanced over her shoulder at Hawk, who winked at her. She turned back to her bio-father for the last time. "When you think about me, *if* you think about me, remember you're the one who ruined any chance of us ever being father and daughter. I would have given anything to have the kind of love and devotion you showed Desiree. Now I'll never know what that's like. But I have him." She pointed her thumb over her shoulder. "So I know I'm going to be better than okay, because he's giving me a new family. One who's already welcomed me with open arms."

"You deserve it, Lucky. I know you don't believe it, but I do love you."

"If only you'd showed it." She glanced one last time down the row of cells at her sister, then took Hawk's hand and walked out, leaving her past behind and looking forward to her future.

Chapter Twenty-Eight

Lucky walked toward the helicopter hand in hand with Hawk. "This is yours?" The sleek black and chrome chopper looked like it seated six. The Gunn Brothers Distillery logo was emblazoned on the rear side panel.

"Ours," he corrected, like every other time she referred to something of his that they now shared. At first, she couldn't wrap her head around how simply and easily he'd brought her into his life and declared them an "us," making it clear that everything they owned, hers and his, was now "theirs" and "ours." She loved the sense of belonging she held in her heart now.

His family had welcomed her with open arms. She sat at their tables, sharing meals with them whenever one of them invited them to dinner. They wanted to get to know her. They wanted to be the family she could count on after she'd lost the one that never protected or loved her the way she deserved. She'd never felt connected to anyone the way she was with Hawk. And their bond was growing stronger every day. And that included his family. "Where are we going?"

"It's a surprise. I want to show you our piece of the world and a place I found a while ago that I think you'll like." He opened the front passenger door for her and helped her up by the hand. He buckled her in and held the headphones out to her. "You're going to need these so we can talk to each other."

Hawk had already spent nearly an hour going over the helicopter while she enjoyed a mocha from the little café in the hanger at the small airport. He took his seat beside her and started flipping switches and checking the many gauges in front of him. He pulled on his headphones and radioed someone, letting them know they were ready to leave. Then he turned to her. "Ready?"

She wiped her sweaty palms over her thighs, straightening her dress. "Yes."

His smile brightened. "Nervous?"

"I've never been on a plane, let alone a helicopter. At least that I remember." She'd been airlifted to the hospital after he found her. That seemed so long ago, but also like it was yesterday that she'd woken up to him holding her hand in the hospital, kissing her head, and telling her that he wanted her to be his.

What a miraculous admission. One she never thought she'd hear from him.

Now, she couldn't imagine her life without him.

"You're going to love it. Trust me."

She put her hand over his on the control he held. "I do trust you. With my life. With my heart. I love you so much." The past weeks had been everything she hoped for and more.

He brought her hand to his lips and kissed the back of it. "I love you, too. More than I ever thought possible. And that you love me the same way...I never thought I'd have that."

She squeezed his hand and showed him all her joy in her smile. "Let's fly."

He loved this and she wanted to share it with him. She wanted to share everything with him.

The helicopter rose steadily until Hawk moved the stick and they passed over the airport, then cut across the land until Hawk's calm voice came over the headset again. "There's our house." He pointed down and to the left. Then he pointed to the right a ways off. "That's Lincoln's place." They flew a bit further and two more houses came into view separated by a long distance.

She waved at the couple out on their porch. "That's your mom and dad!"

As they flew over the other house, another man came out and waved up at them. "Is that—"

"Damon's home." Hawk flew the helicopter down lower before taking them up again. He was laughing.

Damon was probably swearing at his older brother for sending a wave of wind his way.

"Don't worry. He's used to me doing flybys."

"How long has he been home?"

"A few days. I needed his and Lincoln's help with something."

"What?"

"You'll see." His cryptic reply ended with him giving her a tour of the Montana landscape as they passed over towns, rivers, and other notable places until they crossed into Yellowstone territory and the landscape turned into even more spectacular mountains and valleys.

Her stomach tightened as they approached one such mountain top. "Uh, Hawk, what are you doing? We're awfully close."

"We're landing. Don't worry. Sketchy landings are my specialty."

"Um, it doesn't inspire confidence when you use the word sketchy."

He chuckled. "I would never put you in harm's way. We are totally safe. I promise."

She really didn't have to worry. He landed the helicopter like he'd set it down on an air mattress. They sat for a moment admiring the breathtaking view.

"It's so beautiful up here."

He turned to her. "It sure is." His gaze caressed her face. "Ready for your surprise?"

"I don't need a surprise. Being here with you is enough."

He pulled off his headset while she did the same, then he hooked his hand around the back of her neck and drew her into a passionate kiss. "I want to strip you bare on this mountain and make love to you." He kissed her again, stealing her breath and making her melt. "But first, I need you to say yes."

"Yes."

He chuckled and kissed her again. "You don't even know what you're saying yes to."

"If you want to hear it, I'll say it."

"I want you to mean it."

"I do. Because I know whatever it is you want, I want."

"Marriage?"

"Yes."

"Babies?"

"Yes."

"Forever?"

"Yes."

He stared at her for one long moment. "Then come with me." He climbed out of the helicopter, then walked to her door and helped her down. Taking her hand, he led her across an open meadow dotted with wildflowers and shrubs. He stopped her near the drop of a slope, stood behind her, and put his hands on her shoulders. "Don't move. Don't look back. Just give me a few minutes to set up your surprise. Okay?"

"Who could look away from this breathtaking view?"

"I feel that way every time I look at you. I never want to look away." He kissed her on the back of her head, then warned again, "Don't move."

She waited while he went back to the helicopter. There was a lot of rustling behind her, but she didn't turn, just waited patiently, knowing this was important to him.

Finally, she felt him close behind her again. "Turn around, sweetheart."

She did and found him on one knee, holding up a gorgeous set of rings. She didn't even think, she just gave him the word he wanted to hear. "Yes!" Tears blurred her vision before she blinked and saw his eyes lit with delight and a smile so big, her heart overflowed with love for him.

"At least let me say what I wanted to say before I cut the camera and do what I promised I'd do."

She blushed and looked around, but didn't see a camera.

He took her hand, kissed the back like he'd done earlier, then looked up at her, his gaze so earnest and open. "I fell in love with you without spending a single second in your presence. I don't even know exactly when it happened. Maybe it was when I realized that Monday was my favorite day because it was the day you were in my house, making it feel warm and homier than any other day of the week. Maybe it was when I started thinking of ways I could mess up my place, so I could have an excuse to bring you there. Maybe it was when you gave me that first romance book and I finished it feeling lighter, more hopeful than I had in forever. Maybe it was the way every note you left, every treat you made, every distraction you gave me pieced my heart back together because I knew someone cared. Not because you were family, but because you somehow connected with me.

"I don't know exactly how you did it, but week by week, all a hundred and seven of them before I found you in that ravine and almost lost you, you made me want to be a better man. And now I am because you're finally beside me. I'm whole when you're with me." Tears unbidden rolled down his cheeks, telling her how much he really meant every word. "To tell you I love you, just never seems enough. No matter how many ways or times I show you, it never seems enough. But I do love you. I will always love you. So say, yes, one more time and make me the happiest and luckiest man on the planet. Will you marry me, continue living this amazing life with me, build a family with me, and love me the way you do so well?"

She didn't wipe her tears either. "I would be so happy to be your wife, to live my life with you, to have babies with you, to keep loving you, the only man who ever held my heart and protected it and me. Yes. Yes to all of it."

Hawk pulled the big diamond ring out of the box and slid it onto her trembling finger, explaining, "The other one is for you to wear under your gloves while you work."

How thoughtful.

She cupped his face and kissed him with all the love in her heart as he stood and pulled her in close, wrapping her in his strong, protective arms and dipping her back, making her laugh against his lips. He pulled her upright and turned to the side, his arm still around her. "Wave to our family." He pointed to the camera he'd set up on a rocky outcropping.

She did.

Then he kissed her again, took her hand, and showed off the beautiful, sparkling rock.

She still didn't know where the camera was, she was too busy look-ing at the man she loved. Her future husband.

Hawk turned back into her and kissed her softly. "I knew you'd say yes, but I was nervous anyway. I wanted this to be perfect."

"It was amazing. Look at where we are." The majestic mountains overlooking the valley was a beautiful sight on such a warm and lovely day. She couldn't ask for more.

Hawk kissed her again then just smiled at her for a moment before he stepped back and showed her what else he'd set up. A thick blanket lay on the ground with a large wicker picnic basket, a silver bucket filled with ice and a bottle of prosecco, and a huge bundle of red roses.

"I thought I smelled roses in the helicopter. I thought it an odd air freshener choice for you."

Hawk laughed. "Yeah. I had all this stashed in the back seat." He waved for her to sit.

She took a seat while he walked away. "Where are you going?"

"To get the camera." He picked up something off a large boulder and seemed to flip a switch as he walked back to her. "Trail cam with a transmitter. Mom, Dad, Lincoln, Damon, Mason and Lyric, Nick and Aria, my aunt and uncle, and the ladies who all work for you got to see the proposal." He opened the picnic basket and set the camera inside. "Now, we're all alone up here."

She crawled up his legs and straddled his lap, the flowy turquoise sundress she wore fluttered around her thighs.

Hawk's big hands landed on her hips and he pulled her closer, securing her soft folds against his rigid length. "What are you wearing under this sexy as fuck dress?"

She leaned in, brushing her cheek along his, and whispered in his ear, "Nothing."

He pulled the dress up and over her head so fast, she barely had time to put up her arms to help him out.

Naked on his lap, she grinned at the look of awe on his face as he took her in. "Now all I'm wearing is your ring." She held up her hand.

Hawk's gaze sharpened and filled with a possessive look that made her center clench with arousal.

"It's beautiful, by the way. I love it. And the other one." A thick gold band with a smattering of different shaped diamonds embedded in the gold. "You spoil me."

"Oh, I'm gonna." He rolled her onto her back and settled between her thighs as she wrapped her arms around his neck.

They lost themselves in another kiss until she got impatient and undid the buttons on his white button down and pushed the shirt off his shoulders. He pulled the rolled up cuffs off and tossed the shirt. His black jeans were in her way. She attacked the button and zipper, pushing them down over his spectacular tight ass. His cock nudged at her entrance and she rolled her hips to take him into her, but Hawk had other ideas and pulled back.

"Not yet, baby, I want to make sure you're ready. I want you to come on my tongue." He shucked off the rest of his clothes, then settled himself between her wide spread thighs and dove in like a man on a mission. He licked her slit from bottom to top and sucked her clit.

She slid her fingers into his hair and held him to her, rolling her hips against his face as he tongue fucked her, building the euphoria gathering inside her. She could barely hold on, it felt so good.

"Come for me." He sucked her clit and thrust one, then two fingers into her tight channel, pushing her over the edge.

She came so hard her breath panted out and her body quaked. "Hawk," she cried out, riding the wave of her orgasm as he stroked his fingers in and out of her, extending the pleasure. Once she settled into the soft blanket with a sigh, he rose over her and smiled.

"You good?"

"So good." She wrapped her legs around his hips and pulled him to her as she slid her hands up his chest, around his neck, and pulled him down for a searing kiss.

They got lost in the passion again as he sank his tongue and cock into her at the same time. She felt so full and close to him. Protected and loved in his embrace. They made love like they had eternity to spend in each other's arms.

If nothing else, they had the rest of their lives.

Your Next Read

Thank you so much for reading Hawk and Lucky's story. I hope you enjoyed it. Please leave a review for I GOT LUCKY on your favorite retailer, BookBub, or Goodreads. Reviews help more than you know.

Want to know if Lincoln ever gets a date with Mercy, check out WITHOUT MERCY.

And when Damon comes home from his world travels for Gunn Brothers Distillery, a friend reveals he's been betrayed in FOREVER TRU.

Do you like dark romance? Check out SEE ME, book 1 of my She's Mine Duet. Available now!

Brooke has only loved one man. Cody's smart, gorgeous, perfect.
Except he's older. Taken.
Oh, and her *step-brother*.
If only she could prove to him they are meant to be.

Cody has the perfect life.
A sophisticated, supportive girlfriend, a career on the rise.
And an amazing best friend and stepsister. If only he could stop noticing just how beautiful Brooke is. How she gets him. How he *hates* any other guy near her.

When one night of passion turns into a morning-after disaster, Brooke is left to face the future alone. And pregnant.

But little does Brooke know, she's not alone. Someone else has been watching. Waiting. Stalking her every move. And they only want one thing.

Her.

Chapter One

4th of July – Another event his parents dragged him to...

Wow! He hadn't seen her in two years.

She'd changed. Filled out in all the right places.

His gaze traced her curves. Those legs. That ass. Damn.

He wished he could go up to her and say hi.

Lame.

She'd never talk to him. What would he even say to her? No one ever really talked to him. Not unless they wanted something. Usually from his father.

He hated being used. He hated that he couldn't just go up to her, strike up a conversation, and have her begging him to take her out, take her to bed. He wasn't that guy. He didn't know how to be that guy, even though right now he'd do anything to be that man for her.

She made him hard. She made him want.

Then he got lucky and spotted some friends from school, who were friends with Brooke's best friend. He could use them to get close to Brooke. Then maybe he'd have a chance.

Yeah right!

It could happen, he argued with himself.

Maybe it was meant to be.

Chapter Two

4th of July picnic at Brooke's home...

Brooke Banks stared out at the crowd of people milling around the garden and seated at the picnic tables on the patio. Her best friend Mindy Sue was holding court by the pond with her boyfriend, Marco, and several of their college friends. They were entertaining themselves playing cornhole and horseshoes on the grass. They'd all come to support Brooke through this happy but difficult event.

"Brooke! Is that really you!" Mrs. Ellis's mouth hung open as her gaze went from the tips of Brooke's cowboy boots, up her legs and her slightly curvy body, to her green-eyed gaze. "Wow! You were always a pretty girl, but now you're a beautiful young lady."

She appreciated the praise. At least someone had noticed she'd grown up. "Thank you."

"I'm so sorry about your stepfather. We've missed him these last two years." Mrs. Ellis's husband, the mayor, had been friends with Harland since they were boys in school.

Two years ago, her stepfather had died of a sudden heart attack. He'd held the annual picnic for all his friends, fellow ranchers, and community leaders. She missed him every day. She, her mom, and his son, Cody, hadn't been ready to carry on the tradition after Harland's passing. But this year, Brooke insisted they revive it. It was important to keep Harland's memory alive. Traditions mattered and kept them together.

Plus she hoped it would help Cody look toward the future and see this place as *his* now, because he was the one carrying on in his father's absence.

And it didn't hurt that some of the most influential people in the state were here.

As a lawyer, Cody could use the connections with his father's cronies. You never knew when you'd need a favor from someone with the kind of clout many of the individuals here today flaunted.

She nodded to the governor and his wife, who were chatting with her mother, Susanne, nearby. Mindy Sue's father, Doug Wagner, was one of the most highly respected and successful defense attorneys in the state. There were three judges, plus the district attorney and several of his associates here, too, along with most of the business owners from three nearby towns. Everyone they'd invited showed up out of respect for Cody and his father.

And she'd been the one to pull all of this together, from the invitations to the catering, decorations, the music, games, and fireworks show. Every detail, she'd conceived and executed.

She hoped it showed everyone on the ranch that she'd grown up, because from the second she'd arrived home from college, she'd had to remind everyone she was twenty, not ten.

It started with their ranch hand the day she arrived home for summer break calling her little one. Paco didn't mean anything other than affection, but it made her feel like a little girl and not the woman she'd grown into. It didn't help that Cody refused to let her have even half a glass of wine at dinner. He never missed an opportunity to exercise his overprotective streak when it came to her.

Even more annoying, his girlfriend was *Team Cody all the way. UGH! Of course she sided with him to score points.*

Mrs. Ellis pressed her hand to her heart. "Time passes so quickly. We blink and..." She waved her hand up and down in front of Brooke. "Little girls turn into young ladies. Friends pass." She waved at her misty eyes. "Sorry. I miss Harland."

"Me, too."

"And I haven't seen enough of your mother. How is Susanne doing? She must be so proud of you."

"She is." Brooke was lucky to have such a supportive mom, even if she was having trouble giving Brooke her freedom. "And she's well. It was hard in the beginning, but now we're all just trying to keep Dad alive in our hearts."

Mrs. Ellis patted Brooke's forearm. "That's the way, now isn't it? You must be close to finishing college."

"One more year to go until I graduate with my bachelor's degree." She couldn't wait.

Mrs. Ellis leaned in. "And is there a special young man?"

Brooke's cheeks warmed. "No." Just Cody. But he wasn't hers. No matter how hard she tried or wished it were true.

"Well"—Mrs. Ellis nudged her shoulder—"the right one will come along soon enough."

Yeah, I already found him. He's just not into me. Not in that way.

Her mom, Susanne, made her way over to them. "Betty, don't you look lovely."

Mrs. Ellis's sleeveless, fuchsia-colored sheath dress complemented her dark hair and green eyes while showing off a nice pair of toned arms. Mrs. Ellis must work out, because she was in good shape.

Mrs. Ellis waved off Brooke's mother's compliment. "Thank you, Susanne. You're as beautiful as ever. That turquoise dress just makes you glow." The women shared a quick embrace and kiss on the cheek.

"I've missed you," Susanne confessed.

Her mom had retreated from her friends after Harland's death, lost in her grief. But over the past year, she'd slowly started to really live again and reconnect with old friends.

Brooke loved that the party had brought these two back together.

Mrs. Ellis held her hand out toward Brooke. "I nearly didn't recognize your beautiful daughter."

"They grow up so fast." Her mom smiled, even if a bit of sadness crept into her eyes that time had passed too quickly and soon Brooke would be off to school again.

"Yes, they do." Mrs. Ellis was probably thinking of her two children. "Thank you for inviting us to the party."

"Oh," her mother said, "I'm so happy you're here, but the event"—Susanne looked around at all the people, decorations, and buffet nearby—"this was all Brooke's doing."

And today Cody would see she could handle a party of this size and scale and make it enticing for all these people to show up and be here for him. All she'd had to do was call up the governor's wife and tell her how much she hoped she and her husband would attend, and that her stepfather Harland had loved her pecan pie. Mrs. Harris had won first place in the state fair three years in a row and took great pride in showing off her version of the official state pie. She had graciously agreed to not only come to the picnic but to bring a dozen of her homemade pies herself. From there, it had been simple to let others know the governor would be attending, and the RSVPs had rolled in. Not that these people wouldn't come because they respected Harland and Cody. They would. They did. But it never hurt to have a little incentive for those who thrived on being seen in the right circles.

And she'd do anything for Cody.

Mrs. Ellis's smile grew as her gaze shifted to Brooke. "I should hire you for the mayor's next event."

Pride swelled in her heart. She'd worked hard on this picnic. And Mrs. Ellis's approval meant a lot. She attended a ton of events each year. She'd know if something was done well, or fell short. "Unfortunately, I'll have my nose stuck in books for the next couple semesters."

"You should think about becoming an event planner."

Mrs. Ellis's suggestion was nice, but Brooke had other plans. And they included running the ranch with Cody.

Unfortunately, she wouldn't have Cody all to herself. His girlfriend, Kristi Randall, beelined it across the patio toward her and she inwardly cringed.

Kristi barely got out, "Sorry to interrupt, Susanne, Mrs. Ellis." She turned to Brooke. "Have you seen your brother?" Kristi stood before her, searching the crowd with barely a glance for her.

Kristi had never liked her. The feeling was mutual. Kristi wanted all of Cody's attention on her. Brooke? Same. Still, you'd think Kristi would want to befriend Cody's best friend.

Not Kristi. She saw other women as competition.

And while Brooke loved Cody, she also knew she wasn't in the running to be anything more than what she already was to him.

And referring to him as her brother. Yeah, no. She and Cody didn't call each other brother and sister. Their seven-year age gap meant they hadn't been raised together. Brooke and her mom arrived on the ranch when she was ten. Her mother hired on as the cook before Harland fell hard and fast for Susanne and they married. And while Harland had felt like the father she'd never had, she and Cody treated each other like good friends, not siblings.

She'd never, not once, thought of the charming, temptingly hot Cody as her brother.

Kristi huffed out her frustration. "I've been looking for him everywhere." In her long, flowing white dress, pink strappy kitten heels that Brooke hated to admit were super cute, and a tan sunhat over her long golden hair, Kristi made Brooke look like a ranch hand and not the hostess of one of the most sought-after invitations in the state.

Brooke should have put more thought into her outfit like her mother suggested. Not once, but like four times.

She never really paid much attention to what she wore on the ranch or at school. She went for comfort over fashion.

Today she'd thought she'd upped her game by wearing a faded denim skirt that hit mid-thigh and showed off her tanned, toned legs, a short-sleeved, fitted red T-shirt that had lace detail around the arms and hemline but now felt like it wasn't anything special, and her black cowboy boots. She'd pulled her hair up into her usual ponytail to keep it out of the way and off her neck in the hot sun. She could have tried something different. Maybe keeping it down and using some pretty clips to keep it out of her face, even if it would be heavy and hot draped down her neck and back.

Compared to Kristi, she looked plain.

Not exactly showstopping for this who's who party.

Standing next to Kristi, seeing how everyone else around her had dressed in what Mindy Sue would probably call resort chic, suddenly made her uncomfortable. Nervous butterflies battled in her belly as her cheeks heated with embarrassment. She'd tried so hard to make today perfect for everyone. Now, she felt out of place. Not the first time.

Changing now would look too obvious. So she let it go with a heavy heart and tried not to let herself think about it again.

Brooke glanced at Mindy Sue and her other friends out on the lawn, all of them in sundresses or skirts and pretty blouses, hair done, makeup on. Brooke had swiped on some ChapStick and mascara and called it done.

Even the guys were in khakis and slacks with short-sleeved button-up shirts.

She scanned the crowd again and noticed the ranch hands had put on their finest boots, dark denim, and cowboy shirts with pearl buttons, belt buckles shining.

She sighed, thinking that instead of spending the whole morning helping the caterer set up, she could have taken time to actually think about what she wanted to wear and put together something a bit more...sophisticated. Maybe then Cody would look at her like he looked at other women. And she wouldn't feel like the lovesick shadow who followed him around all the time, hoping he'd see how much she loved him.

Ugh. Pathetic. And yet she couldn't squash the undying hope that lived inside her that one day...

Kristi tapped her on the shoulder. "Brooke. Hello. Cody?"

Right. Brooke looked out across the patio, gardens, and grass area where the just-over-two-hundred guests were mingling. "I haven't seen him since we came out to greet everyone."

Kristi huffed out a breath.

Trouble in paradise?

One could hope. Because Kristi had this way about her. She liked getting what she wanted and seemed to be the kind of person who'd do anything to get it.

An only child. Spoiled.

But Brooke had also gotten the sense that pleasing her parents really mattered to Kristi. Brooke got that. You wanted them to be proud of you. It just seemed like Kristi really needed it more than most.

Still, Brooke recognized the longing in Kristi's eyes. She felt it in herself every time she thought about Cody or even looked at him. He had this quality that drew her in.

Kristi and others weren't immune to it either.

But Cody was different with Brooke than he was with the other women who came and went. They could talk for hours or just chill and watch a movie with nothing said. She knew him so well, she could read him like a book. And he was always there for her. Since the day she arrived at the ranch with her mom, they just clicked.

They were friends.

She wanted them to be more.

He ignored all her attempts to get his attention in that way.

She had half a mind to tell Kristi he was off talking to some ex, but that was petty and immature. She'd long since grown past trying to sabotage Cody's girlfriends by conveniently forgetting to deliver messages, or telling them Cody liked something that he hated. He always caught on and gave her a disapproving look that made her feel terrible. She didn't want to be on the wrong side of Cody. She definitely didn't want to lose the amazing connection they shared.

She was really trying to be the grown-up no one on the ranch saw her to be, including her mother and Cody.

Maybe she could do a better job by thinking things through first, like dressing appropriately for the party and presenting herself as the adult she felt like on the inside. Then everyone would see it. Right?

It sucked that everyone still treated her like a child. Well, at least a teen with no sense, despite her stellar grades and the twenty years she'd kept herself alive and well, thank you very much.

Maybe she'd made some mistakes along the way. Thinking Jamie was her friend at middle school summer camp, only to find out that Jamie had hidden a bottle of vodka in Brooke's bag and she got caught during inspection the first day and sent home. Luckily, her mom believed her that she hadn't stolen it from the bar at home. It was a cheap brand they didn't keep in the house. Then there was the time she'd played spin the bottle at Brent's house freshman year with a bunch of friends. She really wanted her first kiss to be with Cody, but Joe came in second, and then the bottle landed on Chris. She'd been disappointed but game to kiss him just to get it over with. But Brent, the asshole trickster, who she'd turned down in front of several of his friends for the spring dance, told her to close her eyes. She did and puckered up to kiss Chris but got a face full of dog tongue instead. Brent got his revenge. Everyone laughed at her. The next day at school, everyone snickered behind her back about her French-kissing Brent's mini poodle. Yeah, high school was not fun with that hanging over her head.

Kristi frowned as she continued to scan the crowd. "If you see him, please send him to me. Tell him my father would like to have a word with him? It's important."

The demand wrapped in the request rubbed Brooke the wrong way. "We're supposed to give a speech while everyone is eating. The lines are forming now. I'm sure he'll find me soon."

"That can wait. This can't. It's an opportunity Cody won't want to pass up. Not if he's smart."

Cody was the smartest guy she knew.

"What's it about?"

"The future. One I think Cody wants, which is why I worked so hard to set this up."

Brooke cocked her head, concerned and suspicious. "What did you set up?"

Kristi huffed. "My father is waiting. Will you just help me find him?"

Mrs. Ellis and Susanne both raised a brow, though Kristi didn't see their curious gazes.

Brooke couldn't let the snappish tone go. "You know, a straight answer would get better results."

"Cody wants to make a name for himself. I can make that happen." Smugness was not becoming on Kristi.

The muscles in Brooke's shoulders tensed. "He doesn't need anyone to make him look good. He's smart, driven, and good at everything he does."

Kristi smirked. "Oh, I know he is."

Brooke didn't like the innuendo. She avoided Mrs. Ellis and her mother's stares. "Whatever." She tried to walk away, but Kristi snagged her arm and halted her.

"Don't mess this up for him."

She turned and looked Kristi right in the eyes. "I want what's best for him."

Kristi grinned again. "Good. Then send him over to me." She smiled smugly and walked away.

Brooke wanted to tear Kristi's pretty blonde hair out.

Mrs. Ellis gave Brooke the same sympathetic look as her mom. "Don't let her get to you. Women like her end up with no friends, wondering why no one likes them."

"I guess. Excuse me. I have to find Cody." She decided if whatever Kristi was talking about would really help him, then she'd do the right thing.

She found him in the garden, sitting in an Adirondack chair next to his buddy Brad Whitlock, the district attorney's son. They'd grown up together and went to college together.

Brad saw her coming and grinned. "Hello, beautiful." He took her hand and tugged, putting her off-balance so that she landed in his lap. He hugged her close. "Where have you been all my life?"

"Right under your nose. But the B word you use for me is usually brat." She elbowed him in the gut, making him laugh as she smiled back at him. Brad was like a brother to her.

Which was weird to think of him as when she'd never seen Cody that way.

And the object of all her desires frowned at his friend.

Brad ignored it. "I think gorgeous suits you better now."

Cody pounded his fist into Brad's shoulder with anger in his eyes as he reached out and took Brooke's hand, pulling her up and out of Brad's lap and into his. "Hands off, asshole."

Brad held up his hands. "I was just saying hello."

Cody narrowed his gaze. "You know the rule. No flirting with *her*."

Brooke cocked a brow. "Is this like the bro code?" She had to admit, she liked seeing Cody possessive over her. And sitting in his lap gave her all kinds of shivery feelings and indecent ideas.

Brad chuckled. "You don't mess with your best friend's sister."

Cody nudged her off him. "Is it time for the speech you want us to make?"

Brooke stood beside him, knowing he'd changed the subject on purpose, but not understanding the wince he'd given at Brad's words or the strange look in his eyes when she left his lap. Regret?

No. That's wishful thinking and my imagination.

She tamped down her hormones and adoration for him and focused. "Uh, Kristi ordered me to find you."

"Excuse me?" Cody didn't look happy about that.

Brooke let it go. "Her father wants to talk to you. Something important."

"Better hop to it," Brad teased. "Don't want to keep the future Mrs. Jansen waiting."

"What?" Brooke nearly choked on the word and the idea that Cody planned to propose.

Cody punched his fist into Brad's arm again as he stood. "Stop joking about shit like that."

She grabbed his forearm and stopped him from walking away. "Are you..."

"No," he said emphatically.

She breathed a sigh of relief that he wasn't planning on asking her to marry him.

Yet.

Shut up, she yelled at that voice in her head.

Cody glanced at the crowd. "Where is she?"

Brooke looked past him. "By the bar."

"How about I get you a drink, Brooke?" Brad offered.

"No," Cody snapped. "Brooke isn't of age."

Brad shook his head. "Come on, old man. We were drinking way younger than she is now."

Cody met Brad's taunting eyes. "Go find one of the couple dozen available women here today. She's not for you."

Brooke wanted to break the tension between these two friends. "I mean, I could do worse."

Cody's lethal gaze landed on her. "Are you serious?"

She rolled her eyes. "No. I'm going to make sure everyone is heading to the buffet line." She walked away, but not before she heard Brad tell Cody, "I was just messing around."

She knew it was to keep his friendship with Cody on good terms, but it kind of pinched her heart, too, that he wasn't serious about her being beautiful, or that he would be interested in her.

Not that she wanted to date Brad. It would just be nice if he thought she was worth Cody's wrath.

You're being ridiculous.

She knew that.

Still, the whole interaction with all of them felt weird. Like maybe Cody didn't want her with anyone but him.

Now that's really ridiculous.

Or was it?

She really needed to stop this train of thought and get a grip.

She made it through the garden and to the buffet line just in time to catch the moment Cody found Kristi and slipped his hand around her waist, pulling her close to his side as he used his free hand to shake her father's hand.

Kristi looked up at him adoringly.

Cody glanced down at her and smiled. People close to them noticed the happy couple.

Was he really thinking about marrying her? Or had Brad really just been joking?

Brooke's heart sank. She was too used to this feeling when it came to Cody. Maybe one day he'd see her as the woman she'd become.

The one who wanted him and only him.

Falling For Owen – The Return of Brody McBride

The Hunted Series

Everything She Wanted

Chasing Morgan – The Right Bride

Lucky Like Us – Saved by the Rancher

Short Stories

"Close to Perfect" (appears in Snowbound at Chrstmas)

"Can't Wait" (appears in All I Want for Christmas is a Cowboy)

"Waiting for You" (appears in Confessions of a Secret Admirer)

Also by Jennifer Ryan writing thrillers as JENNIFER HUNTER

The Ryan Strickland Series

The Lost Victim – The Rose Reaper

About the Author

New York Times and *USA Today* bestselling author Jennifer Ryan writes suspenseful contemporary romances about everyday people who do extraordinary things. Her deeply emotional love stories are filled with high stakes and higher drama, family, friendship, and the happy-ever-after we all hope to find.

Jennifer lives in the San Francisco Bay Area with her husband and three children. When she isn't writing a book, she's reading one. Her obsession with both is often revealed in the state of her home and how late dinner is to the table. When she finally leaves those fictional worlds, you'll find her in the garden, playing in the dirt and daydreaming about people who live only in her head – until she puts them on paper.

Please visit her website at www.jennifer-ryan.com for information about upcoming releases.